Dear Meg,
May you always find delight
in the shadows.
Jenny

The Lure of Evil

Jenny Bassett

Special Offer

Want to know what happens before page one? Unlock the exclusive prequel novella and discover the secrets that set this world in motion—available for **free** on my website.

THE RISE OF DARKNESS SERIES

A Night of Ruin

A PREQUEL NOVELLA

The Lure of Evil

Embracing Evil

TO BE RELEASED IN AUTUMN 2026

This is a work of fiction. Names, characters, places, and incidents either are the product of the author's imagination or are used fictitiously.
Any resemblance to actual persons, living or dead, events, or locales is entirely coincidental.

First paperback edition February 2026

Book design by Author Cultivation
Map by RPG Maps

ISBN 978-1-9192664-0-4 (paperback)

jennybassettbooks.com

For all the girls with book boyfriends...
you'd better clear the roster,
because Keeran isn't the type to share.

MITHRYLAYA
LLMERA
THE FOREST O
ELMAR

EOLANTHEA
DEMUTO
DELIAH'S WRATH
AQUILLA
THE TEARS OF DELIAH
DRIAS
CALLODOSIS
THE JAWS OF RACH-MAH

Trigger Warnings

- Explicit sexual content
- Alcohol consumption
- Blood
- Gore
- Graphic violence
- Indirect discussion of schizophrenia
- Mass murder
- Abduction of adults
- Human trafficking
- Stalking
- Home invasion
- Theft
- Death
- Desecration of a corpse
- Death of a parent
- Edge play
- Rough play
- Primal play
- Racism
- Discriminatory language
- Detailed descriptions of loss
- Explicit language
- Death of a loved one
- Reference to off-page torture

Pronunciation Guide

Aelia *(a-EE-lee-a)*
Aquila *(a-KWILL-uh)*
Artemian *(ar-TEE-mee-an)*
Astraea *(ah-STRAY-ah)*
Beserkir *(beh-SER-keir)*
Callodosis *(KAL-oh-doe-sis)*
Del Awane *(DEL uh-WANE)*
Demuto *(deh-MU-toe)*
Drias *(DREE-as)*
Fenrir *(FEN-reer)*
Ideolanthea *(ih-dee-oh-LAN-thee-ah)*
Jaws of Rach-Mah *(RACK-mah)*
Keeran Draconian-Fafnirean
(KEER-an / drak-OH-nee-an / faf-NEER-ee-an)
Khaled *(KHAH-led)*
Llmera *(EL-meh-rah)*
Mirra *(MIH-rah)*
Mithrylaya *(mi-THRIL-ah-yah)*
Moira *(MOY-rah)*
Otis *(O-tis)*
Peregrinians *(PEH-reh-grin-ee-ans)*
Rhea *(REE-ah)*
Shiva *(SHEE-vah)*
Tears of Deliah *(deh-LYE-ah)*

CHAPTER ONE

Aelia nearly tripped as she ran down the narrow wooden stairs that spiralled around the monumental oak tree she called home. Her hand, clutching onto the crude bannister, was the only thing protecting her from the forty-foot drop from her treehouse to the forest floor.

She puffed her cheeks out in a relieved sigh and slowed her pace, well aware of how close she'd come to bouncing arse over elbow all the way down the steps. So what if she was late? The festival wasn't going anywhere.

She made it safely to the forest floor and straightened her dress. The midnight blue material was interrupted by silver patterns that swirled down her torso, the fabric hugging her closely before flowing over her hips, waving gently around her thighs. It had been a present on her twenty-fifth birthday, and although that seemed such a long time ago now, she still adored it. There were few opportunities to escape the drudgery of life in the forest, and Aelia had relished the chance to pin half her dark curls in a pretty knot, leaving the rest to cascade well past her shoulders. She'd used charcoal to bring her vivid green eyes to life, and a flush of excitement accentuated the high arc of her cheekbones.

As she walked beneath row after row of elevated tree-houses, the path became steadily busier as she joined others on their way to the festivities. Light poured onto the darkening paths through prettily carved windows, illuminating the abundance of sleepy-looking wildflowers that spread throughout the village and the rush of excited villagers. The familiar smell of pine wafted up to meet her as her feet brushed over the thick layer of needles and acorns covering the ground.

Her heart beat a little faster as she came to the edge of the Peregrinian's camp, the travelling band of traders having set up with practised efficiency to transform the space beneath the huge tree trunks into a thriving market.

She craned her neck over the sea of heads to get a better view of the tented stalls that spattered the forest floor beneath the village, full of things to examine and barter for. She had to sidestep out of harm's way more than once as people bustled past her, arms overflowing with whatever they hoped to sell to the Peregrinians, throwing rushed apologies back at her over their shoulders. The atmosphere was intoxicating as the villagers arrived in droves, and Aelia was soon caught up in it, a smile fixed on her face as she sidled through the crowds.

She saw girls she worked with making the most of the rare opportunity to escape their homespun clothes, and young men she had grown up with sharing stories a little too loudly over cups which were refilled a little too often. A brood of children no one had the heart to scold carved a channel through the crowd as they ran past Aelia, leaving a spattering of indulgent smiles in their wake.

Aelia's own smile faltered slightly as she ran her eyes over the traders. Their energy usually matched or exceeded that of the villagers, but to her, they seemed reserved compared to the joviality that surrounded them. Their eyes had a sharpness that Aelia hadn't seen on their previous visits, despite how welcoming the whole village had been.

Aelia sidled to the nearest vendor, her breath leaving her in a gentle gasp as she saw the books that were displayed there. She dragged her fingers lightly over the worn leather bindings, breathing in the yellow pages and the scent of a thousand stories waiting to be told.

Aelia doubted the vendor would have much luck in Callodosis; very few in her village could afford such luxuries. She certainly couldn't.

She pried open the closest book, the leather creaking under her fingers as it spread to reveal a map, the country of Demuto so delicately drawn she had to lean closer to try and take in the detail.

Aelia traced her finger over the dense forest that hugged the southern border, stopping when she found the dot that represented Callodosis, the logging village she called home.

"Are you planning a trip?" the man behind the stall interrupted.

Aelia looked up at the gaunt vendor, his skin the pallor of the parchment he surrounded himself with, the black ring of magic around his irises marking him as an artemian.

"No, I was just curious." She shut the book carefully, her fingers lingering on it a moment longer than necessary.

He slid a heavy tome from one of the piles and offered it to her. "If you're after maps, this book is much more detailed."

"Thank you." Aelia smiled, already backing away. "I was just looking."

The man shrugged and replaced the book, giving her the opportunity to slip away into the crowd.

She hopped from stall to stall, keeping an eye out for

Mirra and Fenrir, but her attention was quickly caught by a small, delicate knife with a carved strand of ivy etched along the blade to form the fuller. It seemed to her too pretty a design for its grisly purpose, and far too fancy for a hunting knife, which was all she had need of. So, she replaced the knife and ran her fingertips lightly over the array of other weapons that lay around it.

The woman, whose build and crooked nose suggested she had no qualms using the weapons she sold, stood behind the stall watching her with a hard, guarded expression. Aelia flinched from her gaze with surprise; usually, the travellers were so friendly.

"Thank you," Aelia mumbled as she made to move away from the stall, turning just as Mirra ran up to her with Fenrir in tow. She was tiny next to his broad frame, her mouse-brown hair clipped carefully up in a pretty twist, leaving a few loose tendrils curling over her pink cheeks. Fenrir was her exact opposite; everything from the way he walked to the proud jut of his chin belied the apex predator in him. The distinct curves of his muscled shoulders were evident beneath his shirt. In fact, the only thing about him that wasn't rock hard were his eyes, the warm pools of liquid amber glinting with boyish amusement as he allowed Mirra to drag him to Aelia's side.

They had all been friends since they were children, and though Mirra was one of the few humans in the village, the difference wasn't noticed by any of them. It wasn't like Aelia could judge anyway.

"What are you looking at?" Mirra peered past her to the weaponry that had been so carefully laid on display. Her fingers reached for the very same dagger Aelia had been drawn to.

"Gods, that's pretty—"

"Don't you touch that." The armourer leapt forward and slammed a fist onto the table so hard the weapons shifted slightly on the dark display cloth. Mirra's fingers froze mid-air as she stared wide-eyed at the furious woman, her mouth hanging open slightly. "Even the likes of you should be able to read. We don't serve humans." She jabbed her finger towards a poster that had been pinned to the far end of the stall.

"Humans are pests, not pets."

Mirra's face paled as quickly as Aelia's darkened.

"What did you just say?" Aelia asked, her voice deathly quiet. She didn't want to believe her eyes, but the sign was right there, the words in unmistakable black and white. How had she not seen it earlier?

"You should know better than to keep such company." The armourer crossed her muscled arms, not so much as an iota of contrition on her face.

Aelia felt Fenrir bristle, looming behind her with predacious menace. She could always count on him to be her wingman in sketchy situations and, as an artemian whose second form was a Wolf, he was one hell of a force to have at her back.

Aelia's eyes narrowed at the vendor, her anger making it hard to think of anything other than grabbing the woman and smashing her face into the poster until it was illegible beneath the bitch's blood. She settled for reaching over to pull the offensive notice free from its pins one by one, locking eyes with the armourer and slowly screwing it into a ball. The woman jerked back as Aelia threw it straight at her head with a dramatic flick of her wrist, but it still bounced off her forehead as she floundered to catch it.

Aelia placed both hands on the table and leant in close, her lips curling as she spoke.

"If I see that back up before you leave, I'll make sure you become closely acquainted with that pretty little knife of yours."

It was a complete bluff. The armourer undoubtedly had far more experience wielding any kind of weapon than Aelia did, but anger could be a weapon too, and right then it blazed so threateningly in her eyes that the woman gritted her teeth and dropped the crumpled paper to the floor behind the table.

"What world do you think you're living in? You don't have a fucking clue what is going on outside your precious little treehouses," she hissed, before jerking her head towards Mirra. "Just get her away from me. Now."

Fenrir snarled and the woman flinched back, her hand reaching for the blade hanging at her hip.

"The acts have already started; we should head over anyway." Mirra grabbed his arm and tried to pull him away from the stall. "Aelia?" Mirra pleaded.

Aelia pushed off the table, her eyes boring into the armourer for a second or two more, until Mirra called her again and she turned to follow. Before they delved too deeply into the crowd, Aelia stood on her toes to cast her eyes over the other stalls, straining to see any other posters of a similar nature. Relieved not to see any, she dropped down and caught up with the others.

"You alright, Mirra?" Fenrir frowned back at the stall, now barely visible through the throngs of people. Mirra nodded emphatically, seeming more worried that he might try to head back over to the armourer than anything else.

"More than alright, we need to hurry though or we're not going to see everything."

"You two go on without me, I'm more interested in the food than the performances anyway. I'll find you later."

"The food… or the ale?" Mirra raised an eyebrow. Fenrir laughed, splaying his hands guiltily as he backed away from them, quickly disappearing in the direction of the tavern.

"I'm sorry, Mirra," Aelia called over the bustle around them, but Mirra just shrugged.

"Nothing I'm not used to." She brushed it off, as though Aelia couldn't see the hurt behind the brave façade. They'd been friends for far too long for Aelia to not know just how deeply that kind of comment cut her, but the Peregrinian's visits were too few and far between for them to let one miserable vendor ruin their fun.

Aelia linked her arm through Mirra's and gave a gentle squeeze, and Mirra returned it with a smile.

It looked like most of the villagers had arrived to enjoy the first night and, judging by the low pounding of drums bouncing off the trees, the celebrations had begun. Excitement pushed aside any residual anger, and they slipped through the crush of people towards the beat.

Aelia let Mirra guide her to a crowd surrounding a pair of artemian dancers; they flowed with the music, soaring around each other, their movements simultaneously graceful and passionate. They moved with perfect harmony; the woman spun wildly around her partner, but he caught her with a gentle strength. Each touch was a caress, their bodies parting and whirling around each other, and yet somehow constantly connected. It was sensual and mesmerising, and Aelia couldn't tear her eyes away. The dance ended as the pair leapt towards each other and, at the last moment, Shifted to form two Doves that flew towards the stars, winding interlacing circles in perfect synchronisation. The crowd erupted into applause, whooping and cheering as the Doves disappeared into the stars.

The spaces between the trees had become a kaleidoscope of natural stages, performers scattered in the flickering fire-light. All of the Peregrinians were artemians, and they flitted between their two forms in their performances, weaving their second natures into their craft.

Aelia and Mirra walked between the artists spread out beneath the trees, seeing as many as they could. They oohed and aahed along with the other onlookers at tightrope walkers that swung precariously before flipping back onto the rope; storytellers; Horses that pirouetted; singers that had people crying with laughter, and women who could bend and contort their bodies into the most unnatural positions.

They were nearing the end of the acts when a burst of flame caught Aelia's attention, with subdued cheers and claps emanating from the spectators around it. A drum resonated in the darkness, hitting a low, carnal rhythm. Curious, Aelia started pushing her way to the front until she could see, but when she did, she froze.

The audience stood unnaturally far back, and not because of the bursts of fire. No, it was the man himself that no one wanted to get close to, seeming to share the same ancient instinct to fear him that ricocheted through her. He stood alone in the ring but towered above them all, wearing only a pair of loose trousers, and Aelia struggled not to gawk at the defined ridges of muscle bunching over his bare torso. When she managed to peel her gaze away from the delicious arrowing v of muscle disappearing below his waistband, her eyes trailed up his body to finally land on his face, and she swallowed. Hard.

His features were made of harsh lines; his nose angular, his cheekbones carved into the tanned skin, whilst the sharp line of his jaw clenched in extreme concentration. A slight frown added to the severe image. But it wasn't just his size or blatant strength that made him so threatening; it was the way he controlled the fire he whirled around him. Both ends of the staff he wielded burned fiercely as he moved in time to the drum, his hulking figure agile as he lunged and spun within the circle of onlookers. The way he moved reminded her of the stories of warriors they had been told as children, his form imposing and precise, and yet he wasn't at war with the flames. It seemed to Aelia as though they danced for him, whirling around him in a torrent, surrounding him in a blaze so ferocious the air crackled. He played with it, exciting it until it raged before him, angry and scorching, before calming it again.

Something about it, about him, had her mesmerised.

They watched him, the man the fire dared not disobey, the man the fire dared not burn. His bare torso glistened with a sheen of sweat; the dancing flames reflected in his dark eyes.

Eyes that flicked up to meet hers.

It was like a punch to the chest. Or more like a fist had punched *into* her chest and squeezed. She took a step back, her hand flying to her sternum, unable to take her eyes off his. The stranger's concentration seemed to falter, the flaming staff falling from its arc for a fraction of a second before he corrected it, his dark eyes wide as he tore them away from hers.

The sensation passed as quickly as it had arrived, and Aelia took in a shaky breath, rubbing her chest distractedly as she continued to watch him. What the hell was that about?

"Here." Mirra wafted a hanky at her.

"What?" Aelia looked at it, confused and resentful of having to look away from the stranger.

"For the drool," Mirra smirked.

Aelia knocked the hanky away, a smile pulling at her lips as Mirra giggled.

"He's just your type," Mirra continued.

"I have a type?" Aelia's attention had already turned back to the man.

"Sure." Mirra shrugged, going back to watching him too. "Handsome, hunky, and crucially, he'll be gone in a few days."

Aelia rolled her eyes down at Mirra, who smiled sweetly at her.

"I'm not going to dignify that with an answer."

"Hey, you know I don't judge, I'm just saying because if you are going to make a move, you better do it fast. It looks like you're going to have some competition."

Aelia followed Mirra's gaze and spotted said competition. Dotted through the crowd of wary onlookers were a handful of women with a certain, unmistakable look on their faces. Aelia couldn't blame them; if you looked past the unadulterated menace that oozed from every pore, he was drop-dead dreamy.

It was the drop-dead part that worried her.

"They can have him." Aelia turned back to Mirra. "I'm quite keen to live to see the morning."

A frown creased Mirra's brow as she looked back at the man behind the swirling flames. "There is something a bit menacing about him, I'll give you that."

"Come on, let's get out of here. I'm starving," Aelia lied, grabbing her friend's arm and tugging her away. The last thing she wanted to do was leave; what she wanted was to lurk in the crowd and memorise every hard line of his body… which was the very reason she needed to get the hell out of there. The last thing she needed was drama, and her reaction to that man was nothing if not dramatic.

She didn't let herself look back as they walked away, but she was certain she could feel the stranger's gaze burning into her back long after they were out of eyesight.

"HOLY CRAP, THAT'S GOOD," MIRRA GROANED, THE WORDS barely audible past her huge mouthful, sauce smeared over the corners of her mouth.

After far too much deliberation, they'd chosen lamb wrapped in some kind of flatbread, the pickled cabbage staining the creamy sauce an irresistible pink. Aelia dropped her nose to it and took a long, drawn-out breath, her heightened sense of smell easily picking out the hints of garlic and rosemary underlying the earthy notes of the lamb.

She closed her eyes and took her first bite, trying to savour every flavour that hit her. She couldn't remember the last time she'd eaten anything this good.

"Oh gods." Her eyes flicked open to meet Mirra's, shaking her head in disbelief; she didn't think she'd *ever* eaten anything this good.

"Right?" Mirra said, before cramming as much of her own into her mouth as she possibly could.

They became too absorbed in the food to talk, the silence between them interrupted by the occasional moan of appreciation. Around them, people milled between the campfires that dotted the forest floor. The smell of foods from all over the country wafted from each one, the Peregrinian cooks selling their wares to the ravenous villagers.

"You two need to quieten down," Fenrir said from behind them, making Mirra jump. "You sound positively indecent."

"Fenrir, you *have* to get one of these." Mirra stuffed another bite in, rolling her eyes towards the dense canopy overhead.

"Or you could let me have a bite of yours?" he said with a persuasive tilt of his head.

Mirra's face fell, eyes dropping to what little was left of her food with a look of utter heartbreak, before holding it out to him. Fenrir took it with a mischievous smile, glancing conspiratorially at Aelia before taking an enormous bite.

"Arsehole," Aelia muttered, lips twitching in a smile as he chewed slowly, exaggerated pleasure etched into his face as he taunted Mirra. She glared at him as he handed her back the pitiful morsel that was left.

"I take it back," Fenrir said, swallowing. "That was absolutely worth all the fuss you two were making."

"I know." Mirra scowled up at him. "It cost more than what my whole family eats in a week."

Fenrir's laugh was contagious; it always had been, and he found nothing funnier than winding up Mirra. Aelia popped the last bite into her mouth as Fenrir wrapped his arms around Mirra's shoulder and pulled her closer, grinning from ear to ear.

"Come on, there are far too many options for you two to only try one thing. My treat." He made to walk towards the campfires, pulling a brightening Mirra with him.

Aelia tensed, spine stiffening despite his sweet intentions. She loved that he looked after Mirra, as a human, she had a tough time of it, but Aelia didn't need his charity. She'd been planning on sneaking off a little later anyway, but if it got her out of having to awkwardly decline Fenrir's offer, she would make her excuses now instead.

"You guys go on," she called. "I'm going to call it a night."

Her friends turned back to her, Fenrir's arm dropping from Mirra's shoulders.

"You're leaving already?" Fenrir's eyes narrowed suspiciously.

Aelia shrugged. "I need to get some bits ready for tomorrow."

It wasn't a lie. Everyone had to bring something for the feast the following evening, and she hadn't prepared anything yet. Fenrir and Mirra exchanged a glance before stepping back towards her.

Mirra checked no one was close enough to hear over the chatter bubbling around them, but spoke in a whisper anyway. "If you're going hunting again, you need to stop. You're going way too often."

"Winter is only a few short months away. If I don't go, we'll have another winter like the ones we grew up with." Aelia tried to keep the frustration out of her voice, fed up with having this conversation.

"I'm not saying don't go at all," Mirra leant closer, still whispering. "I'm just saying you need to be careful or you're going to get caught."

"She's right," Fenrir interjected, all trace of humour having disappeared from his face. "You're pushing your luck as it is."

"Not all of us have the luxury of being admitted into a hunting party, Fenrir." Aelia argued, bitterness coating her tongue. As any artemian, he'd have it easier than either of them. As a Wolf, he had it easier than either of them could dream of. Food, money, respect; Fenrir didn't have to worry about any of it.

"You know I'll bring you back what you need, you don't need to risk pissing off the council for the sake of hunting it yourself," he shot right back, completely unaware how much his generosity stung.

She wasn't human, but she might as well have been. Her irises were ringed with the same black magic that encircled Fenrir's, but for reasons no one could understand, she'd never developed the ability to Shift. Her childhood had come and gone, with all the other artemian children growing into their magic… and yet hers had never appeared. And that's when her life had gone to shit.

Sure, she had other traits besides the tell-tale ring of

magic in her eyes; she was faster and stronger than any artemian she knew, by a long shot, but none of that mattered. She had no second form, so she was treated as human. As less.

"I know, and I love you for it." She tried to unclench her teeth, just wanting to get out of there. "But I won't get caught. Tonight is perfect, no one is going to notice me missing, and no one is going to be out there to spot any sign of me."

She had him there, and he knew it. His mouth tightened into a firm line, the disapproval in his eyes boring into her.

"At least let me go with you."

"Fenrir, rein in the possessive alpha bullshit. I'll be fine," she snapped, needing this conversation to be over.

Hurt flashed behind his eyes, but he blinked and it was gone. Artemians may look down on humans for almost everything, but they clung to their own humanity with a fervour that bordered on the obsessive. They all battled their more animalistic instincts, be they the aggressive tendencies of a predator, or the timidity of prey.

"Fine, just be careful, cover your tracks and keep to the east. We're resting that portion of the forest to let the ecosystem recover so no hunting party will come across your scent there," Fenrir said, his expression hard. "Come on, Mirra, let's get some food."

He didn't wait for her before turning and stalking off.

"He's only trying to look out for you," Mirra scolded, quietly.

If Mirra was pissed with her, maybe she had taken it too far. Regret washed over Aelia, but she steeled herself against it. He would never have let her leave if she hadn't pushed him away a bit. She'd make it up to him tomorrow.

"I don't need his help," Aelia said, watching Fenrir's back

recede through the crowd. Yeah, she'd definitely make it up to him tomorrow. Somehow.

"Everyone needs help sometimes, Aelia." Mirra gave her one last disappointed frown before turning to follow Fenrir. "Stay safe."

"I'll see you in the morning. Have fun," Aelia called after her.

She puffed out her cheeks and pressed the heel of her hand to her forehead. That was not how she'd wanted the evening to end.

With guilt sitting heavily in her stomach, she slipped through the Peregrinian's camp, familiar faces illuminated by the lanterns scattered amongst the trees as villagers milled between stalls.

She couldn't help but scan them for a glimpse of the man with the fire, half tempted to head back to the performer's section to look for him, but she squashed that thought. Everything about that man screamed trouble. There was no sign of him, but as she checked for what must have been the hundredth time since she'd seen him earlier that night, she caught sight of her guardian, Otis.

He was locked in conversation with a group of people she didn't recognise, listening attentively to whatever the man standing opposite him was saying. He stood holding a tankard with his one good arm, his other hidden beneath his jacket, hanging useless and wizened out of sight. Otis had never told her how he'd lost the use of it, and he'd made it very clear it wasn't open for discussion.

Feeling her gaze on him, his eyes lifted to hers, and the crinkles around them deepened in a smile. He raised his tankard to her by way of greeting, and she dipped her head back at him, her smile matching his. With a wave, she left him to his evening, knowing he'd be out until late, prying information out of the

Peregrinians. Their village was small and tucked away, and the news the Peregrinian's brought with them about the rest of the country was just as valuable as the opportunities for trade.

The camp gave way to darkness, the lights from the fires becoming an orange haze at her back, but her night vision kicked in, making the most of what little moonlight filtered through the branches overhead as she made her way back to her treehouse to change.

CHAPTER TWO

Aelia's legs felt leaden as she climbed the stairs that wrapped around the enormous tree trunk to her home. The blue light of dawn was softened by the mist that hung between the trees, distorting the chorus of birdsong that celebrated the new day. Her damp clothes clung to her skin, but she welcomed the mist and the cover it brought. Although the chances of being spotted this early were slim after last night's celebrations, she welcomed any help she could get. The rabbits she'd shot were safely wrapped in her bag, away from prying eyes, but she didn't need anyone asking questions.

She'd been out later than she'd planned, taking longer to reach the eastern quadrant Fenrir had suggested she stick to. She grabbed hold of the bannister to help her exhausted legs up the last few steps. Pausing at her front door, she turned on the balcony that hugged the circumference of the tree-house to look out over Callodosis.

For all its faults, her village was undoubtedly beautiful, and with the gentle light of dawn permeating the thick coverage of leaves above, it still took her breath away. The villagers had tried their best to work with nature when building their little wooden houses, either tucking them between trunks at ground level with ornate simplicity or perching them in the forks of the largest branches, some so high they were barely visible from the ground. Designs varied dramatically, accommodating the unique structure of each tree. Some twisted and curved to make the most of narrower gaps between the enormous branches, whereas others were long and square, spread over two or three supporting trees.

Her own was simple by comparison, a single structure encircling the trunk of the ancient tree that lifted them high into the canopy, towering over almost all the others. The assorted gables tucked between the monumental branches, making the most of space wherever the great oak allowed, and oddly shaped windows had been carved out of the thick wooden walls. Though far from luxurious, Aelia loved every cosy inch of it. With Otis unable to Shift because of his arm, and her own magical failings, she'd had to work damn hard to be able to afford to keep fixing it. Being so high took its toll on the building, and the cost of keeping it safe was eye-watering, which is why so many humans lived at ground level. But Aelia loved it up here, with the beauty of Callodosis around her, and she wouldn't have given it up for anything.

When she could ignore her scratchy eyes no longer, she turned and pushed open the front door, kicking her boots off in the hall and heading straight to the kitchen. She left the rabbits on the kitchen worktop and staggered up the stairs to collapse on her bed, only bothering to take off her soggy outer layers before she snuggled deep into the soft covers, asleep before her head hit the pillow.

AELIA WOKE WITH A JOLT AT THE SOUND OF SOMETHING smashing downstairs. She leapt out of bed, grabbing a jacket and throwing it on as she stumbled down the narrow staircase.

"Otis?" she called as she stepped out into the main room. The sofa that filled most of it was threadbare but made comfortable with an inordinate number of blankets. A pile of dried wood next to the metal log burner, ready for the colder evenings. She made a mental note to check the flue before they used it next; birds had a habit of nesting in it in the spring, and a fire was the worst thing that could happen in a village like theirs.

"In the kitchen," came an exasperated voice from down the arched corridor. She crossed the hall and stepped through the open door into the kitchen to find Otis crouched on the floor, picking up pieces of ceramic from around a rather sorry-looking vegetable tart.

"Oh no," she cried, dropping to the floor to help him.

"I dropped it trying to get it out of the tray. The plate slipped and..." He gestured to the mess in front of them.

"Why didn't you wait for me?" Aelia reprimanded. He'd been her guardian, her only family, for as long as she could remember, and he was just as stubborn now as he had ever been. Aelia fetched a spare plate and scooped up the tart. They might not be able to take it to the feast later, but there was no way she was letting it go to waste. Besides, Otis kept the house clean enough that she'd happily eat it right off the floor if she had to.

"I didn't know what time you'd got back in. I wanted to let you have as much sleep as possible before we had to leave," Otis grumbled, grabbing the work surface to pull himself to his feet with a grunt. He looked good for his years, despite the soft lines forking from his eyes and the grey encroaching into the dark hair at his temples, but Aelia hated seeing the occasional sign that time was taking its toll on his body. He walked off the stiffness crouching had caused as he went to the cupboard to fetch a broom. Aelia cut each of them a huge slice of the tart, her mouth watering at the smell of fresh pastry and grilled cheese. It was nothing special, not compared to what the wealthier artemians would be bringing, but Otis had wrapped the thinly sliced vegetables around each other in a spiralling pattern, giving the effect of petals. The tart looked so much like a blooming rose, it was almost too good to eat—almost.

"What time is it?" she asked, cutting off a piece with the edge of her fork and chucking it into her mouth. Otis had always been a better cook than she was, and the pastry melted in her mouth. She dreaded to think how much he'd spent on the ingredients he'd needed to make it taste this good, but they could hardly turn up with something bland.

"Midday," he said, sweeping up the last few fragments. He paused, leaning on the broom with his good arm as he looked at her. "Do you think you're going out a bit much, Aelia? We have enough stored to get us through the winter now."

"Not you too." She pushed the plate away, her appetite suddenly disappearing.

His eyebrows shot up. "Fenrir thinks you're overdoing it, too?"

It was easy for him to guess who else might be worried about her. The only other people who knew about her little hunting trips were Fenrir and Mirra's family, and they only knew because she'd been filling their stores since she was sixteen.

"I'm not doing any more than I was last year," she protested.

"And people were suspicious last year," Otis pointed out. "We went through the winter without losing a single pound.

How many humans could claim the same? We have to be careful, if you're caught, there'll be no more hunting at all, and then how will we survive?"

"It's fucking ridiculous," she said, her temper getting the better of her. "There's absolutely no reason why the humans shouldn't be allowed to hunt."

"It's the law, Aelia. Only hunting parties are given licences to hunt to protect the ecosystems of the forest. Overhunting is a real worry—"

"That's bullshit and you know it," Aelia cut him off, waving her fork at him. "It's just another way to beat the humans down, to put them at a disadvantage. No artemian would let a human into a hunting party, and it's illegal to form one on their own, so they're left to buy whatever scraps they can afford with their shitty little jobs."

Otis remained silent, just looking at her pensively. Her anger waned beneath his disapproval, even at her age.

"Sorry," she mumbled.

He rested the broom against the wooden walls and came over to her, wrapping her in a one-armed hug. She squeezed him back, breathing in the woodsy scent of him.

"It's not fair, but it's the world we live in and, if you want to keep beating the system, you need to play it safe," he said, pulling away. "So what if we get a little ribby by the spring? My vanity can take it if yours can." He nudged her shoulder, and she relinquished a reluctant smile.

"Your vanity could do with taking a little less, if we're being honest," she pointed at the heavily darned shirt he'd slung on. "There are more patches in that thing than there is original fabric."

He opened his arm wide, peering down at the item in question in faux surprise.

"This masterpiece? Do you know how hard it is to sew

with one hand? Blood, sweat and a hell of a lot of swearing went into making this the work of art it is today."

Aelia rolled her eyes and pulled her plate back towards her, spearing into the tart again. "This is good. Can't say I'm gutted we can't give it away."

"Fortunately, I have enough left to make a spare. Give me a hand?"

"I can give you two."

"Show off."

She laughed and pushed the plate away, clearing space on the surface. Otis grabbed what they needed and they got to work, each of them handing what the other needed wordlessly. Years of cooking together had made them quite the team.

"Have the travellers had much to say about Demuto?" she asked, after a few moments' silence of rolling out the leftover pastry.

Otis paused his chopping and rubbed his forehead wearily with the back of his hand, a worried frown replacing his usually thoughtful expression.

"It's getting worse. Although admittedly they say that every year," he said with a low sigh, grabbing a cloth to wipe himself clean. "But it sounds like they have had a particularly hard time recently with the Astraea attacks."

"Why were the Astraea attacking the Peregrinians?" Aelia's hands froze, the rolling pin stilling in her hands at the mention of the Astraea. They were cold-hearted and merciless; a band of artemians who were convinced that humans should be wiped from existence. Sure, a lot of artemians viewed the humans as the weaker species, but the Astraea took their contempt to a whole new level. One that often involved bloodshed.

"It's not just humans they're targeting anymore, it's anyone who supports them. Apparently, some of the vendors were beaten black and blue just for selling to them."

Aelia felt the world shift under her feet, her mind whirling to a whole new perspective.

"One of the vendors refused to serve Mirra last night." She stared wide-eyed at Otis, the ramifications of what he'd said still hitting home. The armourer's actions may not have been solely out of prejudice, but out of fear. And if she had been scared into behaving that way, how many others would be too?

Otis' eyes snapped to Aelia's face. "I didn't see anything like that?"

"I only saw it at her stall."

"Well, that's something at least. It's surprising more haven't been frightened into similar behaviour, especially after they got hit so badly near Drias. We should be more worried that if they're acting that way, it probably won't be long until the same mentality creeps into the village."

"There were Astraea in Drias?" Aelia's heart dropped all the way to the forest floor. "That's only a day's walk from here!"

"I know, they've gained support more quickly than I would have ever thought possible."

"I thought they were just a small band of outcasts?" Aelia's hand went clammy around the rolling pin. She set it down, the meal forgotten as the threat of change hovered over them.

"Not anymore." Otis shook his head. "They may have started as a bunch of troublemakers, but with Demuto struggling the way it is I'm not surprised people are looking for someone to blame, and the Astraea are pointing the finger firmly at the humans. Every year the Peregrinians bring rumours of them becoming more aggressively active, but this year is particularly disturbing."

Aelia blinked as she processed all that he was saying. "I can't believe they were so close." She shuddered at the thought.

"I know. Try not to worry though, Aelia. Even if they did come all the way out here, which is unlikely, they can see the magic in your eyes as clear as any artemians."

The jet-black circle in his own eyes was a stark contrast against the blue of his irises, almost as obvious as her green ones, but his words did nothing to ease the fear coiling inside her. They might be safe, but what of all the humans? What of Mirra?

As if his thoughts had jumped in the same direction as her own, he asked, "Was Mirra upset about the vendor?"

"Yeah, of course, but she hides it well. Doesn't like any fuss."

It had always been the way with Mirra, ever since they were young, she just wanted to pretend that incidents like that never happened. On the whole, the two of them had been left alone. Aelia had always been freakishly strong, even for an artemian, and she'd made the other children eat their words, alongside a fair amount of dirt, if they tried to pick on them. But there had come an age when smushing someone's face into a mud pie wasn't an appropriate way to deal with their attitude problems, and Aelia had long since passed it.

"After what they were saying last night, I suppose we're lucky it wasn't worse." Otis scraped his strips of vegetables into a bowl and started adding pinches of seasoning, the smell of thyme and lemon adding a zing to the fresh scent of the red onions and purple aubergine. Aelia snapped back into the present and started trying to wrestle the sheet of pastry into the tin.

"Why, what else were they saying?"

"That the trouble in the North is leaking into Demuto. It sounds like we might finally be dragged into their war. Gods knows how the King has kept us out of it for as long as he has."

Aelia immediately regretted asking.

War. There had been whispers of it on the wind for as long as she could remember. Their dark allies in Ideolanthea, the country to the North of Demuto, had invaded the continent across the sea decades ago. Since then, Ideolanthea had sunk its claws into one province after another. The ones left standing were still fighting its dark magic, and they'd been at a stalemate for a few years now. Roping Demuto into their fight might be enough to tip the scales in their favour, but humans and artemians alike would be reluctant to fight alongside the ideolan. It might be a disadvantage to be human, but Aelia would rather have no magic at all than touch the darkness that fuelled Ideolanthea.

"Did the Peregrinians have anything to say that wasn't absolutely fucking terrifying?" Aelia pushed a loose strand of hair off her face with the back of her arm, keeping her flour-covered hand at a safe distance.

Otis huffed a laugh, placing the baking cloth over the pastry before pouring some ceramic beads on top and chucking it in the oven. He added a few logs to the heat compartment for good measure and went back to his filling.

"I take your silence as a no." She washed her hands, noticing the water pressure in the tap was a little low. She'd need to check the water when she checked the flues; they'd had plenty of rain so their supply couldn't be running out. Another thing to add to her bottomless list of things to do.

"Not my end at least." He smiled at her. "How about you? Did you manage to sell any of your pelts?"

Aelia couldn't help but smile. She put her hands into her pocket and pulled out a handful of coins, placing them on the table in front of him.

"They took all of them."

She couldn't sell the pelts to anyone in Callodosis without people wondering where the hell she'd got them from, so she had to sneak them to a Peregrinian who was sketchy enough to keep his mouth shut every year in return for a low price. The money she made from the pelts was nearly as much as she made all year logging in the forest. Her strength had helped her negotiate a little more than the humans, but nowhere near what a normal artemian could earn working the forest. Prejudiced bastards.

"Well, that's the best news I've heard in a long time." Otis grinned down at the coins, relief easing the lines of tension from his brow. "Go on, you go wash up and I'll finish this."

"You sure?" Aelia eyed the jagged fragments of crockery stacked on the worktop. "We're running dangerously low on plates as it is."

He grabbed at the cloth and whipped it at her, making it snap at her thigh with a painful cracking sound. Aelia yelped and skittered across the room. Sometimes she forgot how wickedly fast he could be.

"Cheeky git. Get out of here before I change my mind and let you finish up instead," he said, grinning.

She didn't need to be told a third time.

THE PATHS RUNNING BETWEEN THE TREES FLICKERED WITH dappled green light as the sun streamed through the dense cover of leaves. Birdsong and the gentle caress of the breeze helped to dispel her sense of unease as they walked to the village centre with arms full of the various dishes Otis had prepared for the feast.

Aelia had been trying not to catastrophise, but if Otis was concerned, she couldn't help worrying about what might be headed their way. She mentally shook herself; there was no point in dwelling on such unlikely scenarios. Such an insignificant village tucked away in the middle of nowhere would surely escape all notice, even if these rumours were true. Truth be told, it was a wonder the Peregrinians visited such an isolated place at all.

The forest was busy with people rushing to prepare themselves for the upcoming event, not showing any sign that they shared the apprehension that she felt. So, she pushed such matters out of her mind and focused on the plans for that evening.

Every year, before the Peregrinian's left, the villagers threw them a celebration. Everyone brought something, the spread becoming increasingly impressive year on year as the wealthier artemians tried to outdo themselves. Otis's contribution would be lost amongst their dishes, but that wasn't the point. Everyone brought something, and everyone got to dig in.

In return, the Peregrinians brought the forest to life, transforming their sleepy village centre into a dancefloor that would be full and heaving until dawn.

Aelia dropped off the dishes with Otis and was quickly roped into helping with the set up. She was all too happy to do as she was told, replacing the candles in the lanterns from the night before, and setting up the huge table laden with so much food she couldn't fathom how they'd get through it all in one night. At least, that's how she made herself feel better about sneaking the odd taste here and there.

The excitement was almost tangible as half the village turned up to help, everyone bustling around trying to get everything ready.

Aelia was just finishing arranging a platter full of sweet treats when something caught the corner of her eye. She whipped her head around and came face-to-face with a lithe man with white-beige hair, despite being only a few years older than her. That and the fact that his black ringed eyes lifted slightly at the corners were the main indicators of his second form, one he was all too proud of.

He put a hand on her shoulder and reached past her to steal one of the treats she'd just put in a pretty pattern, ruining the symmetry of it completely.

"Shiva," she said through gritted teeth, shrugging off his hand.

"How's it going, Aelia? Enjoying the celebrations so far?" He rolled the pastry between his fingers, the sugary coating falling onto the perfectly white cloth covering the table.

"What do you want, Shiva?" Aelia had never had time for his games. He was a Lynx, one of several in the village due to their proximity to the mountains. Typically, smaller towns and villages tended to hold families who changed into species that could be found in the local environment. Of course, there were a few families who had migrated and settled from other areas, but most families in the forest had been there for generations. Aelia had heard that cities were completely different, with artemians of all shapes and sizes living harmoniously, but the nearest city was far farther than she had ever travelled.

"Why would I want anything? Maybe I just wanted to see if you needed any help." He smiled, a smug, oily thing that just begged to be knocked right off his face with a well-placed right hook. But now was neither the time, nor the place. So, she just smiled a saccharine sweet smile.

"I wouldn't need your kind of *help* if you were the last man left in the forest. Now stop messing up my table and kindly fuck off."

Shiva tutted, feigning disappointment as he threw the pastry into the undergrowth. "You have such a filthy tongue. One of these days you're going to have to let me see what else it can do."

Shivers literally rolled down her spine at the thought, and she made no attempt to hide it.

"Baby, I'd rather blow a pinecone. Now, where do we stand with you fucking off?" She crossed her arms and waited, her expression carefully neutral.

"Another time then." He winked, completely unfazed, and sauntered away to become someone else's problem.

Aelia started brushing the worst of the mess he'd made off the tablecloth. Shiva had been obnoxious even as a child, but when his second form turned out to be an apex predator, he became outright insufferable.

Sure, he might want to get into Aelia's pants, but she knew it was only because she'd be a particularly challenging notch to add to his already heavily chipped belt. She'd never slept with anyone in the village, and nor did she intend to. She didn't need anything long-term, and it was far too small a place for things to get awkward if feelings got in the way of anything casual, so she had whatever fun she could with visitors passing through.

The hairs on the back of her neck stood on end and her eyes shot up to see the man with the fire standing across the clearing, staring right at her. He was no less imposing in the daylight; the aura of the man screamed danger at anyone brave or stupid enough to look his way. The trouble was, once she'd looked, she found it nearly impossible to stop.

She had no idea how long they both stood there, neither of them moving, but it was far longer than it was socially acceptable to stare at a stranger. Yet she couldn't move, couldn't breathe. Every cell in her body was trained on him, taking in the way his inky black hair tumbled over his ears, the way his brows pressed together in a frown. His dark, devouring eyes burned into her with an intensity that had every nerve in her body screaming at her to get away—and yet she didn't, she couldn't.

Whatever it was making her brain glitch shattered as a crash behind her made her jump out of her skin.

"Look what you did?" Shiva was yelling. His clothes were covered in food, brown chunks dripping down him onto the floor. Mirra stood open-mouthed and horrified in front of him, a tray hanging empty in her hands.

"I'm so sorry," she muttered, leaning to help him wipe it off. He recoiled.

"Don't touch me." He spat. Mirra withered under his look of pure disgust. "As if you haven't done enough, you filthy freeloader."

Aelia's blood boiled. She rushed across the clearing to get to Mirra, fully prepared to tear the contemptuous moron limb from limb. Fortunately, Otis beat her to Mirra's side.

Even with one arm, he was a force to be reckoned with. He grabbed Shiva's hand and twisted harshly, slamming him face-first into the table and pinning him there with his arm wrenched painfully behind his back.

"No one in this village uses language like that." His voice remained calm, but fury flashed in his eyes. "It is vile and beneath us all, even someone like you. If I hear so much as a whisper of such sentiments from you again, I'll make sure you join me in the one-armed club." He leant on the arm meaningfully and Shiva hissed through bared teeth.

Aelia bit her cheek to control her smile, moving to stand next to a shocked Mirra.

Point well and truly made, Otis released Shiva. He whirled around, but when he spotted Otis's hand on the dagger at his hip, he froze. Shiva looked around at everyone watching and curled his lip in a snarl, before slinking away to lick his wounded ego.

"You alright, Mirra?" Otis said gruffly.

She nodded, smiling shyly, aware of the scene they'd caused and the many eyes on them. Aelia gave her a quick hug, and neither of them spoke another word about it. As usual.

When Aelia glanced back to where the man with the fire had been standing, he was gone. She clenched her jaw against the rush of disappointment. She *had* to get a grip.

The hustle and bustle picked up around them as the people drawn by the incident got back to work, and Aelia tried her best to forget about the whole thing, menacing stranger included.

CHAPTER THREE

The Peregrinians showed the village the wild hours of the night. Their music filled the woods, the heavy drumbeat pulsing through the darkness. Callodosis seemed to come alive around them, as though the musicians had awoken the beating heart of the forest.

Keeran strode through the darkness between the ancient trunks towards the celebrations, the thump of the music growing stronger with every step he took. The shadows swallowed him whole, recognising the darkness that lurked inside him and welcoming a kindred spirit into their embrace. He knew how to use them, knew how to walk unnoticed, and tonight, they didn't let him down.

When he was sure no one was looking his way, he stepped into the clearing where the village was celebrating side by side with the Peregrinians he had been travelling with. He scanned the crowd, passing over face after face until he found the one he was looking for.

Ruddy, wrinkled, male; an inoffensive face to most, but just the sight of it was enough to make Keeran's blood boil.

He'd needed to make sure the man was who Keeran suspected him to be, and with the villagers distracted by the celebration, it had been all too easy to break into his house and find the paperwork that had confirmed it.

Keeran's attention drifted from the man, knowing he wasn't going anywhere Keeran wouldn't be able to find him. Instead, he watched the dancers from his position at the edge of the clearing, leaning one shoulder against the rough bark of a tree. Or, if he was being honest, he watched one dancer in particular.

Ever since he'd seen her in the crowd yesterday he'd been unable to get her out of his mind. The moment her piercing green eyes had locked with his, he knew something was wrong. Horribly, awfully wrong.

It was like something had rooted itself deep in his chest, tugging him towards her every second of every minute since he'd laid eyes on her. It filled him with a deep, gnawing ache unless he was near her, which, to his chagrin, he hadn't allowed to be much of a problem.

Something dark slunk in the back of his mind as the woman lifted her brown hair off the back of her neck as she danced, twisting it around her fingers to let the cool air brush against her skin. He ignored it, pushing it back into the shadows of his mind where it belonged, but not before the wall of desire radiating off of it slammed into him.

Keeran clenched his jaw against the power of it, closing his eyes and swallowing hard against the image of her hair wrapped around his hand instead of hers.

His eyes snapped open, unable to look away from her for very long.

Much like he hadn't been able to last night. Or this morning. Or all afternoon.

Shame churned inside him. He'd found her in the crowds

the night before and had hardly let her out of his sight since, following her in the shadows like the monster he tried so hard not to be. Since he'd met her, it was like he was losing his grip on his hard-won control, and he loathed it.

He absolutely fucking loathed it.

He'd nearly lost it when that silver-haired prick had approached her earlier. He couldn't quite hear what he'd said to her, even his hearing wasn't that good, but everything about her body language had screamed her unease. She'd done a good job of hiding it, her expression carefully controlled as she'd shut him down, but he could sense the tension rolling off her from way across the clearing. It was sheer luck she'd managed to get rid of him when she did. Keeran had already been on his way over to teach him that no meant no, and that was a lesson best not taught in front of the whole fucking village. The last thing he needed was to draw attention to himself.

That had been the second time she'd looked at him, her green eyes boring into his soul, as if she had been as incapable of looking away as he was.

Now, watching her dancing, he was just as transfixed.

She danced with her friend, lost in the crowd, the trail of empty tankards left in the evening's wake blurring any inhibitions they might have had. They danced freely, laughed freely, sang freely. It was like she'd become a different person from the one he'd been watching, the tension in her shoulders was gone, the hard glint in her eyes melted by the music. She seemed happy, young.

She spun around her human friend, the lanterns highlighting the softer tones in her dark hair, her dress flaring around her, revealing the curved muscles of her legs. She was striking, mesmerising, so far beyond beautiful he couldn't even find the words.

When the male artemian he recognised from the night

before elbowed his way through the crowd, Keeran stiffened, the bark digging into his shoulder.

The woman threw her arms around his neck as he appeared from among the throngs of dancers, shouting something in his ear. The man said something back, his arms squeezing her tightly before he pulled away and grinned at her with a familiarity that had Keeran clenching his fists so hard his knuckles popped.

The man was an artemian, and Keeran would put good money on him being an apex predator of some kind. That meant he wasn't with the human woman. Relationships between artemians and humans were illegal, and there would be more than enough people in a village like this who'd be keen to see them hang if they were ever caught.

No, he wouldn't be with the human, so did that mean he was with the dark-haired woman? She clearly wasn't human, the black ring around her eyes marking her as carrying magic, so they could very well be a couple.

Suddenly, watching her dance wasn't mesmerising. It was torture.

The creature who shared his mind threw itself against the leash he kept it on, rage and jealousy sweeping over him as he watched her dance with the man. He gritted his teeth so hard he was at real risk of them breaking, fighting for control as the darkness in him snapped and snarled.

The three of them exchanged a few shouted words over the pounding music, and the woman grinned before turning on her heel and elbowing her way through the gyrating crowds to leave the dancefloor and disappear between the trees. Keeran's shoulders dropped from around his ears as he released a slow breath.

At least he didn't have to watch them dancing anymore.

The urge to follow her was overwhelming, but he stomped down on it. Enough was enough. He'd had his fun stalking her through the woods last night when she snuck out to hunt, telling himself he just wanted to make sure she was safe. Though she'd shot those rabbits with enough precision that he should have been more worried for himself than for her. If she'd spotted him, she could have done him some real damage. Probably ruin his last good shirt too.

From the darkened periphery of the clearing, a group of five men broke away from where the rhythmically challenged and the elderly stood drinking. Keeran's expression darkened as he recognised the silver-haired man from earlier, heading in the same direction the woman had gone.

His decision was made for him. Keeran shrugged off the tree, a smile pulling at his lips as he rolled his shoulders. With all the dark, twisted thoughts he was battling, pounding into that smug prick and his little pack of bumpkin badasses was just the outlet he needed for his pent-up rage. All he wanted was for them to give him an excuse.

He waited until they disappeared into the night, giving them enough of a head start that they were hidden amongst the denser foliage that sprang up just past the village centre.

Slowly, as if he had all the time in the world, he stalked after them.

He left the lights behind, the music becoming a dull thud in the background. His senses were fixed on the group he was steadily gaining on, on the scent they left in their wake, mixing with hers. It didn't take long for them to catch up with her, and he settled into the shadows and waited, just within earshot.

"Shiva." The surprise in her voice betrayed her fear, and it made the darkness in him rattle the bars of its cage, its anger sudden and devastating.

"Where are you sneaking off to, Aelia?" The silver-haired Shiva sauntered closer to her, his friend's fanning out around him.

Aelia. Her name was Aelia. Keeran mouthed it silently, tasting the way it felt on his tongue.

She crossed her arms, looking pointedly at the four men standing behind Shiva.

"I'm flattered that you felt the need for so much backup," she said, arching a brow. "Although, after getting your arse handed to you by a one-armed man, I suppose it was wise not to take your chances."

Shiva's face darkened, the smug smile disappearing as he took a step closer to her. Keeran tensed, the muscles in his legs coiled and ready to spring.

"There's more than one way to hurt someone, Aelia. Just because you can't think past your temper doesn't mean the rest of us don't stop to work things through." Shiva tilted his head, exposing his canines with every sneered word.

Aelia rolled her eyes and turned to go. "Give it your best shot, Shiva."

He grabbed her arm and yanked her back, and Keeran's eyes narrowed, a muscle in his jaw twitching as he reined himself in. Not yet. Not quite.

"She wants my best shot, guys?" he said to the men behind him, and they drew closer, their laughter low and menacing. Shiva pulled her close and hissed right into her face. "What if I told you I knew about your little hunting expeditions? That a good enough shot for you?"

Even in the darkness, Keeran could see the colour drain from her cheeks. She tried to pull her arm free, but Shiva held on tight.

"You're going to have to do better than making up bullshit like that, you miserable piece of shit. Following me into the woods and threatening me with what? Lies that you can't prove." She laughed, leaning into him this time. "That's pathetic even for you."

"Oh, I think it would be pretty easy to prove." The smile

returned to Shiva's face, his teeth white in the darkness. "Once I showed them where you stash your bow, I think the council would be all too willing to check your stores. And I bet they'd find contraband in your little human friend's house, too." He tutted, shaking his head slowly.

Aelia didn't reply; she just stared at him, as if her whole world was crumbling around her and she had no idea how to stop it. Keeran did. Shiva was the problem, and oh, how he longed to solve it for her.

Savouring her silence, Shiva grinned round at his friends.

"Have any of you heard her lost for words before?" That elicited another laugh and a few murmured encouragements from the sycophantic morons. Shiva returned his attention to Aelia, his eyes lingering on her face for a moment, savouring the fear she was failing to hide. "You've always been such a cocky little bitch, not knowing how to treat your superiors. Maybe if you showed a little respect, I could turn a blind eye to your illegal little ventures."

This time, she succeeded in yanking her arm free, the anger in her eyes melting the fear that had been there moments before.

"My superior? Just because you can Shift and I can't?" she scoffed, her face twisting into a snarl that had even Keeran blanching. But what did she mean she couldn't Shift? She was no human, of that he was sure; the ring of magic in her eye was unmistakable. He'd never heard of an artemian that couldn't Shift before. "Don't mistake me for some human you can push around, Shiva. You're just a limp dicked prat hiding behind a bullshit macho façade. Well, guess what, buddy, you aren't fooling anyone."

Shiva snapped. With all the speed of an artemian predator, he struck her right across the face, whipping her head round to the side.

Keeran saw red.

He was on them before they could register he was coming, blurring through the night to grab Shiva by the collar and throw him to the ground hard enough to hear the air whoosh out of his lungs. That winded, he wasn't going anywhere in a hurry.

That gave him time to deal with the others.

They rounded on him at once, but he was ready. As one of them ran at him, he took hold of his throat and used his momentum to launch him into two of the others, sending all three sprawling. The one left standing tried to stop in his tracks, his confidence failing now that Keeran wasn't outnumbered. Fucking coward.

Keeran had to really rein himself in, keeping his blows light enough not to kill him, landing a few easily past the man's sloppy defence. Bored, Keeran angled his fist with calculated precision, smiling when he heard the satisfying crunch of ribs breaking. He swiped his leg round, sending the man crashing to the floor in time to face the three others who'd staggered to their feet.

Keeran longed for a challenge; it had been so long since he'd really lost himself in a fight, since he really settled into the blood frenzy of his people. This was all too easy.

He sank into a crouch and beckoned the three over. After an uncertain glance at each other, they charged.

One ended up on the floor with a broken arm, one lost enough teeth that he'd never bite an apple again, and the last might find he had a fertility issue in the future if the crunch beneath Keeran's knee was anything to go by. All before Shiva had caught his breath enough to stand.

The four men didn't wait for their fallen leader; they staggered and stumbled through the undergrowth as fast as their assorted injuries would allow them.

Keeran had his back to Shiva and Aelia, making sure the walking wounded really did leave, and allowing the terrible black he knew would have filled his eyes to settle before he turned to her. It transpired he needn't have worried; her attention was firmly fixed elsewhere.

Aelia had Shiva pinned face down in the dirt, his arms wrenched at a horrible angle behind his back. Any harder and she'd dislocate his shoulder. She leant in close from where she was perched on his back to whisper in his ear.

"If you're going to threaten someone, you really need to prove you can back it up," she hissed. "Like when I say, 'if you or your friends so much as breathe a word to the council I'll cut off that limp little dick we mentioned earlier', I make damned sure you know I mean it." She moved a knee between his legs and shifted her weight back onto it. Shiva screamed, and even Keeran felt like squirming as she squashed it against the hard ground.

"We won't, we won't," Shiva cried, the desperation in his voice pathetic, albeit understandable.

"You sure?" Aelia didn't let up, seeming to enjoy herself.

"I swear."

"Alright then." She shifted her weight and climbed off him, letting Shiva roll into the foetal position to clutch between his legs. She stood over him, legs wide in a power stance that had Keeran's stomach flipping. Who was this woman? "What are you waiting for? Off you fuck."

Aelia shooed him away with a lazy flick of her wrist. Shiva scrambled to his feet, crashed to all fours as his legs gave way, and half crawled, half ran in the direction his friends had gone.

Aelia watched him go with a smug smile, only turning to Keeran when Shiva had disappeared completely from sight.

"Do you know how long I've been waiting for an excuse to thump that prick? And the first chance I get for *years,* and you swoop in and steal it from me," she said, and he honestly couldn't tell if she was joking. A hint of a smile pulled at her lips, but there was an annoyed glint in her eye that surprised him.

She looked up at him with her hands on her hips, taller than he'd guessed she'd be from a distance, but still having to arch her neck back to look up at him. Not many people had the guts to talk to him like that, especially not after they'd seen him wipe out four grown artemians without breaking a sweat. But here she was, scolding him as if he ought to be the one terrified of her.

"I'm sorry." He kept the smile out of his voice, knowing full well it wouldn't help the situation. "Had I known, I would have left him to you. I just thought you were a little outnumbered."

"Oh, don't get me wrong, I appreciate you stepping in. But you could have shared," she countered, looking genuinely put out.

"What? Were you waiting for an invitation?" He cocked his head, raising one brow expectantly, hiding his smile. "I was waiting for some help, to be honest."

Aelia rolled her eyes at his obvious lie, crossing her arms and cocking her hip.

"You didn't give me a chance. One second I was handed a golden opportunity to break Shiva's nose, the next, you had them all running like a bunch of scolded schoolboys."

"Well, in my defence, they needed to be taught a lesson," Keeran said, still suppressing a smile. "Ganging up like that on one person..." He shook his head slowly, tutting. He didn't miss how her gaze darted to his mouth.

"I think if anything, you just taught them that they need even more backup next time."

Keeran huffed a breath through his nose. "I concede that you might have a point there."

She looked in the direction they'd run off in, the slight

irritation in her face slipping to reveal the worry underlying it.

"I don't think they'll go to the council," Keeran said, guessing where her thoughts had disappeared to. From the way her eyes snapped back to his, he'd guessed right.

"You don't?" Aelia uncrossed her arms, subconsciously twining her fingers together and twisting them nervously. "I do. Those men are all ego, and we just seriously embarrassed them."

Keeran fought the darkness rising in him with every fibre of his being, knowing how it would infiltrate his eyes. If he needed to pay them each a little visit before he left, he would, but now was not the time to think about it, not when Aelia was standing right in front of him.

"I think that's why they'll stay quiet," he said, looking for any sign of fear in her face, any sign that the evil in him was visible. "Shame has a way of sealing the lips of cowards."

Aelia's eyes narrowed at him, but he didn't mind. He'd take sceptical over fearful.

"And what about you?" Her fingers had stopped their nervous fidgeting, a hint of steel in her eyes once more. "You obviously heard what they accused me of. Do I need to worry about you, too?"

"After I saw what you did to Shiva?" Keeran opened his eyes wide and shook his head. "I wouldn't dare."

That elicited a smile. At last. It sent a shock right through him, and it was all he could do not to stare. She was so beautiful; fierce, reckless, and perhaps a little violent... but absolutely fucking beautiful.

He stepped closer and her eyes darted round, as if just now realising she was alone with a complete stranger. Keeran knew how people saw him, knew that they picked up on the monster that lurked just beneath the surface, no matter how hard he tried to control it.

His eyes roved over her, trying to read what she was feeling. Her pupils were so wide the green of her irises almost merged with the black ring of magic, and he could see her pulse beating hard at the base of her throat... but was that fear? Or did she feel the same draw he did, the pull that made him loathe the distance between them, as though it would be the most natural thing in the world to take her in his arms and never let go.

Only one way to find out.

He tried to quieten the darkness he knew lived in his eyes, to soften them as best he could before taking another step closer, testing her.

Her breathing hitched, but she didn't step away, her chin tilting to keep her eyes locked onto his.

"I saw you yesterday," he said, his voice low. "In the crowd."

"You did?" He didn't miss the way she swallowed heavily, the way her eyes seemed unable to leave his. His heart pounded as he took a gamble and raised a hand, running his fingers lightly over the bare skin of her arm, praying to the gods that she wouldn't run, that he wasn't misreading this. Because just the brush of her soft skin against his fingertips had his blood racing, his mind a tumultuous mix of desire and trepidation. He couldn't scare her away, he must not frighten her.

"You know I did," he said, letting his fingers glide higher up her arm. "You saw me nearly drop the pole when I spotted you."

Her lips twitched, and some of the tension in his chest eased.

"I saw."

His fingers stopped their gentle caress, grabbing her arm and pulling her so close her chest pressed into his. Her gasp would have made him panic were it not for the way she pressed herself into him, the feel of her breasts against him sending his thoughts spinning. He lowered his head so he was whispering in her ear, the scent of her skin hitting him in an intoxicating rush.

"I've spent every moment since wondering how to get you alone," he admitted, pulling back just enough to read her expression, mere inches from his own. She didn't hesitate.

"And now that you have, what do you plan to do with me?" Her words were cocky, as brash as everything else he'd heard her say, and yet there was the unmistakable trace of apprehension in her eyes.

So he moved slowly, a predator earning the trust of its prey. He kept his grip on her arm, raising his other hand to trace the line of her jaw, tilting her head up until her mouth was level with his own, holding her steady as his eyes burned into hers. Her lips called to him, his body alight with the need to crush into her, to taste and claim, but he held himself back, terrified of scaring her off.

Time seemed to slow as he lowered his lips closer to hers, every breath she took pressing into him as she arched backwards, lifting away from his fingers beneath her chin as she leant into him.

A scream pierced the forest, and their heads snapped towards it in perfect synchronicity. The music, faint as it was, collapsed into silence with a discordant clash of panicked notes.

Aelia didn't even pause to look at him. Without warning, she was sprinting through the trees towards the village centre like a creature possessed.

He took off after her, arms pumping as he caught up. Gods, she was fast. In a matter of moments, they broke through the trees edging the clearing, just in time to see the dark silhouettes that emerged from the shadows step into the light.

They ringed the entire clearing, dark and sinister, too huge to be anything other than the strongest artemians. One broke free from the others, his face illuminated by the lanterns, and Keeran's stomach plummeted like a stone.

Fuck.

Fuck fuck fuck.

CHAPTER FOUR

Aelia stood with her knees bent in a gentle crouch, reflexes taught and ready for action. The celebrations had died, people staring in stunned silence at the figures looming in the darkness, fully encircling the small clearing. One stood in the middle of the band, sagging strings the only thing connecting the two halves of the broken instrument he held in each hand.

Two appeared from either side of her, mere meters away. The man from the woods pulled her closer, dragging her further into the clearing away, putting himself between her and them. She was too stunned to do anything other than let him, to even notice what he was doing.

Several of the shadows moved forward, heading straight for the tables that held the remnants of the feast and flipping them with a crash that had the crowd flinching back.

"What do you think you're doing?" A man Aelia knew to be on the council strode towards them, shoulders squared with all the confidence of a man with his whole village at his back.

One of the strangers left the tables they'd been heaping

on top of one another, her black uniform indistinguishable from those of her companions. In a few strides she was on him, striking him down with cold indifference. He crumpled, his knees barely hitting the floor before she'd drawn her blade, clocking him on the temple with the hilt and stepping tidily aside as he landed face-first on the floor.

Gasps and murmurs sparked through the distressed crowd, everyone shuffling back a few steps to huddle a little further from the unconscious body and the woman who'd put it there. Only then did she look up, her eyes alight and feral, as if daring anyone else to step forward, as if wishing they would.

When no one did, she smiled, sending a shiver scuttling down Aelia's spine, before turning her attention once more to the tables, now piled so high that it took four of them to launch the final one to the top of the heap.

Silence still reigned, Aelia as transfixed as everyone else as they set fire to the tables. The dry timber took quickly, the white cloth Aelia had so painstakingly laid out earlier acting like kindling as the flames billowed up into the night sky.

Fire was a nightmare they all shared, and the villagers began muttering, their fear of the strangers becoming overshadowed by their terror of a forest fire. But before they could act, before any momentum was gained, a figure moved out of the darkness and into the glow of the fire.

He walked assuredly, taking his time as he took to his stage, surveying his audience with unhurried hauteur. He stopped directly in front of the bonfire, his position meaning he was nothing more than a silhouette against the burning orange light. When he broke the silence, his tone was laced with familiarity, utterly at ease with the eyes of so many strangers on him.

"My dear friends, welcome." He held up his arms. His voice, a roar itself, carried easily over the blaze. "This is indeed a night of celebration. Not only for the entertainment and the feast, but as a celebration of us and the magic in our blood, of the power we share as our birthright."

He paced deliberately in front of them, his features still obscured in shadow, but his gait was commanding. The power in his broad, slightly hunched profile was highlighted by the backdrop of flames.

"I am Beserkir, leader of the Astraea, and I stand before you a proud man. I am proud to be with you today. I am proud to be living in Demuto in a time of such potential. I am proud to be able to make these changes with you, my fellow artemians." He was articulate, his words rolling off his tongue with careful eloquence.

Ice shot through Aelia's veins. Otis had been right to worry; the Astraea had come to Callodosis. She dared to look away from the man to scan the crowd. She spotted Mirra and Fenrir deep in the heart of the clearing, and a surge of fear had her fighting the urge to elbow her way to them, grab Mirra and run into the night. They wouldn't make it, she knew they wouldn't, not with every meter of the clearing guarded by the Astraea.

"You have my deepest gratitude, my dear friends, for allowing me to use this night, this gathering of comrades and like minds, to share with you the good news. Tonight, your celebration is added to as we welcome in a new era, one in which the pride of the artemians, and our country, will be reborn." He paused, raking his eyes through the crowd. His demeanour changing until he spat his next words with venom.

"Since our founding ancestors settled in Demuto, the labour of hard-working artemians like you, has been exploited by the human parasites. Riding on the backs of our efforts, they have succeeded in reaping the benefits of our superiority for generations. For too long, this has been tolerated. For too long, you have been subjected to this injustice.

"I, and my fellow Astraea who know this truth, have come here today to light a flame to rid you of the oppression of these injustices, to burn the infestation from your streets, to start a fire that their pestilence *cannot* extinguish.

"In so doing, we make a promise. We will cleanse the streets of all Demuto in the same way we'll purify Callodosis tonight. There will be casualties, artemians so infected by their contact with the human plague that they too must be eradicated. But I promise you once more, anyone who stands in our way will be purged without mercy and we will, *we will*," he shouted, "be victorious". The threat hung in the air, mixing with the smoke in a swirling smog of toxicity.

"Who amongst you has the courage to act on what you know to be right, to stand up for your right to a country you can be proud of? Who will join us this night in our quest to erase humankind from Demuto?"

No one moved.

Beserkir ducked his head low, his gaze swinging slowly over the crowd, looking up at them from beneath his brows.

"Are there none here who recognise the truth in our message, who will stand up for what they know to be right? How many of you have resented the humans, longing for a chance to be rid of them?" Beserkir slammed his fist into his palm. "Now is your chance." He held his arms out wide. "Take it."

The crowd listened without making a sound, the mass of people standing eerily quiet, their expressions hard and guarded. Whether this stemmed from shock or outrage, she couldn't be sure, but the only response he received was deathly quiet.

Until a man edged his way out of the crowd.

Aelia's scowl deepened, her fear transforming to rage as

she recognised the white-blonde hair of Shiva striding towards the leader of the Astraea. He triggered a tide of movement, emboldening others to come forward until more than a dozen people, *her* people, stood before Beserkir.

How could they, how *dare* they volunteer to join him, to join a movement that so unabashedly strove for the genocide of an entire race?

It made her blood boil. She would not, could not, sit back and watch this. She took a step forward, preparing to fight her way to Mirra and kick the living shit out of anyone who tried to touch her, when a hand snatched around her arm and dragged her back.

Aelia's eyes jumped from the hand around her arm, to the hulking lump of muscle it belonged to. His expression was rigid, unreadable, and fixed on her with an intensity that made her blink. It took her a second to recover her thoughts, her mouth opening to tell him what she'd do to his hand if he didn't take it off her right that very second, when a voice broke the silence and her heart spluttered in her chest.

"Please don't mistake the stupidity of the few for the acceptance of the rest," Otis said, the villagers turning to face where he stood at the edge of the clearing. A space opened around him as he walked towards Beserkir, the crowd parting around him like a blade cutting through flesh. "You and your kind are not welcome here. Humans have been a part of our community for too long for us to allow you to spill your poison on the soil we toil over. Leave now and avoid violence that will end in bloodshed on both sides."

Aelia pulled against the hand that still held her, trying to yank herself free, but his grip held firm. Shocked, she tried harder, using all her strength, but it was like it was nothing to him. Never before had anyone been able to overpower her, to make her feel weak, but this man restrained her without breaking a sweat.

"Let me go," she hissed, still trying to wrestle her arm free.

"You saw what they did to that man," he said. "They could kill you."

Who the fuck did he think he was? She was missing what Beserkir was saying to Otis, their voices lost in the scuffle as she tried to break away, so she twisted towards them. Peering over the crowd, she saw a couple of the black uniformed thugs approaching Otis from behind.

"I understand. You may not think I do, but I do." Beserkir's voice carried over the clearing as he sauntered closer to Otis. "I have known many who have been taken in by their pitiful plight, but just because they are weaker than us, does not automatically mean we must protect them, pander to them. They take up jobs that could be better fulfilled by artemians, they eat food that would otherwise sustain those who give back to the community rather than drain it."

Otis stood tall in front of the man, head held high as he stopped in front of him.

"This is wrong." Otis shook his head and waved his good arm at the sea of faces behind him. "And we won't let you hurt anyone else here, human or otherwise."

Aelia chose that moment to spin and knee the towering stack of brawn still holding her right in the fruits. Hard.

She was fast when she wanted to be and, distracted as he was by events unfolding around them, she managed to take him by surprise. She felt a twinge of remorse as she felt them squash beneath her knee, her mind jumping momentarily to how tempted she'd been to pound into them in a vastly different way mere minutes before. But there was no time for such reflection.

He may have looked like the biggest badass she'd ever seen, but even tough guys crumpled with a well-placed knee to the goolies. He dropped his hold on her and bent double, hands cupped between his legs, and she took her opportunity to dash into the throng.

People had hugged closer to one another in their terror, and she struggled to push her way through, sliding and shoving her way closer to where Otis stood, just visible over the sea of heads.

"Your bravery is commendable, my friend." Beserkir rested a hand on Otis' good shoulder. Aelia was still stuck halfway through the muttering mass of people, frantically pushing and sliding between them. "But you're deluded if you think you have a choice in the matter."

In a blur of movement possible by only the most powerful of artemians, Beserkir drew his blade and plunged it into Otis' chest. He twisted it, shoving it in deeper, his face made monstrous by the dark delight contorting his features.

Aelia's scream was lost amongst countless others, the tenuous control everyone had on their fear breaking in a heartbeat. People heaved around her, jostling her from every angle as they tried to flee, but she stood rooted to the spot, unable to look away as Beserkir slid his blade free. Otis stayed upright for one long, agonising moment, before he dropped to the floor, motionless.

Aelia snapped into motion, shrieking his name over and over as she wrestled her way towards him, shoving anyone aside who got in her way. After what felt like an age, she broke free of the wall of people and staggered towards where Otis lay, skidding to her knees next to him. Beserkir had moved away, commanding the Astraea with cold efficiency as they closed in on the panicking villagers, but Aelia hardly noticed.

She rolled Otis over, heart tumbling when he looked up at her, alive and conscious. Her relief was dashed immediately as her eyes fell to the blood pouring from the jagged mess of flesh in his chest. She pressed her hands against it, desperately trying to stop it, but the blood pumped between her fingers in sickening waves.

She chanted nonsense at him, telling him he was going to be okay, as if she could make it real by saying it often enough, desperately enough. Tears streaked her face, dropping from her cheeks and onto his red soaked shirt. Otis raised an unsteady hand and clasped it around her wrist, his grip weak and trembling. Aelia blinked through her tears to look at him, quietening her sobs to hear him.

"Aelia," he croaked, his face twisted with pain. "Aelia, you must leave..."

He broke off, eyes rolling shut as a wave of pain hit him.

"No, no, no," Aelia pleaded, her gaze dropping to the weakening flow of blood around her hands. Otis let go of her wrist and moved his hand slowly to his waist, pulling his jacket aside to free the dagger he always wore from its hilt.

"Take this," he rasped, the effort of holding it out to her making him grit his teeth.

"No," she sobbed, shaking her head vehemently.

"Aelia." His voice was stronger this time, the authority in it unmistakable. "Take it."

She did as she was told, taking one hand from his wound to clutch the familiar hilt, smearing it with crimson.

"Listen to me," Otis said, grabbing her hand. "You must leave. You must take our savings and hire a boat, flee across the sea to Mithrylaya, and find the Del Awane family. Show them the dagger, and they'll help you."

Aelia's face knotted in confusion, her thoughts a tangled mess, but before she could process what he was saying, he squeezed her tight, shaking her arm.

"Say it back to me," he wheezed, eyes feverishly bright.

"The Del Awane family," she repeated, the agony in her chest unbearable as she watched him slipping away.

"Good," he dropped his head back, blood spattering his chin with every breath.

Tears poured from her with every convulsive gasp that wracked her body.

"Please," she begged him, begged the gods, begged anyone who would listen. But no one could help as she watched his last rattling breaths, watched his soul drain from his eyes, leaving them devoid of everything that she had treasured. His hand became a deadweight in hers, and she dropped her head, unsure she could survive the wave of loss that slammed over her.

Beserkir's voice carried over the chaos, and she became aware of her surroundings once more. Aelia's eyes followed him, widening at the devastation that had erupted around her. Some of the villagers had Shifted in their attempt to escape the carnage, and woodland creatures were being torn down in a bloody mess of tooth and claw by the band of some of the most dangerous predators in Demuto. Fear became the perfect partner to her pain, tangling together until she was incapable of feeling anything else as she saw the Astraea meet the villagers with a wall of experienced brutality.

Even in the few frantic heartbeats she watched, the people she had grown up with fell by the dozen, the forest floor already slick with their blood as the bodies piled up. The clearing became a panic-fuelled stampede as the villagers fled, running in all directions to avoid the merciless slaughter.

Movement caught Aelia's eye, and she turned to see several large horse-drawn carts being pulled towards the village centre. Frowning past her tears, she watched with confusion until they rounded the bend and she realised what they were.

Thick steel bars rose from the carts to form huge cages, empty and waiting.

"Round them up," Beserkir ordered, and Aelia's head snapped round to look at him, her grief giving way to pure, unadulterated hatred.

She placed Otis' hand on his chest, squeezing it one last time, and clutched his dagger tightly in her slippery grip. She hauled herself to her feet, eyes dark as they slid to where Beserkir stood with his back to her, several meters away.

Aelia lunged into a sprint, hurtling towards him, a madness descending over her that was impossible to think past. Everything in her longed to kill this man, her very soul seeming to burn with the intensity of her wrath, and she was more than willing to die trying.

Something slammed into her, sending her sprawling to the ground in a winded heap. Her dagger flew from her grasp, rolling across the grass and out of reach. Blinking, she found herself tangled with a human, his eyes wide and ringless as he tried to pull himself free of her.

Before he could, someone hooked under his arms and hoisted him upright, dragging him kicking and screaming towards the cages. The Astraea hardly noticed his attempts to free himself, the human flailing madly as he was launched into the cage with a few others.

Aelia's chest heaved, panic rising in her throat, bitter and overwhelming. She twisted and crawled towards the dagger, feet pounding around her, her ears ringing with the terrified shrieks filling the night air.

Someone tried to jump over her, missed, and kicked her in the stomach, sending the breath whooshing from her lungs. The pain was lost in the panic as her diaphragm spasmed, refusing to draw air in to replace what she'd lost. Seconds ticked by, her entire consciousness homed in on the absence of oxygen, her mouth opening and closing in futile attempts to breathe. Just when she was sure she was going to die, her lungs kicked in, dragging in air in a delicious gasp.

And then the pain hit her.

She groaned, rolling over to reach for the dagger, hissing past the stabbing pain in her ribs.

"Get the fuck away from her," she heard a familiar voice shout.

Fenrir.

Jaw clenched with the pain, she struggled to her feet, one hand clutching her side, the other gripping the hilt of Otis's dagger.

Fenrir had Mirra at his back, arms wide as he snarled at the two Astraeans who were closing in on them. Aelia staggered towards them, horror lurching within her as she saw Mirra peer out from under Fenrir's arm.

"Behind you," Aelia screamed, lurching into a run.

Fenrir whirled around to see the other Astraeans who'd been sneaking up on them. He tucked an arm around Mirra and dragged her sideways, trying to keep himself between her and the Astraeans, but there were too many of them.

One of them grabbed at Mirra and Fenrir tugged her away, bringing his fist swinging into the Astraean's face with a crunch even Aelia could hear. She gritted her teeth and pushed past the pain in her ribs, running faster towards them and leaping onto the back of one of the Astraeans.

She didn't hesitate, plunging her dagger into the man's chest over and over until he gave way beneath her, pushing herself off and managing to stay upright as the artemian collapsed at her feet. She dropped to a crouch and snarled at the others, moving to put herself next to Fenrir, keeping Mirra between them.

"Come on," she jeered, teeth flashing in the firelight, her anger taking her past the point of mania. She burned with the need to kill as many of these fuckers as she possibly could. "Come on, you fucking cowards."

They made no move, the three remaining Astraea looming just out of arm's reach, pulling their blades free from their sheaths.

"We need to get her out of here," Fenrir said without taking his eyes off of them.

Aelia's lip curled. "We have to get past them first."

"Take her and go, I'll hold them off."

"Not fucking likely," she spat, glaring at the steel that glinted dangerously in their hands, wickedly sharp and competently wielded. No way was she leaving him to face that alone. "We push past them together—"

Her words cut off as she realised belatedly what the Astraeans had been waiting for. More black uniformed figures stalked towards them from between the churning mass of people, all armed and ready, a red crest emblazoned on their chests.

Their slim chance of surviving faded to nothing, but as her eyes met Fenrir's, she was filled with an overwhelming determination. He nodded and looked back at Mirra.

"Give them hell," he said, a thousand unspoken words passing between the three of them in the fraction of a second they had spare.

Then the Astraea were on them.

Aelia slashed wildly with her dagger, but her untrained efforts could only keep them at bay for so long. They grabbed her and threw her to the floor, away from Mirra and Fenrir. Boots thumped into her as they kicked at her from all angles, and she curled in on herself, quickly abandoning all attempts to stand as pain took over all her senses. She could see nothing past the legs surrounding her, each of them swinging mercilessly until she felt sure she would die there, tucked in a ball on the floor.

When they stopped, she could barely open her eyes past the agony, unable to distinguish what hurt and what didn't. It seemed like every inch of her had been beaten to a swollen, sticky pulp. She forced her head up, opening her eyes to see Fenrir still standing, lashing out as the Astraea reached past him to grab at Mirra.

There were too many of them, and she watched him succumb, three of them restraining him as Mirra was dragged away. Fenrir roared, wrenching an arm free and throwing it at the man holding her. The Astraean deflected it, pulling Mirra in front of him and wrapping one arm around her neck, locking her in place.

Fenrir threw his elbow back in the face of one of the other Astraeans, loosening his grip enough for him to pull loose, lunging towards Mirra and trying to wrestle her free. The man wrenched her back, dragging her by the neck towards the cages.

Aelia tried to push up off the floor, but only managed to prop herself up on one elbow before her arm collapsed from under her, her cheek slamming into the ground. Fresh waves of pain immobilised her, her body unresponsive despite her terror as she watched Fenrir drop to his knees under the weight of several of the Astraea, his arms twisted inescapably behind him.

His face dropped, anger slipping into horror as his eyes landed on Mirra. Dread, oily and nauseating, washed over Aelia as she twisted her neck to look.

The Astraean was crushing her neck with his arm, mistaking her frantic writhing for a bid for freedom as he suffocated her. A tortured scream rasped out of Aelia as she tried to crawl towards them, watching Mirra fight for air as the unwitting man hauled her backwards to the cages. Her fingers clawed at his arm, her mouth gaping open, her heels sliding desperately against the blood-soaked grass.

Her struggles weakened and her eyes, bulging and bloodshot, turned glassy as her body sagged, a deadweight in the man's arms.

Aelia sank her fingers into the earth, trying to pull herself towards her friend, mouth open in silent despair as the Astraean noticed Mirra had collapsed. He twisted himself round, pausing as he took in her lifeless expression, and dropped her to the ground.

"You just cost me a captive." The timbre of that voice, the distinctive way it wrapped its words in calm familiarity despite their vile nature, would be forever lodged in Aelia's mind.

Beserkir sauntered over, hands in his pockets, stepping past Aelia to address Fenrir.

"You don't look like your second form is anything that can slip through bars," he continued, his gaze running over Fenrir's broad, heavily muscled shoulders. "I suppose it's only fair that you take her place. A life for a life. Load him up."

The Astraeans hoiked him to his feet, ignoring his snarls of pain as they wrenched his shoulders nearly out of their sockets. Aelia cried out, trying to push past the pain to stand.

Beserkir looked down at her and snapped his fingers at one of his thugs, who wasted no time in swinging his leg back and kicking her in the face. Her head snapped back, her neck wrenched to an unnatural angle. Her vision flickered, blurring into black at the edges, and she waited breathlessly for the next impact.

When it didn't come, she tried to blink past the darkness encroaching on her consciousness, but she was only able to make out two pillared legs spread wide, right between her and Beserkir.

She tried to lift her gaze higher, squinting at the hazy image in front of her. Numbly, she recognised the figure, and the last thing she saw before she succumbed to oblivion was the looming shape of the man with the fire. The man who'd held her back.

CHAPTER FIVE

A sombre silence reigned over the forest, even the birdsong seeming subdued in the grey morning light. It was a risk to attempt this in the daytime, but Keeran had missed his chance last night, and he certainly wasn't going to leave without finishing what he came for.

He checked around him, certain no one was watching but needing to make damn sure. There was no movement between the vast trunks; the paths that cut into the dense undergrowth were deserted, the wooden houses perched overhead showed no sign of life, and Keeran doubted they would for hours yet.

The Astraea had taken all the humans they hadn't killed from the village, leaving the surviving artemians reeling. Peregrinians and locals alike had grouped together to try and control the fire, tending to the wounded and moving the dead. It had been a long night for everyone, and those who could had retired to the safety of their homes, whilst those too injured to make the climb were being tended to in the village hall.

Keeran had waited until he saw the last person slip into their wooden treehouse, the Peregrinians having long since disappeared to their camp. And then he'd waited some more.

Finally, he shrugged out from where he hid, and began to climb the stairs up the trunk to the elaborate wooden home that spanned across three trees, each building connected via a gently swinging rope bridge.

Violence shadowed Keeran's eyes as he arrived at the front door, the ornate extravagance of the structure making the creature in his mind slink into consciousness. The tap of its obsidian claws echoed round his skull as it paced back and forth. War crime paid well, evidently. It was one of the rare times he and his other side were in agreement, but the man who lived here must die, painfully.

Keeran dropped to a crouch and picked the lock, fingers steady as he waited for the satisfying click of success. He turned the polished wooden handle and cracked the door open just enough for him to slip into the dark hallway beyond.

Shutting it silently behind him, he began making his way through to the bedroom, his steps silent on the heavily rugged floor. Thanks to his investigations earlier that night, he knew exactly where to go. He'd also made sure that his target lived alone. Yet Keeran still felt a cold rush of relief as he teased open the bedroom door and saw just a single bump beneath the thick duvet.

The beast inside him rumbled an approving growl in the back of his mind as Keeran stalked towards the bed, pulling a dagger free, his other hand reaching to curl around the duvet. He yanked it back in one smooth movement, uncovering the bleary, blinking man beneath.

Fear flooded his black ringed eyes as he focused on Keeran, darting between him and the dagger with terrified surprise.

"General Morbeck." It wasn't a question. Keeran wouldn't be here if he wasn't certain, but the man nodded anyway.

"Y-yes?" he stammered.

"You have been found guilty of treason in the War of Two Kings. You successfully conspired to murder countless of your own comrades, an act which has gone unpunished for decades. I have come to remedy that fact." Keeran felt nothing as he watched Morbeck's expression turn from afraid to downright petrified.

"Who are you?" he choked out, his voice barely more than a squeak.

Keeran leant in close, letting the darkness in him shine through, revelling in the man's terror as he saw the evil enter Keeran's eyes. The beast in him snapped its teeth, impatient for the revenge Keeran was dangling before it. He made it wait a little longer.

"You don't remember me?" Keeran said with a predatory tilt of his head. "Well, I suppose you wouldn't, I was just a child back then. It didn't stop you killing us though did it, from ordering the death of every man, woman and child in the army."

"You're back." Even in the dim light, Keeran could see the colour drain from Morbeck's face. "How many of you?"

"Just me." Keeran tightened his grip on the handle of the dagger. "But that's more than enough for you to worry about."

He slipped the blade between Morbeck's ribs, making sure the tip pierced his pounding heart. Keeran grinned, making sure the last thing the man saw was the evil flashing in his eyes as he watched him take his last, gasping breaths.

He pulled the dagger free and sheathed it, the beast settling back, satiated for now. He eyed the unlit candles on the bedside table and tutted.

"You should know better than to have an open flame so

close to the bed, Morbeck." Keeran raised his hand and snapped his fingers, his magic jumping at his command to ignite a flame at his fingertip.

He raised the finger to his lips and blew, sending the flame skittering over the bedsheets. He didn't wait to see the bed erupt into flames, he didn't need to. He could feel them devouring their target obediently, the dry timber catching alight in a heartbeat. It was only when he began jogging down the stairs that he severed his connection to the fire, his magic receding into the corner of his mind, leaving the mindless flames in its wake, no less hungry for its absence.

By the time he reached the forest floor, the entire building was ablaze, the glass blowing out and raining down around him. A shard caught his cheek as he walked away, and he wiped at the thin trickle of blood, looking at the red stain on his fingers.

When he considered all the blood he had on his hands, he supposed it was only fair he added a little of his own into the mix.

KEERAN SLIPPED BACK INTO AELIA'S TREEHOUSE, WORRIED SHE might have woken whilst he was gone, but his heart quietened when he saw her, tucked up on the sofa where he'd left her.

He crossed the room and knelt beside her, pressing his fingers to the pulse at her neck. When he was satisfied it was steady, he pulled away, allowing himself only a moment to watch her before he left. Okay, maybe two.

Even unconscious, expression slack and mouth open, he found himself transfixed, albeit with a slight smile on his lips.

Determined not to be a creep, or at least not to be caught

being one if she suddenly came to, he rose to his feet and headed to the kitchen. He'd become acquainted with the layout of the place when he'd first brought her here, right after that genocidal maniac had had her beaten to within an inch of her life.

Thanks to his intervention, she'd wake up feeling like she'd been double-barrelled by a horse, but at least she'd be up and walking.

Keeran turned the tap and frowned at the slow flow of the water. He leant over the sink and washed the blood from his cheek, the cut having already healed to a fine red line, running his hands through his now wet hair to slick it back.

He eyed the tap thoughtfully for a moment, wondering if fixing it might be crossing some sort of boundary, before deciding he didn't give a fuck. With a low, decisive grunt, he turned on his heel and left the kitchen, checking on Aelia once more before he opened the front door.

Callodosis was waking up. He ignored the unmistakable smell of smoke, the frantic shouting letting him know the villagers more than likely had it all under control. Besides, the wind was blowing the flames from Morbeck's house away from Aelia's, so they were safe enough for the time being, even if the fire did get out of hand.

Keeran stepped back as far as the balcony would allow, taking in the two-story design of the house, and decided on the best route to the roof. He took all the running start the narrow balcony would allow, launching himself into the air to catch hold of the sloping roof of the gable end, and heaved himself up. The roof was an undulating arrangement of jaunty angles to accommodate the huge branches that the building sat amongst. After a little exploration, he found what he was looking for.

The water tank was suitably full, but his suspicions

proved correct when he found the filter to be blocked with silt. He washed it, replaced it, and was about to head back in when he spotted the chimney flues.

He might as well check those too whilst he was up here.

A little voice nagged at him the whole time he faffed about up there, clearing the flues of any debris, before giving the roof a quick once-over for potential weaknesses or water ingress. When was the last time he'd concerned himself with the drudgery of a stranger's life, let alone helped them with it? Had he ever?

He didn't want to answer that, because the question that followed would be even worse. It flittered to the forefront of his mind anyway. When was the last time he'd opted to save a stranger's life rather than take out one of his targets?

Last night had been awful, not the worst thing he'd ever witnessed, not by a long shot, but certainly in the top ten. Maybe top fifteen. But chilling as the whole experience had been, it was undeniably the best cover-up for the murder he'd come here to commit.

Morbeck had been in the clearing, pandemonium erupting around them, bodies piling up by the dozens. All Keeran had had to do was brush past him, slip a blade into one of his kidneys as he'd passed by, and no one would have questioned just one more body leaking blood onto the forest floor.

But he'd been halfway to Morbeck when he'd heard Aelia scream, the sound turning his blood cold in a way none of the violence of the evening had been able to. When he'd seen her lying on the floor, eyes riveted on the body of the human woman he'd seen her spend so much time with, he'd frozen. Torn between going to her and taking out Morbeck.

It was a no-brainer. Logically, he shouldn't have wasted the opportunity, he should have turned his back on her and killed the traitorous son of a bitch right then and there. Minimal risk, in and out, job done.

But when he'd seen one of those black clad arseholes kick her right in the face, he'd lost it. He was by her side more quickly than he ought to have been, more quickly than any normal artemian, baring his teeth at Beserkir in a reckless display of menace.

He was lucky his actions had gone unnoticed in the mayhem. If anyone had seen him move so fast, he would have had to have left right then and there. Fortunately, Beserkir wasn't interested in losing any more of his men and, having taken one look at Keeran, had decided it wasn't worth the fight.

He'd risked everything to save her and he had no idea why. Just like he couldn't explain why he'd been unable to stop stalking her all day yesterday, hating himself every second he watched her from the shadows, yet utterly unable to stop.

Keeran sat back on his haunches, finally satisfied that the roof would see out the winter, and looked out over the treetops. It was beautiful up here, with the rays of the sun starting to break through the dense morning fog, the thousand noises of the forest starting to fracture the sombre hush that had befallen the village. He watched a squirrel leap into the air, unperturbed by something as inconvenient as gravity as it soared towards the next branch. It landed with an athletic scuttle of paws and skittered away.

Keeran sighed, sick of the same questions circling in his head. In the grand scheme of things, none of them mattered. He would wait until she was conscious, until he knew she was okay, and then he'd leave.

The Peregrinians would be leaving today anyway, though he hadn't yet decided if he'd go with them. Beserkir was a nasty piece of work, and Keeran had a bone to pick with him. Or, if he was feeling particularly vicious, he could pick a bone out of him instead. He grinned at the idea.

He climbed back down, playing with the notion as he walked back into the treehouse, wondering if extracting an entire humerus from a living person was even possible, when a groan made him stop in his tracks.

She was waking up.

His heart flipped in his chest, and he clenched and unclenched his fists, psyching himself up before he pushed into the lounge.

Aelia was sitting on the sofa, her head in her hands, looking for all the world like she did indeed feel like she'd got on the wrong side of a horse, and an ill-tempered one at that. She obviously hadn't heard him come in, and he stood awkwardly in the doorway, not wanting to scare her but equally unsure how not to.

He settled for clearing his throat.

Aelia's head whipped to face him, and she moved more quickly than he'd have thought possible, grabbing a mug from the nearby table and launching it at his head. He ducked, narrowly avoiding the ceramic missile as it smashed into the wall behind him.

"Urgh." Aelia dropped back onto the sofa, her head in her hands again, having gone a ghastly shade of white.

He was next to her in an instant, kneeling by her side as he tried to assess what little of her he could see through her fingers.

"Are you okay?" he asked, wondering if it would be weird to ask to look at her pupils. "Tell me what you're feeling."

"What are you doing here?" she mumbled, weakly.

"I carried you back." Keeran wished she'd drop her hands. He could see so little of her it was hard to ascertain what might be wrong, though her perfect aim with the mug had proved her motor skills to be unaffected by the head injury, and she seemed to be forming coherent sentences. All good signs.

Aelia went still, then her breathing quickened. When she lowered her hands, he almost regretted wishing she would. He could do nothing as a barrage of emotions played out over her face in quick succession, the memories of the night before coming flooding back. Grief, despair, hopelessness, anger and, finally, hatred.

Hatred stuck, easier to bear than the others. He knew from experience.

What he wasn't expecting, however, was for it to be directed at him. When her eyes met his, the loathing that seethed in them had him sitting back on his heels.

"You stopped me," Aelia said, voice low and terrifying. "You stopped me from going to him."

"Beserkir would have killed you then and there, he'd have made an example of you both," Keeran tried to reason, a part of him noting that at least the colour was returning to her cheeks.

"That was not your decision to make," she snapped, lips twisting with anger. He tried not to look, now was not the time to get distracted by her mouth. "I could have made it to him if you hadn't stopped me, he might still be alive."

Keeran had been prepared for tears, had been trying to decide how best to comfort her as she processed her loss. He had never, in all the scenarios that had played out in his head, imagined she would blame him.

"I saved your life," he said, unapologetically. "If I hadn't tried to stop you, you'd both be dead. Actually, I've saved your life twice, and so far, all I've got by way of thanks is a bruise between my legs the size of a watermelon. Was it really necessary to put your whole weight into it?"

That wasn't strictly true. He'd healed already, but she wasn't to know that. She mustn't know that.

"You think this is funny?" Aelia stood, towering over him, and he tried not to think about how close she was standing to him. Much as he liked being on his knees before her, he chose to stand too, rising to tower over her instead.

Her eyes widened a little, as if she'd forgotten just how big he was, but she didn't let it deter her.

"Get out," she yelled, pointing at the door with a shaking finger.

"I don't think it's funny." He ignored her, not wanting to leave her like this. "I'm sorry for last night, I'm sorry for what happened and for everything that you lost. But I'm not, and never will be, sorry for saving you."

"You arrogant, interfering, self-righteous prick." Her whole body began to tremble, her anger seeping out of every pore. "What gives you the right to make that decision for me? Who do you think you are, that you think I need your help deciding what I should and shouldn't do? I don't even know your name, and you think I need you to save me?"

He stared at her, dumbfounded. He watched the anger slip from her face, the anguish that replaced it breaking his heart. He went to reach for her, longing to somehow ease some of her pain, but she recoiled from him, tears welling in her eyes.

"Get out," she yelled. "Get out, get out, get out."

Keeran took a step back, the relief in her expression as he did cutting right through him. She didn't want him here; she couldn't make it any clearer. His gaze dropped to the floor, still not quite believing just how badly he'd misjudged the situation. Then he turned and walked out of the room.

He paused in the hallway, hearing her break down into unrestrained sobs. Realising he might be pushing his luck, he ducked into the kitchen and pulled out the pencil and paper he'd discovered earlier when looking for the things he'd needed to dress her wounds. He quickly scrawled a note for her.

He placed a tub containing the poultice he'd got her on the kitchen counter, next to the instructions he'd written for how often to apply it, before making a beeline for the door.

This time he didn't hesitate as he left.

CHAPTER SIX

Aelia cried until she felt like she didn't have a drop of moisture left in her body. Her grief consumed her.

She wasn't sure what was harder to bear: that Otis and Mirra were dead, or that Fenrir was in a cage headed gods only knew where. The night played over and over in her mind, images of Otis's last moments suffocating in his own blood, and of Mirra clawing at the arm that choked her to death seeming to be burned into her retinas, playing on repeat.

Her only distraction was the pain. When she found the strength to compose herself, she lifted her top and nearly choked when she saw the extensive array of colours decorating her skin. She frowned, her stiff neck complaining as she tried to look closer at the yellows and greens and purples that surrounded the assorted cuts and gashes. Everything looked old, the bruises already yellowing and the cuts scabbed over nicely.

The man whose name she *still* didn't know had said he'd been sorry for last night, meaning she hadn't been out for that long, but the bruises looked days old. Days and days.

Finding it hard to find the will to care, she dropped her shirt and got back on her feet. She couldn't stay in here a moment longer, not when reminders of Otis's life lay everywhere she looked. His pipe sat on the table, his jumper slung over the back of the sofa, his favourite liquor sitting on the side table in its decanter.

She definitely needed to get out.

The stairs took her some time as she half dragged herself up by the handrail, her legs shaking with the pain, but she finally made it up to the shower.

The water rushed out of the shower head, the pressure hitting into her like hot needles, and she groaned as her muscles relaxed under the torrent. It seemed like the water pressure had returned to normal; perhaps they'd had heavy rain whilst she was unconscious. Again, she couldn't bring herself to care.

Aelia was hardly aware of drying herself, slinging on whatever clean clothes were closest before leaving the treehouse as quickly as her aching limbs could carry her.

THE VILLAGE CENTRE WAS A MESS.

Aelia picked her way through the collapsed decorations, the charred lanterns that had been knocked to the ground, the patches of blood soaking into the dirt. Others milled around her, already starting to clear up the debris that littered the floor.

She hadn't seen a single human since she'd left her house.

"Hey, Moira." Aelia stopped beside a woman she knew from work. Although she was older, with more grey in her hair than colour, she was a force to be reckoned with if you got on her bad side. Her second form was that of a Boar, making her stronger than most of the other prey artemians who earned their keep logging the forests. Aside from Aelia, she was the strongest in their team by a long shot.

"Aelia. Glad to see you survived. I was worried when I didn't see you last night, thought they might have taken you too." Moira stopped filling a bag with rubbish and straightened, putting her hands on her hips and stretching backwards. She looked exhausted.

"How many did we lose?" Aelia fought the prickling behind her eyes. She would not cry in public. She would not.

Moira's eyes flicked to Aelia's, before dropping to the floor. "All the humans are gone, either taken or burned," Moira said. Aelia pressed her lips together, not trusting herself not to vomit as she looked over to where several people were shovelling the smouldering remains of the fire into wheelbarrows. "They didn't burn the artemians they killed, leaving us fifty-three of our own to bury, with several more Peregrinians on top of that."

Fifty-three. And every single human was either dead or missing. Aelia felt numb, her shattered heart unable to take any more.

"Do we know where they're taking them?"

Moira shook her head. "No, they filled the cages to bursting and left. It wasn't just humans they took either, if they could restrain the artemians who resisted, they took them too. If not, they killed them."

Pain lanced through the deadened numbness Aelia was clinging to.

"They took Fenrir," was all she could manage to say.

"Oh child," Moira reached over and placed a hand on Aelia's arm, squeezing gently. "I'm so sorry."

"Where are they taking them?" Aelia asked, almost rhetorically, but Moira answered anyway.

"Everyone's asking the same thing, but no one knows the

answer." She smiled, sympathetically, rubbing up and down Aelia's arm a few times before dropping her hand.

Aelia nodded, not trusting herself to speak, blinking furiously at the tears that she refused to let spill.

"Do you want me to take you to Otis?"

It was like ice water had been thrown over her. No, no the last thing she wanted was to see him. She didn't want her last memory to be of him lying there, white and rigid, his skin waxen, eyes already turning opaque. Moira seemed to sense her panic.

"He's been wrapped in the burial shroud already," she added. "And you don't have to see him, there is no right and wrong here. It's whatever you need."

Aelia lost her battle with her tears, and they trickled down her cheeks. She wiped at them furiously.

"When are we burying them?" Aelia squeezed the words through her constricted throat.

"Later today, as soon as the last grave is dug."

"Where?"

"In section fourteen, the one we cleared last week."

Aelia nodded. "Thank you, I'll head straight there then."

"You don't have to, Aelia, we have people on it." Moira was only trying to be kind, but Aelia shook her head.

"No, I want to be the one to dig it for him." If she couldn't stand to visit him one last time, she would make sure she gave him that.

"Alright. Come find me if you need anything, won't you?" Moira pressed her lips into a hard smile and Aelia nodded, thanking her as she turned to leave.

It was a relief to have something to do, and her broken mind clung to the task like it was the last lifeline to her sanity. If she thought about how alone she was for a moment longer, she felt like her grief might swallow her whole, forcing her into a ball on the floor to suffocate on her loneliness.

Keeping busy was the alternative, and she grabbed onto it with both hands.

She walked through her pain, her breath wheezing slightly as she limped away from the forest and towards section fourteen.

Sweat trickled down Aelia's back, her clothes already soaked and sticking to her with the exertion of digging the grave.

Her entire body screamed at her, some parts burning with a bone-deep ache, other areas treating her to a sharp, stabbing pain with every swing of her shovel. It was the end of summer and the ground was baked hard, the roots of the trees they'd recently felled slowing her progress. She'd borrowed tools from the other families nearby, turning down their offers of help but exceptionally grateful for the saw she was using to tackle the roots she couldn't break with her shovel.

Aelia dug until she was throwing the soil up and over her head to hit the pile she'd created next to the grave, and then she dug some more. She hadn't even noticed the failing light until a tentative cough from over her head made her look up.

"Aelia, we were wondering when you might be ready to start the ceremony."

Aelia tilted her head up, squinting. It was one of the council members' sons, his eldest, though he was only just old enough to shave. If she had any room left for any other emotion, she might have felt surprised to see the fading light of dusk settling over the forest above her.

"Yes, sorry," she mumbled, wondering how she was going

to get out of the pit she'd dug herself in. How had she gone so deep without realising? "I'm ready."

"Hand me the end of your shovel," the boy said, offering his hand.

He hauled her out of the grave, Aelia reverse abseiling her way up the dirt walls.

Mortified, she noticed most of the village was in attendance, everyone waiting for her. How long had they all been there?

Turning a brighter shade of red, she scooped her tools out of the way and moved to stand in her place by Otis's grave.

Fifty-three graves had been dug in the coppiced clearing, in no particular order, merely where the family of the deceased found room between the severed trunks for a new sapling to be planted. The families stood by their graves, the rest of the village standing at a respectful distance.

Only then did Aelia notice the stretchers that had been carried from the village, each one with a figure perfectly wrapped in a white shroud. She didn't even know which one was Otis.

The village had no priestess, they were too small to warrant a temple, but one of the councilwomen stepped forward to perform the rites.

The words were lost on Aelia. She'd heard them countless times before, yet they gave her no comfort. The councilwoman spoke of how they were returning to the soil, to nourish the land they had sought nourishment from, to become one with the forest they had called home. All such lovely sentiments, all such bullshit.

Otis was gone, his life taken by a monster. There was no meaning to his death beyond that, and no pious sermons about Mother Nature's circle of life would make her think any differently.

Dusk was a vibrant time in the forest, and nature didn't

pause for burials. Aelia drowned out the monotonous voice of the councilwoman, tuned out the chorus of sobs and sniffs from the grieving loved ones, instead closing her eyes to focus on the life surrounding her. The shriek of an owl, the curdling call of a vixen, the fluttering of a bat's wings.

They gave her peace that she could never have found from the words of the ceremony. Her life had changed beyond recognition, leaving her alone and bereft, but the forest hadn't changed. It would never change.

All too soon it came to the time to bury Otis. They lowered him into the grave, and everyone grabbed a shovel. The peace Aelia had found was short-lived, caving in on itself as she had to accept help turning the soil back over onto Otis.

It was tradition, she couldn't stop it, but she wanted to whack her shovel over the heads of the artemians who stepped forward to help her. Otis was her family, not by blood, but in every way that mattered; it should be her burying him, and her alone.

They planted a sapling over his grave, marking it with a placard with his name on, and Aelia felt something inside of her rip open all over again at the sight of it. His name shouldn't be on a placard, he shouldn't be buried beneath his tree, not yet. It all felt so wrong, like a nightmare she'd wake up from, cold and sweating.

Yet here it was. In undeniable letters.

Otis was dead. Mirra was dead. And Fenrir had been taken.

The villagers started ambling back to Callodosis, arms slung over shoulders and handkerchiefs clasped to faces. Aelia stepped onto the broken earth and pressed her forehead to the sapling, letting the tears come, feeling them drop from her chin and onto the soil at her feet.

"Goodbye," she whispered, eyes closed as she pictured her

guardian. Mirra didn't have a grave, the Astraea had stolen her right to become one with the forest when they'd burned her body, but Aelia knew Otis wouldn't mind sharing his space with her memory. So, Aelia pictured them both, mourned them both, said goodbye to them both.

Aelia didn't return to Callodosis with the rest of the village for the wake, there was no one there she could grieve with. Instead, she stumbled home, unsure what hurt more, her body or her heart.

CHAPTER SEVEN

The climb up the stairs nearly killed her, but finally she staggered through the door. Suddenly, the thought of a house on the forest floor didn't seem so awful.

After another, longer shower, she limped into the kitchen and froze.

There, on the counter, was Otis's dagger, spotless and shining in the light from the lamp she carried, next to a tub and a note.

It was the first time she'd thought about the man all day.

Grumbling, but too curious not to look, she crossed the kitchen and put the lamp down to pick up the note. In perfect, swirling handwriting were instructions on how often to apply the salve she assumed was in the tub.

The petulant part of her wanted to rip it up and hurl it out of the window, with the salve following closely after it, but logic kicked in. Medicine was expensive, and she needed to heal if she was going to go back to work. And she absolutely needed to go back to work if she was going to afford to keep this place from crumbling into disrepair all on her own.

With an angry sigh, she twisted the lid of the tub free, revealing a pink cream she didn't recognise. Not that she'd had the luxury of affording medicine very often before, most of the time she'd had to rely on her own knowledge of the herbs they could find in the forest to treat the occasional ailments she and Otis had suffered with.

She felt a pang at his name and shoved the thought aside.

Dubiously, she pulled off her clothes and started applying the salve. A moan escaped her lips as her pain eased almost instantly. The relief was so heady that a laugh escaped her, sounding maniacal even to her own ears.

She pressed her lips together, the laugh having freaked her out a little, but she couldn't stop the moans from bubbling out of her as she rubbed the salve into every tender spot she could find.

When she was finished, she eyed the pink poultice suspiciously. What was in that stuff, and how could a Peregrinian afford to just give away medicine as powerful as that?

Aelia placed what was left of it back on the worktop, the dagger catching her attention once more.

She thought she'd lost it, hoped someone in the village would be honest enough to return it once she put some feelers out, but here it was, sparkling clean.

Yesterday, she'd killed a man with it. She didn't know if she should be worried that she felt nothing as she churned over the memory, nothing except a grim sense of satisfaction. Even if she dug deep, she felt no remorse, no guilt, no shame. If anything, she regretted not having been able to kill more of the bastards before they'd kicked the living shit out of her, murdered one friend and captured another.

No, she certainly didn't feel any guilt.

What she did feel, was hungry. She opened the cupboard with the plates in, and her eyes narrowed, teeth grinding together as she pulled out a dish already prepared and waiting for her. What was this guy's deal?

Fruit and dried meat, a few boiled eggs and a thick slice of buttered bread were piled high on the plate. Not an extravagant meal by any means, but the best one could do with what was in their stores.

Her stores, she corrected, her breath leaving her with a choked sob.

Too hungry, and far too frugal, to throw the food away out of principle, she carried it to the window. Opening it, she winced as she climbed onto the worktop, ducking out of the window with practised movement to perch on the thick branch just outside. Aelia stretched up to push the plate onto the roof before swinging herself up next to it with a pained groan.

She sat gasping for a moment, waiting for the pain to subside, before she positioned herself in her usual spot, legs dangling over the edge of the roof.

Callodosis at night was her favourite view in the whole forest. Even as low as she was feeling, her grief felt slightly easier to bear at the sight of it.

The light from candles, lanterns, and fires spilled out of the arched windows of the treehouses around her, casting the intricate wooden structures in a cosy light. Each building was a feat of engineering, simple yet beautiful, merging with nature seamlessly. Aelia picked at her food as she looked out over her home, knowing life would never again be the same.

She'd never see Mirra again, never get to talk to Otis again. Which was just as infuriating as it was heartbreaking, because what the hell had he meant when he'd told her to cross the sea to the war-torn continent to the West? Not once had he shown any interest in them travelling anywhere together, nor mentioned any contacts he had outside of Callodosis, let alone Demuto, yet now he wanted her to track down some family on the other side of the world? It made no sense, and her brain revolted at the prospect.

The forest floor was dark, the wooden houses at ground level cold and abandoned, the humans they belonged to never coming back. She chewed slowly, eyes stuck on the empty darkness beneath her.

Her jaw froze mid-mouthful when she saw a shadow pacing purposefully up the path to her tree. It was dark, and the figure was way below her, but she knew with absolute certainty it was him.

Fighting the urge to lob the plate at his head, she watched him stride up the path as if he owned the damned thing. Was he going to come up, uninvited and unannounced, on the day she'd buried her family, right after she'd screamed at him to leave her alone? The audacity of the man, the arrogance. She swallowed the food in her mouth, suddenly resenting every morsel.

He'd followed her into the woods, admittedly saving her from an arse kicking, but what the hell had he been doing there in the first place? And although she was grateful for not having been pounded into by a bunch of thugs twice in one night, she would have *really* loved to land a few punches of her own, broken a nose or two maybe.

She could forgive him for taking that away from her though, she wasn't stupid. No way could she have taken on all of them without coming off seriously worse for wear. But what she couldn't forgive, what had her blood boiling to the point of bubbling over, was that he'd stopped her from going to Otis when he'd needed her most.

If she'd just made it there a few moments earlier, could she have stopped Beserkir? Could she have saved Otis? She would never know; that man had stolen her opportunity to try.

As if she'd broadcast her thoughts to the ground, the man

slowed to a stop. His head tilted backwards to take in the treehouse she was perched on. Aelia fought the urge to scurry back onto the roof, knowing that movement would more than likely draw his attention. If she was still, she highly doubted he would spot her.

He stood there watching for what felt like an age, and she almost wished she could hear his thoughts, could get a glimpse of the indecision that had stopped him in his tracks. He was too far away for her to see his features, and she could do nothing but stare silently back at him, hoping against hope that he'd turn and walk away. The last thing she needed was another argument, and if he dared to knock on her front door, an argument was exactly what he was going to get. Big, brutish stranger or not, she had more than enough anger directed his way to overlook the possible foolishness of antagonising him.

Fortunately, he chose that moment to turn and walk away, his pace slower than before. Aelia frowned at the rush of disappointment that came over her as she watched his back recede into the night. Did she *want* an argument? Did she *want* the opportunity to explain to him in great detail how inappropriate it was for a complete stranger to mooch about her house, cleaning her things and rifling through her cupboards, as if he had some right to meddle in her life?

Her frown deepened as a suspicion bloomed, and she twisted round to where the water tank was hidden. Heaving herself to her feet, she couldn't help but check.

Sure enough, the filter was gleaming. Which it absolutely fucking should not have been, seeing as she hadn't cleaned it since last winter, and Otis sure as hell couldn't get up here.

She had half a mind to chase after him and tell him exactly where he could stick his help. She wasn't some weak, useless creature incapable of looking after herself. She'd kept this roof over hers and Otis's head since she was sixteen, despite the whole of Callodosis looking down on her for not being able to Shift, despite them making her life harder at every fucking opportunity. She had managed, on her own. Who the fuck did he think he was?

Too angry to finish eating, she threw herself back down on the roof, glaring at what was left of the food.

Rage boiled through her, erupting like lava in an explosion that once ignited, she was powerless to control. It overshadowed everything else: her fear, her grief, her pain. But it wasn't all directed at the patronising alpha prick who'd taken it upon himself to look after the first feeble little creature he stumbled on. No, most of it was aimed at Beserkir and the extremist bullies who followed him, wreaking unchecked havoc through Demuto.

Aelia blinked. Why were they unchecked?

They'd always been a nuisance, sure, but last night was nothing short of an extermination, of cold-blooded murder. Why was the King's army not tracking them down and hanging them by their prejudiced little throats?

And what were they doing with the humans they were collecting? Why not just kill them then and there?

Aelia's blood went cold as the question that had been running circles round her mind all day came back to the forefront. Where were they taking Fenrir?

Her mind whirled in a torrent of unanswerable questions, but that last one gave her pause. Here she was moping about being alone, when she was comfortably sitting in her own home, with a full belly. Fenrir on the other hand, was gods only knew where, being taken to gods only knew what.

Her anger turned inwards, twisting to point straight at herself.

If the roles were reversed, Fenrir would already be on his way to save her, of that she had no doubt. Her eyes widened with the awful realisation of how much time she'd lost.

In that moment, her path was clear, her decision made. Maybe one day she would do as Otis said, but for now, her friend needed her.

She pushed herself off the roof, landing on the branch with a grunt, and slipped through the window to pack.

CHAPTER EIGHT

Too wired to try to sleep, despite the obvious logic to wait until daybreak before leaving, she slung the last of what she thought she'd need into her pack, their savings carefully wrapped in some clothes at the bottom.

Otis had more than one belted harness for the dagger, and she tugged it on, cinching it tight over her hips. The dagger was a comforting weight, and she drew it a few times, practicing the angle she'd need to access it quickly in an emergency.

When she could think of nothing else she might need, she shouldered her pack, ignoring her back's protestations, and turned to look around the lounge. The weight of its emptiness crushed her, making it difficult to breathe.

She battled past it, forcing herself to see Otis sitting in his chair, the reassuring constant in her life no matter what else it threw at her. She pictured Mirra chatting away, always smiling, no matter what. She saw her childhood; the happiness, the safety, the love. She closed her eyes and saw Fenrir, her last living friend, the protective goofball who could always make them smile.

She put her hand on the doorframe and silently thought of everything she was leaving behind. For a moment, she allowed her anguish to envelop her, feeling its infinite depth and accepting that it was now a part of her. But so was her rage, and she could either drown in it, or use it.

She sank into the anger, undiluted and pure, and it pulled her from the stupor of grief, giving her direction, purpose. Her future stretched out before her, the path clear and beckoning.

Hoiking her pack higher onto her shoulders, she strode out the front door, shutting it behind her without a backward glance.

IT WASN'T LONG BEFORE SHE WAS LIMPING AGAIN, THE poultice having helped more than she believed possible, but her joints screamed under the weight of the pack. She pushed on, wincing as she realised how much catching up she had to do if she was going to find Fenrir. Usually, a lone traveller would make much better time than a group that size, but in her condition, she wondered if she'd ever catch up.

A light drizzle began to drip from the overhead canopy, and she paused to lift her hood over her head, pulling it down low over her face. Fucking perfect. Not only was she sore, tired, and hungry, but she was going to get wet too.

She left Callodosis behind, following the main road out of the woods. Road was a generous term for the dusty tracks they used to transport the timber they harvested out of the forest, but it was the best they had. As the hours crept by, she found herself crossing the point that took her the furthest she'd ever been from home.

She paused for a moment, hands fisted around the straps

of her pack to stop them digging in so much, doubt creeping in. She swallowed hard and took another step. Now *this* was the furthest she'd ever been. Now this. Now this.

A smile teased at her lips; it was going to be a long walk if she kept this up.

The weak rays of the sun would just be rising above the thick canopy, but she had a while yet before they'd be strong enough for her to follow the physical trail of the Astraea. That was okay though, the tracks were so fresh that she could still smell the mixed jumble of dozens of scents, all mingling to become powerful enough for her to make out.

Her senses weren't human, matching that of the most sensitive artemian, although once Shifted, most of them would have been able to best her. That was where she always fell short.

A regular artemian's skillset was dictated by the animal they could Shift into. If their second form had particularly good hearing, that was transferable to their two-legged form. The same was true for strength, speed, agility, sight, smell, and so on. On two legs, Aelia could beat all of them, at everything. She could outlift, outrun, and outjump the very best of them.

But she couldn't Shift, and that was what mattered in Demuto. That's how your worth was measured.

Aelia was so busy following her nose, so absorbed by her inner monologue about societal injustices, that she was utterly taken by surprise when a hulking shape leapt out at her in an indistinguishable blur and slammed her face-first into the nearest tree.

"Why are you following me?" a voice growled into her ear. Panic flooded through her. The man pressing her against the tree felt huge at her back, and in this position, she was near defenceless.

"I'm not following you," she ground out, face smushed into the rough bark by a firm hand.

Her hood was ripped back, and an instant later, she was let go.

Aelia whirled round to face her attacker, ignoring the pain spiking through her at the sudden movement, her hand reaching for her dagger.

It took her a moment to believe what she was seeing, her mouth dropping open in disbelief as the stranger who'd fixed her water pressure stood gawping back at her.

They both half shouted some garbled version of "what the fuck are you doing here?" at exactly the same moment, the words incoherent over one another, but the sentiment unmistakable.

Aelia glared at him as a slow smile spread across his face.

"If you wanted to get me alone in the woods again, you only had to ask," he said, grinning.

Aelia shoved his shoulder, hard. It was like punching a rock.

She fought the urge to shake her hand against the fresh wave of pain she'd created for herself, refusing to give him the satisfaction.

"You didn't need to shove me so hard," she complained, rubbing at her cheek. She wondered if she had an imprint of the bark on her face.

"I didn't know it was you." The smile leaked from his face, and for a moment she thought he looked genuinely contrite. "Your hood was up, and the rain masked your scent. Are you hurt?"

Great, of course he could smell her. Gods only knew what a man like him Shifted into. She genuinely couldn't imagine any living creature more animalistic than the towering hunk of muscle in front of her.

She threw her hood back over her head, glaring at him the whole time, choosing to ignore his question.

"So you're in the habit of throwing everyone who happens to walk behind you into trees?" she said, not giving him time to answer before she cut in. "Not that I find that hard to believe, after you broke into my house and made yourself at home. How did you even know where I lived anyway?"

Something flickered over his face, too quick for her to register.

"I asked someone in the village when I was carrying you back." He ignored her answering scowl. "And I didn't break in. The door wasn't locked."

"And that gives you the right to just waltz in and start sticking your nose into everything, does it?" she said, voice rising to a near shout.

His expression darkened. Good, she was getting to him.

"I carried you up gods knows how many stairs, tended to your wounds, and fixed a few things while I was waiting to make sure you weren't going to stop breathing. So can you stop acting like I broke in and ransacked the place?" Something changed in his eyes, making their brown depths seem suddenly darker, crueller.

It struck a chord deep within her, an ancient instinct that warned her to be careful. He must have noticed her fear because, with what seemed like a real effort, he controlled his expression, the darkness in his eyes clearing a moment later.

A bit freaked out, she took a step back. His arm lifted towards her, his face regretful for a fraction of a second before he clenched his jaw and let his arm drop to his side.

She replayed his words, eyes narrowing.

"What do you mean you fixed a few things?" She knew about the water filter… what else had he been nosing around?

"Does it matter?" He turned and stalked off to the other side of the track, pulling his own pack from where he'd stashed it behind a tree. "I wanted to make sure you were ok, I had nothing to do whilst I waited, and I thought I was being helpful. I misjudged the situation, I'm sorry."

Her retort died on her lips. He was right, what did it matter now?

"Never mind," she said, not caring how ungracious she sounded. He wasn't the white knight in the story, he was the oaf who'd grabbed onto her with his great big sausage fingers and stopped her from getting to Otis in time. Only when she looked down at his hands, she was proven wrong. His hands were huge, sure, but his fingers were long and tanned, the veins branching up into the tense muscles of his forearm. Something clenched low in her stomach at the sight of them, and when she finally returned her gaze to his, a strange light in his eyes made her wonder if he knew what she'd been thinking.

"You're right, it doesn't matter," she snapped, hoping he didn't notice the colour she could feel stealing into her cheeks. "Let's just go our separate ways and forget all about it."

She didn't wait for him to answer, trying to hide her embarrassment as she turned and strode up the road with as much dignity as she could muster, limp aside.

After a few meters, she puffed out her cheeks in a sigh, trying to dispel the last of her awkwardness, when she heard a twig snap behind her.

Peering over her shoulder mid-stride, her frown slammed back into place.

"What are you doing?" she said, half turning to walk sideways, not wanting to waste any more time.

He shrugged, his pack shifting on his shoulders. "Walking."

She wanted to throttle him.

"Can't you hang back a bit?"

"Can't you? I've already spent enough time trying to do the right thing, it's your turn. You can hang back and wait if you like, but I'm not stopping."

"No," she said, trying to keep the anger from her voice and failing miserably. It didn't help that his lips were twitching in a smile. She didn't know what was worse, that he found her irritation amusing, or that even half a smile took his face from undeniably good-looking, to excruciatingly handsome. Aelia spun back around before she could blush again. She didn't need to explain herself to him anyway.

So, they walked in silence, him hovering a few paces back.

The wind rustled the leaves overhead, the noise comfortingly familiar. The rain finally stopped, and the sun climbed high enough to break through the trees, dappling the path in speckled light. Life chattered and scurried all around them, busy preparing for the change of the season.

And all of it was lost on Aelia, her thoughts fixed unwaveringly on the infuriating presence at her heels. No matter how hard she tried to calm herself, to push aside her anger, he'd make some sound or another, and she'd be back to gritting her teeth, resenting every breath he took.

As the morning gave way to afternoon, he sped up a little to draw parallel to her.

"You pointed out yesterday that you don't know my name. It's Keeran."

She ignored him, not interested in small talk with the man who'd held her back whilst her guardian was murdered, irrespective of his name.

"So where are you going in such a hurry?" he tried again.

Aelia slid her eyes over to him, a biting retort on the very tip of her tongue, when she caught sight of his face. There was no sign of the cruelty she'd been so wary of when she'd first seen him with the flames. The hard angles of his face seemed to have softened, his expression the most open she'd seen it as he held out a conversational olive branch to her.

Weak, pathetic little sucker that she was, she caved.

"I'm trying to catch up to the Astraea," she admitted, only aware of how ridiculous she sounded after the words had left her mouth. She could hardly walk, had nothing but a dagger she had no real clue how to use, and had been pinned against a tree before she'd even left the logging perimeter of her village.

To his credit, he didn't point any of this out.

"Do you mind if I ask why?"

Aelia sighed through her nose, scrunching her lips as she thought about how best to answer.

"You're going to try and get your friend." It wasn't even a question. When she risked a glance his way, she was surprised to see no trace of laughter on his face. So she nodded.

He was silent for so long she thought the conversation was over and was ashamed and confused by the relief she felt when he finally spoke.

"I want to find them too," he admitted.

"Mind if I ask why?" she threw back at him.

"Because monsters like that shouldn't go unpunished." His irises turned black again, not just their normal dark, but black. She suppressed a shiver.

"And you can do that?" Sure, he looked like one giant walking weapon, but there were a lot of Astraeans with Beserkir.

"I'd like to try."

It was just her luck that she found herself stuck on the road with a man who either had an ego so inflated that he was delusional enough to think he could take on a whole party of the most lethal predators in Demuto, or who actually could. She wasn't sure which was worse.

"Why didn't you when they attacked then?" she asked, leaning more towards the ego theory.

"There were too many, and they had the element of surprise. I need to shuffle the deck a bit if I want a winning hand."

She was scrutinising his face, trying to get a read on him, when his gaze lifted to hers. If anything had her dropping the ego theory, it was that look in his eyes. It made her feel like there was something else, something *other,* looking back out at her.

Disconcerted, she glanced quickly away, hoping he'd let the conversation dissolve into silence. No such luck.

"Do you have a plan to free your friend?"

Anger, hot and heavy, reared up inside her again. Mainly at herself for not having a good enough answer, for not having an answer at all, but some of it was directed at him for putting her in a situation where she looked foolish.

Was that fair? No.

Did she care? Also no.

"Not yet." She side-eyed him, daring him to say something patronising.

"That's fair. It's hard to plan until you know what you're up against," he said, without looking at her. "If they followed this road, I suspect they passed through Drias last night. We should be able to get a better understanding of where they're headed there."

"We?" she spluttered, nearly choking on the word.

It was his turn to side-eye her. "You want to go up against them on your own?" His expression emphasised the silent 'How well did that work out for you last time?' tagged on the end.

She didn't answer, turning to look straight ahead, leaning forward against the weight of her pack. Sanctimonious prick.

It didn't help that he had a point.

"You're no good to your friend dead. Which is what you'll probably end up being if you try this alone."

"You're trying it alone," she bit back, eyes flashing.

"I'm trying not to, but for some reason, you're being bloody difficult about it. Something you appear to be particularly good at." His eyes flashed too, the anger in his trouncing hers in a heartbeat. Whatever it was she kept seeing there, it wasn't good. It sent shivers down her spine every time she caught sight of it.

"You don't need to be scared," he said, surprising her. She had always found it hard to hide her thoughts, her traitorous face an open book for all to read. When she looked back at him, he was himself once more, and she caught just a glimpse of sadness in his eyes before he squashed that too.

"I'm not," she lied. He snorted.

"You're a terrible liar." He smiled at her, his eyes back to a dark brown, the sunlight catching the amber flecks in them. "But I mean it, I won't hurt you."

"That sounds like something someone who was going to hurt me might say," she said, wryly.

"It is a conundrum." He skirted round a puddle that had formed in the middle of the path. "Don't say it, and you're scared. Say it, and you're still scared but at least I feel better for trying."

"Maybe stop breaking into people's houses—"

"I did not break into your house," he insisted, square jaw set firm.

"Alright, alright," she said, holding back a smile. It might not be wise to bait him, but the road was straight and boring; what else was she going to do to pass the time?

Aelia certainly didn't remember agreeing to travel together, but Keeran took it upon himself to assume that he'd convinced her and, to be honest, it would have been foolish to turn him down. Unless of course, her initial wariness proved to be correct, and he ended up murdering her in her sleep.

The forest thinned, the shade beneath the trees that she'd spent her life in giving way to bold rays of sunlight, until the woods disappeared altogether to become the vast plains that stretched all the way to Llmera, the capital.

The long grass seemed to be endless, disappearing into the heat haze that kissed the horizon. Aelia turned and looked back at her forest, the trees in front of her enormous in their proximity. The forest spanned for miles behind them until it met the mountain range that jutted from it with unforgiving severity. The cold ridges sent a shiver down her spine. She had known that the Jaws of Rach-Mah existed, but they hadn't been visible from beneath the canopy at Callodosis. Now they broke free from the horizon, their jagged peaks rearing into the sky to form the impenetrable wall that was the southern border.

The wind rushed over the long grasses, tugging strands of hair loose from her braid. She closed her eyes and savoured the feeling, a familiar caress in the new world she was venturing into.

CHAPTER NINE

Aelia was seriously unimpressed with Drias, and Keeran couldn't say he blamed her. As he guided them to the only inn in town, she looked about her with thinly veiled disappointment, and Keeran was struck with the realisation that this was almost certainly the first time she'd left her forest.

If she was used to the quaint little village of Callodosis, the dull efficiency of Drias was undoubtedly underwhelming. The houses were dark and square, erected in a grid-like structure, crisscrossed by uneven cobbled streets that made Aelia's limp ten times worse.

Keeran had tried to set a slow pace on the way here. Seeing as he'd dressed her wounds after the Astraea attack, he was all too aware of how much pain she must be in, but Aelia had stomped towards Drias with no interest in whether he kept up or not. So in the end, he'd just matched her.

And that had generally been the tone of the day, with her making no attempt to hide her obvious resentment of his presence. Every time he'd opened his mouth, she'd shut him down, her answers curt and cutting, and that was if she deigned to reply at all.

He tried not to let it get to him, to bite his tongue rather than snapping back at her. She'd been through a lot, lost almost everything in a few short hours. She was entitled to more than a little leeway. Besides, her being so bloody surly made it that much easier to ignore the connection he felt between them, the connection that very clearly only went one way.

He shouldn't have suggested they travel together. Not only because she clearly didn't want to, but because he'd only just managed to persuade himself to leave her, to try and sever this new little quirk he was experiencing. His people were renowned for their possessive, obsessive nature, but Keeran had never felt anything quite like this before, and he certainly didn't appreciate it.

He'd been so close to knocking on her door last night, the uneasy disquiet he felt at leaving her driving him to try one more time, despite every logical thought telling him not to. Years of overriding his other side, his baser instincts, had meant that logic prevailed and he'd decided to leave Callodosis instead. It was just his luck that there was only one road out of the forest, and that she'd chosen to set out at almost exactly the same time as him. Wasn't that just fucking typical.

Keeran looked at her from the corner of his eye and almost smiled. Aelia had both hands gripped onto her pack, her nose slightly wrinkled as she stepped over a particularly suspicious looking puddle.

"Not what you were expecting?" he couldn't help asking, bracing himself for another rebuttal.

"Not at all," Aelia admitted as she stepped closer to avoid being splashed by the dirty water kicked up by a cart loaded high with felled tree trunks. Keeran frowned as it passed a little too close to the pavement and pretended to squint at a street sign on the house opposite. Once she was a little ahead of him, he caught up, moving to put himself between her and the busy road.

"Drias is just a stopping point for people transporting timber from your forest. They only stay a night before moving on, so there's even less money here than in Callodosis," Keeran explained. He turned left as they came to a junction in the road, taking them away from the main street.

"Can't say I blame them," Aelia said, sidestepping a woman who'd stopped dead when she'd seen Keeran. Aelia took in the woman's fearful glances, the way she instinctively pressed into the wall as she passed rather than come any closer to him than she had to, but Keeran stared straight ahead. People feared him, and rightly so. He'd made his peace with it, but right then, he couldn't stand to see what Aelia might make of it.

They walked the rest of the way in silence, passing more derelict buildings than he remembered seeing the last time he was here. The Astraea were making fast work of anyone who wasn't toeing the line they'd taken it upon themselves to draw, mercilessly ransacking any business that served humans. Keeran had witnessed firsthand how the Astraean influence had changed as he travelled the country. When he had first joined the Peregrinians they had only been targeting humans, and randomly at that. But now the Astraea were organised, anyone who so much as fraternised with a human found themselves on the wrong end of a blade. Or worse, their house was burned down, whole families still inside.

EVENTUALLY, HE FOUND IT; AN INN SO FOUL THAT HE PITIED the sole of his boots. It wouldn't be anyone's first choice, but options were severely limited in Drias. Where there had once swung a sign, someone had scrawled its name in illegible paint. Keeran wondered why the person who'd painted it had bothered; the poor sod clearly couldn't read or write. He pushed the door open, grimaced at the wall of heat that hit him, and stood back to let Aelia pass.

She peered into the dingy darkness beyond, looking thoroughly unenthusiastic as she stepped past him into the tavern. To her credit, she didn't hesitate as she crossed the sawdust-covered floor, elbowing her way through the already heaving room to the bar. Keeran followed, taking note of the rowdiest individuals in the room, clocking the stairs to the right of the crowded space and the door behind the bar that presumably led to the back entrance.

Aelia squeezed herself between two heavily set men, despite the smell of stale beer and sweat that filled the space around them. She leant over the sticky surface to wave at the barmaid.

"We need two rooms," Aelia shouted over the din, holding up two fingers to the girl who appeared to be working the entire room on her own. Her blonde hair was tufting free of its braid at every angle, and she looked in dire need of one of the drinks she was frantically serving.

"For how many nights?" the woman called back, grabbing another tankard and pouring it full of foaming beer.

"Just the one," Aelia said, checking with Keeran with a glance. He nodded. They wouldn't stay a moment longer than they had to. He was acutely aware of the glances directed at Aelia from several of the less-than-savoury looking men in the room. The darkness in him opened its eyes with an audible snick, its scaled lip curling back in a low growl.

The woman skimmed the foam off the top of the tankard and slid it down the bar to an outstretched hand. She reached into a cupboard and produced two keys, handing them one each.

"Up the stairs. Room numbers are on the keys."

Keeran pulled Aelia out of the way, ignoring her protestations, and leant over the bar. He lowered his head so only the barmaid could hear him. Her cheeks flushed, a coy smile playing on her painted lips.

"I'm sorry, I can see you're busy, but would it be possible to get two rooms next to each other?" he asked, leaning in a little closer than necessary.

No way was he trusting the locks in a place like this, not when he could practically smell the intentions of some of the men leering at Aelia. The woman nodded, ignoring the shouts coming from down the bar demanding her attention, reaching back into the cupboard to swap keys. He didn't miss the way her fingers brushed over his as she handed them over.

Yes, people could sense the evil in him, but he wasn't ignorant of the way he looked either, and sometimes that had its advantages.

When he turned to hand Aelia her key, he was surprised to see her looking at the maid with a hard glint in her eye. It vanished almost immediately, but he'd seen it, his chest tightening a little as his mind went into overdrive.

Fortunately, he didn't have time to overthink it too much because, just when they were about to head towards the stairs, Aelia stopped dead in her tracks.

"What is it?" Keeran asked, only just managing to stop without bumping into her.

Aelia raised a hand to point at a sign next to the bar.

Rest easy, no humans served here.

. . .

WITHOUT SO MUCH AS A MOMENT'S HESITATION, AELIA turned and slammed her key down on the bar, making the woman next to her jump so much she spilled half her pint.

Keeran apologised as he reached past her to scoop up the key and followed where Aelia was carving a path to the door. He let her make it out onto the quieter street before grabbing her, pulling her round to face him.

"I am not staying in that place," Aelia hissed, but it wasn't the anger in her face that brought Keeran up short. It was the grief that hollowed her eyes, the first glimpse she'd let him see of the anguish she'd been in since he'd bumped into her on the road.

"We don't have to, just hear me out first?" Keeran said, holding up his splayed hands.

Aelia threw her arm towards the inn, glaring at him as though he'd asked to spend the night in an Astraean camp.

"I am not putting money in the pockets of people who support the Astraea."

"You're not." Keeran forced himself to remain calm, reminding himself just how sheltered she'd been. "Every business in Drias, every business across Demuto will have a sign similar to that, not because they support the Astraea, but because they fear them."

Aelia shook her head violently. "That's no excuse, they're fucking cowards—"

"They are not cowards." Keeran stopped her, suddenly too tired of her attitude to listen to another word. "You saw what the Astraea did in Callodosis. It's no different here. Whole businesses are being ransacked because they still employ humans, and regular artemians are murdered in cold blood for nothing more than serving them. These are normal people, Aelia. Can you honestly blame them for choosing to survive, to protect their families?"

The anger dropped from her face, leaving bitter resentment in its place.

"Fine." She snatched the key from his hand. "I'll eat in my room. See you in the morning."

And without a backward glance, she stormed back into the tavern. Keeran bunched his fists against his rising frustration, raising his head to the darkening sky and letting out a long breath. When he was sure he wasn't going to put his fist through the wall, he made his way to his room. He put his ear to the wall to make sure Aelia was in and safe before heading back downstairs. He needed information, and where better to get it than the local tavern?

Half of Drias seemed to fill every spare inch of the place. He tried to breathe past the smell of sweat as he crossed to the bar, a path clearing before him as artemians squeezed into their neighbours to get out of his way. He searched the tavern and found what he was looking for all too easily.

It was a fact of life that in every sad little tavern, there were sad little men, and this one was no exception. If Keeran was being generous, he would describe his target as middle-aged. His face told of the toll life had taken on him. Thin red veins spidered their way across the loose skin of his cheeks, the grey of his stubble doing nothing to compliment the similar pallor of his complexion, whilst the hair on his head had deserted him completely. He clutched a tankard with a desperate grip, the only lifeline his miserable existence had thrown him.

Although his voice was lost in the din of the room, he was clearly talking just that little bit too loudly into the ear of a younger man who wasn't even bothering to look at him. Keeran's target was undeterred, slinging his arm over the younger man's shoulder whilst he continued, looking earnestly into his face as he persevered with his prattling. It was the last straw, apparently.

The younger man shoved the arm off and got up to leave, hardly uttering a word as he left to find a quieter spot to drink away the day's stresses in peace. In a room too busy to walk in, Keeran's man sat at the only empty table. He looked around the room, too drunk to really mind. That was probably why he drank in the first place.

Keeran went to the bar and ordered two drinks from the all-too-obliging barmaid before joining the man. His eyes boggled as Keeran slid onto the bench beside him, trapping him against the wall, but it wasn't too long before they settled onto the second drink. Keeran slid it in front of him.

"Mind if I join you?"

CHAPTER TEN

Keeran cracked open a bleary eye and was confronted with the dark box the inn generously called a room. The thin sunlight struggling through the filthy glass made it seem no less tragic than it had the night before. He pushed himself off the lumpy mattress, untangled himself from the itchy sheets and swung his legs off the bed. The floorboards were cold on his bare feet, but he hardly noticed, his mind springing into action with its usual unforgiving velocity.

He dropped his head into his hands, his fingers sinking into his hair as the events of the past couple of days hit him.

He'd seen Aelia, developed some kind of immediate obsession, stooped to a little light stalking, had come *this* close to kissing her, and pissed her off royally. Now, somehow, he found himself stuck on the receiving end of no small amount of hostility on a journey he really should have been making alone.

He groaned at the thought of telling her what he'd learnt the night before. If it wasn't so awful, he'd have laughed at himself. There he'd been, explaining the ways of the world to her outside the inn last night, when really he was just as naïve as she was. Never in his wildest dreams had he expected things to have escalated so quickly.

He didn't want to believe it, but several people in the tavern had confirmed that the Astraea were now working under the King's authority. What no one seemed to understand, however, was why.

Keeran's head shot up as he heard movement next door, his hearing easily picking up the sound of her door closing through the thin walls. He shoved himself off the bed, leapt into some clothes, and in a matter of moments, was jogging down the stairs after her.

Keeran's heart sank when Aelia turned to face him, already reaching for the handle of the front door. The purple circles beneath her eyes had darkened overnight, and the redness rimming them suggested she'd spent much of the night awake and crying. Any resentment he felt for her behaviour towards him withered away at the sight.

"Morning." He crossed the room in a few strides. "Where are you heading to?"

"I need some supplies. I wanted to head out early so we can make a move as soon as possible." She shoved the door open and stepped blinking into the sunlight.

"I'll come with you," he said, already heading in the direction of the main street.

"I do not need you to come with me," she bit out from behind him, making him stop and turn towards her. "You seem to find it hard to believe that anyone could survive without your constant intervention, so let me clear this up for you. I do not need your help," she said, emphasising each word.

And just like that, his resentment sprang back into place. When was the last time someone had spoken to him like she did? Had they ever? She was obnoxious, ungrateful, and downright rude. He opened his mouth to tell her as much, the words primed and ready on his tongue, but he managed to stop himself just in time. The tiny fragment of himself that wasn't sick of her shit reminded him she'd been through hell, and him losing his temper was only going to make things worse.

"As you wish. What time do you want to be ready to leave?" he said quietly, anger simmering in his tone despite himself.

"I don't know. When I'm done," she tossed over her shoulder as she sauntered off, limp noticeably improved from the day before. At least she seemed to be using the poultice he'd given her.

He glared after her, quietly seething at the audacity of the woman. He seriously considered marching to his room, packing his bags, and leaving without her. But the moment she rounded the corner, he knew he wouldn't. As soon as she was out of sight, that feeling of anxiousness returned, uncomfortably churning in the pit of his stomach. Grumbling to himself, he stalked in the opposite direction.

He swept down the foul street, letting his frustration radiate off him, the natural aversion people had to him paying off as even the meanest-looking thugs gave him a wide berth. He wasn't the kind of target they were looking for; far from it.

The town did nothing to improve his mood; even in the short time since he'd been here last, the poverty had worsened. The homeless huddled on almost every street; humans, every single one of them. Who knew what position they'd been in a few months ago, where they'd been working, where they'd been living? And now here they were, kicked out and penniless, ripe for the picking when the Astraea next passed through. Keeran threw his hands in his pockets and bowled on, his scowl deepening with every street he passed. The sooner he found Beserkir, the better.

In some ways, it was a good thing that Aelia had fobbed him off. He was running dangerously low on money, and he doubted she would approve of his means of attaining it. The Peregrinians provided the cover he needed to visit most of Demuto without arousing too much suspicion, but travelling with them did not pay well enough, not even close. Fortunately, he could be pretty light-fingered when he needed to be.

Just as he was entering the merchant's quadrant, he saw a human, a young woman, with her scrawny arms wrapped around two hollow-cheeked children, tucked in the corner of the square. Their age was hard to gauge past the dirt on their faces, but it didn't really matter; their dull eyes told him they'd experienced far worse than most adults had.

As he passed, three young artemians approached the destitute family of humans. They were all predator-born, and in fine clothes undoubtedly paid for out of parents' pockets. An alarm bell rang in Keeran's ears, and he slunk into the shade by a nearby water fountain, sipping water from his cupped palms as he watched them.

One of the young men jumped towards the woman with a flying kick, swinging his leg to send her cup flying, a meagre scattering of coins rolling across the road. Her eyes followed the precious money, but she didn't move to retrieve it, only clutched her children tighter.

Keeran kept to the shadows, his expression darkening as another of the men picked up one of the coins. He held it out to her whilst his friends laughed behind him, the noise grating on Keeran like metal on stone. The woman, wisely dubious, made no move to take it, but the man held it closer, waving it in front of her until she finally reached out to take it with delicate fingers. One of the children began to cry, burying its face into its mother's threadbare clothes. Keeran was at risk of grinding his teeth to dust at this point, but still he kept his distance, even when the man predictably whipped the coin away from her, eliciting a chorus of laughter from his companions. What Keeran hadn't expected however, was the force with which the man threw the coin at her, launching it at her face with malevolent delight.

Blood trickled from the resulting cut on her forehead, and Keeran's blood roared in his ears. As the men sauntered off, leaving the woman scrabbling to collect the coins, Keeran ignored the little warning voice in the back of his head to leave well alone, to keep his head down. No, that voice was lost to the snarling of the creature in the corner of his mind that spurred him towards violence. A red mist settled over him, thoroughly clouding his better judgement, and he loosened the leash he kept it on, sinking into the savage brutality he fought day and night.

The men weren't hard to follow. So absorbed in themselves, they didn't notice as death itself began to hunt them, the brown in his eyes all but disappearing as he stalked them through the town. They made the mistake of entering an alley, heading towards the courtyard it opened onto.

Keeran didn't reach for the fire magic that hummed eagerly in the back of his mind, nor did he unsheathe his dagger; no, he wanted to feel their skin break against his, wanted to feel the pain of bone crunching beneath his fist.

The men turned as soon as he entered the alleyway, dropping into a defensive position like the good little predators they were. No flight response here, these cocky little fuckers were all fight.

"Whatever you're planning, I wouldn't recommend it," one of them cautioned as Keeran stalked towards them, exuding menace with every step he took. "We're all armed and know how to use them."

Keeran cocked his head and smiled, a vicious thing that had the confidence leaching from their faces.

"Good," he growled, more monster than man.

The three men pulled their blades free, and Keeran waited for them to spread out into an attack formation. He so desperately wanted a challenge, so desperately wanted to get some of the frustration of the last few days out of his system.

They attacked as one, their thin steels whipping through the air. Keeran sidestepped around the one closest to the wall, moving behind him too fast for him to register. He snapped his neck with one rough twist of his hands. He used the still twitching body to block the blade of his comrade, locking it between its ribs and tugging the weapon free from the shocked man's hands. Disarmed and panicking, it was easy for Keeran to block his clumsy blows before spinning to break the elbow of the third man as he extended his sword arm.

Keeran grinned as he jabbed up into the broken limb with one fist, causing him to drop the hilt just in time for Keeran's other hand to swipe it from the air. He wasted no time in plunging it straight into the eye of the second man, before turning to slam the third man's head into the wall with enough force that even his own mother would struggle to recognise him.

It was all over in a matter of seconds, the bodies hitting the ground one after the other in quick succession. Keeran stood there panting, more from the effort of trying to wrestle his inner beast back into its cage than the physical exertion.

When he left the alley a few minutes later, he left it three coin purses heavier.

THE WOMAN STILL SAT WHERE HE'D LEFT HER, THE COINS collected and the cup now safely empty. Her eyes bulged as he crossed to her, her neck craning back to take all of him in. The same child started crying again.

He dropped to a crouch, hating that she looked more frightened of him than she had been of the three men. Hating that she was right to be.

"Here." He dropped a coin purse in front of her, everything the men had carried, bar what he needed to get Aelia and himself to Beserkir.

The woman's nostrils flared as she tore her eyes from him to glance at the purse, flicking them immediately back to him.

"What do you want?" Her fingers were white where they clung to the clothes on her children's scrawny backs.

"I want you to get out of here. The Astraea will never leave towns like this alone. You stand a better chance heading to the smallest village you can find— the more remote, the better. Leave today, if possible. You never know when the Astraea will be back."

He didn't give her a chance to answer; he rose and turned to leave.

"Wait," she called. He obeyed. "We will do as you say, but please, tell me why? This is a fortune to give to a stranger."

She was well spoken, clearly one of the many victims of the Astraean induced unemployment. Keeran wondered what she had been, how far she'd had to fall, but really, it didn't matter. All that mattered was that she had fallen.

"Because real fear nourishes the worst in us, and your children have already known too much of it. Save them from it before it's too late."

This time when he made to leave, she didn't call him back.

CHAPTER ELEVEN

By the time Aelia got back to the inn, her body was aching again. The uneven cobbles were torture on her struggling joints, but it wasn't the pain that had her heading back to the inn before she had everything she needed; it was the town.

She'd never seen such poverty before, had never seen anyone sleeping rough before. Sure, people struggled in Callodosis, especially the humans, but they all had work, they all had roofs over their heads. The worst thing was how everyone just walked past them, indifferent or unseeing, as if it were the most commonplace occurrence. Aelia supposed that here, it must be.

She wanted to get out of this place as quickly as possible. She'd asked around the few shops she'd stopped in, and learnt that the Astraea hadn't passed through here, which she could have guessed with all the humans still on the streets. One artemian had spotted them leaving the forest and heading north-west, so north-west it was, unless Keeran had heard differently.

Keeran. There was another problem she wished she didn't

have to deal with. She'd be an absolute idiot to pursue the Astraea without him. He'd proven to be more than capable at handling himself in the woods, as if any proof was necessary when he looked like death incarnate.... if death had a jawline you could cut yourself on.

And therein lay the problem. Every moment she wasn't thinking of Otis, or Fenrir, or Mirra, she was thinking of that night in the woods, of how things could have gone so differently between them if the Astraea hadn't shown up. It was indecent, unacceptable. She should be grieving, should be far too distraught for such thoughts, and yet every time he opened his mouth, her heart started thumping in her chest like she was an infatuated teenager.

She made it to the inn and headed straight to her room, throwing what she'd bought into her already bursting pack, and carrying it back down to the bar. The same girl from the night before was behind it, looking less dishevelled but just as exhausted.

"You're working again this morning?" Aelia asked, dropping her pack onto the floor with a thump.

"We're short-staffed," the girl said, not looking up from wiping down the worktop with a cloth too filthy to be doing anything other than smearing grime more evenly across the bar. "We had to let the humans go and there aren't enough artemians in the town to fill all the vacant positions."

"Well, there's an enormous hole in the Astraea's philosophy," Aelia snipped, too wound up from exploring the town to mind her tongue.

"You've only spotted the one?" The girl smiled, wryly.

Aelia huffed through her nose but said no more. The inn seemed quiet, seeing as it was still empty, but who knew who could be listening.

"I need to settle up." Aelia dug into her pocket, but the girl shook her head.

"Your brother paid last night," the girl said. Aelia must have visibly bristled because she stopped wiping and asked, "Is that a problem?"

"No," Aelia ground out, knowing full well why she was prying. "And he's not my brother."

"Oh, my mistake." The girl looked her over before finally asking, "Are you two headed back this way anytime soon?"

"I can't speak for him, but I'm certainly not."

"Oh." The barmaid brightened, a smile lighting up her face at the knowledge they wouldn't be returning together. Not for the first time, Aelia noticed how pretty she was. "Well, safe travels then."

Aelia stared back, trying to ignore the jealousy that was snaking its way through her, more furious than she had any right to be. She'd known the girl was into him when they'd got the keys last night, and much as she tried not to care, she couldn't help but wonder what else he'd been doing when he was down here paying for the rooms.

"Thanks," was all she could muster as she stooped to pick up her pack and made her way out.

Aelia was struggling to process the layers of anger that had stacked up on top of each other over the last couple of days and, as she sank down onto the step outside the inn door, she felt a sudden overwhelming exhaustion that went far deeper than just two sleepless nights.

She'd never felt so alone as she did in this unfamiliar town, with the societal pillars she'd come to rely on crashing down around her. Everyone was gone— a thought she was trying so hard not to dwell on— and she was left to deal with it on her own. Who knew if Fenrir was even alive? And if he was, where the hell were they taking him? Just as she began to spiral, her breathing starting to come in short, sharp gasps, something tugged at her attention. Her head snapped up, just in time to see Keeran rounding the corner.

He was leading a horse on either side, looking for all the world like he belonged on the battlefield, not the bleak streets of Drias. His black clothes did nothing to hide the sheer bulk of the man, the muscles of his arms filling his sleeves in a way that Aelia found hard to look away from. He'd rolled them up, exposing the defined muscle of his forearms, veins popping where he held the leather reins in each hand. Aelia had to look away before her thoughts went to places they had no right to be.

By the time he reached the inn, she was in no better control of herself than she had been. She didn't want this, didn't want to feel this way about him, so when she finally realised he was leading two horses, not one, she latched onto the anger that reared its head instead. First, he'd paid for the room; now he was buying her horses. Why did he think she needed his help?

When he saw her expression, his own darkened.

"Don't bite my head off," he said when he was close enough. "The horse is not a gift, it's so you don't slow me down. I'll sell it after we've found Beserkir, so don't go getting yourself all worked up about it, okay?"

Aelia's eyes narrowed. She opened her mouth to argue, but Keeran cut her off.

"Oh, stop being a pain in my arse and just take the bloody horse." He thrust the reins towards her, and something in his tone made her listen. There was something different underlying it, something sinister she hadn't heard before, and she couldn't help but wonder what had put it there.

"What happened?" she asked, but she stood and took the reins from him.

"Nothing happened, I'm just keen to get out of here." He tied his horse to a hitching post, knotting the leather straps with practised ease. That horse wasn't going anywhere, she noticed, her throat bobbing as she swallowed. "I need to grab my pack, I won't be long."

And he wasn't. In a matter of moments, he was back, fixing his pack behind his saddle and about to spring up into it when suddenly, he paused.

"Can you mount on your own?" he asked over his shoulder.

"Of course I can," she snapped. She'd already tied her pack into place when he was in the inn, so he hadn't had to see her struggle through the pain of lifting it so high, every rib seeming to scream at her to stop. Cursing herself for not being quick enough to have clambered into the saddle whilst he was still inside, she grabbed both ends of it, put her foot in the stirrup, and kicked off.

Her leg betrayed her, buckling beneath her and sending her chest first into the hard leather. Ducking her head to hide her face, she slid back to the floor. The only thing stopping her from collapsing in a heap was her grip on the saddle.

Everything hurt from the beating she'd taken, from the hours spent digging the grave, and the past day of walking certainly hadn't helped. If it weren't for the poultice he'd given her, she doubted she'd be standing. Aelia waited for the pain to subside before trying again. She did better this time, getting high enough that it was her stomach that slammed into the saddle, knocking the breath from her.

Once back on her feet, she had to close her eyes and rest her forehead against the cool leather as she breathed through the pain. Fucking leg wouldn't fucking work. If she could just get in the saddle...

"Will you stop being so bloody stubborn and let me help you?" said a low voice from beside her, making her jump. She hadn't heard him come so close.

She didn't look at him; she couldn't. She felt so weak, so

embarrassed. She would rather the ground opened up and swallowed her whole rather than admit she couldn't get on the horse on her own, but seeing as that didn't seem likely to happen anytime soon, she just nodded.

"May I hold your shin?" he asked, close enough for her to smell the hint of smoke on him. She held her breath, hating that she wanted to do the opposite, that she wanted to press her face into his chest and breathe him in.

Again, she just nodded.

Keeran bent over and wrapped a huge hand around her shin furthest from the horse.

"On three. One, two, three." She flew into the saddle, his free hand grabbing her thigh to stabilise her, his skin hot even through the fabric of her trousers. Her eyes darted to his hand, large enough to almost wrap halfway round her entire thigh, and then flicked to his face, to find his dark eyes locked onto hers.

He moved his hand, jerking it away as if scalded, and took a few steps back.

"You okay?" he said, his voice gravelly, his eyes unreadable.

"Fine. Thank you." She hated how weak her voice sounded. How fucking pathetic.

"I'll be damned." Keeran said to her horse, running his hand over its forehead. "She *does* know those words."

"They aren't warranted when the help wasn't wanted."

"Manners are always warranted," Keeran said as he launched himself into the saddle, settling gently onto the horse's back. He slid his gaze over to meet hers, and the look in his eyes made her toes curl in her boots. "Well, nearly always."

He didn't give her time to answer, putting his heel to his horse's side and making off down the road.

Was… was he flirting? It took her a couple of breaths to

compose herself, her heart doing all kinds of fluttery things whilst she watched his back recede down the street. She took in the broad muscles of his shoulders and wondered what it would be like to be under them, grabbing hold of them...

Aelia sucked in a breath, snapping herself out of it and pushing her own horse on. No, not her horse, Keeran's horse. Keeran's horse, that he'd had to lift her onto.

Mortification doused any other, less desirable emotions, and that led quickly to anger again. Anger that he'd seen her like it, anger that he'd put her in that position, anger that she would never be good enough, strong enough, *artemian* enough.

Fuck him, fuck them all. The sooner she could get to Fenrir, the sooner she could get rid of him. All she wanted in that moment was to run back to her treehouse and bury her face into Otis's shoulder, for him to tell her what to do. Tears welled in her eyes at the knowledge she'd never be able to do that again; the rollercoaster of emotions she was feeling every minute of every day breaking down her resolve. She dashed away her tears before Keeran could see, swallowing hard against the lump in her throat and forcing her head high. She hung back until they passed through the gates of Drias, heading out once more into the vast plains.

CHAPTER TWELVE

Aelia had never sat so long in a saddle, and she soon became aware of a whole new type of soreness. To distract herself from the relentless rocking of joints that pleaded with her for rest, she opted to try and glean what information she could from Keeran.

Drias had made her aware just how sheltered she had been. The Peregrinian armourer who'd refused to serve Mirra had warned them, had told them how clueless they were, but how could they ever have realised just how much their little village had been protected from? Keeran had been travelling with the Peregrinians; she would be foolish not to pick his brain whilst she had the chance.

She pushed her horse on so she was level with him and cleared her throat, breaking the silence they'd both been comfortably riding in.

"Are all towns in Demuto like Drias?" she asked, moving her horse slightly further from his as the huge black beast Keeran rode flattened its ears back and swung its hindquarters towards them, unhappy with their proximity. Keeran soothed it with a hand on its neck, murmuring something too quiet for her to make out.

"They're not all that pretty," he replied once his horse looked less likely to boot her.

Aelia couldn't bring herself to smile, let alone laugh— not when her heart felt heavy enough to drag her tumbling straight from her horse.

"You said the situation was no better anywhere else in Demuto, that everyone everywhere was too scared of the Astraea to stand up for the humans. How can that be? How can they be getting away with this?"

Keeran gripped the reins with one hand and rubbed his brow with the other, suddenly looking as tired as she felt.

"It's got worse, more quickly than I would have ever thought possible. I passed through Drias with the Peregrinians about eight months ago and it was nothing like that. The Astraea stopped us on our way to the forest about a week ago, but we had no humans with us so they just stole what they needed and knocked a few people about, under the pretence of suspecting them of selling to humans. Just flexing their muscles, really. From the number of empty buildings we saw, I imagine Drias has been hit hard. They probably once belonged to humans, or people who were unfortunate enough to be made an example of. The Astraea are scaring everyone into not employing the humans they haven't rounded up yet."

"Where are they taking them?" Aelia stared at him, eyes wide with horror as he spoke. How had it been allowed to escalate so quickly?

Keeran shrugged. "I don't know, but a few people I spoke with suspected they're being taken to the coast."

"The coast?" Aelia repeated, thoughts stumbling over one another too fast for her to untangle them. "Why?"

"No one seems to know."

"That doesn't make sense," Aelia argued. "Why would they risk going so close to Llmera when that would take them right under the King's nose?"

Keeran avoided her gaze, sighing through his nose, before finally answering.

"According to the people I spoke to in Drias, the Astraea have the King's full support."

Aelia looked at him from under her brows, jaw clenched to the point of pain. "What?"

"The red insignia on their uniform belongs to the King. No one seems to know why or how, but there's no doubt that it's true."

"So what do we do?" she wondered out loud, staring off into the distance as she tried to make sense of it.

"We push on. We know they're headed to the coast. If we can't catch up with them on the way, we'll head to Llmera."

Aelia's brows dropped with a sudden realisation.

"Why are you doing this?" She watched his face carefully, but his features gave nothing away.

"You saw the people back there, kicked onto the streets, just waiting for the Astraea to come back and pick them up," Keeran said, staring at the horizon.

"Yeah, but why now? How long have you been with the Peregrinians? You must have seen that all before." Aelia was surprised she hadn't questioned it sooner. He'd left the Peregrinians to chase after Beserkir all on his own… why?

This time, he twisted in the saddle to face her, and she almost flinched at the depth of the black in his eyes. It was as though something other than Keeran was looking back out at her. Whatever it was, it was the very thing that had scared her so much when she'd first laid eyes on him.

"Because after I saw what happened in Callodosis, I decided that man needed to die."

Aelia had to look away. Not because she disagreed, far

from it, but because whatever it was that was looking out of Keeran's eyes sent shivers scuttling over her skin.

"Who is he to you?" Keeran asked, surprising her enough to make her look back up. To her relief, his eyes were dark brown again. "The man you're rescuing?"

Aelia wasn't sure how to answer. He was more than a friend, he was as much family as Otis had been. In the end, she settled with the truth.

"He's the only friend I have left."

Keeran nodded before looking back out at the horizon.

"Then we'd better get him back, but right now, we need to find somewhere to shelter before that hits." He gestured with the reins up ahead, drawing Aelia's attention to the dark storm clouds rolling towards them.

Aelia glared at them with bitter exasperation. It looked like, on top of everything else, they were going to get soaked.

SOAKED DIDN'T EVEN COME CLOSE TO DESCRIBING THE STATE they were in when they finally found a disused barn a little way off the road. Lightning forked through the sky, illuminating the abandoned building just long enough for Aelia to spot it, the clap of thunder reverberating in her chest. The horses skittered sideways across the road, moving in any direction but forward in their terror, and Aelia clung on for dear life as her exhausted legs threatened to give up on her.

Eventually, they reached the barn and Keeran leapt from his horse with more energy than Aelia thought he had any right to have. He encouraged his terrified beast to follow as he tried to open the barn doors.

"Wait there," Keeran yelled to her over the torrential rain, before he disappeared inside to tie up his horse.

There was no way he was helping her out of the saddle,

especially not after he'd had to heave her into it in Drias. Her horse panicked as Keeran's disappeared from sight, and she tightened her reins. She tried to calm it, but all that came out was garbled nonsense as fear tied her tongue in knots. Deciding it was now or never, she freed her foot from the stirrup. The rain had her already tight trousers clinging to her, making movement infinitely harder than it needed to be, but she managed to swing her leg behind her. Her ribs screamed, pain lancing through her chest like she'd been branded, but she clenched her teeth, her momentum taking her past the point of no return. Lightning tore its way through the sky, followed almost immediately by a clap of thunder that broke her horse's self-control. With her not fully in the saddle, she was powerless when it reared onto its back legs, sending her crashing to the ground beneath it.

She curled into a ball as hooves trampled around her, seeming to come from every direction, making it impossible for her to move out of the way.

Just when she thought she would die there, her skull crushed in by her own panicking horse, a booming voice carried over the tumultuous beating of hooves. The next moment, the horse was moved from over her.

"Aelia." Keeran dropped to his knees next to her, the hard lines of his face transformed by worry. "Aelia, are you ok? Where are you hurt?"

"I...I'm not." She thought she wasn't, anyway, either that or the adrenaline was making it impossible to tell if she had any new injuries.

Another flash of light pierced the sky, and Keeran hooked a hand under her arm, hauling her to her feet.

"Get inside, I'll fetch the horse," he shouted and, for once, she didn't argue, splashing through puddles on numb feet into the barn.

Keeran ran in after her, practically dragging the horse

behind him, its eyes rolling as it passed through the wildly swinging doors. The moment he was through, she threw her weight against them, battling the wind to get them closed. Her fingers were like blocks of ice as she tried to slide the beam of wood into place, but after a momentary struggle, she managed to bar the doors shut.

The relief of being out of the rain was instant, the relative quiet blissful after the complete barrage on her senses for the past few hours whilst they searched for shelter. Releasing a shaky breath, she turned to where Keeran was tethering the horse.

She didn't hesitate, moving to help him untack it on unsteady legs.

"I'll do it, Aelia, just go sit down." Keeran didn't look at her as he spoke, but she could hear the irritation in his voice clear enough for her to suspect his eyes would be jet black. She ignored him; it was her horse to look after, even if he technically owned it.

She fumbled with the girth, her fingers next to useless with cold as she tried to wrestle the buckle free. It eventually gave in, and she let it swing beneath its belly, reaching up to try and lift the saddle off the horse's soaked back.

She got it halfway off before her back spasmed and it slipped from her grip. It crashed to the floor, sending her horse skittering into Keeran's horse, with him wedged between them. It was sheer luck that the two horses were too preoccupied with the storm still raging outside to exchange kicks over personal space, and Aelia clapped her hands over her open mouth until she saw Keeran squeeze his way out from between them.

"What the fuck is wrong with you?" he shouted, the barn mercifully too dark for her to see his eyes.

"Nothing," she yelled back indignantly, her temper flaring immediately. It had always been a little too quick to surface, but these days it hardly needed any encouragement. "It slipped out of my hands."

"It wouldn't have slipped from your hands if you'd just listened to me." He took a step closer, throwing his arm back at the horses behind him. "Just like you wouldn't have been nearly trampled to death if you'd just waited for me to help you off."

"I don't need your help, Keeran, and if I do, I'll fucking ask for it," she screamed at him, stepping closer to him, too.

"Oh, you don't? You'd have handled Shiva and his friends, would you? You'd have got yourself somewhere safe when you were knocked out cold by the Astraea after they nearly beat you to death? You'd have stopped that horse from kicking your skull in? I hate to break it to you, Aelia, but everybody needs help sometimes, so can we just stop with the brattish behaviour?"

Aelia's blood thrummed in her ears, her anger boiling over as he dug into her oldest, deepest insecurities. So, she dug right back.

"Who are you trying to fool, Keeran? Who is this white knight bullshit really for?" She stepped closer again, a flash of lightning through the slits in the beams enough to show him glowering down at her, his black hair still plastered to his face. "Because I saw you in the woods, I saw your eyes when you so valiantly came to my rescue. You *loved* hurting them. You're no hero, Keeran, so pull your head out of your arse and stop acting like you've got your shit together when you're clearly even more fucked up than the rest of us."

"Don't talk to me like that," Keeran seethed, the shadows around him seeming darker all of a sudden. She knew she should stop, knew she was being downright stupid to poke at something she didn't even nearly understand, but she couldn't help it. The rage that had been simmering in her over the last few days erupted through her, and she was swept along with it.

"Like what, Keeran? You don't like someone calling you out on your bullshit? Then maybe don't go poking around in other people's. Or are you such a monster that you get off on that too?"

Suddenly, he was close enough that she could feel the warmth radiating off him.

"You think I'm a monster because I enjoyed beating up the men who planned on hurting you?" He barked a laugh, humourless and harsh. "You don't know the half of it. But I promise you, if you keep talking to me like you have over the last couple of days, I'll show you just how much of a monster I can be."

"You don't scare me," she sneered, her anger deserting her as he loomed over her, one enormous column of barely restrained violence. He dropped his head even closer, his face mere inches from hers.

"No?" he asked, his voice little more than a growl. "Then why are you trembling?"

She didn't trust herself to answer, didn't trust her voice not to betray her. Because in that moment, it wasn't fear that was making her tremble, nor was it her soaked clothes. It was his proximity, so close she was surrounded by the smell of rain and spice and smoke. It made her want to throw herself against him, to find out just how wicked that other side of him was, to let him have every vulnerable inch of her to do with as he pleased. Just as she had that night in the woods, just like she'd wanted to almost every moment since.

The energy between them shifted, the silence filled with the sound of the wind driving the rain against the walls of the barn, the tension between them as searing as the lightning tearing through the world outside. He felt it too; she could see it in the shadows of his face, the way the anger melted into something just as devastating, just as terrifying. And gods, how she wanted him to unleash it on her.

He was so close, his head dipped to nearly level with hers; if she just lifted onto her toes, she'd be able to brush her lips against his. Her eyes dropped to them, slightly parted for his quickened breaths, and warmth spiralled through her core as the urge to crush against them surged through her.

One of the horses neighed, voicing its ongoing concern as the storm rattled the barn doors with growing vigour, and the spell was broken.

Rational thought slammed into Aelia, overriding the desire that had overwhelmed her moments before. She took an unsteady step back, stunned by the force of her own emotions. Something flashed in Keeran's eyes, and for a second, she thought he was going to pull her back to him. But it was gone almost as soon as she saw it.

She chose to ignore the part of her that was disappointed.

It took him a while to speak, and when he did, his voice was low and gravelly, the sound shivering down her spine.

"We need a fire. If I finish tending to the horses, would you start one?"

"Of course." She nodded, grateful that her voice didn't tremble.

He turned his back to her and focused on the horses, acting for all the world like nothing had happened. Which, she supposed, it hadn't.

She wanted to kick herself. He'd been in the forest when she'd been held up by Shiva; he'd almost certainly heard that she couldn't Shift. She still had no idea what his second form was, but you just had to look at him to know he was predator-born. He was at the top of the apex, whilst she didn't even make the pyramid.

Of course nothing had happened. And she doubted it ever would.

CHAPTER THIRTEEN

Keeran swallowed heavily—the urge to turn back, grab her by the neck, and claim her mouth roaring through him. The other side of him seethed, its desire a monstrous, twisted thing. It longed to punish her for talking to him that way, and gods, he wanted to as well. Every muscle bunched with the effort of controlling it, of forcing himself to walk towards the horses instead of pushing her to the floor and showing her how torturous pleasure could be. It wanted to explore every inch of her, learning what she liked just so it could wind her to the point of insanity. Until he was all she could think about, until he was all she wanted.

He heaved the saddle off his horse, dropping it to the floor with less care than it deserved. His erection pressed against the restrictive fabric of his trousers, and he was grateful the horses stood between him and Aelia. He palmed it, trying to push it into a more comfortable position, but even that simple touch sent shockwaves of pleasure shooting through him.

What was it about her that had him feeling this way? All she'd done was look at him, and he felt more unstable than he had in years, the beast within vying for control, his grip on its leash slipping from his grasp. He focused on his task, unbridling the horses and slipping on their headcollars, before using one of the blankets in his pack to rub them dry. He followed the grain of their coats, not allowing himself to think of anything other than wicking off the worst of the moisture that dripped off them onto the stone floor.

He was soaked too, but was beyond the point of caring. By the time his horse was dry and he'd started on Aelia's, he was back in control, his other side curled and quiet in the recesses of his mind. Only once his thoughts were his own again did he start to let them wander.

Aelia knew what he was. He'd been so careful to keep the worst of himself hidden from her, trying so hard not to scare her, even when she royally pissed him off. Yet she'd seen right through it. Now that he wasn't at the mercy of the darker side of him, the memory of her words incited nothing more than a resigned misery.

It wasn't a surprise that she'd noticed, not really. Disappointing, sure, but not a surprise. He was, by his very nature, a monster, and no matter how hard he tried to control it, there would always be a part of him that relished violence. The darkest sentiments, the most depraved emotions on the spectrum of the human psyche, came as naturally to him as breathing.

Self-loathing slammed into him, the blanket halting its circles over the chestnut coat of Aelia's horse as shame paralysed him. Had this been his first time battling such sentiments, he might have needed a moment before he could continue. But as it was, shame and self-loathing were his constant companions, and the blanket resumed its rhythmic circles with barely a pause.

Keeran's attention was caught by a soft curse from the other side of the barn, the rain having eased enough for him to hear Aelia struggling with the fire. She'd positioned herself near a hole in the ceiling, clear of the rain falling through it, but close enough for the smoke to have somewhere to go. She'd formed a pyramid from some of the wooden debris that littered the abandoned barn, using some stale hay as kindling, yet her fingers seemed to be too cold to handle the flint properly.

Keeran watched her, and the pang of longing he felt had a bitter sting after what she'd said about him, after she'd stepped away from him. There had been no mistaking the desire she'd felt; it had coursed between them, staining her cheeks a pretty pink that had sent his heart ricocheting around his rib cage. And yet, she'd stepped away.

She struck at the flint clumsily, trembling with the cold. Her clothes clung to her, revealing the impressive curve of muscle she gained from her years logging in Callodosis. Even crouched and shivering, spitting curses at the flint in her hands, she was still strikingly beautiful.

A smile tugged at his lips, despite the heaviness inside him. That flint was getting even more of a verbal beating than he had. He took pity on it and, being careful of timing, reached for the magic that wriggled eagerly at the base of his skull, sending sparks skittering into the hay just as she struck the flint. He teased the fire into taking hold, just enough to get it started before he reined in his magic.

Aelia grinned, looking entirely too pleased with herself, and Keeran huffed a quiet laugh. He fed the horses some of the grain from the saddle bags, piling some of the old hay near them in case they were hungry enough to try it. Then he made his way to the fire with his pack slung over one shoulder.

Aelia had been starting to get some food going from the supplies in her bag, but she paused to look up at him as he lowered himself to the floor opposite her, his wet clothes straining against the movement.

Without a word, she reached over to offer him the water skin.

It was a shitty apology, but he wasn't about to turn down a peace offering, no matter how feeble.

"Thanks," he grunted, taking it from her and knocking back a few gulps.

Aelia said nothing, but she smiled. Shyly. Keeran had to stop himself from staring at the way it softened her face, the same pink creeping into it as earlier. His heart faltered as she quickly looked away, busying herself with fishing for ingredients. She was nervous, he realised with a jolt.

Before he lost himself in a whirlpool of overthinking, he reached for his own pack and dug out some of his own rations.

"These might help?" he said, offering her the dried mushrooms, herbs, and salt.

"Thanks." She took them from him, being careful not to touch his hand as she did. "This is going to need all the help it can get."

Aelia added a few things to the watery soup she had simmering over the fire. He almost had to sit on his hands to stop himself from getting involved; gods forbid he push his luck by offering his help.

Instead, he fetched their bowls and busied himself with collecting more firewood, stacking it in a pile beside the fire.

"At least the storm seems to have passed," Aelia volunteered, leaning over to sniff the soup and adding a little more salt. As if that was going to help.

The thunder had indeed settled from the bone-rattling boom it had been to a comforting rumble, and the wind no longer howled through the gaps in the wooden slats of the barn walls. The rhythmic chomping of the horses, the patter of the rain outside, combined with the cheerful snap and crackle of the fire, brought a comforting feel to the derelict barn.

"Just as well. I'm not sure the barn could have withstood much more of it." He sat down, positioning his pack behind him and leaning back on it. He stretched his legs out, placing his boots as close to the fire as he dared in an attempt to dry them.

Keeran clasped his fingers behind his head, closed his eyes, and arched backwards to stretch out his aching shoulder blades. He didn't relish the thought of another whole day in the saddle tomorrow. When he opened his eyes again, he caught Aelia staring at him, her gaze locked onto where his arms were tense and straining as he stretched. She snapped her attention back to the soup, using a cloth to pour it from the pot. Keeran hardly noticed the unappetising way it sloshed into their bowls, lumps of gods only knew what splashing into the brown water. He was far too preoccupied with that blush that had made an appearance once more.

She must have felt it too, that charge that had crackled between them with more ferocity than the storm raging outside. The thought made him smile quietly to himself as she handed him his bowl.

It quickly vanished as he took his first mouthful. Holy Mother, that was rough.

Feeling her eyes on him, he quickly swallowed, fighting his body's reflex to immediately bring it back up.

"Mmm," was all he trusted himself to say when he finally dared lift his gaze to meet hers. Fortunately, it seemed sufficient to pacify her, and she tucked into her own without so much as a grimace.

He looked down at the bowl, full to the absolute brim, and prepared himself for the challenge of finishing it.

CHAPTER FOURTEEN

Keeran woke to the cheerful twitter of birds, rejoicing in their being alive to see in the new day after the fearsome storm the night before.

He groaned as he pushed himself off the hard ground, his joints protesting a night in wet clothes, on cold stone. Aelia was already up and packing, the horses tacked up and ready to go.

"You're up early," he said, running a hand through his hair and squinting up at her.

"Force of habit." She wrenched the straps of the saddle tight over her pack, securing it in place. "And we lost time yesterday. If we set out early, we can make it up today."

"The Astraea will have lost time too," Keeran pointed out, stretching his neck until it popped, some of the tension in it easing instantly.

"All the more reason to crack on." Aelia gave her saddlebags one final check before patting the horse on the neck. "Means we can gain on them."

"Can we gain on them after breakfast?" Keeran asked, wryly.

Aelia just pointed to a small parcel wrapped in cloth beside him. He reached over and pulled it closer, flipping open the fabric to reveal some sorry-looking berries and some dried meat. He'd take them any day rather than another of her culinary experiments.

"Well, it appears you've thought of everything," he said, hauling himself to his feet and rolling up his blanket.

A few minutes later, they were leading the horses out into the crisp morning air. He breathed it in, the fresh tang only a storm could create. By the time he opened his eyes, Aelia was already swinging herself into the saddle, wincing but managing. She'd applied the poultice again last night, an act that had had him disappearing to check on the horses, and there was no doubt it was helping.

Tugging on her reins, she turned her horse towards the road.

"I'm going to see if I can hunt us something to cook later. If you follow the road, I'll catch up with you," he called after her, making her stop and swivel in the saddle. She looked at him for a long moment before nodding.

"See you later then." She nudged her horse into a trot and took off through the long grass.

Keeran watched her go until his horse nudged him with its dark nose, snapping him out of his trance.

"You're as impatient as she is," he said, running a palm over the long brow of his gentle-eyed companion. "I suppose you're right, though, we should make a move, especially if we're going to catch up with her."

Keeran swung himself into the saddle, careful to lower himself into it gently. He was by no means easy cargo for the horse to carry, and he didn't need to make its job any harder than it had to be.

He clicked his tongue and brushed his heels against its side, heading in the opposite direction to Aelia. The tall grass of the plains surrounding Drias stretched in endless monotony in every direction, all the way back to Aelia's forests in the South. Keeran didn't expect there to be any trouble coming their way from Drias, there were too many people passing in and out of the town for anyone to have associated him with the deaths of the three artemians. But it was reassuring to know that with his eyesight, he'd see anyone coming across the vast expanse of uninterrupted grass well before they saw him.

Unfortunately, the same could be said of any game he might come across. It was far from ideal hunting grounds, with very few places to hide, but that suited Keeran just fine. He was in desperate need of a challenge, of a distraction.

There was little more than a light breeze to ruffle the seeded heads of the grass tickling his horse's belly, but it was enough to carry the subtle scent of a rabbit warren. Rabbit stew sounded pretty damn good after whatever the hell it was that Aelia had made last night.

Keeran dismounted and hobbled his horse, leaving it contentedly tucking into the lush grass, before setting off upwind.

The warren was all too easy to find. Nowhere near enough to take his mind off everything that was troubling him.

Focus, he demanded as he crawled on his elbows through the long stalks up a hill overlooking the unsuspecting rabbits, but it was no good. His thoughts kept scurrying back to Aelia.

She was infuriating. Rude, spiky, antagonistic… and yet, there was an immense vulnerability to her that had stopped Keeran from yelling at her to find Beserkir on her own. Because it was crystal clear that she needed him a damn sight more than he needed her. So far, she'd been nothing more than a liability. An ill-tempered liability.

Keeran just didn't know if the whole "fuck you, fuck them, fuck the whole fucking world" attitude was because of what had happened with the Astraea, or if it pre-dated that. He hadn't known her before; he only had the few moments he'd stolen when he was watching her from a distance to compare her to.

He stopped in his tracks, his elbows relaxing to drop his chest to the ground as he was struck by the memories of the night Shiva had ambushed her. Aelia had kicked off when he'd said he was superior, like he'd really struck a nerve. She couldn't Shift, despite the magic ringing her eyes.

Cogs whirred to life in his mind, the consequences of that flashing before him in a tale of struggle and inadequacy, being stuck somewhere in between human and artemian. There was no doubt in his mind that she was a fighter; in the short time he'd known her, she'd shown herself to be resilient and ballsy. So it was no real surprise that she attacked the world with almost every word she uttered, pushing herself instead of accepting help, and resenting anyone who offered it to her.

Keeran huffed a low laugh, the creature in him opening its slitted eye with a gentle snick. That simply wouldn't do. He clenched his fists so hard the veins of his forearm popped out from the straining muscle. He'd drag that inferiority complex out of her by the throat if he had to.

It wasn't that he couldn't relate— gods knew he was well versed with using anger as a coping mechanism— but he'd be fucking damned before he let her refuse help from him again. Not now he realised where it stemmed from.

He'd just have to find other ways to make her feel powerful, to teach her the pleasure of relinquishing control.

Keeran slammed the bars down on the cage in his mind, shutting off the urges radiating off the creature living in it.

He released a breath and slicked his hair back with a trembling hand.

Just the thought of her was enough to wake it, to stir the primitive emotions it slammed into him. He didn't remember the last time he'd been so vulnerable to its advances. Years, decades, of practice had made his hold over it firm and indomitable, but recently, it had begun to overwhelm him, to push him aside.

Since he'd first seen Aelia.

There was no denying it. That's when it had started. He'd sunk into its urge to follow her, to watch her. It had driven him to protect her, to wait for her instead of heading straight after Beserkir, to suggest they travel together when she'd only slow him down. Common sense had fucking dissipated since he'd first laid eyes on her, the monster in him prying loose his careful hold on its leash.

Keeran closed his eyes, his head hanging low as Aelia's words the night before sliced through him. It made it so much worse that she'd seen through his attempt to be better, that she'd picked up on the evil in him in just a few days. He'd tried so hard to control it, to keep that side of him at bay, and she'd seen right through him. Just like everyone else.

A monster, that's what she'd called him. She had no fucking idea.

Keeran snapped his head up. Fuck it, he shouldn't have bothered pretending; he carried evil with him every breath he took, and there was no escaping it. Not even for a woman like Aelia.

He crawled forwards, creeping over the brow of the hill, and sure enough, rabbits dotted the plains below. His magic leapt to life at the merest encouragement, his aim perfect as tiny balls of fire zipped across the grass to plunge straight through the eyes of three unsuspecting rabbits. The others kicked up their heels and fled, scurrying to safety beneath the soil.

Keeran felt a twinge of remorse as he went to pick up the limp, furry bodies. It was hardly a fair fight. But with someone like him, when was it ever?

A whole day passed before Keeran caught up with Aelia, the rabbits tied and bouncing on his saddle since early morning. The road had met with a river, meandering along its banks until he'd reached the tip of one of the first lakes that formed the Tears of Deliah, a cluster of lakes spanning for miles between here and Llmera, the capital city on the coast. As he looked out over the crystal-clear waters, he regretted not being there when Aelia saw them for the first time.

The break from the monotony of the plains was liberating, the breeze off the lake cool and refreshing on skin that had experienced the unrelenting attention of the sun. The dull plains had transformed into a rolling grassland, full of colourful flowers that supported huge insects the size of Keeran's finger.

Aelia had been easy enough to find, but he'd been reluctant to rejoin her, choosing to follow her at a distance instead. Out of sight, but far from out of mind.

It was shame that kept him away; shame that he'd lost his temper, shame that he'd lost control, shame that she'd seen that which he'd tried to hide. So, he'd put off having to face her again.

But the sun was disappearing beneath the waving grasses on the horizon to warm the other half of the world, leaving him no choice but to join where Aelia was setting up camp.

She'd lit a small fire beside the shelter of an old willow. The tree had bowed in submission to the brutal winds of the plains, all its branches hanging subserviently in the water. Aelia had set up camp on the opposite side, clear of its sweeping boughs.

She looked up from where she was crouched next to the fire, her green eyes sending a jolt through him that left his heart pounding. She stood in one smooth movement, seeming less sore than she had the day before. Pain shot through his ankles as his boots hit the ground, his joints stiff from so long in the saddle, and he paused a moment before turning to her.

Aelia was already halfway to him, her fingers clasped in front of her nervously.

"I'm sorry," she said, coming to a stop in front of him, eyes wary but softer than he'd seen them since he'd watched her at the festival in Callodosis. Certainly softer than they'd ever been when directed at him. "I shouldn't have said what I said, it was completely unfounded and bang out of order. I've been an utter bitch to you since we first met. I'm not even really sure why. I've had all day to think about it, and I feel terrible. I'm sorry."

Keeran had to grit his teeth to stop his jaw from hitting the floor. This was not at all what he thought he'd be coming back to.

"You don't need to apologise," he lied, his past self rolling his eyes at how quickly he'd rolled over. "You've been through a lot, and I'm sorry if I've made that worse."

"You haven't." She sighed, and the anguish in her face tugged painfully at him. The muscles in his arms twitched with the sudden urge to scoop her up and hold her close, as if he could hug away all the hurt and pain she was feeling. A ridiculous notion that he squashed right away. "I'm just so angry, and you were… there. There's no excuse for it."

"Aelia, I get it. Don't beat yourself up," Keeran said, dropping his head to make her look at him. "I mean it, it's fine.

But we don't know what we're riding towards, and if we keep going as we are, our chance at freeing your friend is next to none. We have to be in this together, and that means you need to listen to me as much as I need to listen to you. You can't keep insisting on doing everything your way."

Steel flashed in her eyes, but she tempered it, pressing her lips into a hard line before nodding jerkily.

"I know. I won't do it again," she conceded, so begrudgingly that Keeran almost smiled. She craned her neck past him with a far from subtle subject change. "Did you manage to hunt something? I'll get started on dinner if you want to untack your horse."

Keeran's stomach lurched at the thought of another meal like the night before.

"You cooked last night, it's my turn," he said, hurriedly. "I insist."

Aelia smiled, barely more than a tiny lift of her lips, but all at once, he forgave her everything. He hadn't seen her smile like that since they'd left Callodosis, and it sent a shock lancing straight through his rib cage, his heart stuttering at the sight of it.

"I'll help you with your horse then," she offered, completely oblivious to him trying to remember how to breathe.

They untacked the horse, and he left her rubbing it down as he carried his pack and the rabbits to the crackling fire. She'd already filled a pot with water from the lake, so he got to work skinning the rabbits, dropping them into the boiling water along with a few root vegetables they'd brought with them.

When the stew was simmering nicely, he twisted to reach into his pack for some seasoning, but the sight of Aelia wandering in front of the lake caught his eye.

She ran her fingers through the grass growing along the

banks, wildflowers bursting past the tall green blades, but she seemed oblivious to their dainty colours as she looked out over the vast lake. The setting sun was reflected in the still water, amplifying the pink and orange hues that filled the sky.

The view was breathtaking, but Keeran couldn't tear his eyes away from Aelia, his diaphragm tying itself in knots as she picked one of the flowers, twiddling it between her fingers absentmindedly.

As though she'd felt his gaze, her head turned to him, meeting his eyes unabashedly. Time became irrelevant, the seconds seeming stretched by something delicious and unexplainable that grew within their eye contact. The world around them disappeared as his entire consciousness tunnelled onto her, that tugging in his chest seeming to pull him towards her.

"I'm going to wash in the lake." Her words broke the silence, but not the spell, and she made no effort to move.

"The waters are deep, be careful." The low rasp of his voice betrayed him; his mind jumping to images of her struggling in the dark depths, naked and wet and needing him to wade in after her.

"I will." She seemed reluctant to leave, but she eventually fetched clean clothes from her pack, tucked her dagger away inside it, and disappeared down the bank. Keeran let out a long, slow breath, turning back to stare into the flames unseeingly for a few moments.

What was this? She could knock his legs out from under him with just a look, convincing him that her eyes were his anchor, that her face was the only home he'd ever need. He'd never felt anything like it, not even close. He'd never been in love, but he knew this wasn't it. It went deeper than that; it was an obsession he couldn't control, a tether he couldn't escape.

Trying desperately hard not to think of her naked, mere meters away, he turned his attention back to the food. It took a little fussing and several taste tests before he was satisfied.

Aelia returned to their little camp, her wet hair nearly black as she crossed to the willow and began hanging her freshly cleaned clothes over various branches.

"The water's good," she said, coming close to the fire and folding herself to sit cross-legged before it. She splayed her fingers wide and held them close to the cheerful flames. "Cold, but good."

"I might jump in myself before dinner, unless you're too hungry to wait?" Cold water was just what he needed to control his thoughts. It felt like half the blood in his body had fled south, and the way the tangled snarls of her wet hair hung over her shoulders wasn't helping. It made her look unrestrained and wild, just waiting to be tamed.

The thought crept unbidden to the forefront of his mind, leaching from the beast that had uncurled itself. Keeran shoved it back down, along with all the other diabolical things it wanted to do to her.

Yes, cold water was exactly what he needed.

"No, not at all," Aelia said, shifting to sit more comfortably before running her fingers through her tangled hair.

Keeran looked quickly away, something about the simple action sending his heart into overdrive. His hand clenched involuntarily as he stomped down on the images of all he could do if he replaced her hand with his own.

"Right." His voice was low and raw, eliciting a glance from her. He cleared his throat and tried again. "Be right back."

THE COLD WATER DID FUCK ALL.

Keeran walked the short distance back to the camp just as tortured as when he'd left, as evidenced by the stubborn bulge straining against his trousers. He left his top untucked, trying to hide it the best he could.

He served up dinner into their bowls, saving some for the morning, and sat back against his pack.

A low moan had his gaze whipping up. Aelia had closed her eyes, her empty spoon held halfway between the bowl and her mouth. When she opened them, they dropped straight to the stew, before she plunged her spoon back in for another bite.

This time, the moan was louder, and Keeran vowed to cook for her every night if it meant he got to hear her make noises like that.

"Oh gods, Keeran, that's good," she groaned.

Yup, every night.

"I'm glad you like it." He smiled, his own appetite waning with every bite she took, a hunger of an entirely different nature replacing it. If she kept talking like that, he'd lose the battle with himself and have her crying his name in earnest.

Fortunately, she was too preoccupied with her food to so much as glance his way, and he tucked into his own meal. It was good, sure, but nothing to warrant the sounds she was making. Remembering the meal from the night before, he wondered what kind of food she was used to. Seasoning was expensive, and if the stores he'd rifled through in her home had been anything to go by, food must have been mainly about survival. It made sense if she couldn't Shift— life couldn't have been easy for her.

Regret lanced through him when he thought of all the meals he could cook for her, if he wasn't limited to what he had in his pack. Guilt closely followed it, as he remembered how judgemental he'd been the night before, almost laughing to himself at her inability to cook. What a fucking arsehole.

Aelia scraped her bowl so clean that they probably wouldn't need to wash up. He reached over to where she sat on the opposite side of the fire.

"Here," he said, offering his bowl out to her. "I ate a lot on the road."

She eyed it for a second, almost drooling with temptation before shaking her head.

So. Predictable.

"I can't," she started, staring at the bowl. "It's yours—"

"Take the fucking bowl, Aelia." Her eyes snapped up to his, surprise mingling with just a trace of fear. His tone was soft, but he allowed just a hint of the other side of him to leak into it, the side that very few would dare argue with.

He smiled and held the bowl out closer to her. Aelia reached over and took it. Tentatively, but she took it.

"Thanks."

"Don't mention it," Keeran said, reclining once more onto his pack and dropping his head back on his hands, arching his neck to peer up at the stars. They offered no answers to the questions that circled his mind, a veritable vortex of confusion by this point, but he found some comfort in the familiar flecks of light.

He didn't know what had inspired her to apologise earlier, what had gone through her mind when she'd had a whole day alone with nothing but her thoughts for company. But he was more grateful than he could ever convey for the tenuous peace that had settled between them. It was good that she'd actually listened to him, too, because he was way past the point of letting her stop him from helping her. Not now he understood her better.

If only he could unravel what the fuck he was feeling for her as easily. The darkness in him had never been this reactive to anyone he'd been with before, not even close. He felt volatile, in a way he hadn't since he was a child, before he'd learnt how to control it.

The stars winked at him knowingly, as if privy to wisdom that as of yet eluded him. He sighed up at them before righting his neck to return his gaze to the small camp. Aelia had finished her second bowl and was elbow deep in her pack, biting her lip as she rummaged for whatever she was looking for. Light filled her face a moment before she pulled her arm free, the poultice clasped in her hand, and she smiled triumphantly as she unscrewed the lid.

She shuffled where she sat, angling herself so he couldn't see anything important as she lifted her top and started applying the pink paste.

Keeran didn't let himself look, choosing to busy himself with clearing away the bowls and putting the cooling stew away for the night. By the time he was done, Aelia was trying to contort herself into positions no healthy body could ever achieve, let alone one still recovering from significant trauma, as she tried to rub the poultice into the more awkward places of her back.

A muscle twitched in Keeran's jaw as he fought the urge to roll his eyes. The words slipped from between his lips before he could really think them through.

"Are you going to open the cuts that have barely healed, or are you going to let me help you?" he growled, letting her know the question may as well have been rhetorical.

Aelia's hand dropped to her side, surprise widening her eyes as she stared up at him. The seconds ticked by; his expression controlled, hers an open book. He watched as scepticism, doubt and, finally, resolve flashed across her face.

"It's only my back I can't reach." She narrowed her eyes as she offered the poultice up to him, a hint of her old antagonism leaching into her tone.

"It'll be easier if you stand." He reached past the tub and

grabbed her wrist, pulling her to her feet. Aelia gasped as she came eye level with his chest.

"You could have just asked," she grumbled, looking a little flustered as she craned her neck back to look up at him.

"Asking hasn't got me very far with you," he reminded her before using the wrist he still held to swivel her to face the other way, leaving her no choice but to twist on her feet. Only then did he move to take the tub from her, his fingers lingering on her skin as he did, looming close enough over her that he could smell the soap she'd used.

He watched her closely, reading her body's reaction to his proximity, ready to step back at the first sign he'd crossed a line. Her breathing hitched as his fingers brushed over hers to take the pink salve, the movement of her chest quickening, colour stealing up her neck as a glazed look settled over her eyes.

"May I?" he asked, low in her ear.

"Yes," Aelia breathed, and his heart somersaulted at the sound. The darkness in him stretched to its full height, a growl rumbling from deep in its scaled chest.

Keeran pulled away just enough to lift her top, the shadows from the fire dancing over her bruised skin. The cuts had all scabbed over, the skin knitting together at an inhuman rate; the poultice was working.

"What's in it?" Aelia asked. "The poultice? I've never known anything like it."

"It's an old family secret," he whispered into her ear. "One that's been protected for centuries."

She tensed. "You're really not going to tell me?"

"Not unless I was prepared to kill you afterwards." He smeared some of the cream onto her back, making her jump. He moved his fingers in gentle circles over the soft skin, the muscles of her back tensing beneath his touch. "And I've already told you I have no desire to hurt you."

She tried to hide it, but he didn't miss the shaky breath that passed between her lips as his fingers worked the cream into her skin. A dark smile toyed at the corner of his mouth, the beast within settling low between its shoulder blades, a predator ready to pounce.

"Is that okay?" He knew the answer, could see her body reacting to him, but he needed to hear her say it, to know for certain. "You want me to stop?"

Aelia hesitated, and panic tightened in his chest at the horror of having misread the situation. He was about to pull his fingers away when she finally answered, her words easing the tension in his chest and sending it plummeting far lower.

"Don't stop," she whispered, dropping her head back as if she too felt the aching need that was coursing through him.

She'd closed her eyes, lips slightly parted as she let out slow, unsteady breaths. His chest almost imploded at the slight crease between her brows as she fought the emotions so plainly visible across her face.

The creature in him growled, low and hungry. It didn't want her fighting her desire— it didn't like that at all.

Aelia's eyelids snapped open, as though she'd felt his gaze, and the instant their eyes locked, he knew he was fucked. The other part of him, already straining for control, took the opportunity to seize the upper hand, flooding him with a dizzying surge of lust.

The poultice dropped to the floor as he grabbed her waist and spun her to face him, so quickly she would have stumbled had his hands not dragged her into him.

Keeran was on her before she could even gasp, his lips parting hers with fevered impatience. She collapsed into him, her body curving in to meet his as he claimed her mouth, his fingers locking into the snarling tangles of her hair to hold her in place as he devoured her. Finally.

Her tongue matched his stroke for stroke, each of them

sinking effortlessly into the other's rhythm as though it was an extension of their own. The taste of her sent him spiralling out of himself; immediately intoxicated, eternally addicted.

The frustration he'd felt over the last couple of days merged with his need in a heady fog, an overpowering necessity to possess her, body and soul. Pleasure could break a person just as devastatingly as pain, and he wanted to take her crashing over the edge, fracturing her in a way only he'd be able to piece back together again.

His free hand grabbed her hips and pulled her into him, and she let out a soft whimper as his erection pressed against her. She ground against him, the pressure on his cock a delicious torture.

And just like that, Keeran lost the battle he'd been fighting every day of his life. The beast took charge and wasted no time.

They pulled away just long enough to tease her shirt over her head, careful of her injuries despite their ravenous hunger. She was everything to them; her pain was their pain.

They took in the perfect swell of her breasts, and the defined muscle of her stomach, impatient to taste every inch of her. Her eyes widened a fraction as she caught sight of them, but they didn't give her time to worry about what was burning in their eyes. Their hand whipped up to grip her jaw, tilting her head and fixing it there as their mouth found the sensitive skin just beneath her ear, teasing it gently.

Their lips curved in a smile as her warm breath tickled their ear, coming in little gasps that had their pulse roaring. She liked that. Fuck, they couldn't wait to find out what else she liked.

They worked their way down her neck, one hand still locking her in place, the other brushing gently up over her stomach, making the muscle clench under their touch. By the time they reached her breasts, she was groaning as she arched into them, fingers gripping their shoulders hard enough to leave little half-moons in their skin.

The beast roared its approval— the pain was its reward for a job done well, and it basked in it. They worked her breasts, their teeth nipping at the hardened peaks of her nipples to return the favour, before worshipping her with their tongue. Pleasure, pain, and pleasure again. Her breasts pushed into them with the heaving of her breath as they played, carefully monitoring what she liked and noting it for next time. Because there would be a fucking next time. They were going to learn how to break her, to ruin her, and they couldn't fucking wait.

They tore themselves away from her perfect chest to press their mouth against hers once more, and she kissed them hungrily, pulling them into her with all her fragile little strength. If she wanted more, they were all too happy to oblige.

Their hand dropped to the waistband of her tunic, expertly working at the ties holding it in place. Aelia's hands followed suit, the heel of her palm pressing into the throbbing length of their dick, and it was their turn to groan, their balls tightening at the shock of pleasure she elicited.

Magic swirled awake in their chest, unfamiliar yet unmistakable. It knotted itself around their heart, warm and shining, before snaking out in an invisible thread, reaching towards Aelia.

Fear crashed into Keeran, bringing him back into control enough to slam the other half of him into its cage. He reeled away from her, staggering backwards as the magic of the pair bond steadily receded. A fucking pair bond.

He stood staring at her, chest heaving, mind a swirling maelstrom of emotion he couldn't override.

Aelia stared back, mouth deliciously swollen, the hurt in

her wide eyes stabbing at something deep inside him. But he stayed rooted to the spot, his hand clasped against his chest, completely unable to utter a single syllable.

She dropped to the ground to retrieve her top, clutching it to her as she straightened, but still all he could do was stare at her, fighting the urge to break into a run. His heart beat so wildly he thought it might actually break his ribs, as if his chest didn't have enough to contend with. That infernal tugging deep inside it was stronger than ever, pulling him forwards. Towards *her.*

"What's wrong?" Aelia asked as she threw her top back on, her voice so small and uncertain.

He dropped his eyes to where his hand still pressed to his chest, as if he could see the ethereal thread that had been there moments before. He felt so ignorant for not recognising it for what it was sooner, so stupid. A pair bond; a fucking pair bond.

He shook his head, panic obscuring his ability to find the right words, his eyes still bulging towards his chest where he felt sure he should be able to see the magic that was steadily receding with each frantic breath he took.

If he hadn't been so overwhelmed, he would have answered her. If he hadn't been so overwhelmed, he never would have missed the dark form lunging at him from the shadows.

CHAPTER FIFTEEN

The men appeared as if from nowhere, bowling into Keeran and sending Aelia sprawling into the roots that protruded from the hard earth.

She staggered against the tree, clambering to her feet. She turned to see five men surrounding Keeran where they'd knocked him to the ground, beating him viciously.

"Keeran!" She dove towards them, but something caught her legs, and she landed flat on the ground with a graceless thud. Slightly winded, she struggled to her knees. Somebody grabbed at her hair and pulled her to her feet, wrestling her arm behind her back.

"My apologies for ruining the moment, but I'm afraid it provided too good a distraction for us to miss," her captor panted in her ear, his breath rancid. Aelia writhed against him, trying to free herself from his painful grip despite the warning stabs of pain as her shoulder threatened to dislocate. Throwing her free elbow backwards into his stomach caused him to release her momentarily, but she wasn't fast enough, and he caught her arm again, his fingers digging into her hard enough to bruise.

"None of that now," he said through his teeth and brought his knee up into the back of her ribs. Gasping, she scratched at his hand and threw her body weight against him, sending him stumbling backwards, dragging her with him. It wasn't enough to completely unbalance him, and he sent his fist flying into her face, hard enough to make stars dance in her vision.

"I said none of that!" he growled, and kneed her in the ribs again. She still couldn't see his face, but the scent of stale sweat shrouded him, bad enough to make her want to gag.

"Aelia!" Keeran thundered, and the fury in his voice was startling. She looked towards him, struggling to focus after the blow to her head.

Keeran was already on his feet, and two of their attackers lay on the ground, unquestionably dead. The other three were battling with him simultaneously, trying to catch him off guard, but to little avail. He seemed to blur as he blocked and attacked, spinning around with surprising agility for his monstrous size, dealing out crushing blows. The remaining men darted around him, some wielding knives, some weaponless, but neither seemed able to touch him as he ducked and spun and sidestepped. He was raw and animalistic, terrifying and savage. His attacks landed heavy and accurate, felling another man with a hit to the temple with the heel of his hand.

The man behind Aelia cursed and spat into the grass. Facing her towards him, she got a glimpse of him before he punched her in the face again. Then he threw her on the floor, kicked her in the stomach, and ran to help his comrades. Her vision flickered dangerously as pain wrapped its fingers around her skull and squeezed. Curled in a ball, she clutched at her sides, as if she could stop her barely healed injuries from splitting open. Her face screwed up as she waited for the flickering to settle, for the pain to finish welling.

Moaning, she managed to get to her knees and drag herself over to the bags, rummaging frantically. Finally, she found what she was looking for and, hauling her battered body to its feet, she stumbled towards the group of thrashing men, holding Otis's dagger tightly.

Keeran jabbed one of the men in the throat and he dropped to the ground with a sickening rattle of breath. The remaining two attacked him wildly, doubling their efforts.

Keeran blocked and avoided blows that came with ever-increasing ferocity as fear gave his opponents strength. They had started this fight with the certainty of winning, but now the odds weren't looking so good, and they fought ferociously for their lives. Blood ran down Keeran's forehead, but he showed no signs of tiring, every movement made with calm perfection. He jumped forwards and kicked one man's knee, breaking his leg, before punching upwards under the man's chin, snapping his neck with the force of the contact.

Aelia gasped, and somehow, Keeran heard. His head whipped to her, and she recoiled at the sight of him. There was nothing human in his eyes; the evil she'd caught glimpses of shone bright and unmistakable, fear sending a shiver of goosebumps over her skin.

The black of his eyes flickered as she stepped back, revealing something of the man she'd thought she was beginning to know, an agony she didn't understand creasing between his brows.

The remaining man seized this opportunity and hit Keeran on the back of his neck, quickly following it with a kick to his lower back, sending Keeran onto his knees. She recognised the man as the one who had held her and staggered towards them, unnoticed as he took hold of Keeran's head.

Panic enveloped her; there was no way she was going to make it to him in time. She was going to watch Keeran die, watch this thug snap his neck.

Horror surged inside of her, making it impossible to breathe, overwhelming every thought but one; save Keeran.

He didn't need saving though. In a tenth of a second, he reached over his head to grab hold of his attacker's arms and, with a powerful heave and a roll, flipped the man over and into the dirt in front of him.

Aelia threw the dagger towards him, and Keeran didn't hesitate, swiping it from the air and plunging the knife into the man's throat. Blood poured in horrifying gurgles from his open neck as she stood over him, watching with wide eyes as the noises rapidly quietened, until they stopped altogether.

She stared at the mutilated flesh and tried to feel some remorse or sorrow for the loss of life, but she felt too numb, her hands shaking where they hung by her side. Only then did she look up.

Keeran knelt on the floor a few feet from her. He was hunched over himself, but seemed to notice as she took a step towards him.

"Don't!" he warned. It was more of a growl than words. She stopped where she was, halted by the tone of his voice, and watched him as he knelt in front of her, engaged in some internal struggle.

She recognised it; the desire to Shift artemian's felt, when magic tempted them towards their animalistic tendencies, throwing them into an emotional frenzy. He battled with it, breathing quickly as it warred against him. His whole body shook with the strength it took to control himself, his hands clenched into fists that he pressed into his thighs.

Slowly, moment by moment, he seemed to regain control. His breathing slowed, and the shaking stopped. The campfire seemed to dim, darkness creeping a little closer from the wilderness around them. Finally, he sat back on his feet, running his hands through his hair. He looked up at her for the first time, and relief shot through her as she saw the warm brown of his eyes.

"Oh, Aelia, your face!" he exclaimed. She knelt before him, placing her hand on his knee.

"I'm alright," she mumbled, not letting herself wince at the pain of talking.

Blood trickled down his cheek from a small cut on his brow, but otherwise he seemed completely unharmed. She raised her hand to wipe the blood from his face, but he shrugged her off and guided her back to the fire, sitting her in its warmth.

He left to fill a bowl with water but returned quickly, sitting beside her. Taking off his ruined shirt, he ripped strips from the cleaner fabric and soaked them in the bowl. She glanced at his chest, averting her eyes automatically before realising what she had seen. Gasping, she couldn't help but look back at him.

Her eyes widened as they ran over the multitude of scars that covered almost every inch of him. A few fresh cuts oozed blood, but they were nothing compared to the long, jagged scars that stretched across his body.

The deformed skin shone silver in the firelight. Adrenaline numbed her inhibitions, and she leant forward to trace her finger along a particularly nasty one, feeling the smooth, raised skin. They varied in both size and age, some faint and almost invisible, whilst others would never be so indiscernible, no matter how much time passed. They covered his arms and shoulders, winding their way down his abdomen to his back. He sat still while she examined him, watching her face intently.

"Come," he said finally, and she sat up, looking into his

eyes. Her mind was flooded with questions, all pushing to the front, desperate to be asked, but she bit her tongue. Now was not the time.

The cloth was cool as he carefully washed dirt from the cuts on her face. It stung but she refused to let him see any sign that it hurt. After seeing what pain he had endured, her own seemed comparatively pitiful.

"I saw him knee you, let me see that too."

Lifting her shirt over her back, she showed him. He cursed under his breath. She turned, seeing his dark eyes burning as he glared at her side, and she stretched her neck to try and see for herself. Already the skin was turning a fresh shade of purple.

"Is it that bad?" It didn't feel bad, but shock still numbed the pain. He ran his fingers over her, tickling the sensitive skin. He gently prodded around her ribs, and she grimaced.

"It will bruise badly, but the cuts won't scar if you use the poultice I gave you. He could have broken your ribs, but I don't think he did. You were lucky." He rose to his feet to retrieve the poultice. Aelia couldn't be sure, but his hand seemed to tremble as he gave it to her. "You stay here, I'll dispose of the bodies."

He didn't pause, leaving her kneeling in the dirt as he dragged off the first of the attackers into the night without so much as a glance her way.

Aelia gritted her teeth against the wave of disquiet he left in his absence, fighting to control the rising sense of unease that was constricting her chest.

What the hell had just happened?

The poultice sat forgotten in her lap as she looked back at the camp beneath the willow tree, where he'd kissed her. If you could even call it that. Never before had she experienced anything like it; he'd kissed her like he owned her, dominating her in a way that had her soul screaming for more, winding her need higher and higher until she'd have given him anything. With barely more than a kiss.

Aelia let out a shuddering breath.

Sure, she'd had her fair share of fun in Callodosis when the opportunity arose, but what Keeran had done to her went way beyond fun. She fought the urge to touch her jaw, the memory of his hand fixing her in place whilst he desecrated her chest with his mouth, turning pain to pleasure in a way that was positively unholy.

Right up until he'd stopped.

The unease she felt at the way he'd left was magnified as she remembered him pulling away, looking at her with pure, unadulterated horror.

Shame trickled in, cold and familiar. He'd pulled away, in a moment like that. Why? It couldn't just be because she couldn't Shift... could it?

Because the hypocrisy of rejecting her for being different was just too much for her to accept quietly, not after she'd seen him take out six armed artemians in a matter of minutes. She looked at the bodies spread out amongst the long grass, the memory of him killing them one by one burned into her retinas.

He was fast, unnaturally fast, and she'd never seen anyone with enough strength to snap someone's neck with a single blow. Fear scuttled through her as she remembered the raging evil in his unnaturally black eyes, something utterly monstrous seething in them.

Twisting her neck in the direction he'd disappeared in, Aelia wondered what kind of evil she was dealing with, and what on earth it wanted with her. Frowning, she realised there was a part of her that was eager to find out.

CHAPTER SIXTEEN

Keeran dragged the abhorrent lump of meat that had dared to hurt Aelia away from the camp, without even glancing her way. Like a fucking coward.

It was all he could do to keep moving, the panic roaring through him violent enough to make him tremble, his legs unstable beneath him as he desperately tried to get out of her line of sight. It had taken every ounce of willpower to get away without letting her see how fucking close he was to losing it.

Once he was a safe distance from the camp, he let the corpse thud to the ground. He managed only a few steps before his legs gave way, dropping him into a crouch amongst the long blades of grass. His whole body shook as he tried to breathe away the adrenaline and fear, the creature staying mercifully silent in his mind. Keeran was pretty sure he'd vomit if it so much as purred at him. He raked his fingers through his hair, clutching at it like a madman, staring at the ground as if answers might appear there.

Never, ever, had he lost himself like that. Not as a child,

not in the war, not during any other sexual experience he'd had. Not even close.

It was his deepest, bone-scraping fear. He'd seen first-hand the devastation one of his kind could wreak if they lost themselves to their other side, and the memory still haunted him. Losing control to that side of him could not be allowed. It was evil; vicious, depraved, bloodthirsty, and remorseless.

And he'd just let it loose on Aelia.

The things he'd wanted to do to her, that *it* had wanted to do to her... he placed a hand on the floor to steady himself as his stomach roiled. He was suddenly overwhelmingly grateful he hadn't finished his dinner.

And if all that wasn't bad enough, he had the fucking pair bond to worry about. This whole situation was messed up enough without adding some psycho mating bond into the equation. He'd seen all too well what it had done to Khaled, the man who'd raised him, and he and his mate had never actually completed the bond. Even so, life was torture for him without her, a living hell.

He'd vowed to never make himself vulnerable like that. Not when every day was a battle for control as it was.

He closed his eyes and groaned; the hurt on Aelia's face when he'd pulled away from her burned into his memory. But how the hell could he explain?

Sorry I pulled away, Aelia. You were perfect, the most beautiful thing I've ever seen in my life. But I'd really appreciate it if we kept a good horse's breadth between us from now on. Only, I'm absolutely terrified of fucking you because my other personality wants to dominate you to an extent that verges on cruelty, and it seems like when it comes to you, I'd be completely unable to stop it. Oh, and if you hate every second of it, too bad, because afterwards you'll be tied to me forever by a magical bond I'll be powerless to walk away from.

No amount of good phrasing was going to make that sound any less insane.

Burying his face into both his hands, he groaned again. He was so fucked.

He didn't even know a lower artemian could form a pair bond; he'd never heard of such a thing. They were solely, exclusively formed between immortals; the Dragon's best-kept secret.

Aelia had no idea how close she'd come to being tied to him forever. It would have been so easy to keep going, to give in to that magic, to make her his...

He snarled, screwing his face up at the sky in frustration. Just what he needed, another dangerous part of himself to control.

Maybe if they hadn't been attacked, he could have handled the situation better. Maybe he wouldn't have left her alone, undoubtedly confused and probably frightened. Anger, hot and heavy, swept aside the tangled mess of his thoughts, aimed entirely at himself.

What a fucking arsehole.

He pushed to his feet, back in control of his legs once more, and jogged back to the camp.

Aelia was already buried deep under several blankets, her back to the fire and the bodies he had yet to move. There was no way she was asleep, but he got the message loud and clear; she had no interest in talking to him.

It was just as well, really, because he wasn't ready to face her yet–not even close. He turned his attention to the attackers, the beast creeping to the forefront once more at the sight of them. The audacity of them, to dare to attack him, to attack Aelia.

Magic seethed underneath Keeran's skin, stretching it so thin it felt at risk of tearing. He shouldn't have gone this long without Shifting. It added another layer of volatility to the emotional turmoil he was drowning in.

Anger in its purest form lowered that familiar red haze over him, even as he dragged those it was directed at away from the camp by their already stiffening limbs.

Let the scavengers have them, let them tear the flesh from their bones and fertilise the soil with everything they had once been. They deserved far worse for what they'd done to Aelia.

Keeran would have been all too happy to deliver a more fitting punishment had she not been looking; it had been all he could do to kill them quickly. Especially the last one, the one who had actually laid his filthy hands on her. Had she not been there, he would have taken his time, savoured every second of pain he could inflict before their pathetic mortal hearts gave out.

The red mist thickened around him the more he thought about it, and the air around him shimmered with the threat of magic. He gritted his teeth and controlled his thoughts, the muscle in his jaw twitching with the strain.

When the last of the bodies was dumped unceremoniously on the pile, he walked back to the camp with his shoulders braced as if walking into a strong wind, the last thread of his control fraying by the second.

The flames brightened at his return, reaching up reassuringly as he stormed past. They caressed the fingers he lowered to them, but even their touch could not bring him back, not this time. He needed to Shift. Now.

To his relief, Aelia had sunk into a deep sleep, the slow rhythm of her breathing music to his ears.

Grabbing his sword from where he'd stashed it in his pack, he spun on his heels and ran.

He ran like he hadn't let himself run in far too long, the sweetness of pushing himself to his full potential a small release in itself. The light of the moon was buried deeply behind the clouds, but his steps were as surefooted as they were silent as he tore away from Aelia, as far away as he could before he gave in to the magic.

Alone, in the vast expanse of the plains, it washed his soul clean. His blood bubbled with the intensity of it and he sighed, his eyes closing at the release. When he opened them again, it was through new eyes.

Every living creature held its breath, the night itself seeming to shudder at the Dragon it beheld.

Keeran kneaded the ground with his talons, relishing the power in every sinew of his being for one moment of unadulterated bliss. He unfurled his wings, so black they showed the night what true darkness was made of, swallowing any light that dared to show itself in his presence.

He leant back into his haunches, the muscles of his thigh bunching under him as he launched himself into the sky.

There, defying gravity, defying the world, he felt free. Liberated by the very part of him that he held prisoner, closely guarded and out of sight from the rest of the world.

It wasn't long before he found what he was looking for.

He'd known that their attackers would be part of a larger group, and Keeran wasn't going to risk another ambush from any friends that may come looking when the thieves didn't return. Campfires far below showed the silhouettes of caravans, not dissimilar to the Peregrinians, but these lowlifes weren't interested in trade. Not when there was pure profit to be made stealing from the vulnerable on the roads, of whom there were far too many now that the Astraea were burning whole villages to ash.

Keeran let himself glide to the ground, his wings silently cutting through the night air, and Shifted the moment his talons brushed the grass. His booted feet landed with little more than the sigh of crushed stalks to give him away, and he ran, more beast than man, towards the gentle flicker of flames in the distance.

The encampment was large—an impressive collection of some of the worst depravity Demuto had to offer, a stain on a country already mottled by injustices. A stain he would not allow anywhere near Aelia, not a second time.

He drew his sword, death whistling its approval as he cleaved the air with it, bringing it down into the chest of his first victim. The camp may have been large, but there would be no survivors to speak of the monster who slaughtered with a speed no mortal man possessed, who razed through them like a warrior from a forgotten time.

Keeran didn't need to hold himself back, as he had with Aelia watching. He unleashed the beast inside him, and it roared its way through the encampment.

By the time he was finished, the only movement in the camp was the flickering of the campfires, and even they seemed to cower before him.

GODS, HE HAD MISSED FLYING. ALMOST AS MUCH AS HE'D missed fighting, properly fighting. Now, with the wind carrying him through the night, and the creature in him quieter than it had been in months, he felt like a different person.

He savoured the feeling of the cool air rushing over his scaled body, feeling it part at his nose before rippling over him all the way to the tip of his tail. His venture into Demuto had been productive, having checked off almost two-thirds of the artemians on his list, but not being able to Shift freely had taken its toll.

It was hard for any artemian not to Shift for any length of time, the build-up of magic growing past the point of discomfort, taking them closer towards their second natures. A predator-born artemian might struggle to control their natural tendency towards aggression, dominance, and defiance, whereas those who were prey born might sink into anxiety and subservience. It was no different for a Dragon, only a thousand times worse.

His head was clearer than it had been for days, and the right path lay before him, obvious in the moonlight.

Keeran had grown up with a man who had been wrecked, mind and soul, by a pair bond. Khaled fought it long enough to raise Keeran, being more of a father to him than his own had ever been, teaching Keeran how to use the rare fire magic of their people. In Keeran's eyes, Khaled had rescued him, showing him the power of control when so many of their people had sunk into the worst parts of themselves.

But even Khaled, a Master in the War of Two Kings, renowned for his unwavering discipline, had been unable to fight the devastation of the pair bond. Keeran had seen it firsthand, on the last terrible night the Dragons set foot in Demuto. His mate had died, and Khaled, the most powerful Dragon alive, had burned almost every soul that had turned against them to ash.

So few Dragons still carried the ability to wield fire magic that no one could stop him; no one even stood a chance.

Now, with Khaled gone, it was Keeran who would be unstoppable.

So it was with utter conviction that he made his decision. He must leave Aelia.

He would return to camp, pack up his things, and fly ahead to scout out Beserkir from the skies. Just as he should have done days ago.

The thought tore at him, the tugging in his chest stronger

than ever since he'd kissed her, but now that he knew what it was, he would fight it. With every fibre of his being.

Suddenly, his vision flickered. The grasslands beneath him disappeared, and he found himself standing in a screaming crowd, utter pandemonium erupting around him. Trees, dark and menacing, loomed overhead, their branches reaching skeletal fingers to the sky. Smoke filled the air, and he coughed against the acrid bite of it as it filled his lungs.

Just as quickly as it had appeared, the vision vanished, and his heart jumped into his throat as he found himself nosediving towards the ground. He threw his wings open and beat them hard to regain the altitude he'd lost.

What the actual fuck was that? He blinked and shook his head, utterly disorientated.

He levelled off at a safe distance, too high for anyone to think him anything more than a bird, even if he should be unfortunate enough to fly over a sharp-eyed artemian. His eyes darted around nervously, and just when he thought the whole thing must have been some kind of stress-induced hallucination, his vision shifted again, and he was back under the trees, a stampede of panicking people around him.

His body moved of its own volition, and he saw Beserkir looming over an older man, staring up at him fearlessly despite the wasted arm tucked into his jacket. Horror surged through him as Beserkir raised a blade slowly overhead, as if he had all the time in the world. His body tried to surge forwards, past the people shoving at him, obscuring his view of the one-armed man, but something held him back.

He turned to see what it was, and his blood turned cold when he saw himself standing beside him. All his features were obscured by shadows except his eyes, which burned crystal clear, black as night, and infinitely more terrifying. His own hand restrained him, no matter how hard he pulled and pleaded, his expression remained unmoved, uncaring. By the time he'd turned back to Beserkir, the one-armed man was down, coughing up blood on the floor, alone and dying.

Keeran snapped back to reality with a sickening lurch, freefalling through the air with his wings luffing uselessly towards the sky. He twisted in midair, his wings nearly ripping free from their sockets as they caught him, close enough to the ground that he startled a few deer. They careened away from him, springing through the grass, but he paid them no heed as he landed, Shifting just in time for his boots to touch the ground.

He ran a few steps to slow himself down, his landing far less graceful than usual, before dropping to rest his hands on his knees until he could think past his frantic breathing.

The pair bond snapped to life, ramming into his consciousness like a sledgehammer, nearly knocking him off his feet. Anguish radiated from it, so devastatingly agonising he clutched a hand to his chest, until the bond withered to nothing more than a tug once more.

Realisation slammed into him, and his head whipped in the direction of the camp.

Aelia. It was coming from Aelia.

He ran, leaping through the grass, arms pumping until he overtook the deer that were fleeing his landing, speeding past them in an inhuman blur. He barely slowed as he thundered into the camp, not caring if she saw, only caring that someone was hurting her, was causing her such pain.

But there was no one. The horses reared back as he arrived, heads high, eyes wide, but otherwise, the camp was still.

Aelia was still tucked under the blankets, her breathing a little fast and uneven, but otherwise unharmed. His hand dropped from the hilt of his sword, his chest heaving as he cast his eyes around once more.

Nothing. There was no one here.

A gentle groan came from under the blankets, and Keeran closed his eyes against the fear and torment that flooded the pair bond, rising in a wave before crashing away into nothing.

She was having a nightmare. The visions he'd seen had been of her nightmare.

How was that possible when the mating bond wasn't even fully formed yet? Unless they both accepted it, unless they slept together, it was nothing more than a ghost of a true pair bond, a whisper of its true potential. And if this was what just a whisper could do, he wanted it even less than ever.

Until she moaned again.

She looked so small, so alone.

Keeran's eyes flicked to where his pack lay by the glowing embers of the fire, pretty much ready for him to grab and go, and then back to Aelia. His resolve melted the instant he laid eyes on her.

Fuck it.

CHAPTER SEVENTEEN

There was no escape from her grief, especially not after sleep immured her in its suffocating embrace. Instead, the darkness of her mind was given free rein in the realm of her subconscious. Every thought she worked to suppress whilst awake was unleashed upon her in a barrage of nightmares. The most vicious part of her psyche seemed to turn on itself, her imagination wielding the cruellest of her innermost thoughts, screaming them at her through blackened mouths, in melted faces, from fiery pits. She could do nothing, trapped by the powerlessness of unconsciousness, a victim of her own guilt.

Aelia woke thrashing, her screams piercing in the darkness, but it wasn't that that had woken her. Keeran loomed over her, a steady hand on either shoulder, gently shaking her out of her tortured dreams.

"It's just a nightmare," he said, over and over, although his eyes were wide, worry hiding in the creases between his brows. "It's just a nightmare," he repeated, more softly this time as she quietened.

Dawn teased at the horizon, softening the edge of the

darkness that surrounded them just enough for her to make out his features.

She threw her hands over her face, mortified.

"I'm sorry," she choked out, her breathing still a little erratic. "I'm so sorry."

"You don't need to apologise for a nightmare." Keeran let go of her shoulders but didn't make to move away. Only then did she become aware of his leg pressed against her from where he had skidded to her side.

"I woke you up?" She dropped her hands from her face, not sure she wanted to hear the answer. As if she wasn't embarrassed enough by the way he'd stopped kissing her, leaving her naked from the waist up and gawking at him, she now had to face him knowing he'd had to wake her up from a nightmare like a toddler.

"No, I was already awake."

Aelia pushed herself up onto her elbows, careful not to move away from him. She tried not to think too deeply about why she didn't want to lose the pressure of his leg against her.

"How did you know I was having a nightmare?" she asked, mortified.

Something flashed across his face too quickly for her to understand it.

"You were crying out a little. I thought it better to wake you." The uncertainty on his face made him look younger, as far as possible from the emissary of death she'd seen earlier that night, and some of the disquiet tangling her insides in knots eased. He didn't *look* repulsed by her, by what they'd done; he looked as worried as she felt.

"I'm sorry," she mumbled, dropping her head to her chest. So fucking embarrassing.

"What is it you were dreaming about?" He ignored her apology, his voice gentle and encouraging. Aelia pulled the blankets a little higher around herself, as though that would somehow stop the panic from rising at the thought of talking about it, of reliving the horrors her mind had thrown at her every night since she'd left Callodosis. "You don't have to tell me... but it might help."

Aelia bit her lip anxiously, the band of panic around her chest tightening with each breath she took.

"I see the people I left behind. The people Beserkir took from me," she whispered. "Otis, Mirra, Fenrir... it all replays over and over in my head, and I do nothing. I don't help them."

His eyes darted to her face. "Do they talk to you?"

Aelia nodded slowly, blinking furiously at the tears that were welling in her eyes. She must not cry, she absolutely must not cry.

"What do they say?" he probed, gently.

"They say..." She choked on the words, an invisible hand tightening around her throat that she struggled to talk past. "They say..." She raised her face to the star-filled sky, tears falling unchecked as she remembered all that her dreams accused her of.

"Aelia, you cannot blame yourself for what happened to them." A hint of steel entered his voice. She nodded, but he saw through the empty gesture. His fingers took hold of her chin and turned her to look at him, gripping her gently to emphasise every word. "Beserkir is to blame. Beserkir, the Astraea, the King, even, for letting it happen, but certainly not you."

"I feel so fucking useless," she sobbed furiously. He released her chin, his hand dropping to hold onto hers. "He took them all from me, and I couldn't *do* anything. Fenrir is still out there, and there's not a damn thing I can do about it. I can't even stop a fucking thief." Her voice cracked as she flung her free arm out at the camp.

She bit her lip to stop the sobs that wracked her body, the utter wretchedness she felt threatening to bubble over. Keeran wrapped his arms around her and pulled her into him, rocking her gently until her tears quietened. He brushed her hair away to kiss her forehead, the simple gesture calming the living, breathing pain inside her.

Keeran was quiet for a moment, before he finally said, "you are not useless, Aelia. You are the most determined, stubborn, uncompromising person I've ever met, and if freeing Fenrir is what you've set your heart on, then Beserkir should be trembling in his boots."

Aelia laughed through her snivelling, tilting her head up to look at him. There was such warmth in his eyes, his lips curving to match her tearful smile, that the last of the hollow tension in her chest shrivelled back to being bearable.

She wiped away her tears with trembling fingers, the soft light of the sun threatening them with its presence more with each passing moment. Keeran noticed it too.

"We should try and sleep for another hour or so before we head out," Keeran murmured. He made to get up, but she grabbed his arm.

"Don't." She couldn't bring herself to say what she truly wanted to, her pride limiting her to just that one word.

He hesitated, looking over to his pack, his thoughts hidden behind an unreadable wall, and embarrassment twisted in her gut as it looked like he might pull free.

But he didn't. Slowly, carefully, he lowered himself to the ground next to her, leaving his arm in her grip.

The birds welcomed the hazy light of dawn, but Aelia was asleep far too quickly to notice them, and this time, ghosts didn't haunt her dreams.

Aelia woke up with her arm draped across Keeran, the steady thump of his heart reassuring in her ear. She blinked her swollen eyes, the memories of the night before coming back to her bleary brain with an accompanying wave of embarrassment.

Gods, she'd spilled her fractured heart out to a man who'd practically leapt away from her touch earlier that very night. Fucking fantastic.

Yet here he was, his breath catching softly in the back of his throat, his arm wrapped tightly around her. She couldn't explain the warmth that coursed through her, and frankly, after the cyclone of emotion she had experienced recently, she didn't even bother to try. Instead, she closed her eyes and savoured it.

The sun was high in the sky when she next opened her eyes, stirred awake by Keeran shifting under her. He froze for a second, his mind presumably catching up to the fact that he wasn't alone, before his arm tightened around her infinitesimally.

A smile escaped her, a bubble of happiness breaking through the heaviness that had filled her chest for days. It swelled even more when Keeran pressed his lips to her head, kissing her gently.

"Are you awake?" he asked, his voice thick with sleep.

She pulled back as far as his arm would let her to look up at him.

"Good morning," she said, smiling up at him. Keeran didn't reply, staring at her unabashedly until she felt the need to break the silence. "We've overslept."

He tore his eyes from her to squint up at the sun.

"So we have." He sounded surprised.

"We should get going," she said, her mind jumping to Fenrir and how little sign they'd seen of him and the Astraea. They had a lot of ground to cover today.

"Do we have to?" Keeran squeezed her closer, burying his face into her hair. A laugh bubbled out of her; half relief, half happiness. Whatever the reason he'd pulled away from her yesterday, it didn't seem like it was because she wasn't truly artemian.

"Unfortunately." Aelia fought the urge to snuggle back into him, making herself push up and out of his arms.

Keeran grumbled something about her being stubborn and uncompromising, and she thumped her fist gently down on his stomach, eliciting a deep laugh that rumbled through his chest.

They fed the horses, packed up camp, and had their butts in the saddle in record time, even eating the leftover stew as they rode. The road ran alongside the bank of the lake, and again she was overcome with the beauty of it. This was just one of the Tears of Deliah, the huge, interconnected expanses of water that broke up the plains between here and Llmera. As she scraped her bowl clean, she marvelled at the sheer size of it.

Even cold, Aelia couldn't believe how good the stew was. She could easily have eaten all four portions in one sitting and decided then and there she'd be the one to go hunting today. There was no way she was passing up the opportunity for another meal like that one, even if she had to beg him to cook two nights in a row. Her pride could stoop to a little begging for food that good.

She twisted round to put her bowl in a saddlebag, wincing at the new bruises the thief had left her with. Aelia hated how unhelpful she'd been, leaving Keeran to deal with all six of the men after they'd wiped the floor with her.

In Callodosis, she'd been in the odd scrap here and there, holding her own most of the time, but the reality of an actual fight had found her seriously lacking. She'd had her arse handed to her twice now, whilst Keeran had floored all six men without even breaking a sweat. Literally. It had been nothing to him to kill them with his bare hands.

Aelia side-eyed where he rode next to her, gently rocking in the saddle. She took in the muscle straining beneath the fabric of his sleeves, the breadth of his shoulders and chest that tapered to his trim waist, his huge thighs making the saddle look far too small. Aside from being rather lovely to look at, the sheer bulk of the man screamed of a life spent in heavy training. Physique like that didn't come from performing with the Peregrinians; it didn't even come from something as strenuous as years of logging. She'd know. If the scars she'd seen were anything to go by, it had come from something far darker.

It was beyond time for some answers; she just didn't relish the prospect of asking him. Taking a breath, she steeled herself for the awkwardness, wishing she'd had the sense to quiz him more when she'd still hated him.

Not that she ever really had. He was just an easy target to direct her anger at. It had taken her an entire day on her own to realise it, but it turned out severe boredom was fuel for self-reflection. That and a desperation to think of something, anything, other than the grief that had begun to eat her alive once she was alone.

Shoving that thought quickly aside, she turned in her saddle.

"Keeran, I..." She trailed off, suddenly wishing she'd thought a little further ahead. He looked at her cagily, probably guessing what she was about to ask. She persevered. "How did you learn to fight like that?"

He shrugged. "Practice."

Aelia tried to keep the scowl off her face, but by the smile twitching at his lips, she failed.

"Where? Who with?"

Keeran flicked his reins over the horse's neck, adjusting the leather straps more comfortably in his grip.

"I was a soldier in the King's army."

"What kind of soldier?" she asked, narrowing her eyes at him. The sword he'd revealed this morning looked far too expensive for a common foot soldier. And he certainly didn't fight like one.

"A good one." He smiled devilishly and, for a moment, she was distracted from her line of enquiry.

"You can't have got all those scars in the army, there hasn't been a war since I was a toddler." Keeran's smile dropped, and Aelia could have kicked herself for her tactlessness.

"That's true," he admitted, turning his attention back to the road ahead. "I didn't have the easiest of upbringings. I was born into a society that was much harsher than yours. You had to fight to survive, so that's what I did, and at first I wasn't very good… hence the scars."

"There isn't a society like that in Demuto. No artemian would condone that."

Frustration made her bolder. Despite their animalistic origins, artemians clung to their humane heritage to avoid descending into the incivility of their animal ancestors, fighting their innate instincts that could be so powerful. Did that mean he wasn't from Demuto?

Keeran stared pensively out across the lake for a few long moments before answering.

"There are some things that I can't tell you, for both my safety and yours. But no matter how barbaric my past sounds, I can only ask that you trust me. I know that might not seem fair, but all I can say is that I am not like the people I was born amongst." She opened her mouth to press him further, but he held his hand up to silence her. "I really can't tell you anymore, so there is no point in asking."

His lips were set in a firm line, the black rings in his eyes seeming to darken. Aelia reluctantly changed the subject.

"Who were those men yesterday? Could they have been with the Astraea?" She was surprisingly hopeful at the prospect of his having killed six of them.

"I doubt it, they are more likely to be petty thieves, stealing what they can on the road and selling it at towns and cities."

"I'm surprised they didn't Shift," she mused.

"Thieves tend to be artemians who are smaller, better suited to sneaking and creeping through tight spaces rather than fighters. They were probably more adept at fighting in their human form. What surprised me is that they had no swords, just those knives."

"Would it have made a difference if they'd had swords?" she asked, genuinely curious.

His lips tugged sideways thoughtfully before he answered. "Honestly? Not really."

At least he was honest. Aelia played with her horse's mane, twirling the soft hair through her fingers absent-mindedly.

"What are you thinking?" He sounded apprehensive, his voice quiet, as if unsure he wanted the answer.

"Honestly?" She threw back at him. "I was wondering about your eyes."

His jaw clenched and he looked down at his hands.

"That's something else I can't talk about." This time the quiet in his voice was of an entirely different nature, a hint of danger leaking into it.

Aelia swallowed, hard, but her fear was laced with a hint of intrigue, the memory of how his irises had been jet black when he kissed her sending a cold rush tingling over her skin.

"Is it... dark magic?" she whispered, as if just saying it could summon the ideolan from the North.

"No!" Keeran spat, the astonishment in his voice too genuine to be feigned. Not ideolan then, Aelia thought, with no small amount of relief. That would have been a little hard to swallow. "You think I'm from Ideolanthea?"

She'd never met an Idoelan; one of the terms of Demuto's alliance with Ideolanthea was that their borders remained uncrossable. All she'd heard were rumours of Northerners polluted by their terrible magic. Aelia didn't know how the King had managed to keep them at bay for all these years, especially when half of Mithrylaya, the continent across the sea, had succumbed to them. From what she'd heard, they had a lot to thank him for.

"Well, no," Aelia backtracked. "It's only, I've never seen anyone else's eyes do that. Go black, I mean."

Aelia trailed off, hating herself more with every word she uttered, as Keeran watched her struggle in unimpressed silence.

"I'm artemian, born in Demuto," he said, his eyes meeting hers with unaffected sincerity. "And I would never touch dark magic."

Aelia just nodded, a little ashamed of her probing. Fortunately, it didn't last long.

"Is it my turn to ask the prying questions?" Keeran smiled at her, one eyebrow raised.

"I suppose that's fair," Aelia acquiesced, begrudgingly.

"I heard you in the forest, that night with Shiva," he said. Every muscle in her body tensed, and her horse's ears flicked back towards her nervously. "I heard you say you couldn't Shift."

"I'd guessed you had." She side-eyed him, frowning.

"But you're not human," Keeran stated. That much was

obvious, all you had to do was look in her eyes and you'd see the ring of magic.

"I thought you were meant to be asking questions, not stating the obvious," Aelia replied, wryly.

Keeran huffed a laugh through his nose. "Alright, fair point. Do you know why? Your father, what was his second form?"

Aelia felt immediately less guilty for the invasive nature of her own questions.

"Wow, Keeran, way to keep it light."

"Says the woman who asked about my scars," Keeran said, raising his eyebrows.

"Fair enough," she said, shooting him a grudging look. "I have no idea who my parents are. Otis wasn't my father, he took me in when I was small, just a baby, I think. But even he never knew who my parents were. So no, I have no idea why I am the way I am."

"I've seen you run, you're as fast as any artemian I know. Faster."

"Stronger too. My senses are heightened, my reflexes faster. I just can't Shift," Aelia admitted, matter-of-factly. It wasn't something to brag about, not when Shifting was all that really mattered.

"You've never shown any other signs of magic? Nothing unusual?"

Confusion lined Aelia's brow. "Like what?"

Keeran shrugged. "I don't know."

Aelia looked up at the sky, as if thinking hard. "I once pretended to curse Shiva as a child, and the next day he got sick and was off school? The other kids were particularly nice to me for a little while after that."

Keeran smiled, shaking his head. "Gods help us all if you turned out to be a witch."

"Don't worry, you're safe. Other than a frustrating inability to Shift, I am, to all intents and purposes, artemian."

Keeran looked out across the lake, squinting at something in the distance. Aelia looked too, just about able to make out a dark blur protruding from the water.

"Look, Aelia. That's the town of Aquila."

Sure enough, when Aelia peered out across the still water, she could just make out a cluster of buildings protruding from the lake.

"They're floating!" she gasped, open-mouthed.

Keeran chuckled. "Not quite. The whole town is built on foundations that reach all the way to the lake bed. The people who live there are exclusively artemian, and almost all of them Shift into water creatures of some description."

"You've been there?" Aelia leant over in her saddle, squinting at the peculiar town; if she really focused, she could just about make out the indistinct shapes of people walking between the low, sturdy buildings.

"No, the Peregrinians never stop at Aquila. The artemians there are fiercely independent and don't take kindly to visitors. They won't even allow boats to dock there, so the only way to access it is to swim or fly."

"How?" Aelia stared, uncomprehending. She'd heard of Aquila, but only when it was casually mentioned in conversation. She'd had no idea such a place could even exist. "How did they build a town in the middle of a lake?"

"Centuries ago, water artemians put down wooden stilts into the lake floor. They've petrified over time, making the perfect foundations for the residents to layer stone on top of them," Keeran explained, and Aelia reluctantly twisted away from Aquila to turn towards him. "The buildings sit on that."

"They made an island?"

"Exactly." Keeran nodded. "But the lure of Aquila lies not in the town above the water, but the one beneath it. Apparently, they've transformed the bed into a paradise for water creatures."

Aelia turned to look out over the lake once more. What would that even look like? She would have given almost anything to see it. But even if they'd had time, she had no way of surviving a swim down to the bottom of the lake.

She'd thought she was content in Callodosis, despite the constant struggle to get by, the struggle to prove herself. But as she watched birds flitting over one another towards Aquila, she wondered if she even knew what contentment was. The world was clearly not the place she thought it was, in more ways than she could have ever realised, and she wondered how much she'd been missing out on.

They continued past the town in distracted silence, each lost in their own thoughts.

CHAPTER EIGHTEEN

Keeran didn't waste any time getting a fire going when he set up camp that evening. Aelia had gone out to hunt shortly after they passed Aquila, offering to catch them something if he cooked again. It was an offer he'd leapt at, not only because he wanted to avoid fighting to keep his food down, but because it meant he could whip her up a medicinal tea. Or at least that's what he was going to tell her it was.

He chucked some wood in a pile, flung some flames at it with little more than a flick of his eye, and went to fetch some water from the lake. He set it over the fire to boil, before chucking in an assorted mix of useless leaves to steep.

Keeran raised his head from where he crouched in front of the pot, scanning the grasslands to make sure he was alone, before taking a knife from his hip. It was one of several he carried, most of the others tucked out of sight but within easy reach.

It was fiercely sharp, slicing through the skin of his palm like butter. The pain hardly registered, his heart thumping wildly at the unlawfulness of what he was doing, but it didn't stop him from making a fist and squeezing several drops of blood into the tea. They dispersed amongst the leaves, the green pigment more than enough to obscure the pink.

Dashing back to the lake, he washed the blood from his hand, the cut already sealed in an angry red line. It would soon be just another scar.

Returning to the camp, he put his hands on his hips and stared down at the tea. He could still throw it away. His lips pressed tight, his brows knitting together.

No, he couldn't. Aelia was still recovering from the beating the Astraea had given her. Last night had hardly helped and he needed her fighting fit.

There was no way he could stay with her, not with the pair bond alive and thrumming between them, especially now that he suspected she felt it too. Sure, she had no idea what she was feeling, but that was irrelevant. Keeran would get her to Beserkir, reunite her with Fenrir, then leave them to return to Callodosis. But he'd be damned if he was going to let her walk away defenceless.

He glared down his nose at the tea, his jaw set resolutely. What he was doing may have been sacrilegious amongst his kind. The illegality of sharing the magic in their blood had been drilled into him since he was a child, but there were no Dragons left in Demuto to stop him.

So, he turned his back on the tea and got to work setting up camp.

AELIA RETURNED WITH TWO WATERFOWL BOUNCING ON HER saddle. They plucked them together, but that was as much help as he accepted from her, telling her to go wash whilst he cooked.

His body was acutely aware of her in the water behind

him, hidden by the rushes, but Keeran didn't let his mind dwell on it. Instead, he focused on skewering the marinated waterfowl over the flames and leaving it to cook over the mixed vegetables he was grilling on a huge flat stone he'd positioned in the fire. He used the herbs and spices in his pack liberally, packing the meal with as much flavour as he possibly could. Yes, he might resent that he was magically predisposed to want to make her happy, but he didn't see the harm in putting a little extra effort into dinner.

By the time they'd both washed in the lake, it was ready.

He piled her plate high and handed it to her, along with the tea.

"It has chamomile in it," he explained when she looked at it questioningly. "It will help with the swelling."

"Thanks," she said, looking surprised. She took the tea and set it down, her attention immediately focusing on the food in front of her.

She didn't disappoint. She closed her eyes after the first bite, chewing slowly, and he watched her surreptitiously from over his own untouched plate. He didn't think he'd seen anyone enjoy food as much as she did.

It meant she forgot about the tea until she'd scraped her plate clean, running her finger over it and licking the juices off in a way that would plague him, despite how quickly he'd averted his eyes.

When she finally remembered the cup next to her, she took a hesitant sip, grimacing at the bitter taste, before her expression froze. She blinked several times in quick succession before taking another gulp.

Relief washed over her face as the healing properties of his blood took effect, making him realise the constant pain she must have been in. He'd obviously never seen how blood magic worked before, and he watched with an apprehensive fascination as she continued to shift experimentally where she sat, testing her aching joints. So, when her eyes snapped to his, she caught him looking straight at her.

"That's not chamomile," she said, accusatorially.

"There's chamomile in it," Keeran shrugged more nonchalantly than he felt before popping a generous spoonful into his mouth.

Aelia's eyes narrowed to slits, the green in them glowing in the firelight. "What else?"

Keeran didn't reply, his stare hard and unyielding as he chewed with deliberate slowness.

"Is it the same thing that's in the poultice?" Aelia pushed, undeterred by his silence.

Keeran took his time swallowing, enjoying the flush of impatience creeping up her neck.

"It's chamomile, Aelia." He let a hint of darkness steal into his eyes, noting how she didn't flinch this time. If anything, the flush seemed to deepen. Curious. "Just drink it."

Aelia stared at the tea for a few long seconds, the scepticism on her face fading to grim acceptance, then she necked the rest of it.

She shuddered and closed her eyes, dropping the cup. Keeran's stomach felt like it plummeted ten inches, and it took every ounce of self-control not to call out to her.

A heartbeat later, her eyes flickered open, and Keeran recoiled. The ring of magic in her eyes glowed silver, bright and piercing in the darkness, but he blinked and it was gone. He forced his heart rate to slow, refusing to let her see how much of a nervous wreck he was as they both partook in a crime the Dragons used to kill over. He'd never heard of their magic showing as anything but black, but who knew how their blood affected artemians; perhaps the silver light was normal as his magic worked through her.

Aelia lifted her top and twisted towards the fire, exposing her unblemished ribs. There wasn't a bruise in sight—just toned, golden skin—sending Keeran's stomach lurching for completely different reasons.

"What the fuck?" Aelia whispered, tearing her top up to gape at the rest of her waist, every bruise, cut and scrape having disappeared to leave the fine silver lines of scars. It wasn't long before her attention returned to him. "How?"

"I can't answer that." His voice brooked no argument.

"Why give it to me then?" She was deathly quiet, a trace of fear mingling with the shock on her face.

"Because I'm going to show you how to defend yourself," he stated.

Shock won out over fear, her mouth hanging open for a second before she collected her thoughts.

"You'd do that?"

Keeran set his plate down and brushed his hands together. "It's as much for my sake as for yours. You've been a pain in the butt since we left Callodosis, kicking your arse is going to be seriously cathartic."

He ignored her scowl and jumped to his feet, crossing to offer his hand down to her. Aelia took it tentatively, and he hauled her to her feet, looking for any signs of discomfort and seeing none. Good, that meant he didn't have to go easy on her. They didn't have much time, and there was so much to show her.

"All I have is this dagger." Aelia pivoted her hip to show the weapon she always carried with her.

"You need to learn the basics of unarmed combat before you start throwing weapons into the equation." He almost smiled at the unmistakable look of disappointment that flashed across her face. He continued, regardless. "To fight is to walk the tightrope between offence and defence. Misjudge that balance and expect to fall."

Aelia twisted to look at the floor around them, taking in the rocks and tree roots that jutted from between their numerous bags, saddles and blankets. "Shouldn't we find somewhere a bit clearer?"

"Attackers aren't going to wait to find level ground. You need to concentrate on where your feet are at all times, not just because of obstacles, but also in relation to me."

Keeran shoved her shoulder just hard enough to send her off balance. She looked up at him, her green eyes wide with surprise, but said nothing.

"Stand like this." He demonstrated, planting his feet in a wide stance, and she copied. He shoved her shoulder again, and this time she stayed put. "Good footwork can make up for a lot."

He showed her a few blocks and talked her through the concept of putting your bodyweight into your punch. Everything he showed her she picked up well enough, concentration creasing a fine line between her brows as she absorbed his every word.

It had been an awfully long time since he'd learnt the basics, and it had been a much more vicious lesson to learn than the one he was giving her, but Aelia didn't seem to mind his somewhat garbled explanations.

After a while, they sparred, albeit in the loosest possible sense of the word.

Aelia's lips pressed into a tight line as she tried to block him, failing most of the time despite him dropping to what felt like slow motion. He kept her moving, kept her thinking, and she began to see the rhythm he was setting, gradually blocking him more and more.

There was a rock hidden in the long grass, and when her foot caught it, she flew, propelled by the backwards step she had been taking. His hand was on her elbow in a fraction of a second, but she didn't need him to catch her. With unnatural speed, she righted herself, twisting out of harm's way and safely back onto her feet.

He was caught completely off guard, stunned by the sheer rapidity of her reflexes. The grin that lit her face had his breath leaving him in a ragged sigh, one she completely misinterpreted.

"I told you I was fast." And her smile took on a mischievous gleam.

Aelia was on him with newfound ferocity, throwing herself at him in every way she could think of. Although stunned at first, Keeran fended her off easily, batting her away again and again.

Her grin faded almost immediately, her eyes flashing with frustration as her breathing started to come in gasps. Gods, she was quick, and strong, too. He'd never encountered an artemian like her, her reflexes so fast her body was quickly recognising the patterns in his attacks. She was no Dragon, not even close, but with a little training, she'd be a force to be reckoned with. The thought made him grin, his teeth glinting in the flickering light of the fire.

"How are you so quick?" Aelia asked between breaths.

"How are you?" he shot back. "Stop dropping your left elbow, it leaves you open to attack and makes it hard for you to strike with it."

He demonstrated, swiping his elbow towards her, slow enough for her to block it. She lifted her elbow into a more defensive position, trying to mimic him. He let her practice a few times before he moved on, yelling tips at her, pushing her hard. If her concentration failed, or she forgot something he'd told her, he added a little extra weight to his blows. It wasn't long before she was cursing him.

Keeran turned in a circle around her, yelling a barrage of commands about her footwork, when her elbow dropped. Again.

He gritted his teeth, patience wavering, and swept into

the opening she'd left him to deal her a memorable jab. She cried out, stepping back to hug her recently healed side.

"Elbow up," he reminded her, calmly. There wasn't time for her to keep making the same mistakes over and over again. Dropping into a crouch, he curled his fingers at her, encouraging her back towards him.

"You're a fucking jerk, you know that?" she hissed, glaring daggers at him.

"You've mentioned it once or twice." He couldn't help the lopsided grin that spread across his face. "Now get over here."

"Why, so you can show off some more?" Aelia bit out, folding her arms across her chest.

"Darling, if I were trying to show off, you'd be flat on your back."

A dark smile pulled at her lips, making Keeran's chest tighten. "Well, I'm game if you are."

Keeran's own grin fell from his face as he replayed what he'd said. Her smile had words scattering from his brain like bees from a hive. He opened his mouth, but nothing came out, his chance at a witty reply scuttling off into the silence. He'd settle for any reply at this point, but the thought of Aelia flat on her back, his for the taking, had turned his mind to jelly.

Aelia had no such difficulty. Unfortunately.

"Or are you all bark and no bite?" She quirked an eyebrow, leaning closer with her arms still tightly crossed. "Because so far, all you've done is nibble."

Keeran's blood roared in his ears before it rushed elsewhere, quickly. Any doubts he had about her wanting him vanished, and the other half of him stretched itself into his consciousness, black and scaled and wanting Aelia with a need that had his fists clenching. A few days ago, he'd have killed for her to flirt with him, but everything had changed last night.

The fucking pair bond was not something he was prepared to risk, not even for her. The thought snapped him back to himself, his fear of the bond kicking his brain into gear.

"Why don't we even the odds a little?" Keeran said huskily, his voice betraying what he was fighting to suppress. He gestured to her dagger with a dismissive flick of his fingers. "Take that out."

Aelia blinked, surprised at his cold tone, but her hand dropped to the hilt of the dagger obediently.

"You want me to use this?" The steel reflected the firelight as she unsheathed it, gleaming wickedly. It was a beautiful weapon, worth more than he suspected she realised. Not for the first time, he wondered where she'd got it.

"I want you to try your best to cut me," he said, tone hard, face unreadable.

Aelia scoffed. "You can't be that cocky."

Keeran allowed a little of the darkness to enter his eyes, just enough to trigger that innate fear response in her. From the way her face paled, it worked. He ignored the way his heart sank into his boots; how easily people recognised the evil in him, even her, even now.

"How about we make a deal?" He smiled wickedly, pushing past his self-loathing. "If you manage to draw blood, I'll cook every meal until we find Beserkir."

"And if I don't?" Aelia side-eyed him, suspiciously.

"You have to cook." There was no way this contest wasn't going to be seriously rigged. He'd let her cut him, anything rather than suffer through any more of her cooking, but he was going to make her work bloody hard for it.

"Those are some high stakes," she said, scrunching her

lips into a tight line as she considered it. "I saw you with those thieves yesterday."

"Now who's got no bite?"

Aelia scowled at him, taking a few more moments to think it over before replying.

"Fine."

Keeran opened his arms wide, exposing his broad chest. "Give it your best shot."

Aelia lunged at him, but it was a half-hearted attempt, and he knocked her aside lazily.

"You're going to have to try harder than that," he teased, enjoying the frustrated frown on her face a little too much.

It took her a while to find the confidence to start trying in earnest, holding herself back in case she actually hurt him, but after a few minutes of him batting her away with smug effortlessness, her anger started to get the better of her.

On her next attack, he grabbed her arm and twisted, enough to send her spinning to face the opposite direction. He shoved her between her shoulders and sent her staggering forwards.

"Just because you're attacking, doesn't mean you can lower your defences," he said as she whirled to face him again. "If you're close enough to someone to attack them, they're close enough to attack you."

And so they continued, him barking instructions at her, her trying and failing to hide her growing anger. He was surprised at how quickly she was learning. He was throwing way more at her than she should be able to handle at this stage, but she lapped it up, albeit through gritted teeth. If anything, the harder he pushed her, the harder she pushed right back. And he was more than happy to push, if it meant making the most of what little time they had.

The realisation hit him like a ton of bricks. Who knew how long he had before they caught up with Beserkir? A day, a week? The memory of the thieves attacking her flooded his mind, closely followed by the Astraea attack, then Shiva and his thugs. How many times would she have died if he hadn't been there? The thought broke through the wall he'd thrown up around the tugging in his chest, unleashing a terrible, gnawing anger. He needed to make sure she was safe on the road back to Callodosis. He needed to make sure she was safe, always.

So, with a flash of movement, he disarmed her, popping the blade from her grasp. Her exasperated growl made him grin.

"You're enjoying this far too much," she snarled.

"I warned you I would. Like I said earlier," he opened his hands out in front of him, twirling the dagger expertly between his fingers. "Cathartic."

"Show me how you did that," Aelia demanded, ignoring him. He obliged, handing her back the dagger and slowing the movement down for her to process what he was doing.

"Want me to show you again?" he offered, holding the dagger out to her.

"No, I got it," she said, before lunging at him without warning. The manoeuvre was bang on, incredibly, but without enough power to knock it from his grasp.

"Good." He frowned, impressed again by how quickly she picked things up. "But not enough to disarm me. Try harder, Aelia."

She glowered at him, her green eyes narrowing as she tried again, one hand forcing his wrist down on itself whilst her other made to smack the blade out from the weakest part of his grip. She didn't see his other fist coming.

"Your opponent has two hands," he reminded her, waving his free hand at her with a smug grin.

Aelia rubbed her shoulder, nodding despite the deep frown lines creasing her forehead.

She came at him again, this time ready for the other hand. She was not, however, ready for the leg that swept her own out from under her.

"Two hands *and* two legs, Aelia." He flipped the dagger cockily.

She hauled herself up, not voicing a word of protest. She didn't have to; they were written all over her face.

"Again," he ordered.

This time, she didn't even make contact with his wrist before he had her on the floor again.

"Faster, Aelia."

She was. She blocked his first swing but let the second and third make contact before she landed back on her arse.

"I thought you wanted this, Aelia. You're never going to learn if you spend half the time lying on the floor. Faster, stop wasting our time."

"I *am.*"

"If you were, you wouldn't be covered in dirt."

This time he lunged for her, letting her block the first few before he upped the tempo, pushing her faster and faster. Her technique was still sloppy but anger crackled in those green eyes, driving her on. He just hoped it would be enough to make her forget herself. With a swipe of his leg, he sent her back into the grass. This time she was up almost before she'd landed, the cracks in her restraint showing one of those precious glimmers of her true potential. He didn't give her a chance to recognise it, to slow down.

He pushed her, harder and harder, until her ego was as bruised as her behind and finally, finally, she lost control. With a snarl any artemian would have been proud of, she threw herself at him. His elation was matched only by his surprise at the force with which she came at him.

The dagger was forced from his grasp, and his blows were

knocked aside, one after the other. Something nicked his chest.

Aelia pulled back, chest heaving. Keeran dropped his chin, not believing what he was seeing.

She'd cut him, the edges of the small tear in the fabric darkening with his blood.

He stepped forwards until he was close enough to see her pulse bounding at the base of her throat. The satisfaction in her eyes melted into apprehension as he leant into her, lowering his face until his cheek was mere inches from hers.

"Perfect," he said, his voice low and sinister. "If I see anything less in the future, you will find yourself on the floor until you give me everything. Do you understand?"

He watched her throat move as she swallowed, her lips parting as her breath hitched, but this time, he didn't think it was from fear. He shoved the thought aside.

"Yes," she whispered.

He placed a hand on her shoulder as he passed, just a momentary touch, but he hoped it conveyed what words could not. He couldn't actually apologise, not when he was prepared to push her that hard again tomorrow if it kept her safe. Nor could he express the pride he felt, not when he had no right to feel it. So he hoped something of what he felt came across in that simple touch before he left her looking down at the dagger in her hands.

CHAPTER NINETEEN

Back in the saddle, Keeran grimaced as he adjusted his position. Gods, he hated travelling on horseback. It was uncomfortable, and slow, and such a waste of time. He could have flown the distance they'd travelled since leaving Callodosis in a day. A day and a half with breaks. It was another very good reason for him to have left Aelia…

For the hundredth time in the hour since they'd left camp, Keeran fought the urge to turn and look at her. She'd been quiet since last night, when he'd thrown himself under his blankets and rolled to face away from the fire, away from her. He'd been stiff as a board listening to her get herself ready for bed, tucking herself up in her own blankets on the opposite side of the fire. It had taken everything in him, every single iota of self-control, to stop himself from going to her.

She wanted him to, of that he was now sure, and that knowledge kept him up half the night.

So now he rode next to her, eyes scratchy and trousers tight. He gritted his teeth at the discomfort, his need for her seeming to grow with each moment. Her taunt from the night before played over and over in his head, his embarrassment at his flustered lack of response alleviated only by the thoughts of what he could do to her to prove her wrong. Thoughts that would not go away.

He gritted his teeth, trying to banish the images from his mind, when Aelia's voice jolted him from his purgatory.

"Keeran." Aelia pointed with a trembling finger.

Smoke, and lots of it, rose in the distance from behind a crest of a hill. Keeran looked back at Aelia, and his stomach fell out of the saddle and into the grass. He'd never seen her so angry, the maelstrom of emotion she'd been enduring since Callodosis finally having something real to aim at. He almost pitied the Astraea.

"You don't think..." she whispered, not taking her eyes off the ominous column. He didn't want to answer, not when he recognised the seething rage behind her eyes. In that moment, he dreaded the hatred he saw there, fearing the recklessness that might arise from it.

"It could be," he eventually replied, although he had little doubt as to who was responsible.

Aelia looked into the distance for a single moment, the wind picking up around them, seeming to drive them towards the smoke. It was all the encouragement she needed.

With little more than a touch of her heels, her horse sprang away, reaching a full gallop within a few paces to tear through the grassy plains.

"Dammit Aelia, wait!" He gathered his reins and chased after her. "Wait! Aelia!"

The wind tore the words from him, flinging them back over his shoulder.

Her horse was built for speed in a way that his was not, and she beat him to the brow of the hill, not pausing before she careened back down the other side. Time slowed despite the pounding of his horses' hooves as he lost sight of her, a thousand thoughts racing through his mind as he imagined what might be waiting for her beneath the column of smoke.

He finally reached the top, accompanied by the rhythmic flutter of his horses' nostrils, the beast blowing heavily as he tried to keep up with his friend. There was no time to rest, however, as Aelia was ploughing dangerously down the steep bank on the other side towards the source of the smoke.

He could only assume it had once been a hamlet, one far too small to have been put on any map. Now it never would be. Charred beams lying amongst smoking piles of ash were all that remained of the homes they had once formed, their inhabitants nowhere to be seen.

He drove onwards, checking his horse lest gravity take their descent into its own hands, even as his heart seemed to reach through his rib cage towards the too small figure ahead of him.

Aelia finally slowed to a walk as she reached the hamlet. Only when he reached her side did his breathing return to normal, although his horse needed a little while longer.

He dismounted and tied the reins safely in a knot. Aelia slipped off and copied him.

"Watch yourself, we may not be alone," he cautioned.

The smoke was acrid on his tongue, promising to linger at the back of his throat long after they had left this place.

He walked a few paces in front of Aelia, scanning for some clue as to what had happened, hoping they were wrong in their assumption. They weren't.

In what used to be the centre square sat another pile of ash, smaller than the others and free of beams. Instead, the ash held an array of bones. Too many to count.

A post had been hammered into the ground in front of it,

the poster at its tip whipped at by the sudden wind, folding the paper over on itself.

Aelia walked with heavy solemnity to expose the words the wind had tried to hide from them.

Demuto shall be cleansed.
Rid yourself of your Human pests or face their fate alongside them.

"Aelia..." He tried to reach over to where she stood staring at the words in her hand, to offer what comfort he could... but comfort was the last thing on her mind.

Before he could touch her, she was striding around the pile of ash, her eyes hard and dangerous as they searched the dirt. He watched her read the story it had to tell with an ominous sense of foreboding.

"Aelia, don't be foolish."

She ignored him, bent low as she followed the tracks until the plains opened up before them, uninterrupted by smouldering piles of ashes.

"They went this way," she said, looking out to where the trail undeniably disappeared.

"Towards Llmera. That's hardly surprising," he grunted.

"Good, we won't even need to make a detour." She finally looked at him, not a hint of humour in her face.

"We need to wait. They could have joined a larger unit by now." It was true, the tracks suggested only a small band of the Astraea were guilty of the massacre that smouldered behind them, but who knew what kind of force they could end up chasing down. Aelia turned back to the horses, not deigning to respond. He grabbed at her arm, holding her back.

"Aelia, think this through. This is foolish."

He let her snatch her arm free, her anger momentarily focused on him.

"I'm not asking you to come. Be like everyone else and just walk past the problem that burns at your feet, but I won't." She glared at him, those green eyes boring into him with well-aimed accusation. She spun around and stormed back to the horses, each stride more determined than the last.

"Fuck," he sighed before following.

She'd already leapt into the saddle by the time he reached her.

"Do you have your dagger?" he asked. She lifted her top to show him. "Good."

He pulled his sword out from his saddle and slung it between his shoulders, fighting the urge to mutter under his breath at the lunacy of what they were about to do. She'd snapped at him once and he was in no rush to experience it again, so he gritted his teeth and swung himself onto his horse's back wordlessly.

"See if you can keep up this time." She flipped her braid over her shoulder and urged her horse onwards.

Safely out of earshot, he risked a few mumbled expletives.

THEY ATE UP THE GROUND, THE HORSES EGGING EACH OTHER on as they hurtled towards the murderous pyromaniacs.

Stay in control, stay in control, stay in control, he chanted in time to the beat of the horse's hooves. He was in no doubt that their little game of chase would end in violence, and he just prayed he could keep Aelia alive without showing too much of his other side.

. . .

THE TRAIL LED THEM BESIDE THE TREE-LINED EDGE OF ONE OF the lakes, shielding them as successfully as it blocked their view of the Astraea. So it was with inevitable surprise that they rounded a corner at considerable speed and hit straight into the back of the band of Astraeans.

There were more than he had anticipated, but less than he'd feared; about fifteen armed artemians jumped into action. Fortunately, the only horses they had with them pulled an enormous, caged cart, meaning the Astraeans themselves were on foot.

To her credit, Aelia didn't hesitate for a moment as they ploughed towards them at a gallop. Her dagger was in her hand and bloodied before the first Astraean had a chance to draw his own weapon. Blood sprayed from his neck, his body hitting the floor long after Aelia had passed.

Keeran was hot on her tail, unable to think of anything other than watching her back. She was not ready for this, nowhere near.

His sword whistled through the air, the last sound those who felt its cold touch ever heard. Aelia's dagger was no match for the swords the Astraeans had now had time to draw, not from horseback and certainly not in her inexperienced hands, but in a rush of swinging steel, they managed to emerge on the other side of the Astraeans unharmed.

Wheeling their horses back around, they faced the now ready group of warriors, their blades high and formation held.

"Aelia, be careful of the..."

She didn't wait to hear the rest of his caution. Blood flecked her face as she turned to him.

"They have the humans."

Keeran looked back and felt the familiar red mist start to descend. His attention had been so focused on the threat of the Astraeans, he hadn't noticed what was in the cage they were transporting. It was crammed full of humans, so tightly squeezed that some of their limbs poked through the bars like hay from a net.

He closed his grip around the hilt of his sword and met Aelia's eye.

As one, they charged.

He got ahead of her, breaking into the Astraean formation and sending them scattering. A few of them Shifted, and it was these he focused on, cutting them down as quickly as he could. The more he killed, the less Aelia had to face in his wake.

He twisted to look her way and saw she had leapt from the saddle, sending her dagger flying towards a looming Astraean. She missed. Keeran cursed and dragged his horse back around.

Skidding to her knees, Aelia swiped a sword from a still groaning corpse and raised it just in time to block the blade that swung her way. Her face contorted with the strain, but she flung the Astraean off her. The speed of her reflexes was the only thing that had saved her, but she was facing an experienced soldier, and she couldn't make it to her feet in time before he was upon her once more.

Keeran hacked his way through the soldiers blocking him from Aelia, the blood he spilt dripping from the dark coat of his horse, but he could see another two Astraeans moving to surround her. The red mist enveloped him, pulsing in his ears and boiling his blood.

He kicked his horse, spurring it on, but it could only go so fast, mangling the corpses it trampled over. By some miracle, she blocked another attack from the first Astraean from where she knelt on the floor, completely oblivious to the two that approached her from behind.

He would not make it in time, and there was no way she could hold off all of them, not when she had never held a sword before in her life.

He watched them descend on her, saw the fear of death flash in her eyes as she noticed she was surrounded, the inevitability of it as clear to her as it was to him.

In that instant, he made a choice. He would give up his search for those who had betrayed his kind, he would flee Demuto, he would face Aelia's repulsion.

Because he would not let her die.

THE FLAMES WERE ALWAYS WITH HIM, JUST A PSYCHIC TOUCH away from life, and he reached for them now. In his mind's eye, he guided them even as they woke, already planning their path of swirling incineration, turning the Astraea's weapon of choice against the soldiers who encircled Aelia.

The oxygen was sucked from him when Aelia grabbed hold of the sword she wielded with both hands and slashed at the feet of the man closest to her with enough strength to cleave bone from bone.

The man hadn't even hit the floor before she threw herself over him, rolling away from the other two with unnatural speed. It gave him all the time he needed.

The flames died before they were even created, but the steel in his hands came to life, singing through the air as he launched out of the saddle and rolled to his feet between the two remaining Astraeans. It took every single ounce of self-control to kill them with restrained movements, the beast in him yearning to rip their souls from their bodies with his bare hands.

In a matter of seconds, the road was quiet once more.

Aelia stood looking at him. Her sword hung by her side, her chin held high despite the frantic rise and fall of her blood-spattered chest. There wasn't even a flicker of regret in her eyes, just pure, unadulterated defiance. She'd never looked so beautiful.

His heart thundered in his chest at the sight of her and as he held her gaze, he wondered how the fuck he was ever going to find the strength to leave her.

CHAPTER TWENTY

The road wasn't silent for long. The humans began to cry out, begging for mercy, pleading for their freedom. Aelia quickly reassured them of both.

One of the less gaunt-looking women pointed out the body that held the keys, and Keeran fetched them, thinking it best not to push Aelia too far. Killing someone was one thing, a huge thing, but rifling through their blood-soaked pockets was probably expecting a bit much.

"We need to hurry. This road is quiet, but we want to be long gone before anyone else comes this way," Keeran told them all as he unlocked the cage.

Aelia helped them all out. She was right, they were human, every single one of them. He noticed her scanning their faces, and watched the hope fall from her when she realised Fenrir wasn't among them. He'd doubted he would be, but that didn't make seeing her grief hit her anew any easier.

He squeezed her arm, a small, understanding smile tugging at his lips. She just nodded and turned to help the weaker humans out of the cage.

Keeran spotted crates stored on top of the cart and climbed up, prying one of them open with a grunt. There were enough supplies here to last the humans for at least a week.

"Help me get these to the ground," Keeran called to one of the younger men. He jumped forward to help, two others close behind him. Together, it was easy enough, and Keeran was soon back on the floor.

"Where were they taking you?" Aelia asked the woman who had pointed out the keys.

"They never said," the woman replied. "Some of us were in that cage longer than others, but no one ever heard them mention what they were going to do with us. Trust me, we listened."

"You're not all from the hamlet back there?" Keeran interjected, handing her a cloth bag full of food. She opened it immediately and pulled out an apple, taking a huge bite with closed eyes. It was a few seconds before she replied.

"No, they've been collecting us one stop at a time," she said through her mouthful, already rifling through the bag and pulling out a stale chunk of bread. "Each time I thought they couldn't cram any more of us into that cage, we'd pull up somewhere else."

"I don't understand. Why would they be collecting you?" Aelia wondered out loud, touching her fingers to the hilt of the dagger at her hip.

"None of us know, but we've been headed in the direction of Llmera," one of the others said as he limped over; his clothes hung off him, torn and dirty. Keeran dreaded to think how many 'stops' he must have witnessed.

"I just hope I never find out," the woman added before tearing into the bread, her jaw working hard on the stale crust.

"Where will you all go?" Aelia asked, looking out over the

small group of humans. They had to have saved about thirty of them, and all because of Aelia, he thought with a tinge of shame. He'd have just ridden past the smouldering hamlet.

"As far from here as possible. I don't know if anywhere is safe for us anymore, but we'll put our heads together and come up with a plan." The man sighed as he took in the massacre on the road around them. "Whatever we do, we can only do it because of you two. We all owe you our lives."

"There is no debt." Keeran looked towards where their horses had fled to, looking warily down at them from halfway up the gentle rise of the hill. "Just get off this road quickly and we'll do the same."

"Thank you, we will."

Keeran turned, making to step over the prone form of one of the Astraea to get to the horses. He paused as he did, looking at the body for a moment.

"And take their swords with you," he said, before stepping over it without a second glance.

"We will," the man repeated, more quietly this time.

"Good luck," Aelia said before starting to follow Keeran.

THEY MADE IT TO THE HORSES, REASSURING THEM WITH gentle murmurs. When the whites of their eyes were no longer visible, they swung into their saddles and trotted away without looking back, oblivious to the humans watching them disappear behind the trees.

THEY RODE LONG INTO THE NIGHT. ONLY WHEN THE HORSES could go no further did they finally set up camp, washing them off in the water before leaving them to graze. They'd managed to find what little remained of a farmstead on the lakeside, the moss-covered stone walls having crumbled away to varying heights. The tallest stretch of unbroken stone came to no more than shoulder height, but they settled down behind it gratefully, escaping the wind that still tore across the grasslands.

Keeran hunted whilst Aelia washed, making sure she was well out of eyesight when he shot a tiny ball of fire into the eye of a waterfowl. Usually, he wouldn't take the risk so close to her, but the blood that covered him had well and truly dried by now, and he wanted to jump headfirst into that lake more than anything. He hid the mark by slipping a throwing knife into the smoking hole, the laceration obliterating the evidence.

Aelia was teasing the knots from her hair by the fire when he returned. All thoughts of the lake deserted him when he caught sight of her. The firelight played over her skin, shining a spotlight on every beautiful inch of her. He could have stood watching her all night, lake or no lake, but he guessed he only had another second or two before she looked up.

He made the most of both of them before finally moving, holding up the waterfowl for her to see.

"You go wash. I'll sort those out," she suggested.

He took her up on the offer and headed for the water.

He stripped in the privacy darkness provided, washing first himself, then his clothes. Only when every speck of the day had been scrubbed off did he return to camp, the luxury of clean clothes one he deeply appreciated. He'd thrown on a vest until he was dry enough to swap it for a shirt, no longer feeling the need to hide his scarred arms from her.

He hung his wet ones to dry next to Aelia's, and the domestic simplicity of the task struck him with an overwhelming gratitude that she was here, alive. Today could have gone so differently. It sent that strange twist in his chest into overdrive, as though his heart had been rung out like his bloodstained clothes.

CHAPTER TWENTY-ONE

What the hell had come over her?

The same question had been rolling through her mind on a loop since they'd left the humans. She had killed people, had been desperate to kill them, but even now that the adrenaline had left her system, she couldn't bring herself to regret it.

She sat next to the collapsed ruin they'd found, the wall half standing, the rubble lost to time. The wind was dying down, but it was still enough to make her drying clothes flap where they hung. She sat as close as she dared to the fire to try and dry her still-wet hair, wearing only an oversized top she'd brought with her because she was sick of her hair soaking whatever top she then had to sleep in. She'd change properly once her hair had dried a little more, and frankly, after the day they'd had, she couldn't care less about propriety.

With her legs tucked carefully underneath her to hide how little she was wearing underneath it, she used a cloth to tease the last stubborn lines of dried blood from the intricate marks on the dagger's hilt, having to use her nail at times. No matter how much she scrubbed, the hilt still looked tainted.

She had killed three people, two men and one woman... at least she thought they were. Truth be told, from horseback, she hadn't had time to notice much more than where to aim, her dagger slicing through flesh as if it were nothing. Aelia couldn't decide whether that was a good thing or a bad thing.

She turned her dagger over in her hands, angling it in the firelight to make sure every speck of blood was gone. The blood itself didn't bother her, she'd have been useless out hunting if it did, but she didn't want any trace of those monsters to linger.

And that's what they were. She'd reminded herself of it a thousand times already, whenever panic started running circles in her mind, waving doubts around like streamers at a festival. They were monsters.

The last thing she remembered with any real clarity was racing around the corner and seeing what was in that cart. And then she had run in like a wild thing, charging into them as if she'd lost her mind. Maybe she had. Only a lunatic would think they stood a chance against so many. She would have died if it weren't for Keeran.

Keeran. She let her eyes slide over to him for what felt like the millionth time that evening. He was hanging his clothes to dry next to hers, as silent and unreadable as he'd been since they'd left the humans. She couldn't tear her eyes off him.

Aelia's chest tightened at the memory of him charging at the Astraea. She felt like she had seen him as Mother Nature had intended him to be, wielding death with every sweep of his sword, the closest thing to perfection she had ever seen. She hadn't even known such beauty existed in death, but it did, and Keeran was it.

She had seen it in him countless times over the last few days when his control slipped. That same irresistible darkness that had flickered beneath the surface, a mere glimmer of what she had seen today, but just as beautiful.

Aelia got to her feet and walked tentatively over to him. She'd put him at risk today, too, and his silence made her suspect he wasn't best pleased about it.

"I'm sorry," Aelia whispered when she was a few steps from him.

After a moment's pause, he turned to face her. She met his eyes unflinchingly, all too aware that he was reading every sentiment raging within her. Embarrassment, guilt, sadness; there they sat for him to see.

"What for?"

"For my naivety. If it wasn't for you, I'd be dead."

He walked over to her, stopping only when she had to arch her neck to look at him.

"If it wasn't for you, all of those humans might have died."

She swallowed heavily and tried to look away. He grabbed her chin and made her look at him. She didn't resist.

"The only thing you have to apologise for is not waiting for me."

Only then did she try to free her chin. He didn't let her.

"We're in this together, remember? I have your back, you have mine." His irises flickered to an unnatural black, and her breath caught in her throat. "How can I have your back if you take off like that?"

She said nothing. There it was, that *otherness* about him. It sent a shiver of goosebumps over her skin. She wasn't completely foolish; she was still absolutely terrified of it, but now that fear had a tinge of something else, something curious, something eager.

He dropped his face closer to hers, still gripping her chin.

"Promise me you won't do something like that again." His

voice dropped to a menacing growl that had her toes curling, even as alarm scurried down her spine, her muscles tensing involuntarily in response to the danger in his eyes.

"I promise," she breathed. She would have promised him anything.

She fought to control her hammering heart, but his eyes dove to the hollow at the base of her throat, and the subtle lift of his lips told her that her pulse had betrayed her. When they returned to meet hers, there was something enticingly predatory in their depths, and she found herself leaning fractionally closer, an innate curiosity taking over her.

Keeran dropped his fingers from her chin and took a step back, his eyes locked onto hers, the indecision in them warring with a hunger she could relate to. Whatever it was that was holding him back, she was no longer under any misapprehension that he didn't want her. From the way his breathing had picked up, the heavy rise and fall of his chest making something tighten low in her stomach, she knew he wanted her as much as she wanted him.

And she was sick of waiting.

He ran his fingers through his wet hair, slicking it back and out of his eyes. She doubted he was conscious of the way it made the muscles in his arm flex, but her gaze followed the movement ravenously.

The coiling tension she felt in that low and sensitive part of herself almost every time she looked at him had been settled by the freezing water of the lake, but just a few glances at his bare arms had her biting her lip as filthy images flitted through her mind. Of those arms holding her up, of them pinning her down, of her nails digging into them.

As if he could read her mind, his eyes slid over her, fixing on where her teeth sank into her lip. She had to clear her throat before she trusted herself to speak.

"The way you fought earlier, Keeran... I've never seen

anything like it." Aelia shook her head incredulously. "It was beautiful."

Keeran's eyes widened, an expression she couldn't pinpoint flashing over his face, making him look younger, vulnerable. Then it was gone, disappearing behind the hard wall of his usual expression, a small smile replacing it instead.

"That was nothing, Aelia," he murmured, little more than a rumble in his chest.

She believed him. Whatever he was, he wasn't like anyone she'd ever met before. Even when she tried her hardest, he was still quicker, stronger, more dangerous than she would ever be.

"Remind me not to get on your bad side then," she managed to say past the nervous excitement building inside her.

Keeran's smile darkened, making her breath hitch. Something dangerous gleamed in the darkness of his eyes as he slid them over her. He took a step closer to her, then another, until he was right on top of her again. Her breathing quickened in anticipation; her world shrinking to just the space separating them, to the magnetism that made her want to close it.

He towered over her, so tantalisingly close she had to tilt her head back to hold his gaze; she breathed him in, the now familiar scent of spiced musk and smoke. Anticipation curled inside her as he brushed his fingertips up her arms, bridging the gap between them; she couldn't tear her eyes from his to check, but it felt like they left a trail of flames in their wake, her skin tingling at his touch.

"You might like my bad side." His deep voice sent a cold thrill right down to the pit of her stomach. Lower in fact.

She was suddenly acutely aware of how little she was wearing under her shirt. Each rise of his chest brought him so close to touching hers that she longed to arch her breasts into him, craving the feel of him against her.

"Why don't we find out?" she purred, her lips curling upwards at the molten desire burning in his eyes.

Slowly, so deliciously slowly, he dipped his head to brush his lips against her neck, making coherent thought fade from reach.

"Are you sure that's what you want, Aelia?" he said, a dark rumble in her ear.

She tilted her head, exposing her throat, silently begging for more. His mouth found the hollow at the base of her throat where her pulse pounded, smiling a satisfied smile against her skin as he felt how fast it was beating, before he trailed his tongue up her neck to nip at the soft skin beneath her ear. She gasped as his teeth teased, his tongue soon soothing the sting.

"I need to hear you say it," he demanded, his breath hot against her neck, his lips so tantalisingly close to her skin. His fingers curled around her arms, as if begging her to agree.

"Yes," she breathed. "Yes, that's what I want."

Keeran growled, his face still buried in her neck, a taste of that other side of him, a promise of what was to come.

He lifted his face, and she melted at the need in his eyes, all of it focused entirely on her. Her whole body ached at the sight of it. Keeran held her jaw with one huge hand, gripping her throat with the lowest fingers—and crushed his mouth against hers.

His tongue claimed her, devoured her, explored her. And she let it, his kiss a demand that she was all too happy to submit to. She tangled her fingers in his hair, pulling him closer, arching into him desperately, needing to feel as much of him against her as she could.

His free hand lifted the fabric of her top up her thigh,

higher and higher, the ache in between her legs throbbing as he drew closer to where she needed him most.

He froze, realising how little she was wearing under the shirt, and groaned deeply into her mouth, grabbing her bare arse and drawing her into him, pressing the hard length of him against her. His kiss deepened, possessing her as his grip on her throat tightened slightly, pulling her mouth harder into his.

She longed for his touch, her body already trembling, and she moaned pleadingly. He released his grip on her arse to hook under her thigh, wrapping it around his waist and lifting her off the ground. The hard stone of the wall behind them slammed into her back, the bite of it only heightening the need she felt coursing through her as his hand drifted to cup between her legs. His smile darkened as he felt how wet she was, how desperately ready she was for him.

Aelia's fingers clawed into his shoulders, the fabric of his vest bunching under her grasp, her mind unable to think of anything other than his hand. With one leg still wrapped around him, she lifted herself up onto her toes, pushing herself into him pleadingly. He was so torturously close.

Keeran pulled his face away, watching her reaction as he gave her what she needed, his thumb circling that most sensitive spot with the gentlest of touches. A predatory smile played on his mouth as her head dropped backwards against the wall, her eyes closing as his fingers teased her. Aelia wasn't aware of her grip tightening on his shoulders, she didn't see the thrill her nails caused burn brightly in his eyes, all she could think of were those fingers. Pleasure began to build over her like a haze, the need for more, for him to fill her, to fuck her. She needed it, she needed more. A whimper escaped her, her breaths coming in shallow gasps as she clung to him.

He read her mind, her body, and plunged his fingers deep

inside her. Gone were the gentle touches, the soft strokes of his thumb. Now his fingers slammed into her hard enough to make stars dance behind her closed eyes. She cried out as the haze thickened, and he caught it with his mouth, devouring her moans of pleasure as he took her closer to the edge. The promise of release built inside her until she could feel it on the horizon.

The heel of his hand brushed that bundle of nerves each time his fingers filled her, and she bit her lip to stop herself from crying out again. Keeran noticed her restraint and growled, pressing his mouth into hers and prioritising her clit, focusing on the friction he knew she craved until she moaned into his mouth uncontrollably. He swallowed the sound greedily, his approval rumbling in his chest.

Release rushed towards her, threatening to wash over her, and she reached down, wanting to feel the hard length of him in her hand as she came.

Keeran went rigid at her touch, his fingers halting. Confused, she opened her eyes and flinched at the wall of control suddenly in his, the muscle in his jaw feathering with forced restraint. But he must have noticed the hurt in her face, something flickering over his before the wall he'd thrown up melted as quickly as it had appeared, replaced with a resolve she didn't understand.

Before she could think anything else about it, his strong arms scooped her around him, lifting her off the ground, his warm hands gripping her arse as she wrapped her legs around him, the wetness of her pressing into his abdomen. The hunger in his eyes told her he was aware of it too, that he knew the friction of his vest against her was delicious torture, just enough to tease, not enough to build. She couldn't look away, their eyes fixed onto one another as he lifted her off him and on top of the ruined wall, the muscles of his arms bulging.

Aelia looked down at him from her perch and couldn't breathe at the heat that blazed in his eyes. There was no hint of the restraint that had been there moments ago as he placed a hand on the inside of either thigh. His eyes locked with hers as he opened them, spreading her legs wide to reveal the glistening warmth between them.

Then and only then, did he tear his gaze from hers, looking greedily at what waited for him at eye level. He had never looked as predatory as he did then; she'd never seen him so unleashed, the power in him darkening his eyes, turning them so black they swallowed the light. She didn't need to remind herself that this was what she had wanted, her whole body throbbed with need at the sight of him so raw, so himself. She lifted her shirt higher, offering herself to him with a shift of her hips.

Keeran needed no further encouragement. His fingers squeezed into her thighs as he lowered his face towards her. He ran his tongue up her in one breathtaking sweep, as if he couldn't wait to taste every inch of her, and the growl that escaped him sounded more beast than man.

He pulled away, shutting his eyes to savour her taste for a few rapid heartbeats, swallowing with a throaty moan. And then he feasted on her in earnest. There was no other way to describe what he did. He feasted, as if he were a man starved.

All thought of self-control was forgotten as his tongue set to work. She wasn't even aware of the cries that escaped her as he set about discovering what she liked, playing and flicking and sucking until she quivered on the wall, only his grip on her thighs keeping her from falling as her body turned to liquid.

Her hips ground against him with a mind of their own as her pleasure coiled tightly, on the brink of exploding through her, so close her entire consciousness held its breath. And at that exact moment, Keeran pulled away.

Aelia gasped at the absence of his tongue, the need inside her desperate and frenzied. But when her eyes jumped to his, her heart twisted in her chest. She'd seen glimpses of the darkness in them, seen the black overtake the rich brown of his irises, but this was something else. Keeran was gone, and the creature looking out at her from the obsidian depths of his eyes made her blood run cold.

"You already told me once you would work with me," Keeran said, his voice dark and gravelly, "that you would stop insisting on doing things your way."

His thumb brushed over her clit with firm, deliberate strokes, sending tremors of pleasure up her spine. The shock of his eyes had brought her down from the brink, but just a few passes of his thumb had her biting down on a moan.

"And then you go and do it again today, putting yourself in harm's way because you won't stop to include me in your decisions." It wasn't Keeran talking. There was nothing familiar in the menacing growl of his voice, but as his thumb worked over her, she found it difficult to care. "So you have no one but yourself to blame for this."

Aelia barely had time to register what he'd said before his fingers slid into her. She felt herself clench involuntarily around them, her body needing him in a way she'd never experienced before. He curled his fingers inside her, hitting something that had a delicious ache building within her in mere moments. He settled into a rhythm, curling his fingers towards him over and over until her head hung back, her mouth dropping open in a silent cry of previously unknown pleasure.

Then his tongue got involved.

In seconds, she was close to the most earth-shattering release she'd ever felt. It rippled through her, building to the point of breaking, and then he stopped again.

Aelia groaned, her fingers digging into his shoulders as she tried to stop him from pulling away, but to no avail.

"How can I protect you if you keep doing things like this?" Keeran tilted his head as he looked up at her from under his brows, no hint of playfulness in his expression, and Aelia's stomach flipped nervously. He wasn't teasing her for fun, for any sense of enjoyment. This was her punishment, and by the look in his eyes, he was going to make her pay.

"I... I'm sorry," she stammered, heart racing.

"So you've said." Keeran bent to kiss the inside of her thigh, tightening his grip on her possessively. "But you apologised last time too, and it didn't stop you tearing off without me today. There could have been anything waiting for you over that hill. Anything."

The hand holding her let go, making her cling to him for fear of tumbling backwards off the wall.

"Hang on tight, Aelia," he said, with a wicked smile.

His mouth latched onto her clit and sucked, sending her eyelids fluttering closed at the wave of bliss that washed over her. His fingers followed, slipping into her and curling up to match the rhythm of his tongue. The fabric of his vest bunched in her hands as she cried out, her legs wrapping around him to try and pull him closer. She felt his satisfied smile, but he didn't change his pace. Instead, the fingers of his free hand slipped under her shirt to gently push her back, before his fingers trailed down her stomach with the lightest of touches. Her muscles bunched under them, and her neck dropped back as she lost herself to the sensations building within her. When he reached her pelvis, he pushed down with the flat of his hand, pressing against the relentless curling of his fingers.

Her world realigned, pleasure she hadn't known existed coursing into her as his fingers fucked away her sanity, as his tongue devoured her inhibitions. Her legs shook, bliss wracking her body until she thought it would break her, until she forgot who she was.

She wanted to scream when he stopped the next time, pulling his mouth from her and leaving his fingers motionless, ignoring the way the walls of her clamped around them desperately.

"I wonder how long it will take for you to learn your lesson?" he asked, rhetorically. "I wonder how long it will take before you break."

Her heart was already thundering in her chest, her breathing uncontrollable and ragged. An icy shiver of fear flooded her veins, his words making her wonder how long he planned to do this to her. Her whole body was already trembling like one giant exposed nerve, every touch, every sensation sending her whirling.

The answer came in time.

Over and over again, he took her close to the edge, each time more intense and spine curling than the last. But he stopped just as release was about to crash over her, scolding her as he waited for her to come down.

She cursed him, begged him, cursed him again, but it made no difference. He edged her until her heart thundered so loudly in her ears she was sure it would give out on her, until her need was so intense she felt like she would buckle under the force of it. And there was nothing she could do to stop him. She was stuck on the wall, his hulking form blocking her escape, with nothing but a sheer drop onto rubble behind her. She was utterly at his mercy.

And she'd fucking agreed to this. She'd asked to see his dark side, like a fucking sadist.

Sweat glistened on her skin, sticking her hair to her face, her cheeks hot and burning. Her muscles gave out on her, leaving her half draped over him.

So that time, when he stopped, he had to support her

head to talk to her. His hand cupped her cheek, stroking her tenderly, and when she forced her eyelids open, the monster in his eyes looked back at her with warm satisfaction.

He pressed his lips to hers, so gently.

"We're a team," he whispered against her mouth. "Promise me."

Aelia nodded frantically, her voice barely more than a whimper. "I promise."

"Do you mean it?" he urged, reaching his hand between her legs once more.

"I do," she breathed.

"Good girl."

His mouth slanted over hers as his fingers worked into her, one hand fisting into her hair to pull her close, the other slamming into her so hard her whole body rocked with the force of each thrust. This time he didn't stop, and she found herself almost wishing he would as the pleasure spiralled tighter and tighter inside of her, every muscle in her body tensing in anticipation of the torrent of sensation that threatened to slam into her. And yet it kept building, the intensity growing. A spasm of fear spiked through her, unsure she could take it, unsure she could stand it.

When it finally broke, she screamed, trying to pull away from Keeran, but he kept his mouth firmly locked onto hers, as if the sound was his and his alone. It was the most earth-shattering, bone-breaking, eye-watering, life-altering, out-of-body orgasm of her life, and all she could do was cling to him and hope she survived.

Something in her chest ripped open, filling her with a warm golden light. It knotted itself together, winding out of her and reaching towards Keeran. The waves of pleasure slowly subsided, but the insistent pulling in her chest did not.

Panic took over, and she pulled away from Keeran, eyes dropping to where her hand clasped at her sternum. The golden thread was invisible yet real, intangible yet undeniable.

After a few moments, it began to fade, coiling back into her chest until it disappeared altogether.

Only then did she become aware of Keeran watching her.

"Did you—" she stammered. "Did you see that?"

Keeran shook his head, his eyes back to brown, and filled with such sadness she flinched. He lifted her off the wall, sliding her slowly down the length of his body until her feet reached the floor, never once taking his eyes off hers.

Her legs wobbled under her, threatening to give way. Without hesitating, he hooked under her knees and swept her into his arms. He sank down by the fire, keeping her tucked close against him, his arms firm and unyielding around her, as if he never wanted to let her go.

CHAPTER TWENTY-TWO

Her heart had calmed down enough that she was no longer worried that it would give out on her, and yet something had changed in her chest, a pulling sensation that had her wanting to lean in as close to Keeran as she could get.

She rubbed at her sternum, trying not to panic. That couldn't have been some kind of sex fuelled hallucination. She'd *felt* it.

Her eyes narrowed, a memory swimming to the surface of the only other time she'd felt anything like it. It had been the first time she'd seen Keeran, when he'd been performing in Callodosis. There was one unignorable common denominator there, and when she raised her eyes suspiciously, it was looking right at her.

"Say something," he said, almost pleadingly.

"What was that?" she whispered.

"Which part specifically?"

He had a point. Was she referring to the fact that he'd pinned her on a wall, used sex to punish her, given her an orgasm that had altered her perception of pleasure, or the fact that it seemed to have triggered some kind of… she didn't even know how to describe what she was feeling now, a tether, an ache? Whatever it was, he was undoubtedly at the other end of it.

"I felt something…" she spread her palm over her chest. "I can still feel it."

She was too scared to care how crazy she sounded, and something in his expression made her think he knew exactly what she was talking about. Her mind flung the memory of his eyes at her, black as pitch, staring up at her. There was something he wasn't telling her, something he hadn't wanted her to see.

"Did you do something to me?" she whispered, hating how small and frightened she sounded.

Hurt ripped across his face, and for once, he couldn't hide it. His torment took over his features, flooding her with guilt that she'd been stupid enough to suggest as much.

"No," he said, averting his eyes, hiding something from her.

She twisted in his arms, trying to make him look at her. "What aren't you telling me?"

Keeran swallowed heavily, still staring unseeingly at the blankets beneath them.

"Keeran," she said more loudly, snapping his eyes back to hers.

He sighed, the worry in her gut snarling more with each passing second. How bad was this going to be?

"It's not something one does to another person," Keeran started, reluctantly.

"What is it then?" Aelia pushed, growing impatient.

Keeran opened and shut his mouth a few times, looking for words that wouldn't come.

"Spit it out, Keeran," she snapped, her fear getting the better of her. What was happening to her?

"Have you ever heard of a pair bond?" he said, pressing his lips into a hard line the moment the words had left him, as if regretting ever letting them out in the first place.

Aelia frowned, the words seeming familiar, but she couldn't remember why.

"I don't think so?" she said, uncertainly.

Keeran nodded, unsurprised. "It's a bond that forms between two individuals. No one really understands the magic behind it, but each pairing is unique to the couple, connecting them in ways specific only to them."

"And that's happened? To us?" Aelia stared up at him, her fear easing slightly. It was something Keeran seemed to understand, and just putting a name to what she was feeling made her feel better about it. At least she wasn't losing her mind.

"It would appear so."

"Why?"

"No one knows," Keeran said.

"No one knows," Aelia repeated, sceptically. "Who are these people who don't know? Because I've never heard of any pair bond forming between artemians before. And that's what you told me you were."

"I am," Keeran insisted, so quietly she almost missed it.

Aelia blinked as she remembered where she'd heard of pair bonds before, the blood draining from her face as realisation hit, and hit hard.

"A mating bond," she whispered, thoughts whirring. Her eyes flicked to his, looking for the darkness in them with renewed fear. She tried to pull away from him, but his arms tightened around her.

"Aelia, please," Keeran said, imploringly.

"Let me go," she made her voice go cold, not letting it tremble with the fear that pulsed through her veins.

His arms loosened enough for her to stand, but his fingers clung to her wrist.

"You need to let me explain." He looked up at her, the anguish in his face tearing at her heart, quietening her terror. She gulped, trying to control the panic, the emotional turmoil of the day leaving her wired and volatile.

The wind tickled past her bare legs, reminding her how little she was wearing, and how close she was standing to him.

"I need to have clothes on for this conversation."

He released her wrist, watching her closely as she rifled through her pack and threw on a pair of trousers, as though worried she'd make a break for it. She hopped gracelessly into her boots, nearly falling backwards in her rush to pull them on.

"I'll answer anything you ask," he said, when she was done. "Just let me explain."

Aelia stood facing him, legs planted hip-width apart, heart still racing.

"You know what I am?" he asked, barely audible from across the clearing. He sat with one leg bent high, his elbow resting on his knee, yet he seemed coiled and ready to spring. She could feel the tension radiating off him.

"I think so." It made perfect sense; it explained why he hadn't Shifted in the days she'd known him, why he was so fast, so strong. It explained the scars, and the evil she saw in him. She felt so stupid for not seeing it earlier. "You're a Dragon."

"Ask me something," he demanded, softly. "I'll tell you anything you want to know."

He hadn't denied it. Aelia felt all the blood rush from her face.

"What are you doing here?" She folded her arms over her chest, trying to fight the pulling feeling that was trying to drag her back to him.

"I came to settle some old scores," he replied immediately.

"What does that mean?" Aelia shook her head, refusing to accept any more of his vague bullshit. Not now she knew she might be tied to him by some freaky, magical bond.

This time, he hesitated, pursing his lips as he thought of his answer.

"When we were exiled, it was a massacre. Our own generals turned on us, poisoning every man, woman, and child in the King's army, making us near defenceless. They slaughtered nearly all of us. The lucky ones were murdered in their beds, rendered completely paralysed by the neurotoxin they'd slipped into our food. The rest died slowly, only half in control of their bodies as they tried to flee." Keeran's expression had darkened, a hint of cruelty entering his tone. "That night will haunt me for the rest of my life."

"You were there?" Aelia gasped. He looked too young to have been fighting in the War of Two Kings. She was only a few years old when the war had ended, far too young to remember anything of it, and he was only a few years older than her. Or was he…

The Dragons were immortal, she realised with a jolt. She suddenly wished she'd paid more attention to the stories told in Callodosis about the Dragons. As a child, she'd been too engrossed by the legends, the warriors, the battles. If only she could remember some of the details.

"I was there," he admitted. "I was a child when they turned on us but, by the end of the war, both sides had recruited the children of Dragons into the army. Once Shifted, even a young Dragon is a formidable force on the battlefield."

Her historical knowledge was limited, but even she'd

known that the Dragons had begun to involve their young in the bloodiest war in Demuto's history. But knowing it had happened and seeing someone it had happened to were two very different things. Aelia shut her eyes against the horror that rose like bile in her throat.

"You still haven't answered my question," she said, shakily.

"In some ways, I can understand why they did what they did," Keeran continued, picking up a twig and twirling it absentmindedly between his fingers. "The Dragons had lost themselves, had succumbed to the darkness that lives within us all, and we were tearing the country apart in a pointless war. But Aelia, if you'd have seen it, you'd understand. Dragons fell screaming from the sky on wings that couldn't support them or were shot down by the artemians they'd fought alongside. Some couldn't even get airborne, so they were butchered on the ground, speared over and over until they succumbed to blood loss."

"Why. Are. You. Here?" Aelia bit out, despite the nausea curdling in her stomach at his words.

Keeran lifted his chin, his eyes defiant and unapologetic.

"I came back to kill the generals who turned on us. To track down any of them who still live and make them pay for what they did to us."

Aelia's shoulders slumped a little, and she dropped her eyes to hide her relief from him. He wasn't back to try and reclaim Demuto; she hadn't stumbled upon some immortal uprising. The Dragons had ruled them for centuries, the closest things to gods to walk the earth. There were other immortals across the world, other forms of magic that blessed the immortals of other countries, but in Demuto, Dragons were the pinnacle of power. The last thing she wanted was to be involved in their return.

Revenge, however, she could understand.

"Us?" Aelia said, wrapping her arms more tightly around herself. "There are more of you?"

A muscle in Keeran's jaw twitched, his fingers clenching and unclenching where they rested on his knee.

"I fled to the mountains to the South with one other Dragon, Khaled. He died last year. To my knowledge, there are no other Dragons in Demuto."

"I'm so sorry." Aelia didn't know what else to say. In a few short minutes, the little he'd told her about his past revealed more trauma than any one lifetime should hold. She couldn't imagine what it must be like to be the last of your kind, how lonely that must be.

"What are you thinking?" he ignored her apology, his eyes searching hers.

"I'm thinking I'm an idiot for not working it out sooner," she admitted, with an attempt at a smile.

"About the pair bond?"

"No, about who you are," she said quickly, her eyes narrowing. "Why? When did you figure out the … pair bond?"

Her tongue tripped over the words, feeling unnatural and alien to her. She'd heard of mating bonds being formed; many of the legends told over campfires revolved around them, but none of them spoke of one formed between a lower artemian and a Dragon. She didn't even know it was possible. It was a type of magic reserved for the immortals, a connection tying two souls together in a bond so powerful, so unbreakable, that death itself was the only thing that could sever it… and even that rarely ended well.

"When I kissed you, the night the thieves attacked." He flicked the twig he'd been playing with into the fire, watching it burn with a hard intensity. The light of the flames flickered over his profile, drawing attention to the perfect line of his jaw. She hadn't had much of a chance to unravel her feelings about whatever it was connecting them, but he had, and he definitely didn't look happy about it. The realisation knotted painfully in her stomach.

"Is there nothing we can do about it?" she asked, half hoping he'd say he didn't want to, half terrified that there was no escaping it.

He didn't look away from the flames, but a muscle in his jaw feathered.

"It's not fully formed yet. We'd have to accept it to complete it." He finally looked back up at her, catching her expectant expression and sighing. "We'd have to sleep together."

Aelia took a step backwards.

"Was that what that was about?" Aelia pointed to the wall he'd had her perched on. Would he have stopped had she not panicked? Or would he have kept going, committing them to this bond without ever consulting her?

"No," Keeran insisted, anger permeating every line of his body. "You think I'd do that? Take that decision from you? Who the fuck do you think I am, Aelia?"

"I don't know who you are," Aelia snapped back, hackles rising at his tone. "I don't have a fucking clue. You've lied to me every moment we've been together, which I can't exactly blame you for, all things considered, but it does mean you forsake the right to get defensive when I then struggle to piece it all together."

Keeran leapt to his feet, shoulders tense and fists bunched. How had she not realised what he was? Standing before her now, he was every inch a warrior, a beast, a Dragon.

"You may not have known what I am, but that doesn't mean you don't know me," he said, with careful restraint. He couldn't hide the black encroaching into his irises, though.

"What *is* that?" Aelia took a step back, not sure if she was on the verge of raging at him or bursting into tears. It was too much; she felt emotionally wrung out, physically exhausted. After everything that had happened in Callodosis, this was tipping her over the edge of her control. "It's like there's something else looking back out at me."

Her voice trembled. Great, her body was opting for tears. She pressed her lips together, squeezing hard as she tried to hold them back. Keeran's face softened immediately, the darkness vanishing as soon as he saw her distress. He took a step closer, arm outstretched towards her. Aelia recoiled, knowing she'd lose the fight with her tears if he was nice to her, if she let him take her in his arms.

He froze and lowered his hand.

"I'll tell you anything you want to know, Aelia, just please, come here." Worry creased his brow as he took her in, reading the panic threatening to overwhelm her.

But she just shook her head, taking another step away from him.

"I can't think here." Her voice broke, and she cursed her own weakness. "I need some space. Don't follow me."

Aelia spun on her heel and stalked to her horse.

"Aelia, wait, it's pitch black out there." Keeran crossed the clearing in a matter of strides, watching her untie her horse and slinging the rope around its neck to tie the loose end to the halter. "You can't seriously be going out without any tack."

Aelia sprang onto her horse's back, grabbing hold of the rope and touching her heels to its flank. The horse skittered to the side, pivoting around where Keeran held it firmly beneath the chin.

"Let go," she snarled, too desperate to get away, to hide her tears from him, to think about anything else.

Keeran looked silently up at her, a world of pain and fear buried in his eyes. For a moment, she didn't want to go, she wanted to slip right into his arms and cry until the world started to make sense again. But then he released his hold on the rope.

They stared into each other's eyes for a second that stretched for an eternity, before she gritted her teeth and pressed her horse on. It dropped into a canter and took off into the night.

CHAPTER TWENTY-THREE

Keeran watched as Aelia vanished into the darkness, staring long after she'd disappeared. When it was clear she wasn't coming back, he spun with a carnal roar, sending his fist flying into the nearby stone wall. It went right through it, sending fragments of stone crashing into the grass. He shook the dust from his fist and closed his eyes, trying desperately to control the seething rage that threatened to take over him.

With an almighty battle, he wrestled the beast within him back into its cage, where it threw itself against its constraints. It wanted to take off after her, both protective and wrathful in equal amounts. She'd left him. She'd worked out what he was, and she'd bolted.

He dropped his head into his hands, wishing he could erase the way her face had paled the moment she'd realised what he was. A beast from times gone by, the tyrants her people had struggled under.

And what had he done? Had he explained why he was doing what he was doing calmly and concisely? No, he'd fucked up royally, choosing instead to make it seem as though he was some revenge-obsessed vigilante.

Which he was. But not in the way he'd made himself out to be.

He dropped his hands in exasperation, wishing he could rewind time and start again, explaining everything to her properly.

The Dragons had fucked up, causing a war that spanned decades, decimating whole families as the twin princes fought for the throne. It was a ludicrous situation. Even as a child, Keeran was aware of the madness of it.

But the night that their people had turned on them had been the night his guardian had been about to seize the throne. How different Demuto would have been with Khaled and his unit in power. They were one of the few who still maintained control over the darkness all Dragons battled with, and they could have brought the rest of their people back.

Instead, Khaled's mate had been murdered, shattering the man he'd been permanently, leaving a shadow of what he had been.

If only the artemians had conspired with those who were still good, still honourable, the world would be a much better place. And that's what really pissed Keeran off. That they'd chosen to poison and murder all of them, irrespective of who they were. That was what he couldn't forgive.

But he hadn't said any of that to Aelia. He hadn't emphasised how he wasn't like the Dragons of the war. Khaled had taught him discipline, taught him how to rise above their baser instincts.

His eyes landed on the pile of stone he'd just punched his fist through. Well, he tried to rise above them, anyway. Admittedly, it had got a whole lot harder since he'd met her.

Keeran scooped up a small rock and threw it in the air,

watching it tumble over on itself before catching it again. He kept throwing it, needing something to focus on to stop him from tearing after her.

The creature in him bared its teeth at the thought, urging him to do just that.

"As if you haven't done enough," he said aloud, shoving back at the beast with enough anger to send it slamming into the walls of his consciousness. It picked itself up, obsidian eyes gleaming, but it stayed silent.

His throat bobbed as he looked over at the wall he'd lifted Aelia onto, his eyelids sliding shut as he remembered what he'd done to her. What they'd done to her.

He'd lost control again, losing himself to that coercive, overbearing, domineering bullshit. What must she be thinking? No wonder she'd run from him. From them.

Keeran let the rock roll from his fingers, his heart so heavy it dragged his shoulders down into a slouch.

His actions had sent her careening through the night, in lands full of thieves and the Astraea, and here he was sitting pretty, waiting for her to return.

Fuck that.

Keeran squared his shoulders and stalked out of the ruined farmstead to the open grassland beyond. When he was clear, he Shifted, taking the form of nightmares, of winged death. He didn't hesitate, launching himself into the sky and climbing high.

She said she'd wanted space, so she could have it, but he'd be damned if he wasn't going to watch her from the skies to make sure she was safe. Besides, what she didn't know couldn't hurt her.

CHAPTER TWENTY-FOUR

Adrenaline dried Aelia's falling tears in a way nothing else could, her horses' hooves pounding on the hard earth, matching the thundering of her heart. The wind tore at her, flinging her hair out behind her, and she laughed wildly.

This was exactly what she needed: the freedom, the joy, the excitement. It cleared her head, lending her the perspective she'd been searching for.

She didn't know how long they'd galloped for, her horse coiling and springing beneath her in a tireless rhythm, the muscled athleticism of the beast unlike anything she'd ever known. She felt a surge of affection towards him as she reined him up, smiling as he fought her, not ready to stop yet, but she kept a steady pressure on the ropes in her hands until he came back to her. He worked hard all day, it wasn't fair to push him hard at night, too.

He slowed to a stop, ribs pushing into her thighs as he blew hard, the gentle fluttering sound of his nostrils warming her heart. She ran her hand over his neck as she waited for his breathing to settle.

"Shall we take off, just you and me against the world?" she asked, smiling down at him as he looked wide-eyed into the darkness, the muscles of his back pushing into her as he craned his neck for a better view.

Aelia looked out over the grassland, sucking in a breath. The moon had peeked out from behind the clouds, hitting the seeded heads of the grass and lending them a metallic sheen. They rippled in the gentle wind, turning them to liquid silver. Mesmerised, Aelia tried to take it in, trying to lodge this moment into her memory.

The moon slipped back behind the clouds, taking the magic of the moment with it. The euphoria of her flight waned, leaving her as grey and monotone as her surroundings. She puffed out her cheeks and dropped her head back, looking at the clouds overhead.

He was a fucking Dragon.

Out here, it didn't seem like such a big deal. She'd already known he was different; having it confirmed shouldn't have been such a huge surprise. But that revelation, combined with the fact that there was some predestined connection between them, had just been too much.

And it probably hadn't helped that she'd found out just after he'd taken her body to the point of breaking, pushing her harder than she knew was even possible. It had been terrifying, overwhelming, cruel… and just the thought of it had her wanting to do it again.

Sex would never be the same. But that definitely wasn't reason enough to stay, she reminded herself, firmly, but she couldn't help but wonder what more would be like.

Ice water flooded her veins. There couldn't be more, not without completing the pair bond. From what Keeran said, if they had sex, that would be it. There would be no escaping this insistent tugging in her chest, this feeling of unease that had her wanting to scuttle back to him with her tail between her legs.

Would he be cross with her for taking off? What would that look like now that he didn't need to hide his identity from her? Aelia shook her head. He'd had plenty of opportunities to hurt her, but other than pushing her a bit hard when they'd fought, he'd never given her any real reason to fear him. Quite the opposite really.

Aelia was pulled from her reverie by her horse plunging its head violently into the grass, pulling her forwards with such force that her head snapped back and she nearly slipped down its neck.

"You'll give yourself a tummy ache," she ground out through gritted teeth as she tried to haul it back up, battling with it as it tore a few mouthfuls of the long grass. "Just wait a bit, will you?"

She reached forwards to pull some of the long stalks from its mouth, tutting to herself.

"If we walk home, you'll be able to eat then, okay?" she scolded, guiding it round towards the camp.

A breeze danced over her skin, and her stomach rolled at the scent it carried.

There was a group of people, a large group, and close.

Her pulse ratcheted up, roaring in her ears with a mix of excitement and fear. They'd been chasing down the Astraea for days now. Could it be that they'd finally caught up with them?

Aelia looked back in the direction of the camp, torn between going to get Keeran and scouting out the group whilst she was here. There was no point in dragging him out if it wasn't the Astraea, and what was the harm in just looking? It wasn't like she was going to storm the place, even if Fenrir was there.

Her heart flipped at the thought of finally finding Fenrir.

She raised her nose to the wind, but her senses weren't strong enough to make out his scent amongst all the others. That decided it. There was no way she could wait to find out if Fenrir was with them; she had to know.

She hobbled her horse and slunk towards the scent, keeping low in the grass as she climbed a steep, rocky bank. They were making no attempts to be quiet, and the wind carried the sound of raised voices to her, boisterous and masculine. As she neared the top of the bank, she dropped to her stomach and crawled the rest of the way on her elbows, ignoring the sharp rocks digging into her skin. She followed the longer grass where it interspersed the stonier ground, keeping herself hidden as she approached the camp.

The smell of cooking meat, unwashed bodies and testosterone met her, making her wrinkle her nose. They were Astraea alright; the red insignia on their black uniforms had been burned into her memory like a brand. There were dozens of them, most of them sat around various campfires, some milling around idly. A few trees grew on the top of the hill, providing them a little shelter from the wind. She peered around the camp, the light of the fires making it hard for her to see if anything hid in the shadows beneath the trees, but her hopes sank to her boots when it became clear there were no caged carts here, not a single one.

She'd assumed the band they'd interrupted earlier were on their way to rejoin this larger group, but perhaps they weren't… perhaps they send those they capture on ahead. The realisation triggered a heavy weariness to crush down upon her.

Was this even the same group that had been in Callodosis? She couldn't see their faces from here, but she had to know. Inch by careful inch, she crept slowly closer until their features came into focus. She could even hear the conversation around the nearest fire but soon disregarded it as the inane drivel it was. These were the people tearing their communities apart? How had such morons got away with it for so long?

Aelia scanned their faces, praying her memory wouldn't let her down, but none looked familiar.

A voice broke across the clearing, sending the camp into silence. It reverberated around her skull, like a nightmare come to life, and she lay frozen in place by the intensity of her hatred.

"Well, well, well, look what we have here," Beserkir said, unfolding himself from the floor. His back was to her, facing the treeline, but she would have recognised him anywhere.

She was so absorbed by her hatred, she almost didn't notice the figure that stepped out of the trees, but something made her drag her eyes off Beserkir. The tugging in her chest amplified at the sight of the faceless shadow.

A thousand spiders seemed to scuttle over her skin as the man stepped out of the darkness and into the light of the fire, walking towards Beserkir with the ease of familiarity.

"Beserkir," Keeran said in greeting.

CHAPTER TWENTY-FIVE

"Keeran," Beserkir threw his arms open in welcome, and the other side of Keeran snarled its dislike. "What brings you back to us, my friend?"

"Let's drop the pretence, shall we, Beserkir?" Keeran sidled closer, unperturbed by the Astraea moving in closer. "You're a raving psychopath, and the charm offensive's fooling no one."

In some ways, it would have been nice if Aelia had been here to see Beserkir meet his end, but Keeran couldn't risk her finding out that Beserkir knew him. It had worked out perfectly.

He'd spotted their camp soon after leaving to find her. If he could wipe them out before he tracked her down, he would eradicate any chance of her ever finding out about his association with them. And killing them might even be enough to get him back in her good books.

That might be pushing it, he admitted to himself. She was more likely to be pissed that he'd attacked them without her, but some things couldn't be helped.

"Such animosity," Beserkir tutted. "Is that any way to treat someone who's been as forgiving as I have? Who's overlooked so many of your little misadventures?"

Keeran's jaw clenched shut. The desire to rip the skin off the man in front of him, one strip at a time, was almost too much to resist. But he needed information first; Fenrir wasn't here, and he couldn't kill Beserkir until he'd found out where he'd been taken.

"We're even, Beserkir, I did what you asked of me."

Beserkir laughed, a cold, hollow thing.

"Even? You poor deluded soul, no, we're not even. Not even close." He smiled, his teeth flashing white. "How many is it we found you guilty of murdering?"

"Forty-eight, sir." A woman piped up from Beserkir's right. Keeran wondered if she kissed his arse literally as well as figuratively.

"Forty-eight." Beserkir shook his head, disbelievingly. "Of our finest veterans. You can't seriously have thought you'd walk away scot-free after giving us one little crumb of information."

"That crumb of information led to the deaths of more people than you accuse me of murdering." Keeran stalked forwards, not bothering to hide the rage that darkened his eyes. The monster in him snapped its jaws, eager for the taste of blood. "You never told me what you were going to do."

"Oh, don't delude yourself. You knew who I was when you came to me with information about Callodosis. You have our thanks for that one, though. Rounding up the humans can be such a messy business." Beserkir sighed at the difficulties of what he considered a good day's work. "It was so much easier to know they'd all be in the same place, at the same time. It made our job infinitely easier."

"I didn't know who you were," Keeran retorted with a snarl. "You told me you were an officer of the King's army, you never said anything about being the leader of the Astraea."

"But I am one and the same." Beserkir opened his arms wide, presenting his chest to Keeran with a proud smile. "Elder Beserkir, at the King's service."

"I know that now." The monster inside Keeran lunged, yanking on its leash as it goaded him into taking Beserkir out. "But I'd never have told you about the festival had I known who you were."

Self-loathing vied with his hatred of the man in front of him. He'd allowed Beserkir to trick him, to play him, and it had cost Aelia everything. Just one flash of fire would be enough to take out his comrades, then he could have his fun with Beserkir.

No. What if Aelia wanted to see the bodies? She didn't know about the fire magic yet, and presenting her with dozens of piles of smouldering ash wasn't going to help her trust him. He'd need to ease her into that one. He'd have to take them out the old-fashioned way, not that he minded.

Beserkir leant in closer, his expression suddenly hard and unyielding.

"You're forgetting you had no choice. It was help us, or face the noose," he reminded Keeran, with dark satisfaction.

It wasn't strictly true. When Beserkir had confronted Keeran, it had been an inconvenience, sure. But to hang him, they'd have to catch him, and that was never going to happen.

He'd had a choice. He could either have killed the man who claimed to be an officer of the king and risk drawing attention to the area, which would get in the way of the murders he was actually interested in committing. Or he could pretend to be under the man's thumb, feeding him seemingly harmless information about the Peregrinian's plans in Callodosis.

In retrospect, it was a stroke of genius on Beserkir's part. He knew how whole towns and villages came together for celebrations when the Peregrinians were in town, and knowing when and where meant he could swoop in with the knowledge that all the humans would be gathered in one place.

Keeran had made the wrong choice, and he'd carry the consequences with him for the rest of his life.

"I came because I wanted to understand," Keeran said, half truthfully. "You made me complicit in what you did. At least show me the courtesy of telling me what you're doing with the humans you captured."

"Arrested," Beserkir corrected. "We're arresting the humans on the King's orders. Then they're transported back to Llmera, where they are examined. If they pass that stage, they are shipped to Ideolanthea as part of the treaty the King has established between us and our volatile neighbours to the north. We give them our humans, and they allow us to stay out of their war. Be grateful, Keeran. Were it not for the King's ingenuity, we'd be across the sea in Mithrylaya fighting in their armies quicker than you could say 'genocide'."

Before Keeran could process this information, he was flooded by a wave of rageful terror, so powerful he almost swayed where he stood. Beserkir was still talking, but the noise was lost in the barrage of emotions coursing into him. It took him a few moments to realise they weren't his own.

Aelia. She was in danger.

He had no idea how the pair bond worked, and thus far, it seemed a temperamental thing, utterly uncontrollable. But he sank into the emotions pummelling into him, trying to feel something past them, to catch a glimpse of something, anything that might help him locate her.

An intangible force drew his eye across the clearing, just in time to see a shadow slink over the brow of the hill.

The other side of him dropped to a crouch, tail flicking in agitation. They knew that shadow, that was *their* shadow.

His heart turned cold, sending shivers of panic through his veins. How much had she heard? Keeran forced his eyes back to Beserkir, not wanting to draw any attention to where Aelia was making her escape down the bank opposite.

"You're right, sending them to Ideolanthea is the lesser of the two evils. I'll do anything I can to keep Demuto out of that war. What do you need from me?" Keeran lied, needing this conversation over as quickly as possible.

Beserkir smiled. "Rather them than us, right brother?"

Keeran forced himself to smile. He would come back and murder these bastards, but right now, he had to get to Aelia.

KEERAN STORMED AWAY FROM THE ASTRAEA, TREMBLING FROM the effort of not stalking right back and putting each and every one of them on the wrong side of the grass. His cheeks burned with the strain of smiling with Beserkir, saying anything that would get him out of there as quickly as possible.

His palms were clammy at the thought of what Aelia might have heard. The pair bond had gone cold, and he had no idea how to trigger it again. So, he jogged into the darkness, making sure he was well and truly out of sight before he Shifted and took to the skies. It was risky this close to someone with the ear of the King, but Keeran couldn't give a fuck. He had to find Aelia.

His wings beat the air, taking him high enough to survey the ground below. She had nothing with her, not even a saddle, but would she even return to the camp?

To his immense relief, she had. He spotted her tearing through the grass at breakneck speed, low over her horse's neck as she raced back to the speck of fire in the distance that marked their camp. He circled over her, too high for her to sense his presence, just in case she came off, but she made it back without any trouble.

He landed a safe distance away before sprinting towards the camp with every iota of strength he possessed. The muscles of his thighs bunched beneath him as he strained towards her, terrified she'd be gone before he got there. He almost sagged in relief when he rounded the corner of the ruined walls to find her buckling her pack to her saddle. She leapt out of her skin when she saw him, but her fear turned to hatred so quickly it almost stopped him dead. Almost.

"Stay the fuck away from me," she seethed, teeth flashing in the night.

He didn't listen. There was no way he was letting her get on that horse. Not before he'd explained himself to her. He was still several strides away and, seeing him making a beeline straight for her, she tried to swing herself into the saddle. He was by her side in a blur of movement, grabbing her thigh and pulling her back to the ground.

"No," he hissed. "You don't get to run off again. Not without hearing me out."

"Oh, I think I've heard enough, Keeran." She must have been pissed, because there wasn't even a hint of fear in her eyes, despite the unnatural black that had overtaken his. "You were an informant for the Astraea. You *told* them when to attack Callodosis."

He flinched at the venom in her voice, and she seized the opportunity to try and mount her horse again. He grabbed her arm and forced her to face him, knowing that if she left, she left for good. Something inside him cracked at the thought, fractures appearing in places he hadn't even known existed until he'd met her. If she left now, he knew they'd shatter into agonising shards that no amount of time would ever be able to piece back together again.

"I didn't know." He drew her closer to him, desperate to make her see. "You heard that too. I didn't know who he was or what he was going to do."

"You think that matters?" Aelia spat, leaning so close to him he could see her bloodshot eyes, the skin around them puffy from tears he hadn't been there to wipe away. That she hadn't wanted him to see. "Because of you, they knew exactly when to attack. If it wasn't for you, Mirra and Otis might not have been around when they arrived, and Fenrir might not be headed to Ideolanthea for gods only knows what."

"You can't hold me responsible for something I had no way of knowing," Keeran protested, the excuse ringing hollow even in his own ears. But he had to try, he couldn't just let her walk away. He'd been such a fool to think he could ever leave her, a delusional fool. He was hers from the moment he first laid eyes on her, undeniably and irrevocably.

"No? Remind me, why was it you had to help them?" Aelia shouted, with a sarcastic tilt of her head. Red was starting to creep up her neck as her anger boiled over. She wrenched her arm free from his grip. "Don't touch me, you fucking murderer. Forty-eight people, Keeran. And you have the audacity to try and convince me of your innocence?"

Her words stole the air from his lungs like a punch to the gut. He could do nothing but stare at her, chest heaving. He was everything she accused him of being: a murderer, a monster, a liar. He had no defence, not when it was a truth that had haunted him every day of his life.

She turned to put a hand on either end of her saddle, the leather creaking beneath her grip. She twisted her neck to look at him, and the loathing burning in her eyes crumpled any lingering hope he had. "As if the gods thought I'd accept a pair bond with someone like you."

A silver ring flashed in her eyes, very faintly, and only for a fraction of a second, but it was enough to stun Keeran into leaning back. It was all the space she needed to swing into the saddle, kick her horse into a canter, and disappear without a backwards glance.

Keeran didn't know how long he looked out after her for; any concept of time was lost on him as the consequences of the night picked at his sanity. The grasslands began to wake up around him in anticipation of the imminent arrival of the sun, the light turning from black to grey.

And still Keeran stood staring after her.

CHAPTER TWENTY-SIX

Aelia's first glimpse of Llmera should have been one of the most exciting moments of her life, and yet she couldn't muster the enthusiasm she knew the massive mountain that housed their capital city deserved.

The few days since she'd left Keeran had been torture, leaving her with too much time alone with her thoughts. Her masochistic subconscious had plagued her. It made her relive the horror of that night in Callodosis every time she closed her eyes, before replaying Keeran's conversation with Beserkir over and over again, all day long. And just to really piss her off, it hounded her with the memory of how Keeran had looked when she'd screamed at him, the way she'd seen something in him crumple.

So Llmera, if nothing else, presented her with the distraction she had been so desperately waiting for. The mountain stood in the otherwise uninterrupted horizon, a lone sentinel guarding Demuto, marking where the waves of grass gave way to the endless undulations of the sea.

It was a masterpiece of engineering, but the real wonder of the city could not be credited to any mortal power;

Mother Nature was the true architect. As a tidal island, the mountain on which the Dragons had built their capital city protruded from the ocean, commanding the attention of everyone Aelia shared the road with.

Initially, she'd been uneasy when it had started to become steadily busier, the tracks webbing across Demuto merging to form the wide stone road to the capital, but none of the merchants or tradesmen around her so much as looked her way. They were all too preoccupied with making it safely to the city, a note of apprehension hanging over them as they shuffled forwards, aware that their time to cross to the mountain was limited.

As the tide had withdrawn, it had exposed the stone road embedded in the soft sand of the seabed, linking the shoreline to the city. If they didn't cross in time, at best, they'd arrive in Llmera with wet boots. At worst, they would be swept away by the rising tide. Despite being unimpressed with the potential consequences for her, Aelia had to concede that it made for a stronghold which must have been unrivalled in its defensive abilities.

The ocean floor stretched indefinitely on either side, a strip of wet sand hugging the shoreline as far as the eye could see. The traffic into the city was slow-moving, which gave her ample opportunity to appreciate the world usually hidden beneath the sea. Aelia had no idea how many times she'd heard people marvel at the fresh air of the coast, waxing lyrical about the smell of the sea, but now she was here, she wondered what the hell they'd been talking about. The ocean was undoubtedly breathtaking, humbling her with its vast magnificence, but the cloying smell of fish and marine decay was not something she thought belonged amongst the many wonders it was credited with.

As she drew closer, the mountain loomed above her

imposingly. She'd grown up on stories of the Dragons of Llmera. Of how they had excavated it to create a multitude of tunnels, branching in a complex system from base to peak to form the Inner City, home to the wealthiest of the wealthy.

The rock that had been removed during the excavation of the Inner City had been used to build the enormous sea wall that ran the perimeter of the mountain's base. It seemed poetic that the sea defended them from assailants, and the wall defended them from the sea, like a guard dog kept safely outside the home.

The same stone had been used to build the Outer City, a crowded network of houses, temples, stables, and warehouses that sprawled up the mountainside. Aelia craned her head back to take in the buildings that seemed to have been thrown against one another with disorderly charm.

The density of the Outer City faded as it crept higher, the terrain becoming too rocky and sheer to support buildings past a certain point. Aelia ignored her protesting muscles for as long as she could, but eventually she had to right her neck before it got stuck that way.

The crowd on the road slowly shuffled around her as she rode forwards amongst the trading trains, carts, and people. Hundreds and hundreds of people. With rest tantalisingly close, she climbed up the winding road to the sea wall, finally coming to the main gates. The guards on either side of it were leagues apart from the one they'd seen in Drias. Their gleaming plated armour was immaculate and well-fitting, their expression was stern and alert, surveying every face that passed with unnerving severity.

Aelia guided her horse towards them, troubling them for recommendations for an inn. They supplied her with directions, which she repeated in her head a few times as she passed through the gate.

A flicker of pride stirred in her chest as she looked around the chaotic streets of Llmera. She had made it.

They stood in the lowest ring of houses and shops at the base of the mountain. The streets of the Outer City, the part of the city that covered the outside of the mountain, were heaving with people. She walked aimlessly for a while, listening to the cacophony, breathing in the city. Life surrounded her and after her few days in isolation, she relished it. The houses were simple but cherished; not a speck of dirt covered the walls. Nor did she see any beggars, not a single one.

Aelia examined the people as they walked. Most were simply dressed, much like those in her village, but occasional flashes of expensively coloured fabric caught her eye amidst the browns and greys. It seemed popular to walk around once Shifted, so Animals of all shapes and sizes crawled, loped, and flew down the streets.

Guards were everywhere, monitoring the crowds tirelessly. Massive Dogs roamed the streets, the Llmeran flag wrapped tidily around their neck. They were soldiers in the King's army, artemians in their second form with an unparalleled sense of smell, for which they were renowned across Demuto. They sniffed the air as they walked, detecting everything from which animal a person Shifted into, to what they had for lunch.

Aelia's stomach lurched. What would they make of her scent? She wouldn't have the scent of a human, she was sure, but how could she smell of an artemian if she didn't have a second form? Unsure, she decided to give them a wide berth.

The inn turned out to be infinitely nicer than the one in Drias, much to her relief, but she found out why when she came to pay for the room and stable. Whatever she had to do to free Fenrir, she needed to do it quickly, because anything more than a couple of nights would have her near penniless for the journey back to Callodosis.

So, she left her horse with instructions for him to be treated like royalty, the horse she'd inadvertently stolen from Keeran, and headed straight out on aching legs to find the docks.

ALTHOUGH QUIETER THAN IT HAD BEEN EARLIER IN THE DAY, Llmera still hummed with the energy of a capital city, with music wafting from closed doors alongside spiced scents that had Aelia's mouth watering.

The subtle smell of brine permeated the city, but it grew stronger as shops and restaurants gave way to the warehouses and grimy taverns that lined the streets leading up to the docks. Although it was still early evening, many people on the streets looked like they'd already seen the bottom of one too many tankards. Aelia resisted the urge to find the hilt of her dagger as their leering followed her down the street.

Aelia only slowed when she reached a break in the sea wall, the paved streets giving way to a dock full of ships being readied for the open water. Gulls soared between their masts, their sharp calls in harsh contrast to the soothing rush of the waves lapping against the rocks below.

A few were warships, proud and intimidating; some were preparing to transport the wares of merchants around the world; but most of the vessels looked as though they simply sailed the coast and returned with fish to feed the city. The smell was overpowering, clogging the air as the day's catch was unloaded, but Aelia was too wired to notice.

Somewhere in amongst the floating beasts before her, was a ship readying to transport humans to Ideolanthea.

Aelia swallowed the familiar nausea she'd been fighting since she'd heard Beserkir tell Keeran about the King's deal, to save the artemians from war by forsaking the humans. She had no idea what the ideolan would want humans for. All Ideolanthea cared about was their war, and the humans would make weak soldiers against the magic wielded in the Mithrylaya.

She'd spent the last few days praying to gods she didn't really believe in to let Fenrir still be in Llmera. If he'd already been shipped off to Ideolanthea, she doubted she'd ever be able to track him down.

Aelia stopped at the water's edge, leaning onto the handrail atop the sea wall with crossed arms. She looked out over the array of ships; she had no idea what she was looking for, but somehow she had to work out where they were keeping the humans.

Ships came and went, the black waters beneath them making Aelia's stomach churn as their hulls slipped silently through the waves, their sails tucked safely away. It took her a while to work out how they were heading so surely out to sea without any visible means of power, but when she saw a jet of water explode out of the ocean into the air, her mouth dropped open.

An artemian, in its second form, was dragging them safely out to deeper waters. Now she knew what to look for, she could see monumental shadows lurking beneath the surface, huge creatures of the deep ready to tow ships in and out of the docks.

Smaller marine creatures accompanied the fishing vessels, leaping and flipping out of the water in a way that brought a reluctant smile to Aelia's lips. She wondered what role the Shifted artemians played; whether they helped detect the fish, or perhaps even helped to guide them towards the nets. It was a different world; one she could have watched for days.

Aelia sat and dangled her legs off the sea wall, leaning her chin on her arms as she peered over the lower metal bar of the handrail. Minutes turned to hours as the cries of the men and women working the ships washed over her. Watching them work was bewitching, so vastly different from what she was used to in the forest, and yet the teamwork necessary made her think of her logging team with a pang of homesickness. They worked even as the sun set, loading and unloading until Aelia's back ached for them.

She noticed a constant presence amongst the chaos as the hours passed. A young woman in a perfectly pressed uniform Shifted frequently, flying from ship to ship on the black wings of a raven. She meticulously documented the contents on her ledger, searching every nook and cranny for contraband, unperturbed by the late hour.

Aelia watched with growing exhaustion, thinking of the overpriced bed waiting for her in the inn. Now she'd formulated something of a plan, her thoughts started to wander. They quickly got stuck on Keeran, as they so often did. Memories of the night she'd left him whirled round her head, starting with seeing him with Beserkir, flitting to the pair bond revelation, before landing on the way she'd found out…

The moment thoughts of being perched on that that wall in front of Keeran snuck in, she slammed down on them, forcing herself to focus on the clerk still flitting around the dock. The woman's work ethic was not to be sniffed at, and Aelia watched most other workers leave before the conscious clerk finally tucked her ledger into a black leather satchel and made to head home.

Aelia uncurled herself from the hard ground, her joints stiff and uncooperative after so many days in the saddle. Still, she hardly minded a little stiffness, not when she was still so relieved Keeran's 'tea' had eradicated her pain. She guessed she'd never know what he'd put in it, which was a damned shame because it was nothing short of miraculous.

After a few awkward steps in which her legs gradually agreed to function again, Aelia took off after the clerk, keeping enough of a distance so as not to draw attention to herself. Her nerves started to get the better of her, and she rubbed her clammy palms on her trousers, struggling to control the shallow gasps of her breathing.

If she was caught, she'd be flung straight into a cell for assault, and Fenrir would end up in Ideolanthea. But after hours of sitting up there, she hadn't been able to think of a better plan, no matter how hard she racked her brain.

So, when the woman turned onto a deserted street, Aelia picked up the pace and barrelled her into a dark little alleyway. The clerk was so petite she would have been knocked to the floor had Aelia not grabbed her, slamming a hand over her mouth to muffle the woman's predictable squawk of surprise. She was careful to keep the woman firmly facing away from her. Too pumped full of adrenaline to feel guilty, Aelia dragged her back into the shadows, easily overpowering her flailing attempts to get away.

"Stop struggling," Aelia panted in the woman's ear, sticking her dagger into her abdomen just hard enough to make its presence known. "If you tell me what I need to know, you'll be home in time for dinner. If you don't—"

Aelia pressed the blade in firmly enough to make the woman gasp, her breath dragging against Aelia's palm.

"Do you board all the ships that pass through Demuto's docks?"

The woman hesitated, and Aelia could have sworn she sensed the woman's surprise. After a brief pause, she nodded.

"Even the ones carrying the humans to Ideolanthea?"

This time, the pause was longer, but a nod still followed it.

"Do you know what's happening to them when they get there?"

She immediately shook her head.

"Do you know where they keep the humans before they're shipped out?"

Another nod. Aelia sucked in a relieved breath, getting a waft of the woman's floral perfume.

"I'm going to drop my hand now. If you scream, I swear to all the gods I'll put a hole straight through your spleen. Do you understand?" The woman nodded, trembling so hard that Aelia's resolve nearly shattered. But there was no going back now. She lowered her hand and breathed a silent sigh of relief when the woman stayed quiet.

"Good," Aelia said, to herself as much as the woman, swallowing down on the nerves that kept threatening to make her lunch reappear. If anyone peered into the alley, she was fucked. If the woman screamed, she was fucked. She gripped her shaking fingers more tightly around the hilt of her dagger. "Where do they keep the humans?"

"In a..." the woman tried to speak, but her voice cracked, her abdomen heaving against Aelia's restraining arm. "In a w-ware..."

Aelia's gut clenched as guilt coursed through her.

"It's okay. Take a second. Just breathe." Aelia scrunched her eyes closed for a moment, hating herself for doing this to someone. "What's your name?"

"R-rhea," she gasped, her breathing erratic.

Aelia tutted and sighed, wishing she could harden herself against the woman's obvious terror. Get in, get the information, get out. That had been the plan. But if she carried on, she was going to leave this poor woman traumatised.

"Rhea," Aelia said, resignedly. "I'm not going to hurt you. My friend was taken, and I just want to get him back. I'm not a murderer, I'm not a thief. Until a few days ago, I was just like you, just trying to get by."

"Your friend is human?" Rhea asked. She was still trembling, but her breathing wasn't quite so frantic.

"No," Aelia replied, a hard edge entering her tone, unsure why she'd be asking that. Was she a supporter of the Astraea?

"Then he'll be transported separately," Rhea said, appearing to have mastered some of her fear. "The humans are shipped out daily, but there aren't as many artemian prisoners, so they wait for there to be enough to fill a boat before shipping them out."

"Why ship them separately?" Did that mean Fenrir stood a greater chance of still being in Llmera? "When was the last shipment of artemians?"

"Artemians are logged as high-value cargo. They're shipped in better conditions than the humans to reduce the risk of fatalities on the journey." Rhea swallowed audibly, her voice still laced with terror. "There hasn't been a shipment of artemians for a fortnight."

"Where do they keep them?" Aelia swallowed the bile that rose at Rhea's words. She dreaded to think what conditions the humans were being kept in.

"In a warehouse, not far from the docks." Rhea didn't hesitate, the words pouring out of her now. "Well, it used to be a warehouse. The Astraea have kitted it out more like a prison now."

"You've been inside?"

Rhea shook her head. "No, I'm just a dock clerk. I don't have anything to do with cargo before or after it leaves the ship."

"But you know where it is?"

"Yes," Rhea breathed, her voice thick with horror. "Everyone does. They make no secret of what goes on in there, to scare the rest of us into submission."

"Looks like it's working," Aelia sneered, accusatorially. Rhea may just be keeping her head down to survive, but if more people had stood up to the Astraea, maybe things wouldn't have got so fucked up.

Rhea paused before answering. "You don't know what they do to us if we don't cooperate."

"Oh, I have a pretty good idea," Aelia said, darkly.

Rhea whimpered, her body wracked with another bout of tremors.

"Just tell me where the warehouse is," Aelia said hurriedly. She'd already spent too long talking, it was time to leave.

Rhea rattled off directions, repeating them word for word on Aelia's request.

"You better not be lying to me," Aelia lowered her voice threateningly. "Remember, I know where to find you."

"I'm not lying," Rhea said grimly.

Aelia could do no more, she had no choice but to believe her. She moved as quickly as she could, loosening her grip on Rhea and flinging her hood up in one smooth movement, before she spun and legged it out of the alleyway.

CHAPTER TWENTY-SEVEN

Keeran was about to storm into the alley when Aelia rushed back out of it, hood low, eyes downcast. He threw himself back into the doorway, obscuring himself in the shadows until she was far enough down the street for his heart to stop pounding.

If she saw him here, clearly following her, he dreaded to think what she'd do, but she'd been in the alleyway for such a long time, he'd started to think her ambush had backfired. Out of curiosity, he waited to see if the woman she'd targeted left the alley too. He was a little relieved to see her peek her pale face round the corner, look both ways, and scurry off down the deserted road. The last thing Aelia needed was more trauma to deal with, and he was glad she hadn't needed to kill the woman.

He pinched the bridge of his nose, exhaling away some of the stress of the last few minutes. The indecision had been torture whilst he waited for Aelia to reappear out of the alley. If he waited too long, he might be out here twiddling his thumbs whilst she was being hurt, or worse, but if he rushed in too quickly, then he'd reveal that he'd been following her for days now. It was a conundrum he had a horrible feeling would keep presenting itself.

With a gentle shake of his head, he pushed out from the doorway and went after the woman. He'd worked out what Aelia was doing whilst he watched her at the docks. The clerk was fastidious, checking every corner of every ship, so the chances were high that she'd have some information on the boats that shipped the humans out. It was a solid plan, Keeran conceded, so long as the woman hadn't lied or didn't go running to the Astraea.

So Keeran followed her, unseen despite the clerk's nervous glances over her shoulder. He longed for that uneasy feeling he had to be wrong, for the woman to go straight home and stay there, but experience had taught him to trust no one. So, he let her lead him through Llmera, climbing well away from the lower levels of the Outer City and up into a far more prosperous area. A sinking feeling settled low in his gut, his suspicions growing as the houses became far too expensive for a clerk to afford. She wasn't going home.

Music and laughter began to fill the air, the streets becoming busier despite the late hour. His stomach growled as the scent of spiced treats wafted from heaving restaurants, but there was no time to stop and savour it.

The woman stopped outside a huge stone building, the enormous front door framed by an extravagant, columned porch. A muscle twitched in Keeran's jaw as he saw the black uniform of the guards stationed outside it. He would recognise that uniform anywhere; she'd gone straight to the Astraea.

The clerk looked both ways, fingers white where they clutched the leather strap of her satchel, before making her way up the stone steps that led to the heavy wooden front doors. Keeran sighed, wishing he had better options available to him, but there was no way the woman could enter that building.

He flicked his attention to the part of his mind where his magic waited, jumping to action at his touch. He soothed it, guiding it towards the woman with such careful control that he forgot to breathe, his whole being focused solely on limiting the effects of his power. He willed the magic to life, just a quick flash of heat, perfectly aimed within the base of the woman's skull. She paused mid-step, blinked once, and crumpled face-first onto the floor, dead before she hit the ground.

The guards rushed down to her, turning her over and shouting for help. Keeran didn't know if they noticed the tendrils of smoke wafting from her nostrils, he was already headed back the way he came.

BEING BACK IN LLMERA BROUGHT HIM GREATER PLEASURE than he'd ever anticipated. This was his home, the city he'd grown up in. Admittedly, he'd spent most of his time in the Inner City, but just being back on the mountain had hit him with a warm sense of nostalgia.

He doubted he'd get to see the Inner City, which added to the deep, permeating sadness that had gnawed at him since Aelia had left. Even here, in the Outer City, he was risking too much just with his presence.

Every time Keeran sensed a Guard Dog, he had to hightail it in the opposite direction, out of fear of them catching his scent. It might be they were too young to have ever scented a Dragon, but there were plenty in the city who had been around when the Dragons had ruled.

Worst-case scenario, if they did recognise it, he was sure he could elude them for long enough to get off the mountain, but if he ventured into the Inner City, his chances of an inconspicuous escape were nonexistent.

Regardless, getting caught wasn't an option. Aside from the fact that he'd be the first Dragon to be seen in Demuto in decades, and the consequences of that weren't something he wanted to consider, he'd also have no choice but to leave Aelia if he was caught. So, he gave the Guard Dogs a wide berth.

The stone buildings that lined the streets were immaculate. The paving slabs on the streets were even and tidy, without a speck of grime or rubbish, and the plants that sprung up to climb over the buildings were artfully manicured. Llmera was somewhere people were proud to live, and the slobbish laziness he'd witnessed in Drias would never be tolerated here. Keeran remembered the sentiment all too well. His childhood may not have been a happy one in the typical sense, but he had always loved Llmera, had been proud and protective of everything it represented. Its beauty was unparalleled; nothing he'd seen elsewhere in Demuto had come close, and even now, he felt a deep connection to the city his ancestors had built.

Keeran caught up to Aelia easily, the combination of her scent and the pair bond guiding him to her. The bond had grown stronger since the night she'd become aware of it, with him getting flashes of emotion and even the occasional glimpse of her surroundings. That aspect of it was beyond his control, the connection temperamental and unpredictable, but the familiar tugging in his chest was a constant, like his own internal compass guiding him to her.

It took him a while to spot her, as she was standing inconspicuously in a patch of the street just out of reach of the overhead lamps, but when he did, his stomach lurched. Just as it did every time he lay eyes on her. He longed to go to her, to try to explain himself, but really, what was there to explain?

He'd hidden the truth from her, about what he was, about what was going on between them, about his involvement with the Astraea attack. He couldn't blame her for walking away from him, but he'd never forgive himself for not making sure she got back to Callodosis safely, and if that meant resorting to creeping around after her, so be it. He'd done worse.

Aelia surveyed the huge warehouse in front of her, taking in the small windows that peppered its tall walls, the guards leaning casually against the enormous doors that led onto the road. It was no different to the other warehouses that surrounded it, each building squashed between its neighbours in the typical Llmeran style. Space was a luxury few could afford on a mountain that had been crammed full for centuries.

And yet, despite its unremarkable appearance, there was no doubt that it was what Aelia had been looking for. The whole place reeked; of fear, of death, of sweat. He dreaded to think how many people were crammed in there.

Aelia wisely didn't stay long enough to draw attention to herself, choosing to walk a circuit around the building before heading back towards the inn. Keeran followed at a safe distance, breathing a sigh of relief when she entered the inn without venturing on any side quests. No city was completely safe at night, and if she was attacked, he'd have no choice but to reveal himself. Now she was safely tucked away for the night, the chance of him being put in that situation was next to none. Until tomorrow, anyway.

Keeran waited outside until he saw the light come on in her room, before venturing in himself. It had taken a little persuasion for the innkeeper to give him the room he'd wanted, but a full coin purse had been enough to make him move some of the other occupants around to give Keeran a room next to Aelia's. One of the good things about Llmera was that there was no shortage of wealthy artemians with full pockets, so Keeran had parted with the money all too willingly.

He ordered some food and took it to his room, not wanting to risk Aelia coming down and spotting him. He ate without noticing much of what was on his plate, his appetite having all but disappeared over the last few days, and kept his ear trained on the room next door.

There was hardly any movement, so he assumed she'd gone straight to sleep. He rubbed his own sore eyes with his thumb and index finger, all too aware how late it was. He pulled off his clothes and headed into the shower. It was hardly lukewarm, the log burners heating the water tank must need topping up, but he was just grateful to be washing in something other than lake water. He rubbed the soft towel over himself, tousling his hair dry the best he could before lying down on the bed. He sank into the soft sheets with a groan, grateful that Aelia had picked a nicer inn than the one they'd stayed at in Drias.

This was the closest he'd been to her in days, with only a thin wall separating them. The thought of her being so close was torture, sweet, agonising torture. His thoughts spun to the night that he'd slept with her in his arms, her cheek pillowed by his chest, and he loathed the moronic part of him that had pulled away from her, that hadn't seized the opportunity to spend every night with her cradled against him.

He would give anything, absolutely anything, to be in that room with her. He'd always been content on his own, but since she'd left, he'd been devoured by a loneliness that had burrowed into him, leaving him feeling hollow, like a part of him was missing.

He knew it was the pair bond, but he no longer resented it. The only thing he resented was himself, for ruining what could have been, for not grabbing it with both hands whilst he'd had the chance.

He reached for it, the sliver of connection he could sometimes feel between them, but there was nothing besides cold, empty space. Unless they accepted it, this was all it would ever be, a tenuous ghost of everything they might have shared had he not been so fucking stupid.

All of a sudden, it flickered to life, flooding Keeran with an onslaught of emotions that had him flying upright in bed, his eyes locked onto the wall between them. It only took him half a heartbeat to realise it wasn't fear that was coursing into him, far from it. His pulse ratcheted up, his lips parting in astonishment at what Aelia was feeling.

Just as quickly as it had hit him, the connection began to wane, but he gritted his teeth and sank his mental claws into it, straining with everything in him to keep the link between them open. To his immense relief, it obeyed, widening in his mind until he could feel her like he'd never experienced before.

CHAPTER TWENTY-EIGHT

Aelia was sick of feeling like this. Keeran had done something to her that night on the wall, and it had been all but impossible for her to ignore it. She didn't know if he'd flooded her with so many hormones that he'd permanently altered her brain chemistry, or if it was just a side effect of the pair bond thing, but whatever it was, she couldn't stop thinking about him.

She despised him for the lies, layering one on top of the other until she had no idea who the hell she'd been travelling with. He was just as much a stranger to her as he had been in Callodosis, only now he was the stranger who had led Beserkir right to her front door.

And yet, despite all that, every second, of every moment, was accompanied by the deep, yearning need he had awakened in her. She had tried her best to ignore it, refusing to give in to it, but here, buried in a cosy duvet... she couldn't help herself.

The soft sheets pressed against her bare skin and she closed her eyes, trailing her fingers lightly over her stomach, the sensation causing her abdomen to clench in anticipation.

She would allow herself this on one condition; under no circumstances would she think of Keeran. She would not think of what he'd done to her on that wall, the way it had plagued her thoughts every moment since, or how much she longed to see what else that other side of him could do to her.

Her fingers froze. No, she would not think about him, not now. This was to help her get him *out* of her mind, not allow him to worm his way deeper into it. She needed to get this out of her system. Now.

She slid her hand between her legs and groaned at how wet she was, the lightest touch of her fingers against her clit making her gasp and throw her head back into the pillow. She couldn't remember ever having been so aroused, despite, or perhaps because of the looming danger the following day held. Her whole body ached with a desperate need for release, and she couldn't fight it any longer.

Her fingers brushed gently over her clit, and she bit her lip to stop herself from crying out at the immediate pleasure that radiated through her. Why had she denied herself this for the last few days? It seemed so nonsensical now. What did it matter if he was the reason she felt like this? No one but her would ever know if she gave in to it, and surely something that felt this good wasn't something to resist.

A low groan escaped her as she resolved to do this all night if she needed to, her fingers leaving her clit to slip into her opening. Her walls clenched around her, desperate for more than just her fingers, and the thought of Keeran's cock rushed unprompted into her mind.

She worked her fingers into herself, adding a third to try and satiate the desperate need for more as she imagined Keeran pressed down on top of her, thrusting into her with enough force to send her mind whirling.

Her eyes flew open, and her lip curled in frustration. She

would *not* think of him. She forced herself to think of previous partners, to try and remember some of the more exciting moments she'd shared with them, but they paled in comparison to what Keeran had done to her. How he'd effortlessly given her the most bone-trembling orgasm of her life, as if that were just a taste of what he wanted to do to her.

Desire flooded through her at the memory of it, and her fingers took on a mind of their own, pumping into her with hard, delicious strokes. She remembered the way he'd read her body, his tongue exploring her every need whilst his fingers teased her pleasure to heights she hadn't even known existed. Suddenly, she didn't care that she was thinking about him, her mind turning to jelly as tension began to coil its way through her, desire washing away conscious thought until it was like he was there with her. His presence seemed to fill her mind, coursing into her in a way that had her crying out for more.

"Aelia," she imagined him growling, his voice reverberating through her skull.

"Keeran," she cried out in response, past the point of caring about the thin walls, oblivious to anything but the thought of him there with her.

"Wait for me, Aelia." An image filled her mind of Keeran's hand around his cock, her imagination working in overdrive as he stroked it from base to tip, the velvet head slick with his arousal.

Aelia moaned, her back arching as she slowed down. Her palm pressed into her clit with every thrust, but the thought of tasting him, of licking every delicious drop off him, was enough to send her spiralling. It took every ounce of self-control to slow her fingers, but even in her fantasy, Keeran's tone didn't allow for any disobedience.

The image flickered, but something inherent in her latched onto it, clinging to it, her teeth sinking into her lips with the strength of her desire to see more. His hand had gained speed, and his hips lifted slightly as if he were arching. Aelia panted as she watched the muscles of his forearm straining, the veins tracking up his arm popping, and she longed more than anything to have that hand back round her throat.

"Is that what you like?" his voice rumbled through her mind, sending a shock of pleasure shooting straight between her legs. *"Then, by the time I'm done with you, my hand will be the only necklace you'll ever want to wear."*

Aelia trembled, her chest heaving as his words sent her careening towards release.

"Please," she breathed, entranced as she watched him, her hand picking up speed to match his. She heard him groan, his ragged breathing awakening something primal in her, and she gasped at the intensity of the tension that started to build inside of her.

"That's it, ride your fingers for me."

She didn't need telling twice. She slammed them into her, deaf to her own cries, her attention fixed onto his as he pounded his hand over his cock.

"Come for me, Aelia, I want to feel you come for me."

His words tipped her over the edge, freefalling into an abyss of pleasure so deep she didn't know if she'd ever come out the other side.

"That's my good girl."

Aelia's back lifted off the bed, her body writhing with the strength of the orgasm that rushed over her, intensified as she watched him reach his own release. His pleasure somehow merged into hers in a way that had her vision exploding with blinding white light.

Time seemed to stand still, her control of her body whisked away from her, and all she could do was ride it out. It seemed to take an eternity to pass, and simultaneously be over all too soon. By the time she regained control over her senses, her mind seemed suddenly smaller, empty.

Aelia opened her eyes, finding herself alone in the room, her breathing steadily slowing. She swallowed, the usual afterglow of an orgasm fading all too quickly as she realised her imagination had run wild with her. It had all felt so real, so wonderfully, intoxicatingly real, but of course it couldn't have been.

She breathed a puff of air through her nose, feeling ridiculous. She turned onto her side to face the wall, rubbing her chest against the awful tugging feeling that refused to leave her alone. She tossed and turned for a little while, before wriggling closer to the wall. Only when she was pressed right up against it, was she able to finally fall asleep.

THE NEXT DAY PASSED IN A BLUR, WITH AELIA TOO NERVOUS about the coming evening to pay much attention to Llmera. She walked the streets in a daze, trying to take it in, but the thought of breaking into the warehouse had her fighting down her panic every step she took.

She had been a stone's throw from Fenrir, and there was no way she was going to desert him now, but that didn't make what she was going to do any less terrifying.

Time slipped by painfully slowly, but finally the sun abandoned the city and Aelia stepped out into the cover of darkness. She was completely unable to appreciate the buzz of the city, awake and vibrant around her. She jumped out of her skin at any sudden noise, and it was with some relief that she left the busier higher streets and descended to the warehouses nearer the docks.

When she was several buildings away from where they were keeping Fenrir, Aelia found the rundown warehouse she'd scouted the night before, ducking into a backstreet behind it. Several of the windows were smashed, the wooden frames rotting in the strong sea air. She stepped back as far as the narrow street would allow, checking to make sure she was alone before hurling herself forwards. Using all the momentum she could muster, she launched herself towards the window, her fingers reaching to grip onto the filthy ledge. Curling her lips back to bare her teeth, she hauled herself up until she was perched on the windowsill, crouching low as she checked once more that no one had entered the street. Confident she was alone, she dropped into the warehouse.

Her boots hit the ground with a thud that made her wince, but one quick look around confirmed what the outside of the warehouse suggested; no one had stepped foot in here in an awfully long time. A canopy of cobwebs stretched overhead, and Aelia supressed a shudder. Beams hung rotting and broken from the ceiling, and she heard the scurrying of rats as they fled the intrusion.

Her night vision had been ruined by the street lamps, but after a few minutes she felt confident enough to continue. She needed to get to the roof, but she pursed her lips as she saw the staircase on the other side of the abandoned space. It looked barely stable enough to support the rats, let alone her.

She cursed under her breath and made her way towards it, not having an alternative, and started to climb. She went up on all fours, so when two of the boards gave way beneath her, she was able to stop herself from falling to the stone floor with them. With a thundering heart, and enough cursing to make a demon blush, Aelia finally made her way up the precarious flights of stairs to the rooftop.

She had to shoulder the door open, flinging her whole bodyweight against it before it budged, but she was able to force it open just wide enough for her to slip into the cool night air. She breathed in a few delicious gulps, grateful to have not ended up buried under a pile of debris on the warehouse floor. Only then did she notice the view.

Llmera was beautiful, the lights of the city spread out over the steep mountain side, the stars winking down from above. The ocean was even more beautiful at night, a slice of the moon's light spearing through the darkened water, the waves appearing to fight off the celestial attack as they lapped against the silver rays. It gave her a moment of peace, the vast expanse of water making her problems seem insignificant, negligible. She allowed herself one more deep breath, inhaling what could well be her last taste of freedom, should she be caught, before turning to face the edge of the warehouse roof.

She was six buildings away from the one she needed, each one pressed tightly up against its neighbour, so in theory, she'd be able to leap from roof to roof without too much trouble. At least, that's how it had appeared from the ground. Standing at the roof edge lent a slightly different perspective to the situation, but she didn't allow herself to hesitate. With a running jump, she cleared the first gap, sprinting over to clear the next, and the next. She found herself grinning, her smile so wide it made her cheeks ache, and she had to stop the bubble of exhilarated laughter from rising out of her as adrenaline met relief in an intoxicating rush.

Aelia landed on the roof next to the warehouse she needed and ducked into the shadows behind the low wall that rimmed it. She could make out the darkened silhouette of a guard patrolling the roof, although patrolling was a generous term. He stood on the far left and appeared to be watching something happening on the street below. Aelia crept closer, waiting until she was almost level with him, before leaping to her feet, launching herself across the gap separating the roofs and hurling herself towards the guard.

Her dagger was in her hand before he'd even registered her presence, and she clamped her free hand over his mouth as she raked it across his throat. He thrashed in her grip, but she held on tight for the few moments it took for his legs to sag underneath him. She let him drop to the floor, patted his pockets until she found a bunch of keys, and used them to open the hatch that led into the warehouse.

The stench that hit her when she hauled it open was enough to make her retch. Sweat and excrement and disease; she'd never known anything like it. She buried her nose in her sleeve and climbed in.

She blinked past her watering eyes, desperately trying to make out her surroundings. She found herself on a set of basic metal stairs, at the bottom of which was a narrow corridor lined with barred cells.

As her eyes adjusted, she finally realised what she was seeing. She lowered her hand from her mouth, her eyes wide with horror. Each cell had so many humans crammed into it that they could barely all sit, let alone lay down. They were pressed up against one another, filthy and reeking, their sallow skin clinging to their visible skeletons. Some looked up as she walked down the corridor, trying to tread lightly as she passed, but others didn't even seem to register her presence.

A man stood up in one of the cells ahead of her, his eyes alert but wary. He was the only one who'd come close to acknowledging her, and she stopped in front of him. His gaze landed on the keys in her hands, and she held them out to him.

"I can't stay to help you, but if you get everyone out, there should be enough of you to overpower the guards outside." Her voice was barely more than a whisper, her throat constricted by the overwhelming despair she felt at seeing what her country had allowed to happen.

The man reached up and took the keys from her.

"I'll get them out," he said, his voice rattling in his too-thin chest. The others were stirring around him, hauling each other to their feet as whispered hope spread between them.

"Where are they keeping the artemians?" Aelia asked, looking round at the cells once more. There wasn't a single artemian amongst them.

"Downstairs." The man pointed down the corridor before setting to work finding the key he needed to open the cell door.

"Good luck," she whispered, meaning it with all her heart, before she turned and hurried away. She didn't know how the humans would ever make it out of Llmera, but right now, her priority had to be getting Fenrir out, and the humans were about to create enough chaos that it would be that much easier to smuggle him to safety.

She could hear the clang of cell doors being opened behind her, and she broke into a run, tearing down the corridor until she reached the stairs. She flung herself down them, two at a time, until she reached the ground floor. The smell was less horrific here, the cells nowhere near as crowded, and she ran between them, frantically searching for that one face she was so desperate to see.

The artemians were in much better condition than the humans upstairs, and they quickly began shouting and pleading for her help.

"Fenrir?" Aelia cried. The noise from upstairs was quickly becoming thunderous as hundreds of humans stumbled to various exits. She sprinted from cell to cell, ducking and peering to try and find him. "Fenrir?"

She ran around the entire warehouse floor without catching sight of him, and her chest tightened at the horrifying possibility that he wasn't here. The artemians were rattling the bars of the cells, pressing themselves against the cold metal as they tried to reach out to her, but Fenrir wasn't amongst them.

A door burst open, slamming into the wall behind it, and a stream of Astraea flooded in, their black uniforms sending a pang of cold dread lacing through Aelia. She backed up a couple of steps, ready to run in the opposite direction, when a door at the other end of the warehouse swung on its hinges and more Astraea swarmed in. They filled the warehouse, most disappearing up the stairs to the humans, some remaining to surround her. All too quickly, screams erupted from overhead, and Aelia closed her eyes against the unmistakable thump of beaten flesh.

A slow clapping echoed around the room, and Aelia's eyes snapped open again to see Beserkir walking through the open door. The artemians shrank away, their despondent cries fading to silence at the mere sight of him. He walked towards her with a humourless smile on his face, his hands still clapping a slow rhythm.

"Bravo," Beserkir said, with the same eloquent familiarity that haunted her dreams. He stopped clapping to point a finger directly at her. "We have all been so impressed."

Her blood ran cold, draining the colour from her face.

"To think, you followed us all the way from Callodosis, killed a unit of my men, lost me a cartload of humans, and planned on releasing countless more tonight." Beserkir spread his arms wide. "I'd have to be made of stone to not recognise such a remarkable feat of bravery."

"You give me too much credit," Aelia said, trying not to panic at how he knew so much. "I don't know anything about killing your men."

"Come now, this is not the time to be shy." Beserkir smiled, making Aelia's skin crawl. "I admit I probably wouldn't have remembered you from Callodosis until one of my men reminded me, one with a particularly good nose. He recognised your scent amongst the bodies of my soldiers, along with the scent of a male I'd seen just the night before. The same man who stopped me from killing you in Callodosis."

Beserkir's smile fell, and although he was still on the other side of the room, Aelia took an involuntary step back.

"I firmly believe it's important to acknowledge one's mistakes," Beserkir continued, "and letting you live was undoubtedly one of mine. But we cannot change the past, we can only take action to make the present more tolerable."

Beserkir snapped his fingers and, a moment later, a man appeared in the door. The Astraean dragged someone behind him, straining as he heaved the motionless body across the room to dump it at Beserkir's feet. It was only when Beserkir grabbed hold of it and hauled it up onto its knees that Aelia recognised it.

"Fenrir," she gasped. Her legs felt like they might give out from under her as she cast her eyes over her friend. The strong, capable man she had loved since she was a child was barely recognisable, lost beneath the swollen flesh that distorted his features. "What have you done to him?"

Aelia's anger rippled through her, stripping her of her fear. Fenrir was barely conscious, one eye completely invisible beneath the red, puffy skin around it, the other glazed and unfocused.

"Well, once we knew who you were, we remembered you'd been fighting with this one for the little human bitch." Beserkir shook Fenrir hard enough for his head to loll forwards. "So, it wasn't too much of a leap to work out that you were probably coming for him. I admit I perhaps let my temper get the better of me a little whilst we waited for you, but in my defence, you did royally piss me off."

"Not used to not getting your way?" Aelia tilted her head to one side and pouted. "Poor baby."

Beserkir paused, surveying her with cold, hard eyes. "No, I'm not, nor do I ever intend to be. You see, I'm lucky enough to have the King's authority to do exactly what I love doing. He wants the humans rounded up and shipped off, and I'm all too happy to oblige. All I ask for in return is a little freedom, a little room to play."

Beserkir drew his sword with his free hand and held it to Fenrir's neck, his eyes never leaving Aelia's face. He watched her closely, his lips curling in a smile as he saw the dread fall over her.

"You like games?" Aelia tried to control her breathing, to keep the fear from her voice. "Then come play with me instead. I'm the one you're angry with, not him."

"Oh, but I am playing with you." Beserkir touched the edge of his blade to Fenrir's throat, just enough to break the skin. The pain caused Fenrir to stir, his head raising on his unsteady neck to peer at Aelia through his one good eye.

"Aelia?" he managed to say, his jaw moving at an awkward angle where they'd broken it. The light in his eye when he recognised her broke her heart, a glimpse of the man she knew. She'd done this to him. In trying to get him out, she'd made everything ten times worse. Time seemed to slow as Aelia watched the blood drip from Fenrir's throat onto the floor. She tore her eyes from the red droplets that beaded down the edge of the steel to look at the man responsible.

"Let him go, and I'll do anything for you. I'll walk right onto one of those ships to Ideolanthea, I'll let you punish me however you see fit, but please, let him go. Please." She had no power here, and she knew it. She had nothing to bargain with, but if there was even the slightest chance she could save Fenrir, she was prepared to beg.

"No, Aelia," Fenrir mumbled, wincing at the effort of talking.

"Anything?" Beserkir asked, taking her by surprise.

"Anything," she agreed, knowing it to be true. She had nothing left to lose, this man had taken it all from her. There was nothing she wouldn't do to save Fenrir from him.

"And you won't fight me?" Beserkir narrowed his eyes at her, sceptically.

"Not if you let him go."

Beserkir pressed his lips into a line, watching her closely as he considered it.

"I prefer my first plan," he said with a shrug, and drew the blade clean against Fenrir's throat.

Blood poured out from the wide gash in his neck, bubbling out from his mouth to pour down his chin. Beserkir still held him upright by his collar, keeping him in place for Aelia to watch every agonising moment of his death. Her last friend on this earth, the last person she loved.

Something raw and vicious sparked inside of her, alien and yet inherent. Her rage was its kindling, her grief igniting a power in her she didn't know she possessed. Aelia sank to her knees and screamed, unleashing every pent-up emotion she'd been carrying with her since Callodosis. They exploded out of her in a torrent of anguish and agony, of loss and confusion, of heartbreak and fury. They burst out of her, throwing her head and arms back with the violence of their release, erupting from her in a blinding flash of silver light. It channelled out of her with a mind of its own, destructive and beautiful and hateful.

The light faded as quickly as it had appeared, withdrawing back into her, and her scream died with it. She dropped forwards onto her hands, with hardly enough strength to look at where Fenrir's body lay abandoned before her. Gasping for breath, she could barely process the destruction that lay around her. Half the warehouse was gone, the Astraea and artemians flung away from her in assorted heaps, some struggling to move, some obviously never going to move again. Some of the cages had burst open, and the artemians took their opportunity to run, stumbling through the rubble to the gaping hole in the side of the warehouse.

A pile of stone in front of her shifted and, to her dismay, Beserkir appeared from beneath it, struggling to push free from the debris. His eyes landed on her with a hunger she couldn't understand.

"You..." he said, laughing manically. "Oh, they'll be thrilled if I send them you. A hundred gold coins to the artemian who secures her."

Beserkir waved his dust-covered hand in her direction, grinning at her like a man possessed. Aelia twisted her neck to see a fresh wave of Astraea flooding into the building, and her heart sank. She tried to push herself to her feet, but whatever had just happened had wiped her out, draining her of every drop of energy.

She didn't understand what had happened, and there wasn't time to think about it. She pushed herself back on her heels and, with the last of her strength, pulled her dagger free. She would not allow them to take her alive, not if it benefited Beserkir, and she'd rather die than let them ship her off to Ideolanthea.

She pressed the tip of the dagger to her chest, took one last look at Fenrir, and closed her eyes.

"Aelia," Keeran's voice ricocheted around her skull, and her eyes flicked open in shock. *"Don't you dare."*

There, emerging from the hole in the warehouse, like a warrior of legend, was Keeran. He moved through the Astraea like a god, his blade singing as he whirled it through the air, and her broken heart stuttered to life at the sight of him.

He'd come for her.

Her arms were too weak to hold the dagger aloft any longer, her muscles trembling with the effort of staying seated, but she couldn't take her eyes off him. Blood sprayed from his sword in arcs as he cleaved his way through the Astraea to get to her, the controlled fury in his jet-black eyes triggering something deep inside of her.

He'd been in her head; she'd heard him, loud and clear. Her thoughts jumped to the night before, but were whisked quickly away again as Keeran skidded to his knees beside her.

"Can you walk?" he asked, peering deep into her eyes. Worry drew his brows together, despite the otherness looking at her from under them.

"Can you walk?" This time, he spoke right into her mind again, cupping his hand over her cheek. She shook her head, her tongue too thick and heavy to obey her.

He swept her into his arms, standing as if she weighed nothing, and carried her from the building. She clung to him with what little strength she had as he moved to hold her with just one arm, freeing the other to swing at the remaining Astraea, clearing their path.

Once they were outside, he hugged her close and ran. She bounced against him as they sped past the dark buildings lining the streets. Keeran dove down little side alleys she would never have spotted, taking them on a convoluted route through the city, but it made no difference. She could still hear the baying of Guard Dogs hot on their tails.

Keeran slammed his shoulder into a wrought iron gate, forcing his way into the courtyard garden that lay behind it. Trees filled it, their heavy branches forming a dense canopy overhead, with flowerbeds and benches tucked between the dark trunks. In any other situation, it would have been beautiful.

With her arms still wrapped around Keeran's neck, he sank onto the grass, hiding them behind the heavy foliage of the garden.

"You need to drink this," he said, using the edge of his sword to cut his palm before raising it towards her.

"No," she pulled away, disgust curling at her lips.

"Don't argue with me, we don't have time for me to explain." His eyes flashed black, and although it didn't scare her, the urgency in them made her listen. She looked down at the red line of welling blood that glistened on his skin. "Please."

He held it closer to her, and she sighed, finding enough strength to glare at him. It earnt her a small smile, cracking through what little remained of her animosity towards him. With a grimace, she lowered her head to his hand and placed her mouth over the cut.

The moment his blood touched her lips, she groaned, grabbing his wrist and pressing it harder to her mouth. She'd never felt anything like it, never tasted anything like it. Warmth coursed through her, the power in it making her skin tingle and her bones hum. The space in her mind seemed to expand, exposing a filament of light that felt wholly and unmistakably of Keeran. He was there, in her mind, tethered to her via a connection she'd never even known she'd been missing, and yet now couldn't fathom being without.

"That's enough," he said, huskily, gently teasing his hand from her. She let him pull away, but her tongue followed, stroking the length of the cut once more. She felt him groan, rather than heard him, the vibration travelling through him and into her.

Aelia blinked, amazed by the strength coursing through her, her brain suddenly clear again.

"Give me your jacket." Keeran slid back to give her room to move, his arm outstretched and waiting.

"Why?" she asked as she pulled it off and handed it to him.

"To confuse the Guard Dogs." He wrapped the jacket around his waist and stood. Aelia was on her feet beside him in an instant. She felt like she could run laps around Llmera. "You need to stay here."

The baying was getting closer, the Dogs leading the Astraea to where they were hiding.

"As if that's something I'd ever agree to," she snorted, shaking her head, but Keeran grabbed her by the shoulders.

"We don't have *time,* Aelia. I need to get them away from you. If they catch me, I can get myself out if I have to, but I don't know if I'll be able to get you out, too." He peered through the dense greenery to the street beyond. "You need to leave the city, as soon as the tide changes. Promise me?"

Aelia opened her mouth to argue, but Keeran's eyes blazed black.

"*Promise me?*" The words burned down that tether in her mind, and the desperation in them made her shut her mouth. She looked up at him with wide eyes as the pair bond stretched between them, weak and flickering, but undeniable. Before she could say anything else, Keeran crushed his mouth against hers and gravity shifted, the whole axis of her world seeming to veer towards Keeran with that one, hurried kiss.

The baying of dogs was nearly on them, so loud it sounded like they could have been in the garden. He tore his mouth from hers, ducked out of the gate, pulled it shut behind him, and was gone. She stood there staring after him, feeling like the most useless wretch to have ever wasted oxygen.

CHAPTER TWENTY-NINE

Keeran ran, his legs easily carrying him away from the baying hounds behind him. He kept his pace slow, making sure they caught up to him, that they got him in their sights before they scented Aelia hiding in the garden. He heard them round the corner, their baying picking up as they spotted him, and he picked up speed. He was still holding back, running no faster than a regular artemian, slow enough not to arouse suspicion.

He picked his turns carefully, taking him in the general direction of the busier part of the city, where the restaurants and taverns would be open and heaving until the early hours. He could still lose them, he could still get Aelia out. There were enough dark corners in this city for them to hide until the coast had cleared, even if they had to lie low until the tide was out. All he had to do was lose them.

The streets became steadily busier, the smell of alcohol and smoke wafting amongst the partying artemians. They didn't have time to move out of his way, but he didn't need them to. He skimmed past them, little more than a rush of air between his skin and theirs, before he was gone.

He heard the thud of music and sprinted towards it, picking up the pace until he rounded a corner and ploughed into a square crammed full of dancers. He skidded to a stop, apologising to the grumbling artemians he'd nearly slammed into, before edging past them deeper into the thrum of people. He dropped Aelia's jacket from around his waist and slouched his shoulders to help him blend in with the crowd, stooping so his head wasn't sticking out over everyone else's. He doubled back rather than going the obvious route directly across the square, positioning himself immediately next to a street vendor cooking skewers of meat. The succulent aroma made his mouth water. For a moment, he wished he could find out what the chunks of chicken had been marinated in, wondering if he could replicate it for Aelia, but the baying of hounds snapped his attention back to the present.

The crowd scattered as the Dogs charged into them, closely followed by the Astraea. They shoved anyone who wasn't quick enough to the floor and screams quickly broke out as people rushed to move out of their way. Keeran waited until they'd ploughed right past where he was hiding behind the strong-smelling meat, then ducked out and pushed his way back the way he'd come.

He broke into a jog to keep up with everyone else around him, his heart in his throat as he forced himself to keep the pace slow, but as soon as he was a few streets away, he broke into a sprint. He tried his best to follow the route he'd taken, trying to overlap his scent as best he could, just in case the Dogs came back this way.

When he was a couple of turns shy of the garden, he ducked into an alley. Breathing heavily, he risked a glance into the street. All was quiet, no one was giving chase, yet he couldn't shake the feeling that someone was watching him. He hung back, hugging the wall as he waited for guards to come tearing past. No one did.

Still, he waited. He couldn't risk leading them straight to Aelia

Aelia. The moment he'd seen the flash of light from inside the warehouse, he'd known it was her. The power of it had been electrifying, charging down the pair bond like lightning. Keeran dropped his head back against the wall, breathing heavily from both exertion and shock. He should have known Aelia wasn't artemian, he should have recognised it sooner. She couldn't Shift, was phenomenally strong, *and* they'd pair bonded. He closed his eyes as he remembered seeing the silver light in her eyes; he'd been so stupid for disregarding it.

Keeran pushed off the wall. This was no time for retrospection. He hugged the wall to peer around the corner, only leaving the alley once he was sure he had lost them, his gait much calmer than his erratic heartbeat.

Get her out, get her out, get her out, it seemed to pound.

The garden was only a few turns away, with no sign of an armoured pursuit behind him, and he felt a little of the tension ease from his shoulders.

Something caught his eye, and he jerked his head skywards to see a Bird circling over him. His heart sank into his boots. It was a mark.

He'd *felt* someone watching him and he'd just sat tight and waited. He cursed his stupidity as a band of soldiers rounded the corner. He turned back the way he'd come, only to find a second band closing in from behind.

There were no side streets, no exit points, nowhere for him to run.

Keeran looked at the sky and felt the lure of freedom it offered. Instinctively, he reached for the magic that hummed at the base of his skull, ready and waiting to transform him into the stuff of nightmares. The soldiers closed in, but it didn't matter. In mere moments he would wipe them all from existence like the insects they were before vanishing into the sky.

Then his chest tugged uncomfortably, and the magic stilled, his hand pressing to his sternum. If he Shifted now, the city would be on red alert, and the only road out would be closed off. Aelia would never get out.

The pair bond was silent, even when he reached for it, and for the first time, he wished they'd cemented it so it was less fucking unreliable. He would have done anything to have felt her, to know she was still safe.

In that moment, brief as it was, his mind was made up. Without a shred of remorse, he let the magic slip from his grasp.

And then they were upon him.

He didn't draw his sword. No mortal man would be able to kill so many soldiers, and that's what he must be in their eyes if Aelia stood any chance at escaping—a mortal man like any other. It didn't mean he was going to go easily though.

A grim smile played on his lips as he dropped to a crouch.

THE GUARDS DID THEIR BEST TO RESTRAIN HIM, AND FOR THE most part, he let them, allowing them to take him to the main gates of the Inner City for the relatively meagre price of a little payback.

"Pack it the fuck up," the guard to his immediate left said, his voice notably more nasal since Keeran had head-butted him square on the nose.

"Make me." Keeran grinned through the blood on his own face, not all of it his.

They'd put him in manacles, so tightly bound in front of him that his wrists screamed every time he moved, but he couldn't resist having a little fun. The guard snarled and went to ram a gloved hand into Keeran's stomach, but he came a little too close, just enough for Keeran's knee to slam into his groin. The others holding Keeran yanked him roughly back by his manacled wrists, his hands threatening to fall off altogether, but he forced himself to smirk through the pain.

"Ah, don't worry too much, it's not all that bad," Keeran said as the guard doubled over, groaning. "Now you have a matching pair, a squashed nose and a squashed—"

Keeran saw the fist coming from his right, but he let the punch land. A mortal man wouldn't have been able to avoid it, and so, as far as these idiots were concerned, neither could Keeran. The guard who had thrown it smiled smugly, though the gap Keeran had created between his teeth ruined the effect somewhat.

"How's that for making you?" he leered. "Now fucking walk." He shoved Keeran, knocking him forward a few steps.

"Would be a whole lot more impressive if you could say it without a lisp."

Keeran did walk, though, escorted by his whole bleeding entourage through the gates and into the tunnel to the Inner City.

A small part of him was elated at being taken into the belly of the mountain. He hadn't expected to see the Inner City whilst he was here and the thought of laying eyes on his home, his true home, set something ablaze in his chest.

What he didn't understand was why they weren't taking him to Llmera's commoner's prison; to the cells that dimpled the mountain peak like a well-made Gouda, only nowhere near as savoury. They couldn't know what he was, no fool would have sent so few men to bring him in if they did, so where were they taking him?

They reached a blockade of guards that had never been necessary when the Dragons ruled. It appeared that the new

King liked to keep the Inner and Outer City divided, however. They were let through with a few raised eyebrows at the state of the guards escorting him. Keeran smiled, a dark, cruel thing, and they quickly averted their eyes.

The tunnel, polished and beautiful as it was, became more so with each passing step. Columns erupted from the floor, each with a colossal dragon perched atop it, supporting the weight of the mountain on their backs whilst their outstretched wings connected tip to tip to form the vaulted ceilings. Keeran walked between them and felt his pride awaken, ugly and demanding, as he was reminded of all his ancestors had been. Walking obediently in the shackles of mortals wounded that pride, and the beast it belonged to snapped at his control, urging him to kill them all for their insolence.

The statues glared at him from their posts, but he ignored them, just as he ignored the Dragon within him. Aelia had to have a chance to get out; once she'd had time to leave the city, he could make his escape. Until then, until she was safe, he would play the prisoner.

The moment Aelia crossed his mind, the beast within him settled, and with far less resistance than he was used to. Keeran huffed a breath through his nose. The pair bond wasn't even formed yet, and there it was, tamed into behaving itself by one fleeting thought of her in danger.

The tunnel opened into the enormous chamber that formed the main portion of the Inner City, tiered and sprawling and glorious. Every single building was one with the stone, bricks flowing into the rock face as if Mother Nature had created them herself, each one as magnificent as the last as they spiralled around the mountain's largest cavern. By day, light would pour from channels that allowed access to the surface, some of them Keeran himself had flown through all those years ago, but the Dragons were not ones to accept the limitations of the sun's benefaction.

The Inner City at night was exactly as Keeran remembered, with every inch illuminated by flames. It flickered in the open mouths of the dragon statues that balanced on every corner of every building, a testament to the mastery the Dragons had over fire. The statues drank the oil the Dragons had invented, their bellies filled with it every day by designated servants so that Llmera never had to sleep. Even the plants that climbed over almost every surface had come alive in the absence of the sun, glowing lights streaking through the dense foliage with ethereal bioluminescence.

The vibrancy of the city hit Keeran with a shock of nostalgia, and he would have given almost anything to stop and take it in, just for one moment. Music and laughter and the smell of food he hadn't dared to remember filled the air around him, the best parts of home so nearly within his grasp.

The guards had other priorities though, and he was shoved roughly on. They tried to keep him out of the way of the artemian aristocracy, lest the sight of him offend their more delicate sensibilities. They might not have seen much of him, but he saw enough of them to realise the city wasn't the only thing that hadn't changed.

He had always hated the superiority the people of the Inner City wore, and he could see it still, the condescension draped over them like another layer of their self-indulgent clothing. Fortunately, he didn't have to look at it for long.

Dragged, jostled and pushed, he was taken via the backstreets to an innocuous townhouse. Tall and towering, it bled into the cliff of the cavern, no doubt extending far back into the depths of the mountain. It was into this that Keeran was finally deposited, the old guards handing him over to the new with a word of warning. Rather unnecessary, Keeran thought, as he watched them limp away, each of them bleeding from one orifice or another.

He had already had his fun though, and he went quietly with the wary-looking replacements, more interested in where they were taking him than the guards themselves. The marble floor gleamed in the light cast by the chandelier in the hall, and a wide staircase swept up and around to meet the galleried landing that loomed over them. This was not his to explore though, as he was taken through a comparatively ordinary-looking door tucked into the far corner of the entrance hall.

The humble doorway turned out to be entirely misleading. Despite being far from the most grandiose aspect of the hall, it turned out that the reception room behind it housed one of the most powerful men in the country.

Keeran bit back a snarl as he came face-to-face with Beserkir.

CHAPTER THIRTY

It was only through years of careful practice that he managed to control his expression, fixing his face into hardened neutrality.

Beserkir had no such inhibitions. On the far side of the room, he leant against one of the most ostentatious desks Keeran had ever seen, smiling like a spider that had just caught something in its web. As ridiculous as it was, the desk wasn't out of place in the room. One quick sweep of his eye was enough for Keeran to realise what Beserkir lacked in taste, he made up for with money.

After ascertaining that the guards behind stood between him and the only exit in the room, Keeran finally slid his attention to the man who so clearly wanted to be the centre of it.

Beserkir had cleaned himself up from the incident in the warehouse, changing into a well-cut suit that highlighted the broad sweep of his shoulders, but the grazes on his face belied his less-than-savoury day job. Irrespective of the marks Aelia had left on him, Beserkir was as impressive in the study as he had been before the backdrop of his burning victims in Callodosis. He had the air of a man who was used to being the most imposing person in the room.

"My old friend," Beserkir started, his voice as slippery ever. "I'm sorry to have dragged you here so unceremoniously, but patience has always been a virtue I've struggled with."

Keeran remained silent, giving him nothing.

"I would offer you a drink, but I'm told you can't be trusted to behave. Rather an animal, apparently." Beserkir tilted his head to peer at Keeran down his nose.

"The country really has gone to the dogs if one of its Elders is too much of a coward to give a man in chains a drink," Keeran said, raising one dark brow.

One of the guards pushed him hard enough that he fell to his knees. Pain lanced through them as the bone slammed into the hard marble.

"That won't be necessary, but thank you," Beserkir cautioned, shooting the guard a disparaging glance. He pushed himself off the table and took several slow, deliberate steps closer, stopping just out of Keeran's reach. "Now, I think you're confusing cowardice with practicality. It took me far too long to get free of all the dirt after my run-in with your little friend, and I have somewhere I need to be. So, for now, we must keep this civil." He slipped his hands into his trouser pockets. "Funny you should mention dogs though…"

Beserkir jerked his head and Keeran heard a door open behind him, followed by the gentle click of claws on marble as a Guard Dog padded across the room to stand beside his master.

"This fine young man tracked you all the way from the abandoned corpses of the soldiers you and your friend saw fit to murder."

Keeran's mind reeled. They'd been tracking them this whole time.

"I don't know what you're talking about," he replied, keeping his voice calm.

"Oh, sure you do." Beserkir crouched closer. "By the lakes. My soldiers all murdered, the humans released and only two other scents mingled into the mix. Yours was one of them, of that I'm sure. My Dogs don't make mistakes."

"I hate to ruin their track record, but it would seem they're not as infallible as you want to believe." Keeran let a little of the cruelty in him shine in his eyes. "I insist you give credit where credit's due. It was me who killed your little soldiers, each and every one of them, and trust me, I didn't need any help."

Beserkir's smile widened. "Oh, bravo. I had hoped you two were close. I was rather depending on it actually, so thank you for confirming my suspicions. We know she was there, there's no point in lying. What we didn't know, is what she was." Beserkir tilted his head, searching Keeran's face. "Do you?"

Keeran couldn't help the muscle that twitched in his jaw. It was all he could do to stop from ripping free of the manacles and tearing Beserkir's head right off his smarmy body—but he had to play along to give Aelia time to escape. For the hundredth time, he strained into the space where the pair bond sometimes was, but he was met with nothing but silence.

Beserkir laughed and Keeran's lip curled as the sound scraped down his spine. "Maybe you do, but from what I saw earlier, I suspect she doesn't. Am I right?" Beserkir opened his hands expectantly, before grinning at whatever truth he read in Keeran's expression. "I thought as much. The trouble I have now is that my friends in the North, the ones who are so very grateful for our two-legged contributions, would pay more than you could possibly comprehend to get their hands on her.

"Now, catching you is still a win. You are the lesser prize, admittedly, but you did still murder my men, and that can't go unpunished. Usually, such a crime would warrant a public execution, which our prisoners usually end up begging for after a little time with some of our more creative prison guards, but today I am feeling unusually magnanimous. I will offer you your freedom, right here, right now. All you need to do is tell me where the girl is."

The beast inside him crouched low, seething quietly with a predator's patience, a spring coiled and ready for the moment it was safe to pounce. A slow smile revealed the sharp points of Keeran's canines as he relinquished a little control, letting a hint of the beast show. The Dog beside Beserkir whined softly and backed up a step, leaving its master to face the brunt of Keeran's focus.

"If you touch her, I'll finish what she started and crush every bone in your body. One at a time." The calm in his voice was laced with violence, every word spoken by that darkest part of him.

"Oh, I plan to do far more than touch her. Revenge is a dish best served in many courses, and I have had plenty of time to plan all the ways I'll make her suffer." A little colour had drained from Beserkir's face as Keeran had spoken, but otherwise his cockiness remained unscathed. He waved at someone behind Keeran, and he heard the door open once more. Three more Guard Dogs entered the room.

"Her scent has already been found in the Outer City, and I have no doubt that my most experienced…"

Beserkir was cut off as one of the Dogs, one with grey around its muzzle, Shifted the moment it reached his side.

"Sir." The guard jerked his head, requesting a private audience. Beserkir leant closer to hear the whispered message, clearly unimpressed at the interruption. Keeran strained to hear, every sinew in him ready to react at the slightest provocation.

Beserkir was still for a few long moments after the guard pulled back, his face tilted away from Keeran, but when he turned, that smile was back in place.

"Well, get out and see to that at once. Now." Beserkir shooed the four Guard Dogs out with bored impatience. Only when the door swung shut behind them did he allow his eyes to settle back onto Keeran. He sighed, a slow, exaggerated thing.

"It appears I won't be making it to my function after all." He turned and bowled his way to a cabinet on the far side of the room. Crouching low, he rummaged in its depths before standing once more, whatever he was doing concealed by his broad back. "I think I will risk having a drink with you. Perhaps it'll soften that temper of yours."

"You know as well as I do I won't be drinking that." Keeran raised an eyebrow at Beserkir as he crossed the room with a crystal glass in each hand.

"Oh, my friend, what would be the sense in poisoning you? You have information I need." Beserkir didn't hesitate as he came within arm's reach of Keeran, a glass held out for him to take. Keeran didn't so much as glance at it.

Beserkir stared at him expectantly, so close that he could see a droplet of blood at the edge of one of the deeper cuts on Beserkir's forehead, so close that Keeran only just had time to block the glass that came flying at his head. The guards were on him a fraction of a second later, pinning him as Beserkir's sleeve covered his mouth.

Keeran roared and flung himself backwards, loosening the guard's grip enough for him to send his chained fists up into Beserkir's abdomen.

The Elder grunted but held his ground, keeping his sleeve firmly pressed over Keeran's mouth.

The room started to spin, colours leaking where they shouldn't as lines blurred in and out of focus.

"Besides, I don't need you to drink anything for me to drug you," Beserkir managed to say as Keeran flung one last blow his way. He couldn't tell if it made contact, he couldn't tell if his arms even moved. He fought whatever drug was coursing through his system, fought it with everything he had.

He was unconscious before he even hit the floor.

CHAPTER THIRTY-ONE

Aelia waited in the garden as the baying of the Guard Dogs drew close again. They'd been circling the area relentlessly and it was only a matter of time until they found her, but she had no idea how to escape with them so close. The buildings that backed onto the garden were all secure, and she wasn't a capable enough climber to shimmy up the narrow windowsills and drainpipes that led to the roof.

She was trapped. Panic gave way to despair as she whipped her gaze around the small garden, desperately looking for a way out. She reached to touch her fingers to the bark of a nearby tree and tears welled in her eyes, spilling before she could stop them. She collapsed against the tree, pressing her forehead into the trunk and closing her eyes. She envisioned herself back in Callodosis, Otis in their tree-house, Fenrir and Mirra safe and bickering somewhere nearby. She breathed in the scent of the bark, knowing it was likely the closest to seeing her home again she would ever get.

She shouldn't have left, she shouldn't have tried to save Fenrir. All she'd done was make things worse. If she'd just stayed home, Fenrir would still be alive, and Keeran wouldn't have a target on his back.

Keeran. He'd saved her, again. Shame squeezed more tears from her eyes, her mouth hanging open with her silent cries as she banged her head against the bark. This was all her fault.

He'd been right about her. She was stubborn and selfish and wouldn't listen, insisting on doing this on her own. If he'd have been there, he could probably have saved Fenrir, but she'd been too fucking stuck up to hear him out.

How dare she judge him, when she was ten times the monster he was? How many had she killed back there? How many artemian prisoners had she seen lying mangled and broken after her outburst? She had no idea what had happened, what kind of magic that had been, but right then, she loathed herself too much to care. She guessed it was part of the pair bond, just another surreal twist of magic that she didn't understand. Like how he'd spoken to her in her mind, how she kept feeling these uncontrollable flashes of him, like how his blood healed her. She huffed a humourless laugh. At least she knew what was in the suspiciously pink poultice now. And the tea.

"I know Callodosis is full of tree huggers, but I think you might be taking it a bit far."

Aelia spun to face the low voice, blinking through her tears at the tall figure lurking in the darkness. At first, she didn't believe what she was seeing. He was a ghost from her past, someone she thought she'd never see again. She'd thought she'd never see anyone from home again. Her eyes lingered on the uniform, the armour, the red royal insignia on his breastplate, and her lips pressed into a hard line.

"Shiva," she gasped, stunned.

"Hello, Aelia," Shiva said, quietly.

It only took her a second to remember what he'd done.

"You joined them," Aelia snarled.

Shiva held his hands up imploringly. "I made a mistake."

"You filthy, traitorous bastard," she seethed, taking a step towards him. "They murdered everyone in cold blood, rounded them up like animals, and you *joined* them."

"No. Yes," he stammered. "No."

She lunged at him with teeth bared and shoved him in the chest, hard. He staggered backwards.

"Aelia, listen!"

She had never liked him. He had always been arrogant and cocky, letting his apex predator get the better of him, but this? She shoved him again, anger blurring her thoughts until she could only think in red; in the red of the flames feeding on the ones they'd burned, in the red of the blood they'd spilt in the clearing, in the red of the insignia he wore on his chest.

"Bastard," she hissed and drew her dagger, swinging it at him with a snarl. He was quick enough to block her, but he didn't attack back.

"Aelia, stop," Shiva pleaded, but she barely heard him over the blood roaring in her ears.

Again, she swung, and again he blocked. Over and over, until she had him backed against the wall with her blade against his neck.

Rage boiled inside her; all she could see was Mirra's face when he'd shouted at her. When he tainted her last day in this world with those vile words. Blood appeared at the tip of her blade as she snarled at the memory, the steel pricking his throat.

"They caught Keeran," Shiva gasped, his hands held by his head in surrender. "I came to help you."

Her eyes sliced to meet his, terror tainting the anger she was hiding behind. They'd caught Keeran. He'd tried to lead them away from her so she could escape, and here she was, just as trapped as he was.

"Why would you help me?"

"I can't work for them anymore," his voice cracked, the desperation breaking through. "I had no idea what they were capable of until it was too late."

"Beserkir made it pretty fucking clear, Shiva. What part of his wanting to cleanse Demuto didn't register?" she spat sardonically.

"I know." Shiva gulped past the steel at his throat. "It was only after they started attacking everyone I knew how fucking stupid I'd been. I can't sleep, I can't eat… that night will haunt me for the rest of my life."

"That makes two of us," she sneered, but she pulled the dagger back an inch.

"I just want to go home," Shiva choked out. "But how can I face my family with everything I've done? If I can get you out of here, at least there will have been some point to all of this."

The cries of the Guard Dogs broke through the silence and Shiva twisted his head towards them.

"We have to leave. If they catch us, we'll both be on the next boat out of here," Shiva said, his pupils wide with fear.

"I don't trust you," Aelia snarled.

"I know," Shiva bit his lip, gaze flicking between her and the street, the sound of barking getting steadily louder. "But you can't get him out on your own."

Aelia sucked in a breath. Keeran's words echoing round her skull, mixing with Shiva's. All the times she'd refused his help, she'd failed. Years of trying to be good enough, trying to prove herself just as capable as any artemian, and when it really mattered, she'd failed. She was as useless as they'd all believed her to be. She couldn't let her stubbornness cost her

Keeran, too, and Shiva was right, she couldn't get him out on her own.

Aelia reluctantly stepped back, letting her dagger drop to her side.

"How do we get out of here?" she asked, her voice cold.

Shiva breathed a sigh of relief. "We need to make it to the sea."

Aelia barked a humourless laugh. "And how do you propose we do that?"

The Dogs' barking was almost on them.

"We run." Shiva grabbed her wrist and broke into a sprint, dragging her with him through the iron gate and onto the lit street.

Aelia tore her arm free from his grip but kept pace beside him. Any trace of her earlier weakness had disappeared, her legs buzzing with energy from Keeran's blood as she pounded after Shiva.

There was every chance he was leading her straight into a trap, but at least with him, she stood a chance. Alone, she'd never make it, not least of which because she had no idea which was the quickest way to the sea. Downhill, sure, but unless she made it to the docks, she'd just find herself trapped between the hounds and the sea wall. So, she followed him as he took turn after twisting turn, gravity lending them speed as they ploughed down the steep streets, the scent of brine growing steadily stronger.

She began to recognise where she was and her heart skipped in her chest as hope lent her legs another burst of speed. Shiva was struggling next to her, his second form built for short bursts rather than endurance, so she grabbed his arm and half dragged him towards the docks.

The baying of Dogs picked up behind them, but she didn't dare turn to look. Shiva cursed beside her, his breath coming in ragged gasps.

"Nearly there," she panted, her lungs burning. *Nearly there.*

She chanted it to herself in time with her frantic breathing, willing them to make it. They skidded round a bend and Aelia nearly whooped when she saw the fragmented light of the moon reflected in the sea, the skeletal masts of the great ships protruding from them like the emaciated limbs of great beasts.

"Where now?" Aelia wheezed, slowing slightly.

"We...jump," Shiva managed to say past his desperate breathing.

"Gods, Shiva," Aelia grumbled, tugging him towards the harbour. "If we survive this, you have to start doing some cardio."

She turned as they made it to the water, just in time to see the shadows of the Hounds charging round the corner. She jumped, her feet hitting the water a fraction of a second after Shiva's. The water sucked her in, rushing over her head. She resisted the urge to burst back up, instead swimming alongside the slimy stone harbour as far as her straining lungs would allow. When they eventually threatened to take matters into their own hands, she slipped her head above water and took a deep gulp of air before submerging herself once more.

She could feel Shiva brushing against her as he followed. At least she hoped it was Shiva. She suppressed a shiver, trying not to think of the creatures she'd seen in these waters just yesterday. They kept swimming, coming up for air as quietly as possible as they navigated their way to the edge of the harbour, where the enormous wall sprang out of the sea to encircle the city.

Aelia pushed herself into the corner where the two structures met, clinging to the wall as the waves gently lapped at her, sucking her out just to push her back in again. Now she was in it, the ocean felt like a living creature, with an alien sentience that made her skin crawl. The sooner they could get out of it, the better.

"What now?" she whispered, nearly choking on seawater as a wave forced itself into her open mouth.

Shiva put a finger to his lips, before pointing at an enormous hole in the sea wall. A trickle of water flowed from its open maw, and Aelia looked from Shiva, to the hole, and back again.

"The *drains*?" she hissed, suddenly filled with immense regret for trusting him.

Shiva just slammed a finger back to his mouth, his head jerking angrily to where the Astraea were searching the docks, the Dogs whining at having lost their scent. Aelia huffed through her nose, keeping her lips pressed firmly shut against the salty water. He didn't wait for her to agree, he just took off towards the hole, his arms slipping silently through the waves.

Aelia glowered after him, wishing to the gods she had another choice, any other choice, but to follow him.

AELIA CURSED SHIVA FOR WHAT FELT LIKE THE MILLIONTH time in the last hour. The drain was vile, filled knee deep with the city's waste, and even breathing through her mouth hadn't been enough to stop her from vomiting at the smell.

So here she was, lost in a network of tunnels she wasn't utterly convinced Shiva could navigate, covered in countless people's excrement *and* her own vomit. Right at that moment in time, she wasn't sure if she'd rather be on a ship to Ideolanthea.

"Will you stop moaning?" Shiva said, shooting her an

exasperated look. "You think I'm enjoying this any more than you are?"

Aelia snorted. "You belong here, just as much as every other piece of shit we're wading through."

Shiva stopped and spun to face her, the brown water splashing around his knees.

"I don't need to be here, Aelia," he reminded her with a snarl, their surroundings seeming to have worn away at his earlier remorse. "I could very easily leave you to rescue your friend on your own."

Aelia averted her eyes and waded past him. His sigh echoed off the circular stone walls, but she heard him start to slosh towards her.

"Did you know Fenrir had been taken?" she asked, after a while.

Shiva hesitated before answering. "I was going to get him out, that was always the plan. He didn't trust me when I told him as much, but I swear I was waiting for the right moment for us both to make a break for it. That's the only reason I stuck around." His voice darkened. "Then Beserkir found out it was someone from Callodosis who'd killed his men by the lakes, and he worked out the connection between you and Fenrir. The next thing I knew, Fenrir had been taken from the warehouse. You know the rest."

Aelia's lower lip trembled and she shut her eyes against the prickle of tears, grateful Shiva was still behind her and couldn't see. She'd been so foolish to think she could help; if she'd just stayed in her little hole in Callodosis, Fenrir might have got free. How egotistical had she been to think she could do anything of any worth? She was nothing, she had always been nothing, and she'd got Fenrir killed trying to prove otherwise.

"I'm sorry, Aelia," Shiva said quietly. "They're monsters."

"And they're working for the King." Aelia slowed down to

let him catch up, having regained control of her expression. "How did that even happen?"

Shiva shrugged. "The King's scared of the ideolan. Aren't we all?"

"But what do they want with them?"

"I honestly don't know." Shiva sighed, looking as exhausted as she felt. "I don't even know how we could stop it."

"There must be people working against the Astraea? There must be some kind of push back?" Aelia sounded almost pleading, even to her own ears.

"Beserkir has the Astraea *and* the King's Guard at his disposal. I don't know how anyone could fight against that."

"No, me neither," Aelia admitted.

"Look, this Keeran guy, do you know he worked with Beserkir?"

Aelia shot him a look of surprise; she'd considered that Shiva might know about that.

"I know a little," she said hesitantly, wanting to hear what Shiva had heard.

"Do you know he was arrested by Beserkir for murder?" Shiva raised his eyebrows at her. "Multiple murders."

"Yes," Aelia said reluctantly. What Keeran had told her about the last night of the War of Two Kings had haunted her. He'd been involved, had been there to see his friends and comrades hewn down like beasts, and she could no longer bring herself to blame him for wanting revenge. Especially as the desire for vengeance was something she was coming to understand all too well.

"And do you know he told Beserkir when to attack Callodosis?"

Anger sparked in Aelia's eyes. "He didn't tell them when to attack, because he didn't know who Beserkir really was. He gave them information he thought was harmless."

Shiva looked at her closely, and Aelia averted her eyes to hide what she wasn't willing to show him. What she'd barely admitted to herself yet.

She'd forgiven him. The seething anger she'd been clinging to had dissipated, leaving nothing but dejection in its place. She'd pushed and pushed and pushed him away, and yet he'd never left, he'd never stopped looking after her. And it had got him locked up.

"I think this is it," Shiva said, breaking the silence.

Aelia narrowed her eyes at the rusty ladder hugging the wall, curving up to meet a hatch in the ceiling.

"How could you possibly know that? Everything down here looks the same." He'd only been here a few days more than her at most, how had he had time to learn its sewers, and why?

"Well, to be entirely honest," Shiva yanked uncertainly on the ladder, testing to see if it would hold. "I'm not one hundred per cent certain we're in the right place."

Aelia folded her arms and scowled at him.

"You led us through the sewers, through literal shit, without knowing where you were going?"

"I didn't see you coming up with a better plan," Shiva bit back. "And I had a rough idea where I was going. This was how I was going to get Fenrir when I found out he'd been taken to the Inner City to become Beserkir's latest plaything."

Aelia sighed and dropped her arms. "You're right, I'm being a dick, sorry. Let me go first. That ladder looks like it's going to crumble the second one of us touches it."

Shiva looked down at her but didn't move away from the ladder, a strange light in his eyes.

"What?" she asked, panicking that something awful might have splashed onto her face without her noticing.

"Just…" Shiva shook his head, an incredulous smile lifting

his lips. "Well, if someone had tried to tell us a few weeks ago that we'd be here, in a sewer in Llmera, working together, either one of us would have beaten the fucker up."

"Yep, isn't life just fan-fucking-tastic," Aelia said, looking up at the rusty bolts securing the ladder to the wall. "Give me a leg up, would you?"

Shiva snorted and grabbed her shin, boosting her up onto the ladder. He pressed his hand into her back as they both waited to see if it would hold her weight. He gingerly let her go as she began to climb.

Aelia made it to the hatch and twisted the lever with a screech that made them both wince. With her heart racing, she pushed it open as carefully as she could before peeking her head through.

"It's a changing room." Aelia twisted her neck round to peer past the hatch door to make sure the room truly was empty. She wrinkled her nose at the damp smell that permeated the darkness. "A really old changing room."

Shiva punched the air and let out a quiet whoop. "That's how it's fucking *done*."

Aelia rolled her eyes and pulled herself up into the room.

"I take it this is where we were meant to end up, then." The Inner City was meant to be the height of luxury, the physical embodiment of the Dragon's wealth and power. Aelia spun slowly on her heel to take in the filthy, derelict changing room with pursed lips. This was not at all what she'd imagined.

Shiva grunted as he climbed out of the hatch, jumping to his feet and looking around with a smug smile.

"Ready to be impressed?" he wiggled his eyebrows at her.

"More so than I am now?" she asked, her voice dripping with sarcasm. "Impossible."

He strolled to the door and scrambled around in the dim light.

"What are you looking for?" She peered over to him, not able to see past his back.

"You'll see."

With a satisfied grunt, he reached up, standing on his toes to strike the flint he'd found against the wall. It took a few attempts, but finally sparks flew and flames erupted in a shallow trench near the ceiling, snaking around the room until they ate their own tail.

"Admit it, that's pretty impressive," Shiva smirked.

"How?" Aelia gasped, turning to follow the ring of fire that sat in a gentle lip well above head height, encircling the whole room.

"Oil. The whole city is lit with it. And that's not even the best part." He crossed the room and put his hand around something on the wall. Aelia's eyes opened wide when she realised what it was. "Get ready to love me."

He turned the tap and dove out of the way of the water that sputtered from the rusty head in the ceiling.

"Oh, thank the gods." Aelia nearly stripped off right then and there, desperate to get under the pouring water. She'd never felt so unclean in her life.

"Uh, did the gods make sure there were clean clothes here? It's me you should be thanking."

Aelia tore her eyes from the shower to look at where he stood in front of a wall of lockers, holding two tightly wrapped leather bags. She could have hugged him, honestly, truly could have hugged him.

"I thought if Fenrir and I held them up high, we could keep the worst of the filth of the sewers off them." He chucked one of the bags at her. "Means yours might be a bit big, but beggars can't be choosers."

Aelia snatched the bag from the air and looked at it in wonder.

"You really were trying to save him." She turned the bag

over in her hands, opening it wide enough to see the black uniform of the Astraea tucked neatly inside. She frowned.

"It's all I could get my hands on," Shiva explained, reading her confusion. "But it works out well for us now. It'll make it that much easier to get to the cells they're keeping Keeran in."

"You know how to get there, too?"

"It's the same place they were keeping Fenrir. I mean, I've only seen it on maps, but I think I can get us there."

Aelia took a deep, shaky breath as she looked at Shiva anew. He smiled back at her, and it held none of the snarky arrogance she was used to.

"No one uses these rooms anymore, but we still need to be quick. You shower first, just come out when you're ready, and I'll swap with you." Shiva turned and made for the door.

He was just about to disappear through it when Aelia stopped him.

"Thank you, Shiva," she said.

He just smiled and nodded before ducking out of the room. Aelia stared after him for a moment, until her gaze was caught by the flames once more. An idea sparked to life at the sight of them, and she smiled as she stepped forward to have the most thorough shower of her life.

CHAPTER THIRTY-TWO

"I really don't think this is a good idea," Shiva grumbled for what must have been the tenth time since they'd left the changing rooms.

They were running up the stairs two at a time, climbing through the servants' quarters that the changing room had been part of. The stairs were crudely cut into the rock of the mountain, curling in a wide spiral above and below them, centuries of footsteps having worn a smooth dip into the middle of the dark stone. Their feet trod where countless others had as they climbed higher out of the lesser-used tunnels in the depths of the mountain, to ones that were still in daily use. Aelia supposed there had been a time when all the tunnels had been a hive of activity, when the Dragons ruled probably. She wondered if Keeran could remember what it had been like.

So far, all Aelia had seen of the Inner City was the network the servants and guards used to get around without encroaching on the Main Chamber, because gods forbid the upper classes laid eyes on the people serving them.

"So you've said, but your plan of just waltzing into the prison left a lot to be desired."

"We have uniforms," Shiva gestured impatiently to his black attire, his chest heaving as they climbed past yet another door leading off the spiralling stone staircase. "We *could* just waltz in there."

"I'm not taking any chances." Aelia grabbed the handrail to help haul herself up, her legs feeling like jelly. "What we need is a distraction."

Shiva grumbled something under his breath but kept climbing. Sweat streaked down his face as he tried to keep running, charging forwards as if he wasn't likely to end up dead or in a cell for helping her. And all she'd done was throw his past in his face. Guilt prodded her into opening her mouth.

"Shiva, I --"

He stopped so suddenly she nearly ploughed into the back of him. "This is it."

He held a finger to his lips and cracked the door open. It was chaos inside, with guards running past in either direction. Shiva shut the door again quickly.

"Something's happened," he said, looking worriedly at the handle in his hands.

"What?" Aelia panted, her heart racing from more than just the climb. She was about to walk into the guard's quarters, like a rabbit stepping into the fox's den.

"I don't know, but something's got them riled up." Shiva eyed her apprehensively. "Maybe it will help? Maybe they'll be too preoccupied to notice two more guards running around."

"Unless it's us that's got them riled up," Aelia pointed out with a flash of fear.

Shiva shook his head. "No, whatever this is, it's big." He pressed his lips into a firm line, cogs almost visibly whirring behind his eyes before a hard resolve crept into them. "There's no turning back now. Agreed?"

Aelia didn't even hesitate. "Agreed."

Shiva looked at her once, then he flung the door open and dove into the corridor at a sprint, trusting her to be hot on his heels.

She took off after him, heart freezing in her chest when she bumped into a guard, but he didn't even break a stride, just sprinted off without looking back. She was just another uniformed face.

Shiva yanked open another door and disappeared inside, the hammering of boots on rock becoming muffled as the heavy wood swung shut behind them.

They both leant with their backs against the door, breathing heavily with pent-up adrenaline.

"That was the easy part," Shiva said wryly, looking down at her with a gleam in his eyes.

Aelia laughed, clapping her hand over her mouth.

"Come on." He tugged at her black uniform sleeve. "Just walk as if you belong here."

The servants' door had opened onto a small backstreet, not too dissimilar from one you might see in any wealthy part of town, and he guided her down it, looking every inch the Astraean guard. He leant in to the arrogant swagger she knew from Callodosis, fixing a sneer on his face that was all too believable. She tried her best to mimic him, pointing her nose in the air with what she hoped was haughty confidence, but her expression melted as she passed a gap in the houses.

Her mouth hung open as she saw her first real glimpse of the Inner City, framed by the two houses. It was nothing like she'd envisioned; no imagination could possibly have dreamt up anything close to what stood before her. Palaces and castles grew as if from the mountain itself, their towers and turrets joined by bridges in a thousand different connections, every corner of it aglow with flickering firelight. Beauty and power rarely joined hands, but in the Inner City, it was a partnership that had thrived.

"Aelia, come on." Her glimpse of paradise was dragged out of sight as Shiva tugged her away by the arm. She blinked hard, trying to hold the image in her mind's eye a moment longer.

They walked around the outer edges of the chamber, trying to remain as inconspicuous as possible. Glimpses of the city came into view, but Aelia kept moving, resisting the urge to stop and stare.

A King's guard rounded a corner up ahead and they ducked into an alley, not looking back until they were far up the adjacent street. When they finally did, there was no sign they were being followed.

"How much further?" Aelia whispered. It felt like they'd been walking for hours. Just how big *was* this chamber?

"I'm not sure. Just keep walking." Shiva risked a glance over his shoulder. "I don't think that guard saw us."

And so, on they went, Aelia fighting the urge to run with every step they took. The streets were surprisingly busy considering they were approaching the early hours of the morning. Some seemed to be enjoying every last minute of the city's nightlife, and others looked as though their day was only just beginning. Each passed the other with mutual respect and equal affluence, their wealth dripping from every inch of them. Aelia had never seen such clothes, such colour, such elegance.

She'd also never felt so out of place.

Aelia's heart raced more quickly with every minute that passed, the moment of discovery seeming increasingly likely with each corner they rounded. When Aelia thought she couldn't bear it any longer, Shiva finally stopped.

"I think this must be it." He cast his eyes over an

innocuous building, one of the few without a flaming Dragon perched on its roof.

"How do you know what we're looking for if you've never even seen it?" Aelia said, concern furrowing a crease between her brows as she scanned the empty street.

"That's the sign for flashfire, the oil they use." He pointed to a symbol etched above the door, right before kicking it open.

They both held their breath, but the street stayed empty, so they disappeared inside, pulling the door shut behind them.

A small flame flickered in a glass lantern by the door, the only one in the whole room, casting just enough light for her to see the drums lined up in stacks against the walls. Aelia grabbed one and pulled the cork free with a satisfying pop, quickly slopping the oil everywhere.

"Are you sure you want to do this, Aelia?" Shiva stood unmoving by the door.

Aelia righted the drum and hugged it against her chest. "Yes, I'm sure. Whatever's got the guards so riled up might not be enough to get us into the cells, Shiva. We need chaos." She swung her arm over at the drums. "Help me make it."

Shiva ran a hand through his hair and looked up at the ceiling. "This is not going how I thought it would go."

Aelia laughed, turning to slosh more oil around. "When does it ever?"

Shiva groaned and grabbed a drum, helping her cover most of the room.

"It doesn't need to be that thorough. They mix a little flash powder with the oil to help it catch, so when this lot goes, it's *really* going to go," he explained, begrudgingly.

"You think that's enough?"

"I think that's plenty," he said with a grimace.

Aelia chucked her drum back on the pile, whilst Shiva

poured a careful line of oil to the door, tore a thick strip of cloth from his tunic and rolled it into a straw. He dipped one end in the oil before setting it down, the undipped end *just* touching the line of oil. Aelia handed him the flint she'd taken from the changing rooms.

"Ready to run?" he asked, looking over his shoulder from where he crouched.

She opened the door and nodded. The oil-covered tip of the fabric caught on the first strike of the flint against the stone floor, and they both bolted from the building, arms pumping furiously.

They made it two streets over before the oil ignited, the core of the mountain trembling with the force of the explosion.

Shiva threw her against a building, shielding her with his body against the wall of heat that battered them, and stayed there until the world stopped shuddering.

"That should draw some attention," he grinned down at her, his earlier reservation seeming to have disappeared in the rush of adrenaline. She couldn't help but grin too, looking back at the column of smoke billowing over the buildings.

"Come on." He pushed himself upright and took off down the street once again, with Aelia in hot pursuit.

Screams began to infiltrate the peace of the Main Chamber, and soon the people they passed were running just as wildly as they were. In the chaos, they were just another terrified citizen, fleeing the scene of an attack.

The prison was easier to find than she expected, buried beneath an enormous arena, a landmark even they couldn't fail to miss. As they drew closer, Shiva slowed to a walk, allowing them time for their breathing to settle.

"Remember, you have every right to be here," he ducked

his head to whisper in her ear. "You're a member of the Astraea. Make sure you act like it."

And just like that, the Shiva she knew from home was back in place. He nodded to the guards at the entrance and strode right past as if he owned the place. They gave him a long, hard look before their eyes settled on Aelia, but they didn't stop them.

As they entered the twisting tunnels that swept down into the underbelly of the mountain, Aelia could almost taste the blood in the air. She dreaded to think what atrocities these walls had seen, but the very stone seemed polluted by violence. Even the fire that burned in the overhead lip seemed dimmed, spluttering as if it too was struggling to breathe in the heavy air.

These cells had been designed to contain the most dangerous creatures their country had ever seen, buried too deep within the rock for any Dragon to Shift without crushing itself. It was utterly inescapable.

Aelia found herself grateful her stomach was empty after her experience of the sewers as she contemplated spending even a few nights in one of these cells, trapped in the unforgiving rock, behind metal doors thick enough to contain a god.

Shiva strode past the few guards they did see without seeming to bat an eyelid, and she forced herself to emulate his confidence, to walk as though she had every right to be there.

And yet, everything about this place felt wrong.

CHAPTER THIRTY-THREE

Keeran leant back on the chair, taking the pressure off his shoulders. His arms were pinned painfully behind him, the frame of the chair cutting into his bicep, and his shoulders felt like they might pull free of their sockets if he kept straining. The chains that bound him to the floor were inescapable, reinforced to be able to restrain even a Dragon but, after a little wiggling, he'd discovered that the chair had a weak spot. He tested it once more, feeling it creak beneath him and smiled. If he could break it, he could stand, and if he could stand...

Maybe he'd be able to get one of those guards around the neck, show them just how unbreakable those chains were. It was the only happy thought he'd had since he'd woken up down here.

Keeran had known where he was the moment he'd opened his eyes. The cells beneath Llmera were infamous, the only prison capable of holding a Dragon. And if Beserkir had drugged him to bring him here rather than the commoner's prison at the top of the mountain, that meant he knew what he was.

That older Dog must have recognised his scent the moment he walked into the room. The city had been full of it just a couple of decades ago, he'd been lucky someone else hadn't picked it up sooner. He'd been such a fool to come into the city, but what choice had he had?

After that, everything had gotten a little boring. The guards had asked him a few questions, and he'd relinquished the basics, sprinkling lies amongst the truth like dust on mud, indistinguishable. They had his name, Keeran Draconian-Fafnirean, and that would tell them everything they needed to know: what lineage he was from, his military record, his kill count in the war. The only thing they couldn't know was his pyrokinetic ability; that he'd learnt after he'd been exiled. Keeran would be damned if he gave Beserkir any more information about himself than that.

Keeran had to hand it to him, Beserkir had kept his cool for a man finding himself face-to-face with the only Dragon to have set foot in the Inner City since their banishment. That was twice he'd got one up on Keeran. It would not happen a third time.

He strained towards the hole where the pair bond ought to be and felt nothing. He pried at it, willing to feel something, anything, that would reassure him that Aelia was alright, but the bastard thing stayed dormant. If they'd accepted it, it would be a constant in his mind, as reliable as the rising sun. But they hadn't, and so he was left waiting in the dark.

The monster raged at the back of his skull, ferociously demanding control. Keeran could feel the murderous desire coursing through it and into him. The utter wrath that these mortals would dare imprison him, that they would stoop to drugging him as they'd drugged his comrades all those years ago, was almost too much to bear. The beast battered at

Keeran's defences, wanting to blast their way out of here and drown the city in blood.

Because that was the one thing the cells couldn't contain. No pyrokinetic could be stopped by mortal means; it took magic to restrain magic. Keeran could melt the chains should he want to; it would be bloody painful, but he'd heal quickly enough. Then the next time a guard dared enter, he'd open the door to a firestorm the likes of which the world hadn't seen since Khaled had raged his way across the battlefield all those years ago.

But Aelia was probably still in the city.

The beast in him snapped its jaws shut and growled, low in its belly. Its slitted eyes narrowed as it reined in its blood-lust. Keeran sighed at the quiet, as his emotions became his own once more.

They couldn't break free if she wasn't out. He couldn't leave knowing she might still be here, being hunted down like a criminal.

What if they'd already caught her?

Keeran dropped his head back against the chair and pressed his eyes shut, trying again to feel something down the fragments of the pair bond. If he could just get a glimpse, he'd know what to do.

Very little sound reached him through the thick metal. So, he had no warning when the door opened and Beserkir stepped into the room. Not that Keeran was surprised; if anything, he'd been expecting him sooner.

Keeran smiled, an ancient evil looking out from his eyes as the beast inside him roared for revenge, for this creature who'd *dared* to drug him to be punished. Keeran flicked open the lid in the corner of his mind in which his fire magic lay curled and waiting, rearing its head and quivering as it waited for his instruction.

Now that he had eyes on Beserkir, his decision became

that much easier. If he had to burn the city to the ground to find Aelia, to keep this man from getting his hands on her, he'd do so without a moment's hesitation.

Beserkir spoke from the doorway, a folder held loosely by his side. "Now, before you do anything reckless like squash us both into the rock, I'd like to caution you that doing so would mean the imminent death of your dear little friend."

The fire magic sizzled and died, the lid slamming shut on top of it.

No.

Beserkir stepped into the room, making a show of inspecting every corner of the dingy space, raking his eyes over the uneven surface of the crudely chiselled walls. The door grated shut behind him with a resounding *thunk.*

"Well now, I imagine this is a little different to the quality you were used to in the Inner City before the Dragons fell." Beserkir sniffed, slowly pacing the perimeter of the cell. "I do regret not being able to offer you something a little more comfortable, but we are all so terribly concerned you might take it upon yourself to raze our little city to the ground."

Beserkir disappeared behind Keeran and came close enough to test the chains that bound Keeran's arms behind his back, secured to not just the chair but to a huge iron ring embedded in the floor itself.

"It seems we have that little eventuality under control now, though. So, there are some things I wish to discuss with you."

"Where is she?" Keeran kept his face expressionless, his tone bored. Only he knew the battle that raged inside him, the beast thrashing and writhing at the thought of this monster capturing Aelia.

"Oh, she's safe. I can't promise she'll stay that way, though. That all depends on your cooperation." Beserkir came back into view, choosing to stand dangerously close to

Keeran. He leant in to pick a piece of fluff from Keeran's shoulder, dropping it to the floor with a satisfied smile. Keeran fought back the snarl that threatened to tear out of him.

"How do I know what you say is true?"

"You don't trust me? How sad," Beserkir said, looking quite the opposite. He looked like the cat that had got the cream. "Well, she's rather an impressive girl, I'm a big enough man to admit that. She managed to escape from the very jaws of our tracking Dogs, break her way into the Inner City, and set a good portion of it on fire in what was undeniably one hell of a distraction. All in an attempt to get to you."

It was all Keeran could do to keep the horror from his face. Aelia had broken into the Inner City? The whole time he'd been hoping she was getting as far away as possible, she'd been doing the exact opposite. He wasn't sure if he wanted to laugh or break something.

"Not impressed yet? Tough man to crack. That would be enough to have me smiling. Not to worry, she didn't stop there. With almost every guard in the prison trying to extinguish the fire, or busy making sure you didn't have any slightly scalier friends coming to your rescue, she used the stampede the fire caused to try and break you out of here." Beserkir lowered his head, not a shred of humour in his smile. "Fortunately, my Dogs are every bit as good as I told you they are, and her scent was picked up before she could do any more damage. Anyway, enough about her, she's taken up more than enough of my time. You are *far* more interesting."

"I disagree." Keeran looked Beserkir right in the eye. "She's just one artemian, and she's caused you more trouble than I ever have. Bit embarrassing for you really, isn't it?"

Beserkir laughed, nodding his head as he resumed his slow pacing, this time staying in front of Keeran.

"Well, both of us know that whatever she is, she's not artemian," Beserkir said, dismissing the topic with a wave of his hand. "But no, it's you who has my undivided attention now. You see, the other Elders and I are keen to know how a Dragon came to be in Llmera."

"Maybe I just got homesick."

The hard heels of Beserkir's boots clicked on the stone floor as he spun to face Keeran, any trace of a smile long gone. "Or maybe you were scouting for a future attack. Seeing what's changed since your kind fled."

"Perhaps I just missed artemian company. You guys sure do know how to throw a party." Keeran jangled the chains at his back.

Beserkir paused before changing tack. "Indulge my curiosity. You look too young to have known Llmera under the Dragons' rule." He scrutinised Keeran, squinting as he got a closer look. "So how old are you really?"

Keeran just stared back, teeth clenched.

"Oh, now that's no fun. Play the game, Keeran, or I'll have to use my trump card." Beserkir straightened with a satisfied smirk. "Every question you don't answer is another scar I'll put on your friend's pretty little face."

Keeran snarled. He couldn't help it, it ripped out of him so viciously that even Beserkir took a step back, the colour leaching from him.

"You want to know how old I am?" Keeran said through bared teeth. "You have my name, check the records, you lazy piece of shit."

Beserkir nodded gently, his expression back under control even though his face remained distinctively peaky. "You're right, we have people searching the archives as we speak. I was just too intrigued to resist asking. It's not every day you get to meet an immortal. But you're right, my friends would be quite displeased if I wasted this opportunity satisfying my own curiosity."

"Are these your friends in the North?" Keeran asked, with a predatory tilt to his head. "You seem a little too keen to impress them, which makes me think they're not your friends at all. Do they have you by the short and curlies, Beserkir?"

"Oh, you'll be sure to meet them soon enough, so you can see for yourself just how friendly they are. But I want to get as much out of you as I can before they whisk you away." Beserkir came a little nearer, leaning so close that Keeran could see past the bravado, could see the dilated pupils and the quickening of his pulse where it beat in his throat. "So, tell me, Keeran, how many others are there?"

Keeran didn't get a chance to answer. The door opened, slowly, one grating inch at a time. Beserkir straightened with a sigh, clearly not expecting an interruption.

The sigh died on his lips when Aelia slipped through the open door.

Keeran didn't waste a second.

He threw himself back into the chair, heaving all his bodyweight back into the weakness he'd found earlier. It splintered with a crack, and Keeran caught himself, crouching as he strained with his arms to shatter what remained of the wood. In a matter of seconds, he was free of the chair, his chains swinging loosely.

It made no difference.

Beserkir was a man used to battle, a warrior to his core, and Keeran had barely managed to straighten before he was kicked viciously to the floor. Beserkir stood one foot on his chained hands and wrenched Keeran's head back, holding a dagger to his throat hard enough to draw blood.

Aelia froze, halted mid-stride in her run to make it to him.

"That's it. Stay right there unless you want a repeat of the Fenrir incident," Beserkir drawled, seeming immensely pleased with himself. "It's such a pleasure to finally meet you."

"The pleasure is all yours," Aelia spat.

"Aelia, run," Keeran shouted. If she would just leave, he could remove Beserkir from her life for good. One brush of his magic and Beserkir would be ash, but he'd already lied to her so much. What would she make of the fire magic that made him even more of a monster than she could ever fathom? "Run!"

"But she only just joined the party?" Beserkir crooned. "Oh, I appear to have been caught in my lie. How uncivilised of me. I can only apologise, Keeran. I couldn't think of another way of keeping your leash nice and tight. My only defence is that it was only *half* a lie. See, I knew she was in the Inner City, I just wasn't quite sure where. I was damn sure she'd make her way here, though, and I just couldn't miss the opportunity to be here when she did."

As if by silent command, Shiva stepped into the room. His hands were buried in his pockets, as though he were strolling into a tavern, not into a prison cell with a known Dragon. Keeran's lip curled back in a guttural snarl, despite the blade still pressed to his throat.

"No, it's okay, he's..." Aelia trailed off as Shiva strolled straight past her, crossing to stand next to Beserkir. Keeran watched the heartbreak roll over her, and it was all too easy for him to work out what had happened. "You... you bastard!"

"You did well." Keeran heard Beserkir say from behind him, his hand still fisted in his hair. "Did all go to plan?"

"Yes, sir, other than the explosion. But she wouldn't be dissuaded, and I couldn't risk arresting her at that point in case I triggered another outburst of magic."

"You got her here, that's all I care about."

"Thank you, sir."

"Everything you said... was a lie?" Aelia said, her voice deathly quiet.

"A hundred gold coins were well worth a bit of acting," Shiva leant closer to her, conspiratorially. "One might say I gave it my best shot."

Aelia's lips parted, a frown flicking over her brow as Shiva's words hit home. The pair bond flared to life and a wall of devastation slammed into him, the hurt of Shiva's betrayal enough to make his eyes water. But there was something on the other end of it, burning and bright and ruinous. Keeran's jaw slackened as he saw the black ring in Aelia's eyes turn bright silver.

"Guards," Beserkir roared.

A wall of a dozen soldiers flooded into the room, blocking Aelia from the exit. Some held swords aloft, some had arrows nocked and ready. Her eyes met Keeran's, and the raw power in them sent a bolt of ice through his heart.

He felt it surge through the pair bond, the only warning he had that she was about to lose control again.

Keeran reacted on pure instinct, unleashing his fire magic with a snap of his will and sending it roaring over himself in a flaming cocoon. The weight of Beserkir pressed into him, regrettably close enough to be enveloped within the shield, and his screams vibrated painfully in Keeran's ear. He felt the barrage of Aelia's magic against his own, rageful but uncontrolled. All he could do was lie there and grit his teeth as he shielded himself from her wrath.

He felt her magic start to wane, both against his wall of fire and through the bond. The instant it vanished completely, he withdrew the fire magic and unclenched his eyes. He shoved Beserkir off and rolled himself to his feet in one rapid movement. He needn't have bothered, Beserkir was out cold.

Keeran snapped his eyes up to Aelia. She still stood by the door, swaying slightly. Her gaze raked across the bodies that surrounded her, mangled past the point of recognition. Keeran had seen some pretty disturbing things in his time, but this made even his stomach roil.

Only Beserkir had been spared her unique brand of death, but Aelia hardly seemed to notice.

He reached for her through the pair bond, nearly sagging with relief when he felt it still intact. He sank into her mind, feeling the turmoil she was suffocating in. She felt so fragile, like her sanity was on the brink of shattering. She latched onto him, and he wrapped his presence around her, wishing he could shield her from all she was feeling.

"What's happening to me?" she whispered, sounding so broken he knew he needed to get her out of there. Now.

"I don't know," he said truthfully.

"I can't control it," she spoke to him through the pair bond, a brush of her lips against his mind. He nearly closed his eyes at the sweetness of it, the delicious purity of her mental touch.

"Let me get you out of here." Keeran jangled the manacles. "And we'll work it out, okay?"

Aelia stared vacantly at the body of Shiva, barely recognisable now.

"I didn't kill you." Her eyes flitted back up to him, a slight frown creasing her brow.

"No, you didn't." He smiled grimly, relieved the blinding light of her own magic had prevented her from seeing his. "Now I need you to get the keys. Check Beserkir's pockets."

She glanced at the manacles still fixing him to the floor and nodded. Her legs wobbled beneath her as she crossed the room, but she made it to Beserkir before she let them fail her. Keeran winced as her knees struck the stone, but Aelia hardly seemed to notice. She started patting him down, pulling items from various pockets until he heard the sweet jangle of keys.

She hauled herself to her feet and fumbled with the keys until she found one that fit. The clunk of it turning in the lock of his manacles was pure bliss. He shook his wrists and ankles free and spun to face Aelia, his hands hovering over her head, her neck, her arms, as he checked every inch of her. She didn't move, but her eyes were locked onto him, as though he were the anchor in the storm he could still feel raging in her mind.

He threw his arms around her and pulled her close, wrapping his mind around hers as tightly as his arms. She hugged him tight, burying herself into him, body and soul.

"I'm so sorry," he whispered into her hair, pressing his lips against her over and over again. She'd lost Fenrir, Shiva had tricked her, and whatever magic had awakened in her had wrung her out to the point of collapse. He had to get her out of here.

CHAPTER THIRTY-FOUR

Aelia felt warmth starting to seep back into her, emanating out of Keeran and breaking through the numbness that had encapsulated her. He filled her mind, the sensation as inherently him as the heady smell she was burying her face into.

She still felt weak, her muscles trembling with the effort of standing, but her mind no longer felt like it was on the verge of tumbling into insanity. So she pulled away, prying free of his arms to look down at the man who'd done this to her.

She sank to her knees beside Beserkir, looking down at him with a cold numbness she hadn't expected. In her dreams, she had revelled in this moment, and yet she felt next to nothing. She flung Beserkir's coat apart, grabbed hold of the dark fabric of his shirt, and tore it open. His chest was the toned perfection of a warrior, but no amount of muscle would protect him from her now. He hadn't stirred yet, not so much as a twitch, but there was no way she was letting him die so easily.

She withdrew her hand and put every iota of strength she

had left into a slap that had his head slamming into the rough stone. Beserkir groaned. She pulled Otis' dagger free and kissed the hilt before leaning over him, her hand right next to his head. She had relived the exact moment Otis had died enough times to remember exactly which ribs Beserkir's blade had slipped between, and the tip of her dagger found the equivalent spot on Beserkir's chest.

When his eyes opened, the fear in them spiked right through the numbness she'd been feeling. A vicious satisfaction coursed through her at the sight of it, and she pressed the dagger in just enough to break through the skin. Beserkir tried to writhe, but she pinned him with her free arm, pressing it against his neck with all her strength.

"I wish I had more time," she whispered as she sank the dagger in a little further, relishing in the terror she saw blooming in his wide pupils. He tried to beat her off him, and Keeran's boots slammed down to pin his arms to the floor. "But life so rarely gives us what we want, so I'll just have to savour this moment."

Her forearm locked his head in place, rammed under his jaw so he couldn't scream, so he could barely breathe. Inch by careful inch, she slipped the dagger between his ribs with exaggerated slowness. She felt no remorse as he choked on the blood that gurgled up his throat, splattering his chin with his desperate attempts to breathe. Something in her had died with Shiva's betrayal. The last remnants of the girl she'd been had shattered, leaving something hard and jagged in their place.

And that part of her smiled as it watched Beserkir's last, excruciating moments. Her lips parted, sneering down at him as she shoved the dagger in to the hilt, twisting it with a violent wrench of her wrist. Beserkir's eyes rolled back in his head, staring unseeingly at the ceiling.

Aelia yanked her dagger free and wiped the worst of the

blood on his tunic, smearing it over the expensive fabric. She struggled to her feet, turning to find Keeran watching her with a strange expression. She didn't have the willpower to analyse it, or maybe she just wasn't prepared to face his judgement.

"We need to go," was all she could bring herself to say.

Keeran held out his hand to her and his warm presence brushed against her mind. Her eyes flickered shut for a moment before she took his hand and let him guide her towards the door.

They picked their way through the horrific remains of the soldiers to the corridor outside. It was dark despite the fire that lined the ceiling, but Aelia had memorised every turn she and Shiva had made. She stumbled over nothing, and Keeran held her by the elbow, helping her stay upright despite her trembling legs.

Whatever she'd done in that room, it had wiped her out again, draining her to the point of collapse. It was only with Keeran's help that she made it to the exit, blinking in the light of the Main Chamber. The sun had risen and the crevices in the ceiling funnelled its light into the Inner City, illuminating the rows of guards that encircled the prison entrance.

A volley of arrows came whistling towards them, and Keeran stepped forwards so quickly she couldn't register the movement. With a wave of his hand, the arrows turned to ash, the metal heads clanging to the floor, slowly followed by the grey ash that wafted down after them.

Aelia sucked in a breath, her brain struggling to comprehend what she had seen. Keeran stiffened at the sound but didn't turn around.

"All we wish to do is leave. Your commander has fallen, and our fight isn't with you. Let us walk away, and we will let

—" Keeran broke off as a lone arrow was loosed towards them.

In a blur of movement, he tugged Aelia to the side. Aelia gasped, shock at the speed at which he moved numbing her to anything else. It was only when his lips pulled back in a snarl, his eyes fixed on her arm, that she became aware of the stinging pain. Looking down, she saw a slight rip in her sleeve, revealing the deep scratch the arrowhead had sliced into her skin. It was nothing, hardly worth bandaging, but if Keeran hadn't moved her…

Keeran spun to face the soldiers with a roar that had even the bravest of them recoiling. As if from nowhere, a wave of flame rolled off Keeran, his rage crackling within it as though hell itself had been unleashed. The soldiers were dead before they could scream, the empty shells of their armour crashing to the floor where they'd stood. Dozens fell in seconds, nothing left of them but the white-grey piles of ash on the floor.

Chest heaving, he turned to face her painfully slowly, as if only just realising what he'd done.

"Aelia…" Every inch of him pleaded with just that one word, his whole body imploring.

Fire magic. The words echoed around Aelia's skull as she looked at all that was left of the men who'd tried to kill them. Keeran wasn't just a Dragon, he was a pyrokinetic, and a fucking powerful one.

At least that explained the magic that had surfaced in her. It must be coming from him.

"You could have done that sooner," Aelia said, wryly.

Keeran stared at her warily, disbelief etched into every perfect line of his features. She felt such bone-deep regret at having called him a monster, for sensing his vulnerability and using it against him. He wasn't a monster; he was death, he was power, he was everything she was not. And he was perfect.

"Teach me," she breathed. There was nothing she wouldn't do to have that kind of strength, to be able to stand up to the people who tried to take those she loved from her. If she had even a fraction of his power through the pair bond, she wanted to wield it with him.

Keeran's throat bobbed as he swallowed the emotion that glistened in his eyes. "Let me get you out of here first," he joked, thickly. "Do you trust me?"

"Implicitly." The word tumbled from her mouth before he'd even finished asking, and his sharp intake of breath squeezed at her heart. She wished with every fibre of her being that she could take back what she'd screamed at him by the lake. She could feel how deep those wounds went, and she loathed herself for adding to them.

"I'm going to fly us out of here." He grabbed her hand and pulled her towards the arena the prison was buried beneath. "We need space."

Aelia's heart flipped as she realised what he meant, but she stumbled after him, her feet dragging on the smooth stone. The arena was ringed by a huge seating area, half of it carved into the mountainside, half of it standing tall and free. Keeran led her confidently through the outer portion of it to the arena within.

"This is where we used to train," he called over his shoulder, and her stomach flipped at the thought of him fighting other Dragons. "Are you strong enough to climb on once I've Shifted?"

"I think so." In truth, she honestly didn't know, but there was only one way to find out. Nervous anticipation coiled low in her stomach. She was going to see him Shift. She was going to see a Dragon.

Shouts began to bounce around the empty stone structure behind them, the unmistakable rattle of metal armour getting steadily closer. Keeran nodded to her.

"Stay here." He didn't take his eyes off her, jogging backwards through the dirt of the arena until he was nearly in the centre of it. The shouting was getting louder, but she was utterly transfixed by Keeran.

Magic shimmered in the air around him, and she just had time to see his eyes widen at something behind her before he broke into a sprint.

"Aelia!" he roared into her head.

There wasn't time to react, one moment he was running towards her, the next he'd transformed in a ripple of magic. The scaled beast bounded towards her, wings spreading wide as it covered the distance in a few leaping strides. Its body was a hulking expanse of rippling muscle, its wingspan so wide that she couldn't see both tips at the same time. Black scales covered its angular body like flint, but the skin of its wings was so thin it was nearly translucent.

It was on her before she could think, and she spun away from it, dropping to a crouch with her arms over her head as the columns of its front legs slammed down on either side of her, blocking out the morning light of the sun.

She peered through her eyelids, just in time to see the soldiers Keeran had spotted pouring into the arena. They froze as they came face-to-face with the monster of legends, the god of death. Her god of death.

She stood slowly, hardly coming level with the obsidian talons that pierced the dirt on either side of her. The soldiers scrambled to escape, shoving past each other as they tried to push their way back through the arched door through which their comrades were still pouring out. They all bore the red insignia of the King, and Aelia wondered how many humans they'd each captured, how many artemians they'd silenced.

Whatever their number, it would climb no higher.

Thunder rumbled in the great expanse of Keeran's chest, his neck snaking lower.

"Do it," she said with a nudge of her mind against his.

His jaws parted, and the thunder above her became a roar of flame, exploding from him in a column of fire no mortal could hope to survive. The stone building glowed, roasting those who lurked within it, their screams lost to the billowing flames. By the time his jaw snapped shut, there wasn't a soul among them left living.

He stepped carefully over her, and she craned her neck back to take in the rippling black scales that passed overhead. His tail whipped over her, the black giving way to the deep crimson of fresh blood as it tapered to a fine point.

He settled into a crouch beside her, his reptilian eyes watching her with a predatory gleam she recognised all too well. This was what she'd seen lurking within him, the otherness she both feared and craved. Her lips curved in a wicked smile as she took in the violent beauty of him, and a metallic rumble rattled from deep within his chest.

She tentatively reached out to touch his nose, and the rumble intensified approvingly. She ran her hand over the smooth armour of his scales. They were almost iridescent where the sun struck them, showing the subtlest shine of red within the black that seemed to swallow all light.

The bones of his skull protruded in elegant arcs, the minute scales around his nostrils flaring slightly with each breath he took, his lips hiding the razorlike teeth he'd bared when running across the arena.

She trailed her fingers over him as she walked to his side, looking up at the mountainous expanse of muscle. The skin on his wings felt like silk under her fingers, and her eyes followed the line of them up to where they'd folded tightly to his side. They attached to his shoulders at the base of his long, graceful neck, creating a slight indentation in the otherwise perfect curve of his back.

Her lips pressed together with grim determination. He'd tucked his front leg beneath him, and she reached as high as she could to try and grip onto the angle of his foot. Her fingers hooked over it, but her arms failed her almost immediately, and her knees buckled as her feet hit the dirt.

His head lifted from the ground and snaked towards her. She climbed to her feet, her muscles still wobbling beneath her. Keeran rolled his head to the side, and she hesitantly draped herself over his muzzle. She just had time to notice the warmth of him, before she was lifted off her feet with an undignified squeak.

The ground fell away from under her as he lifted her onto his back, waiting until she had slid safely between his wings before he swung his head back around.

Aelia tried to reach him through the pair bond, but it had disappeared. The loss of it slammed into her, leaving her gasping.

Keeran began to move, standing and spreading his wings wide. She fell forwards, nestling between the prominent curve of his shoulder bones as his wings beat at the air. He lifted himself onto his back legs, rearing towards the slips of sky visible from within the crevices in the mountain. Without warning, he launched them into the air, gravity relinquishing its hold on them as they left the arena and climbed over the city.

The wind tore at her, pulling at her hair and making her eyes water. She blinked frantically, peering at the Inner City as it sprawled beneath them.

It was glorious. Waterfalls gushed down the mountainside, cascading past the palaces that climbed out of the rock. Flowers of climbing plants had burst open to greet the sun, splashing colour within the vibrant greens that crawled over the buildings.

Keeran circled over it, seeming as reluctant to leave as she was. His wings found a steady rhythm, and her body rocked with his, absorbing the movement more easily now that they were airborne.

Aelia's stomach plummeted as Keeran rolled sharply to the side, bunching his shoulder blades to keep her firmly in place, but saving her cost him altitude. They dropped a few feet before he corrected himself, allowing Aelia a glimpse of the javelin they'd narrowly avoided. The artemians were firing at them.

Aelia sank low onto his back, swinging her head as she frantically tried to see where the javelin had come from. With a sickening lurch in the pit of her stomach, she spotted the enormous machines lining the upper portion of the cavern, each being loaded with a javelin so huge it took three artemians to carry it.

Keeran must have seen them too. His bellow reverberated around the Main Chamber, loosening fragments of stone and dust from the ceiling. He beat his wings furiously, seeming to lengthen as he tore through the air towards a sliver of light in the cavern's ceiling. Aelia couldn't breathe, fear closing her throat as the rockface loomed closer. The crevice was too narrow, just a slit in the rock. There was no way they were going to fit.

Her mouth opened in a silent scream as they barrelled towards it, certain that death was imminent. At the very last second, Keeran flattened his wings against his side, scrunched his shoulders in close to pin her in place, and pinwheeled into the gap in the rock.

Her vision flickered from dark to light as they spun through the crevice, erupting on the other side with a burst of his wings. He roared his fury to the open sky, and she felt the world beneath quake at the force of it.

But Keeran didn't stop, didn't turn back for revenge, despite the rage she didn't need a pair bond to sense seething within him. He levelled out, his wings settling into a steady beat as he carried them away from Llmera, away from the Astraea.

She was hundreds of feet in the air, on the back of a monster, a world of enemies beneath her. And Aelia had never felt safer.

CHAPTER THIRTY-FIVE

The Jaws of Rach-Mah rose around them, and Keeran flew lower now that they were out of Demuto, soaring through the green valleys between the enormous mountains.

They hadn't stopped since they'd left Llmera, and Aelia didn't know how he was still functioning. Not only had he flown straight through the night, but he'd also kept some kind of heat haze around her when she'd started to shiver. It glimmered across her skin, as beautiful as it was warm. She knew very little about magic, but her momentary experiences had left her more exhausted than she'd thought possible. She dreaded to think the kind of strain it was taking for him to maintain the magic around her. She couldn't tell him to stop, that she'd be ok without it, because the pair bond had stayed fractured and silent since they'd left Llmera, no matter how hard she tried to reach out to him.

Initially, she didn't think she'd be able to sleep whilst being jostled by the movement of his flight, the hard scales of his back rubbing against her uncomfortably, but she was out cold as soon as the adrenaline had left her system. She found herself opening her eyes to a new day, her fatigue having let her sleep through a whole day and night.

Other than being beyond ravenous, she felt infinitely better for the rest, and looked out at the jagged guardians of the southern border with open-mouthed awe. Snow already capped their rocky peaks, but the dense foliage that carpeted their sides flowed down into the valleys between them to form a forest that rivalled hers in beauty. Even from such a height, she could see the ancient magnitude of the trees. She longed to disappear amongst them, to let them hide her from the horrors of the world her own forest had shielded Callodosis from for so long.

THEY'D BEEN AMONGST THE MOUNTAINS FOR THE BEST PART OF the day, and the sun was starting to slip from view before Keeran finally angled them down towards a clearing on the side of one of the mountains. Trees ringed half of it, giving way to the grass that flowed uninterrupted until the rock gave way to a sheer cliff's edge. He aimed right for it, the air from his wings rippling through the long grass as he landed.

He twisted the moment his talons touched down, and magic shimmered around her. Aelia shrieked as Keeran disappeared from under her, and she fell through the empty space he'd filled. Two thick bands caught her, and she opened her eyes to find Keeran holding her close, his arms wrapped tightly under her.

"Don't *do* that," she yelled, slapping his chest.

Keeran laughed, and the vibration of it had her insides turning molten despite herself. She released a shaky breath and tried to wriggle free. He set her down but didn't let her go.

"Some warning would have been nice," she grumbled, but she didn't try to pull away.

"It's a little hard to talk to you in that form." His voice was liquid warmth, pouring over her skin and leaving goosebumps in its wake. How had she never noticed before?

She swallowed heavily, remembering just how blind she'd been, how cruel.

"Keeran, I..." She didn't even know what to say. She was sorry for so much. For everything she'd said, for pushing him away, for getting him arrested. "I've been so stupid."

He cupped a hand to her cheek, the rich brown of his eyes looking knowingly into hers.

"Me too." His thumb stroked her cheek, and she leant her head into his palm. "There's so much I should have told you."

"I know why you couldn't." She'd have run for the hills if he'd told her what he was, what she was becoming to him. "I just wish I'd handled everything better."

"You've had to handle too much, all at once." She heard the truth in his words, knew how close she'd come to breaking. How much of that had he felt in the cells, when he'd found his way into her mind? "I'm just sorry I added to it."

Aelia shook her head. There was no point denying that he had, but it hadn't been in his control. Neither of them had had any say in the pair bond.

"You were in my head." Aelia peered up at him, a thousand questions forming on her tongue all at once. It was so hard to pick one. "Is that normal for the pair bonds?"

"Yes, but only once it's been accepted, that's why it's so intermittent."

"Is it why..." Aelia struggled to find the words. "The light, the magic... is that the pair bond too?"

Keeran tensed against her, and she pulled back slightly to better see his face.

"No," he said, shaking his head. "That's nothing to do with the pair bond."

Aelia gulped, confusion slipping into panic at the consequences of that.

"I can't control it," she whispered, brows pinching together. "I thought you'd be able to show me how. I killed all those artemians in the warehouse. I could have killed you."

Keeran placed his other hand on her face, brushing the loose strands of hair back in place.

"We will figure it out. There is always a solution." He dipped his head so it was level with hers. "Always."

"What is it, if it's not coming from the pair bond?" she asked, struggling to control the dread rising inside of her.

Keeran sighed through his nose, his brows pinching together as he struggled to find the words.

"I don't think you're an artemian, Aelia. I think you're from one of the realms in Mithrylaya."

Aelia blinked up at him, Otis's last words ringing in her ears. Had he known? Had he known what she was?

"Otis told me to go across the sea and find the Del Awane family. It was the last thing he said to me."

Keeran shrugged reassuringly, dropping his hands. "Then maybe that's where we need to go. But for now, we need to find somewhere safe and think everything through."

"Where?" Aelia looked around at the mountains barricading them from all sides.

"Where Khaled and I used to live." Keeran smiled down at her. "But first, we need to talk some things through. I'm sick of keeping secrets. I'll answer any question you have, and I hope you'll answer some of mine."

Aelia nodded. "Of course." She opened her mouth, one of the hundreds of questions she had leaping to the forefront, but he held his hand up to stop her.

"Let me hunt us something to eat first. If I don't eat something soon, I think I'll keel over." He didn't look like he was about to pass out; he actually didn't look even remotely tired despite his long flight. Aelia, on the other hand, was so hungry her stomach felt like it was eating itself.

"Okay, I'll get a fire ready."

A gentle smile creased Keeran's cheeks, softening his face in a way that made her knees feel weak all over again. The energy shifted in the air between them, and she saw a hint of darkness flicker in him. She bit her lip at the sight of it, and his eyes homed in on the movement, watching it hungrily.

But when he leant in to kiss her, it was gentle, his lips parting hers with a tender reverence, his tongue dancing against hers. His hand gripped the back of her neck and pulled her closer, seeming to breathe her in. Her arms wound around his neck, her fingers sinking into his hair, desperate to get as close to him as was physically possible. She had found her home, and she never wanted to let go.

So when Keeran began to pull away, she felt such an immense disappointment that all sense of pride and propriety evaporated in a puff of longing. Her body followed his, arching into him as he pulled back, not wanting to let the moment end. His lips curved against hers in a smile, but it didn't stop him from breaking free of her grip.

He huffed a laugh through his nose at her evident frustration, the warmth in his eyes appeasing her somewhat before he pressed his lips against hers once more. Even the gentle brush of his mouth sent sparks skittering through her. He broke off the kiss and pressed his forehead against hers, closing his eyes.

"I know the concept of a pair bond is something you've never had to consider, and I swear I will respect whatever decision you make. But before you choose, you need to know that there is nothing I would not do for you, no line I would not cross to keep you safe, irrespective of what kind of monster that makes me. There is no part of me that does not love you. I am yours, wholly and completely." He pulled away to look at her, the black depths of his eyes darkening further as his voice lowered, her heart skipping in an uneven beat at the heavy suggestion that rumbled in it. "I also know that I have had far too long to think of all the things I want to do to you, of all the ways I'm going to take every delicious part of you. But when I do, Aelia," he said, her name little more than a growl on his lips, the sound curling in her chest as he leant closer. "It is not going to be on a cold clearing, with you anxious and exhausted. No." His teeth nipped at her ear. "When I do, you're going to need your strength, because I plan to make you come until you're seeing stars long after the sun has risen."

If her pulse had been uneven before, it was positively racing at the promise in his words.

Stunned into silence, she watched him walk backwards, eyes locked onto hers until he reached the cliff edge. Then he stepped right back off it.

Aelia's heart stopped beating altogether, leaping into her throat as she took a staggered step towards him.

A thud shook the air, vibrating through the rock she stood on. Another followed shortly, even more powerful than the last, the pressure in the air hitting her ears.

Thud. Thud. ***Thud.***

They seemed to be getting louder, reverberating through her like thunder. Slowly, powerfully, Keeran rose into the sky, soaring over the trees and away into the distance. Aelia puffed out her cheeks and released a ragged breath.

Damn.

She raked her fingers through her hair.

He loved her. All the hurt and anguish and panic that had been threatening to overwhelm her were brushed aside by the warmth ballooning inside her. It bubbled out of her in a disbelieving laugh as she watched him shrink into the skyline. A smile still played on her lips as he disappeared behind a mountain, and she dropped her hands by her side, feeling lighter than she had in weeks.

She started collecting firewood, readying the fire and stacking some in a pile beside it. She didn't bother lighting it. She wasn't going to go in search of flint when she had her very own fire god flying back to her.

So, she folded herself onto the grass, sitting cross-legged as she took in the view. She shielded her eyes from the low rays of the sun, peering into the sky. Aelia broke into a smile as she spotted a shape flying high, too large to be a bird. Keeran was on his way back.

Still high above the valley floor, he soared out of the sinking sun towards her. She squinted, taking the opportunity to watch him fly as he came steadily closer. The sun blinded her, but she strained past it to make out the detail in the shape hurtling towards her.

Dread hit her like a wall, fear rolling over her as she shook her head in horrified denial. The Dragon barrelling towards her was too small, too lithe, too long. Its scales glinted, the evening light bouncing off its golden sides.

It wasn't Keeran.

She lunged to her feet and ran, her legs pounding the ground in a frantic sprint towards the shelter of the trees. Blood rushed in her ears, her arms pumping by her side, her breathing already coming in gasps as she dove between the enormous trunks of the mountainous forest.

Before long, she could feel the vibration of the Dragon's wings in the air, thudding in her ears like a drum. It was close, but she didn't dare look up. She willed her legs to move faster, praying the trees gave enough cover to hide her progress down the mountain.

The downhill gradient worked to her advantage, gravity

urging her forwards. So she ran, hardly aware of the acid burning in her muscles. Her feet tackling the uneven ground, skimming over roots and fallen branches, focused entirely on escaping.

The branches in the trees above her bent and swayed ominously, the air from the Dragon's wings buffeting them from above. Panic threatened to take over; it knew where she was.

For the time being, the cover of the trees protected her, but she couldn't hope to outrun a Dragon. Her thoughts were frantic, terror making it hard to think clearly. All she could do was run.

The trail was steep and uneven, and tree branches whipped across her face. She fell once, sprawling across the hard earth, tearing the skin of her hands and knees. The pain didn't register, and without a second's hesitation, she was back on her feet, tearing through the trees once more.

She was focused so intently on the trail that it took her a while to notice that she couldn't hear the pounding of wings. She didn't ease up her pace, ploughing through the trees, her chest heaving with the exertion. Her legs were on fire, and sweat streamed down her face, but she ignored it, overriding it. The trees to her left gave way to a wall of rock, thick with moss and ivy. The forest started to thin, the protective green breaking to expose her to widening patches of ominous blue, but she had no choice but to keep going.

She spotted the dark mouth of a cave ahead, just on the other side of a rocky clearing, and hope began to leak into the fear that pumped through her with every ragged breath.

She daren't look up without risking falling again, but she couldn't hear the Dragon above her. The narrow slit in the rock wall was within reach. Her tired legs felt like they were wading through water, but she grimaced through gasping breaths. She was going to make it.

Aelia barely had time to register the ground shuddering beneath her feet before her legs were swept out from under her. Caught mid-sprint, her momentum sent her crashing into the ground, and her head slammed against the rocks.

She saw stars, dancing in time to the ringing in her ears. Blinking past them, she raised herself onto her hands, urgency overriding pain.

Something large and unyielding pushed her firmly to the floor again, holding her there. She looked with chilling trepidation over her shoulder, her face a mask of unadulterated terror as she saw the enormous mass of golden scales that stood over her.

She shrieked. It was involuntary, her body bursting with so much fear the excess screamed out of it, piercing the air and echoing off the rocky mountain sides. But there was no one to hear it, no one to save her; there was only the great, golden Dragon pinning her in place.

Forthcoming

Aelia yearns for power—but will her dazzling magic be her deliverance or will she bring the whole world crashing down around her?

Out in Autumn 2026

Want early access to sequel news? Sign up for updates—and a free prequel—by using the QR code or visiting the website: **JennyBassettBooks.com**

Check Out Our Kickstarter

Want to dive more deeply into the world of Demuto? Check out our Kickstarter!

A Kickstarter campaign is a genius mix of preordering and crowdfunding, set up to help creatives raise money for projects ahead of time. If targets are met, you receive your order when the project is complete; if they aren't, then your card isn't charged!

I have adored writing *The Lure of Evil* and would love to create a **special edition** beautiful enough to stand out on even the most spectacular bookshelves.

If funding goes *really* well, I'll be producing an **audiobook**, too. This would be professionally directed and produced, with duet narration.

In addition, you'll have the chance to purchase exclusive rewards:

- A set of character art bookmarks
- Art prints
- Bespoke earrings
- Art print jigsaw puzzle
- "Immediately intoxicated, eternally addicted" mug

Sign up for early updates and receive a launch alert the moment the campaign goes live at **JennyBassettBooks.com**.

About the Author

Jenny Bassett is the author of the Rise of Darkness series. Living in a world sadly devoid of dragons, she decided to create one that is full of them. When she's not tip-tapping away at her laptop, she's probably being squashed by her 35kg 'lapdog', Loki.

Getting this book into the world has been one of the most exciting experiences of my life and I can't tell you how much it means that you've read it. If you enjoyed *The Lure of Evil,* I hope you won't mind me asking a small favour: leaving a review on Amazon makes an enormous difference to a debut author like me. If you have a moment to spare, I'd be incredibly grateful if you'd share your thoughts.

Venture to **jennybassettbooks.com** and sign up for my newsletter to claim your free ***Rise of Darkness*** prequel novella, receive news on upcoming releases, deals, Kickstarter launches, and so much more.

Head to **@JennyBassettBooks on TikTok** for daily glimpses into the creation of the next Rise of Darkness novel, book recs and exclusive content for readers who prefer their romance sharp, shadowed, and a little unhinged.

Acknowledgements

There are so many people I have to thank for helping my dream become a reality, this page would be nearly as long as the book itself if I thanked them all as earnestly as they deserved. So, for the sake of sparing the rainforest, I will endeavour to be succinct.

To my parents, for their endless patience and guidance. At 31, there's still not much I don't do without consulting you, and I'm so grateful you're there whenever I need you. Always.

To Roy, for being able to make me laugh, even on difficult days.

To Alicia, for your endless patience and encouragement.

To Carol Bellhouse, for reading each drafted variation of this story with equal eagerness every time. You never doubted that this book would see the light of day, often giving me confidence when I needed it most, and for that, I am eternally grateful.

To Bryony, Alicia, Charlotte, Maria, Craig, Rosanne, Sandra, and Arya. Imposter syndrome is real, and it wasn't until I got your feedback that I really began to believe this book could really be something. There were times when your messages had me dancing round the kitchen, and I consider myself incredibly lucky to have had your encouragement and enthusiasm.

To Eliza Osborn, I am so glad you agreed to take me on. Your insight and knowledge have been absolutely invaluable. You have been wonderful, so thank you. Very much.

To Ian, for all the help and advice, especially when you had MUCH bigger fish to worry about. I am so grateful to you for talking everything through with me.

And to Loki, who has been by my side for almost every word I typed. One of the best things about writing is getting to spend the day snuggled up with you.

Read More
of *The Rise of Darkness* Series

* 9 7 8 1 9 1 9 2 6 6 4 0 4 *

BV - #0120 - 130226 - C0 - 203/127/21 - PB - 9781919266404 - Matt Lamination